K. R. CONWAY

LAST LIGHT

To Emma -
Smoking Talus
again?! WOMAN!
Stop that!
KR Conway

WICKED WHALE
PUBLISHING

First Edition September 2017

Conway, K. R.
Last Light / by K. R. Conway

Summary: Now actively hunted and in a race to seize control of a notorious time altering device known as the Gabriel Gate, Eila Walker must come to terms with what it means to be a true warrior in the face of a deadly enemy.

ISBN: 978-0-9973737-1-4

Wicked Whale Publishing
P.O. Box 264
Sagamore Beach, MA 02562-9998

www.WickedWhalePublishing.com

Published in the United States of America

For My Kids:

Though I admit to dreaming of monsters for under your beds when you're trying to sell each other on Ebay, you two lunatics are the loves of my life. On a side note, there's a spider the size of a Fenway frank in the bathroom and I'm not getting him. So, ya know, just be brave, like Eila.

(stop laughing, you brats).

K.R. CONWAY

LAST LIGHT

BOOK 4

Dear Reader:

When I first started writing LAST LIGHT, the final installment of Eila Walker's outrageous story, I knew it was going to be a sizable book. What I didn't anticipate was just how large it was destined to become.

After numerous conversations with my "Beta" team, and some insurmountable problems with binding it as a print book due to its size, it was decided that LAST LIGHT would be split into two parts:
LAST LIGHT is now Part 1.
DAYBREAKER is now Part 2.

While most authors and editors would cut a story down to fit a more appropriate size, my team (and myself) felt that doing so, in this case, would result in a less robust end to the Undertow series.

At nearly 200,000 words, Last Light is twice the size of Undertow. To put that in perspective, Last Light is bigger than any of J.R.R. Tolkien's Lord of the Rings books, some of Stephen King's Dark Tower series books, and about half of the Harry Potter books. Combined, the entire series is more than a half-million words long.

So, without further ado, I present to you LAST LIGHT.

DAYBREAKER will debut in November 2017.

Sincerely,
K.R. Conway

PROLOGUE

TERREBONNE PARISH, LOUISIANA

For fifteen-year-old Jared Marlowe, midnight in the Terrebonne bayou was like drowning in a flask of ink. It was an endless, glorious swath of ebony; a place of drifting shadows and swaying moonlight, all of which served to tip one's imagination toward tales of mythic beasts and prowling snakes complete with pearlescent eyes. Among the ancient cypress trees and lacy Spanish moss, the swamp had always crooned a rich, sweet song that thrummed through the bones of those like Jared.

Those born of the bayou.

His home since birth, Jared knew every inch of the tangled waterways and black swamps of Terrebonne. He knew the tangy taste of the lakes that fell away into the crawling fog, and he knew the pebbled tracks of the lone dirt road that offered humans a rare, tempting peek into the edges of his dangerous world. Those few foolish souls who did wander further than the road never saw daylight again. Humans, Jared's mother would say, were far too tasty to leave to the jaws of the uncultured gators.

This had always been his clan's territory, centuries before the humans ever settled the area. At over a thousand square miles, Terrebonne's human residents kept mainly to the few scattered towns, leaving the rich expanse of swampland to the Wreckers like him. And his kind – his family – owned this world by blood and right. His ancestors had ruled the endless bayous with ruthless yet balanced hands. His own family history was written in the detailed scrimshaw etched over his moon-white fangs - a right of passage gifted to all Wreckers on their thirteenth birthday. Theirs was a rich tale of treasures plundered, lives taken, wars fought, and peace won. Century upon century of stories. Century upon century of tradition, handed down a thousand times over.

And perhaps he was young and foolish to be so naïve, but Jared always believed that Mayhem was an unshakable fortress – a labyrinth-like expanse untouched by the other ancient, gifted clans. None dare set foot in Wrecker territory. None dare tempt the wrath of their ranking Elder, Midas, or the fierce water-born people he ruled.

Yet as Jared stumbled through the thick mud and sharp grasses of the swamp, his arms burning from carrying a little girl away from the carnage and into the safety of the deep bayou, his mind couldn't come to terms with what had happened. Because to Jared, the Wrecker village of Mayhem, and her central citadel, were unraidable. Unconquerable. His home was a vibrant, hidden jewel among the Louisiana swamps . . . until tonight. And nothing - NOTHING - prepared him for what he'd witnessed hours earlier through the warped glass of his grandfather's golden spyglass, the celebration between Midas' crew and Lawson Waite's turning from excitement to extermination.

He should've been inside Mayhem when the attack happened.

He should have been there, fighting alongside his family.

Someone should've been wary the moment Lawson Waite came to Terrebonne with fifty Mortis in tow, offering to renew trade with the Wreckers. Everyone had been hopeful. Perhaps too hopeful. Too desperate.

So, instead of being inside Mayhem when celebration turned to carnage, Jared had been more than two miles upriver, pulling chilled copper kegs of River Whiskey with the other young mooncussers so that those inside the citadel could toast to a new era of trade and bootlegging with Waite. Dredged out of the thick mud at the edge of Lost Lake, the priceless liquor was what the Wreckers were known for among the supernatural world - a moonshine so strong that ingesting too much could easily kill you, immortal or not.

The celebration was supposed to be a new start for the Wreckers; a new bargain with Lawson Waite who'd finally agreed to begin transporting the high potency cocaine leaves once again. No one knew what made Waite cut Midas off from his drug smuggling business two years ago, but the effects of no longer having access to the best coca leaves in the world, which the Wreckers used in their whiskey stills, devastated their moonshine business. Buying sub-quality cocaine from a drug runner in the Caribbean led to Maia Moriarty ending her long-standing relationship with Midas, and soon other underground clubs followed suit. For two years, the Wreckers barely survived. But then Waite suddenly contacted Midas mere days ago and agreed to start running the coca leaves to Mayhem once again.

Everyone rejoiced.

Now everyone might be dead.

"Where's my mom?" whispered the little girl in Jared's arms, her cropped hair smeared with dirt.

He couldn't meet her eyes as he pushed relentlessly through the swampland, more teens and kids around his age carrying younger ones. Taking to the rivers was not an option, the fear that their magic could be felt by the Mortis too much of a risk if they entered the waterways. "I'm sure she'll come get you soon," Jared lied, rage burning through him at every word he spoke.

It was by the grace of Fate that most of the children had not been inside the village when the assault began. Instead, they'd been shooed to the deep moat outside Mayhem's towering walls to catch frogs in the dark water as the adults partied with Waite and his Mortis inside the main citadel at the heart of Mayhem.

Jared's best friend, Farraye, who had delivered a barrel of whiskey to Midas with a few of the other mooncusser teens, had stopped to play briefly with the little kids, including his four-year-old sister, Neela. He told Jared that they'd only been in the moat with the kids maybe five minutes when the first screams started.

Thank God he'd stopped to catch tadpoles with his little sister.

Thank God he and the other mooncussers grabbed the children and ran.

It was the only reason the littlest of his kind were still alive.

Through the rippled moonlight, Jared could see Farraye trudging through the mud, Neela clutched to his back, her umbratael, Poe, squished tightly in her arms, its smoky raven form nearly unrecognizable in her tight grasp. Even at a distance, Jared could hear Poe offer quiet cackling sounds as Neela held it; as if the shadow tail was trying to calm its young mistress. Moving swiftly through the reeds, Raye's own umbratael, Edgar, had maintained its form - that of a badger, complete with broad back and clawed feet. Edgar made no noise as it moved in time with Raye, a true reflection of Farraye's own personality, focused and driven.

Raye's Aunt had been inside Mayhem. All the elders had been in there, and Jared fought back the nausea as his stomach rolled with the brutal knowledge that his mother had also been at the party. Was she even alive? Was she wounded?

At some point, Waite would realize that the Wrecker children were missing from the carnage, which meant that reaching the Barrie forts, miles away, was their only hope at staying hidden and protected.

"Farraye," Jared whispered as they passed on either side of the cypress trees cloaked in shadows and moss. Raye's exhausted face met his in the shadows. "We'll get the rest of them out, I swear. This shit ain't over. I'm not leaving my mom in there. No way."

"I should've been there," Raye replied quietly, hoisting his sister a little higher. Another child, maybe seven years old, had woven through the reeds to clutch onto the bottom edge of Farraye's worn leather vest - as if doing so could ensure the little one made it to the Barrie treeforts alive. Everywhere, fading in and out of the cypress, were children and teens, some walking on their own, others being carried in the darkness. They were a moving tide of exhaustion and grief, each one of them accompanied by their equally devastated umbrataels.

"We had a job to do. We weren't screwing off," Jared urged, desperate to ease Raye's guilt and his own. "Had we known . . ."

"Had we known, they would've never been allowed anywhere near Terrebonne," growled Farraye. His gaze went back to the abyss of swampland ahead of them. They had to make it around Lost Lake, nearly ten miles across, and then head north, to Barrie. They had hours to go on foot before salvation welcomed them. "This is why we were always taught that Mortis couldn't be trusted. This is why we do not align ourselves with such . . . such evil. I can't believe Midas let them in!"

"Midas was desperate, you know that. We all were. I just can't figure out why they attacked. What do they want?"

"They wanted us gone! And now everyone is . . ." He glanced at the little ones around them and mouthed the word 'dead' as a tear trailed down his cheek. He brushed it away roughly with his shoulder, trying not to jostle Neela who had nodded off. Poe slid carefully out from her grasp and landed on the ground, shaking out her shadowy feathers. She ran on stick legs to catch up with Jared's umbratael, Sprout. The two tails began chattering to one another, the discussion not sounding all that friendly.

"They are NOT all gone! I refuse to believe we are all that's left, do you hear me?" Jared snapped, trying to battle back his own tears. "I just don't understand why? The Mortis entourage that came with Waite seemed to be made of stone - no reaction, no emotion. We have not been at war with the Mortis for centuries. The treaties have held! Why attack us? Why now?"

"They are soul thieves, Jared! Mindless killers," hissed Farraye. "They are not of the natural world. They are not like us. They were designed, created, by forces that should not meddle in the order of things. They should all be exterminated. This, THIS, is war. This ends the treaty."

Jared sighed, hiking the little one in his arms a bit higher. At only two years old, she'd yet to develop her umbratael fully, so all that drifted along on the ground behind them was a thin layer of smoke - her shadow tail, which would eventually take on its final form in another year or so. Thankfully, in Jared's warm grasp, the toddler's head finally lolled onto his shoulder as sleep claimed her. By his feet, Sprout slinked along, now arguing in an indignant, chirpy voice with Poe.

The two umbrataels halted suddenly in front of Jared, and he nearly kicked right through their smoky forms as he stumbled to a stop, trying not to wake the girl. "Sprout! Dang it, can you two stop arguing for two seconds?"

Sprout turned his slug-like form to Jared, his black, featureless face looking right at his owner. He chirped sharply, showing off his two stubby fangs as he relayed the insult that Poe had flung his way. Jared glanced at Poe, who simply ruffled her foggy feathers and turned her beak up at Sprout.

Jared sighed, "Jeez, you're not fat, Sprout. You're just . . . wrinkly," he urged, shaking his head. He couldn't even believe two shadow tails were arguing about shit like this right now. Sprout glared at Poe, demanding an apology in his squeaky voice.

The raven turned back to Sprout, stomping over in his direction. She squawked out what had to be the worst version of an apology ever, then took off, choosing to fly between the branches above her master, who Farraye carried, rather than hang on the ground with Sprout anymore.

Sprout watched Poe go, his shadowy mouth hanging open, horrified. He then turned back to Jared and let out a string of disgusted squeaks.

"Dude, yesterday, you accused Poe of having chicken legs! What did you expect?" Jared argued.

Shaking his head, Jared knew one thing to be absolutely true: dealing with umbrataels was far easier when they were fused to their owners as actual TAILS. Unfortunately, such a shifted state only occurred when a Wrecker took to the water. On land, however, a Wrecker's tail transformed into an opinionated, smoky little creature who literally followed their owners everywhere, like a shadow. Hence their nickname: "shadow tail."

Sprout muttered something less than civil under his breath as Jared started walking again, his wrinkly, CHUBBY umbratael sulking as he followed along. Silence seemed to slowly infect the group of young Wreckers, voices dropping away as hope seemed to bury itself in the mud, like whisky casks.

For a long while, no one spoke as they made their way through the swamp, midnight's clutch on the sky slowly falling to the demanding light of dawn.

Throughout the long trek, memories of what Jared had seen through the spyglass stirred over and over in his mind on an endless, terrible loop. He recalled how Farraye and the others had come running through the cypress trees after the attack, yelling for Jared. He'd and a few other 'cussers had been hauling up whiskey from the boggy ground, oblivious to what had happened.

Confused as to what was wrong, Farraye had quickly explained to Jared what he had heard through the towering walls of Mayhem - the screams, the sounds of things being smashed and orders being shouted. He told Jared he'd grabbed the kids and run, but Jared had to know more. Had to know what was happening inside the village.

So he'd climbed the largest Cypress near the lake, Sprout weaving through the branches alongside him, his flowing form of starlight and shadows allowing the umbratael to perch on the thinnest branches. Jared finally wedged himself in a large fork in the tree, brought the spyglass to his eye, and froze. The citadel and the surrounding homes and villages were being shredded. Bodies of his people were strewn like trash among the glittering buildings and dark rivers.

It was absolute carnage.

Even at a mile distance from Mayhem, the gently swirling current of water that rippled around the gnarled roots of the cypress trees had begun to run red with the blood of his people. Above him, Sprout's mournful wailing was unlike anything Jared had ever heard, freezing the blood in his veins. Gutted, he'd ripped the spyglass from his eye, breathing hard as panic and rage, fear and nausea flooded his body. Sprout had reacted immediately to the change in his master and quickly descended the tree, wrapping around Jared like a second skin, ready to phase into his master's aquatic form. But Jared had eased Sprout from his body, and instead called down to the other mooncussers and children, all of them confused. All of them terrified.

"We need to stay off the river and head to the Barrie treeforts," he told them, his eyes landing on Farraye, whose little sister was clutching tightly onto her big brother. Farraye simply gave a tight nod, knowing that Jared was right. The Barrie treeforts, built by the children over the years as a fun hideaway, represented the one safe spot among the bayous. The one place wrapped in such powerful spells that only Wrecker children up to a certain age could enter - only Wrecker children could even find the skeletal treeforts built from the pieces of the shipwrecks their parents had caused. Whatever wasn't deemed valuable to the elders became the spoils of plundering little hands for their beloved hideaway.

Many of the 'cussers demanded to go back to find their parents. To ditch the Barrie idea and head back into Mayhem.

In his heart, Jared wanted to as well.

But he'd seen what was happening and he knew the reality of

what awaited them if they returned to the heart of Terrebonne. Waite's fighting Mortis had ripped Mayhem apart. They were unlike anything he'd ever seen. Unlike any chilling horror story he'd ever been told. They moved like phantoms, wrapping themselves in the blackness of bayou shadows and making themselves near impossible to track in the night. Their strength was . . . endless. They had beheaded people in one move.

As the memories of what he'd seen hit him all over again, Jared staggered with the girl in his arms and she startled. "I'm sorry," he whispered to her and she let out a sad, broken cry - so soft, it was barely more than a whisper. In the dim light of the rising dawn, he could see a small bruise on her cheek, no doubt from when she ran on her own little feet through the bayou with Farraye and the others.

Jared swallowed as he eased her head back down to his shoulder. "We'll be to Barrie soon, I promise."

"I want my mama," she whispered, and Jared bit his lip, trying choke back the rage and pain. Tears flowed down his face silently as he patted the girl's back, her body relaxing once again in his strong arms. Beside him, Sprout slipped by his leg offering a soft caress, as if to let Jared know he wasn't alone in his sadness. Unable to take another step, Jared leaned back against a tree, Sprout curling up next to him and purring sadly. The girl in his arms drifted back to sleep as others walked by, all of them bone weary.

"Jared? You okay?" asked one of the 'cussers who paused before him, another smaller boy clutched to his back. On the ground near him, an umbratael in the shape of an otter waited patiently. The kid couldn't be more than thirteen, and now here he was, slammed suddenly into adulthood by Lawson Waite. By Mortis. As the kid stood before him, Jared realized that he'd never even taken the time to know his name. The knowledge that life could be snatched from those around him was a punch to the chest.

"I just need a second, uh . . .?"

"Sam," the 'cusser offered. "Name's Sam."

"Thanks. For helping, Sam," Jared replied, looking at the boy on Sam's back.

Sam tightened his jaw and simply nodded, no longer able to speak lest the pain of what had happened tore from him in a tidal wave.

Jared knew the feeling well and simply offered a brief nod in return. The cusser gave him a long, sad look before moving on, the little boy on his back watching Jared as they disappeared through the high reeds.

One minute.

Jared would give himself one minute to stop shaking. To halt the memories and to focus on the tasks ahead.

He dragged in a breath as he looked down to Sprout, "We're gonna need help."

His faithful umbratael paused and watched Jared, his small, smoky shape rippling as if tickled by the dawn. Jared's older cousins had joked that Sprout looked like an oversized slug, but Jared loved him. Shadow tails like Sprout were the truest confidants to a Wrecker – a piece of oneself, reflected in a sliver of smoke that traveled alongside their master, day and night.

As Jared studied Sprout, he realized that he didn't even know if his cousins were alive anymore.

He swallowed hard, "I've got an idea. It's one messed up plan, but it's the only people I know that may be able to help us. But Farraye ain't gonna go for it, so I got a feeling it's just gonna be me and you, my friend."

Sprout cocked his head and chirped out a question, demanding details, but Jared just shook his head. "Not here. I can't tell you here, but I will. I promise. As soon as we have everyone in Barrie, and we are certain all the wards are solid, you and I . . . are leaving. On the sly."

Sprout's little lip curved into a devious grin, revealing one stubby fang. "*Caaa chee neek ta?*" he squeaked.

"Yup," Jared replied, trying in his mind to map the best route north that would avoid the Lesser territories in the Blue Ridge mountains. "Let's just pray she's still just as ruthless as Midas said she was and that she's willing to cut a deal."

Sprout's grin widened and he purred darkly in response.

Jared pushed off the tree and started walking once again, the little girl in his arms. In front of him, dawn was slowly transforming the eastern sky, painting streaks of purple and pink on the horizon. And though his feet were slowed by the mud, and his skin was sliced over and over by the whip-sharp reeds, Jared felt nothing - no pain, no sadness.

For now he had purpose. He had a plan.

And if he was lucky, he'd also have Madame Moriarty.

And revenge.

CHAPTER 1
TORRENT ROAD, CAPE COD
SATURDAY, 1:05 PM

Truth be told, I'm not a big rule-breaker.

Okay, well . . . *before* I met Eila Walker, I wasn't a big rule breaker.

Actually, come to think of it, I did kinda ditch the rules two summers ago, before Eila, when I went against my canine-code of "nice doggie" and attacked Kian's sorry butt at the beach, sinking my teeth into his arm. At the time, I'd just realized he was a soul thief *and* probably sucking the lips off my best pal, Ana, so I was riding the emotional crazy train hard and fast at that moment. And I wasn't aiming for his arm, if I'm being entirely truthful. My intended target was his fat head, but, *oh well.*

Sometimes, I reflect on that moment (especially when I'm stuck watching the two of them shamelessly eyeball-flirt from across a room) and I'm really pissed I missed.

Now, however, that one insane summer felt like a lifetime ago, rather than eighteen months. Actually, the Breakers fiasco back in October, a mere FIVE months ago, felt like decades ago.

Standing on the balcony of Torrent Road, I drummed my fingers along the railing, studying the same irritating, dog-bitten soul thief out of the corner of my eye. He was leaning against the railing next to me, his forearms draped over the cherry wood as he systematically cracked each knuckle, the tension in his body palpable as he watched Eila below us, James' package containing a cheap cell phone on the table in front of her.

Her strong voice filled the massive open space as she explained her idea of recruiting (which sounded a helluva lot like *bribing*) Christian's old boat-buddies, the notorious *True North* pirates, into working for us. I was fairly certain Eila had finally cracked completely, as her entire sales pitch was basically, *"When fate kicks ya in the balls, pull yourself back up with the help of some hired sociopaths."*

At least, that's how my brain was translating her speech.

As she stood on the first floor, her hands braced on the round oak table arguing her point to the rest of our gang, all I could think of was how we all ended up knotted together as a crew. From our point above them, Kian and I were spectators to what felt like a turning point for us all. As if there were two paths: one REALLY suicidal, and the other one a little less so.

Great options, obviously.

I'd always do whatever Eila needed; whatever protected our friends and took Lawson Waite and his time-jumping Gabriel Gate out of commission. But I could tell that Kian wasn't just thinking about goals and vengeance and keeping the supernatural Gate from a drug-dealing, wanna-be terrorist.

He was also thinking about Ana and her safety.

He was weighing whether or not Eila's plan was wise and if it would put the girl he loved in even more danger.

I knew Kian loved Ana. That he'd always be there for her and protect her despite the doubts I had about him when we first met (in my defense, he was a total prick back then). But I'd never really understood that level of love – the type that isn't born of blood, but of obsession, lust, and a selfish desire to never be apart. It seemed so all consuming, like an inferno, and I used to pity those people for what I believed were the trappings of a mindless crush.

But as I watched over the argument growing below, Raef, Rillin, and Eila now talking over one another, I knew I had already taken a side in the debate raging. And it wasn't because I, at my most basic, wasn't much of a rule breaker, or that the whole pirate thing was FREAKIN' INSANE. No, it was because, for the first time in my life, I started to understand – to *feel* – what Kian did for Ana.

My eyes drifted from Eila's spot at the table to the auburn-haired girl standing near her and gesturing with her one good arm as she too got into the argument. The robe I'd given her from Christian's guest room hung from her shoulders, entirely too huge for her five-and-a-half foot tall frame, and her useless left arm remained tucked in the terry pocket.

I was so screwed. Dumb, DUMB dog.

I'm not sure exactly when I began to like (and I mean *really* like) Nikki Shea. Part of me thinks it was when I broke into her house with Eila a few months ago and saw the formal, cold home she lived in. Part of me thinks it was when I stood over her as Marsh and defended her against a very high, very desperate Basil Moriarty, and then beat the snot out of him in the cafeteria to seal the deal. Or maybe it was the snide remarks Nik shot my way on a regular basis, or how she wondered at the color of my human hair compared to Marsh's onyx fur.

And part of me says that I fell for her when I held her in the backseat of Raef's truck, trying to keep her awake and warm, Rillin's knife still jutting from her shoulder as Ana drove like a maniac to Faust. I remember, vividly, how her eyes would drift closed and I would urge her to stay awake, the streetlights strobing in a ghostly yellow haze over her face and bloodied shirt as Ana sped for New Bedford.

I told her, over and over, that she'd be okay and that I wouldn't let her go. I think I said it more for my benefit than for hers. To convince myself she wasn't going to die in my arms and that I wouldn't be the last soul to talk to her before Death came calling.

In that moment, surrounded by my bruised and reeling friends, I no longer saw Nikki Shea as the epic bitch she'd been for years. She wasn't the ruthless, curvaceous overlord of our high school, but a fearless, selfless girl who'd put her life on the line to stop Rillin and Sara Booth from taking Eila. She even had it in her, somewhere, to help Rillin despite what he'd done to her.

At the end of the day, she was just a girl, with crappy parents and no friends, save for our motley crew. Somehow she'd weaseled into my heart.

And like Kian, I was thinking of her safety in whatever we did next, especially given her injured arm, insanely cool metal-warping powers be damned.

Beside me, Kian cracked another knuckle. "I'm giving you ten seconds to grow a pair, Hairball, and speak up, otherwise I'm pulling the plug on Sparky's dumb-ass plan."

"What makes you think she'll even listen to me? I mean – look at her. She's rocking her soapbox right now and ain't looking to be knocked off anytime soon."

Kian turned to me, one eyebrow curved upwards in an irritatingly perfect curve. "So, you think using Christian's pirates is a good idea?"

"Frak, no. Only suicidal idiots would do such a thing!"

Kian grinned, yelling out over the room in a booming voice, "MJ SAYS YOU'RE A SUICIDAL IDIOT, SPARKY!"

I was going to murder Frat Boy.

Everyone stopped talking and glared at us from the lower level. My hands itched to shove Kian off the balcony.

Eila, her fist planting firmly on her hip, eyed me from her spot by the table. "Oh, does he now?"

"YUP!" called Kian.

"Uh, NO – that was taken out of context, E. Totally a sensationalized soundbite, used for shock value and nothing more. AND without permission, I might add." I shot a deadly look at Kian, who just smirked. *What a freakin' ass –*

"Speak up, MJ. Why do you think this is a rotten plan?" asked Eila, still watching us.

Crap. I sucked at debate when I was forced to take it Junior year. This was going to turn out like a wordy version of roadkill.

"Well," I glanced at Kian, who looked smug. I was gonna go rabid on his butt the next time I phased. "Well, it's just that . . . uh . . . we don't really know these pirate people."

"Oh my, God," muttered Kian under his breath.

"Yeah, and well – just take *True North's* crew. Christian himself said that he killed half of them and then basically forced the others to join him by being flippy-switched into Mortis."

"Flippy-switched?" asked Raef, his arms crossed.

"Ya know – turned, or whatever you soul thieves like to call it." I glanced at Eila and she seemed to actually be listening.

"Go on," she commanded, slowly. Suspiciously.

"Well, what if they didn't actually like being pirates? What if, in reality, they hated Christian's guts because they were forced to be part of his crew?"

"Ha, that sounds familiar!" said Nikki, shooting a look at Eila.

E stuck her tongue out at the Ironess, then continued on. "Okay, so what you're saying is they may have an axe to grind with Christian, and thus, me. Is that what you're getting at?"

Well . . . yeah. That works. "Yes! Yes, that's what I'm getting at!" I bobbed my head like a freak, totally pleased I had actually argued my point without going down in flames.

Suck it, Debate Team!

Eila looked around the table, her eyes landing on her broody boyfriend. He pressed his hands to the table. "He's right, E. Bringing in a crew like that, who may in fact be gunning for Christian due to some pent-up anger issues, would NOT be the people to call on for aid."

Eila tossed her hand. "Well, then – what do you suggest?"

"Call Moriarty," Raef replied. "Ask her if we can stay at Faust for a while and regroup. Tell her everything we know so far and that more than our lives are on the line. Tell her about the Gate."

"We just left Faust! I don't think Maia is desperate to have us back anytime this century."

Raef offered Eila a sly smile. "Do it for me?" he asked.

Kian rolled his eyes so hard I think he glimpsed the back of his skull.

Eila sighed, "Fine. I'll call Baz – see if we can crash at Faust while we figure out what to do." She rubbed her face, looking exhausted. Honestly, Eila hadn't been looking too great for a while now - almost since Polaris. And she'd scared the crap outta me when I thought she was going into Light overload in Moriarty's club, which I guess was a false alarm, but still . . . I was starting to really worry that stress, exhaustion, and grief were taking their toll on my pal.

Ana studied her from across the table. "You sure you don't want to use Collette's place? That doesn't have any connection to Christian, so it should be safe. Waite shouldn't be able to track us there."

Eila shook her head. "I can't take the risk that Collette didn't spill secrets before she was killed, like the location of her Chinatown loft in Boston."

I nodded in agreement. As annoying as she was in person (and distractingly built like a real life Assassin Barbie), Collette had been an asset to us. I prayed her death had been swift during the second raid on Christian's island, Polaris, which had happened only a few days ago.

Eila frowned, "Even if Collette didn't reveal any of our secrets to her attackers, the reality is they got into the vault. They sacked the house. Any information that Christian had in his office or vault would've been free pickings. Plus, James apparently believes that Christian's mainframe, Halee, could've been hacked."

Ana tossed her hands, "Exactly! Wouldn't info on Faust be in there as well?"

That stopped Eila cold for a moment. She thought carefully before she spoke. "When I first met Maia and we talked about

Christian's involvement in Faust, it sounded like he was more of a silent partner. I don't think anything was officially on the books. It was more of an old-school agreement – handshake and trust and whatnot."

"Faust isn't a sitting duck, either," added Raef, leaning against the table with one hip, his arms crossed. "Maia keeps that place well-guarded. My guess is her nightclub has a lot more than just a few infrared security cameras. I bet Faust is secretly built like a fortress."

Ana frowned, "Eila – we could bring the heat onto Maia and Baz. We could put them in the line of fire and drag them into this . . . *war*, with us."

Rillin's voice rumbled from the corner of the room in reply as he slowly flipped a small dagger between his fingers. "Ana, the fact that Lawson Waite has a time gate means that everyone has a stake in the war with him now. No one, not even the human world, can afford neutrality."

He stopped playing with the knife, grasping it hard in his wide hand as he turned and stalked back to the table, looking over to Eila. "Call Moriarty and fill her in on what we've learned and what we believe Waite is up to. Ask her if we can come to Faust and regroup while we figure out a plan of attack. Let her know that she has the right to turn her back on us without shame. That we understand the risks she is accepting by sheltering us and that the decision to do so is hers alone."

Eila glanced at Raef who gave a short nod. "I agree. It's a workable plan."

"And if Moriarty says 'no'? What then?" asked Nikki, playing devil's advocate.

"We cross that bridge when we come to it," Eila replied.

"Christian owns many properties throughout the country and the world. We have options if Maia says 'no'."

The girls, Raef, and Rillin got down to logistics as I looked over at Kian. "Happy? No more pirates."

He smiled at me, showing more teeth than necessary. "Yes. Very. So glad you did it and not me."

I narrowed my eyes. "Why's that?"

"Because, if this plans goes into a landslide, I can say it was your idea in the first place to ditch the pirates. Me? Crap free. You? Loads of dog poo if this was the wrong choice."

I rubbed my face, "I really can't stand you some days. Most days. Actually, nearly all the time."

"Only nearly?" asked Kian, giving me a light punch in the shoulder that may've crushed a bone or two. "Well, heck, Cujo – we're basically best pals!"

Forget pushing Kian.

I was ready to jump myself.

CHAPTER 2

408 MAIN STREET, CENTERVILLE, MA

SATURDAY, 2:07 PM

By the time I was twelve, Scrabble had become more of a religion than a game. I can still remember the day Mae bought our very first beat-up set from a yard sale in Mullville, not far from our apartment complex. I was ten at the time, and I can still remember how the breeze seemed to vibrate with the angry hum of June bugs and how the air felt too thick for my lungs.

It had been sweltering hot that day, the sun cooking the blacktop into a sticky kind of tar that caked my flip-flops and caused the soles of shoes to warp and mutate. It always seemed worse – the melted asphalt – the farther you got from the city and the closer you got to our neck of the woods. It was a damning ooze reserved especially for the lower class, I swear.

We had gone there in search of a cheap bookcase for my bedroom, but as we wandered through the folding tables, all we saw were mementos, once precious, now tossed aside for mere pennies.

I always wondered if those people regretted what they sold. Did they take the time to remember each memory that wrapped around every little glass cat and faded doll, or was it easier *not* to remember? Was it easier to block out the history in order to move on? And with every item sold, did they themselves change? Did bits of their hearts close off with each trinket exchanged for the sake of a quarter?

Did they feel the loss of something once loved, now gone forever?

Standing in Mae's room on the top floor of 408 Main Street, I let my fingers trail over the careful row of random letters that she had set upright on her side of the window seat. We'd brought the faded board game with us from Mullville when we moved to Cape Cod. Mae had insisted that we start our new adventure off right by christening the house with a game of Scrabble that very first night, so many months ago.

We'd set up our aging board on the floral cushions of the window seat in her room, the view of the old backyard barn warped and watery, thanks to the leaded glass of the window. And then we started playing, teasing and trying to put the pressure on one another. But that was the thing about *our* version of Scrabble – we would play a single game over the course of days. Weeks. Even months.

Our little letters were the equivalent of a chess fanatic's rooks and pawns. We played when we had a spare moment, me wandering up to her room to make my move when she wasn't home or was busy with whatever, and then she would do the same when she had a free moment. To us, Scrabble was a sacred rite that only the two of us were allowed to partake in.

I studied the array of letters. There were a bunch of words

already spelled out across the worn crisscross pattern of the board. Apples, wheat, visionary, and turnpike were just a few of our creations.

I'd forgotten about the board and in my neglect, the letters had acquired a thin layer of dust. Mae wouldn't be happy that our little tiles were less than pristine, but I was afraid to attempt to blow the dust off, terrified that the tiles would scatter as well.

In some odd way it felt as though Mae still lived within the game. That if I closed my eyes and the house was silent, I could hear her voice echo down the staircase as she called that it was my turn. She would say I was going down in flames and that she just claimed some double or triple word score. I would then yell back something in regards to her being delusional and that I'd stolen her Thesaurus (or something stupid like that), and she'd laugh.

Such simple moments I'd taken for granted and thought nothing of when they were happening. I thought our Scrabble games were dime-store memories, my twenty-five cent trinket. It was only now, when she was gone and never coming back, that I realized how very priceless each moment with her had been.

I swallowed hard, shoving back the burn in my throat as I looked over her tiles, trying to decode what she was going to do next. It was her turn. It would remain her turn. I couldn't bring myself to put away the set, nor to help her play.

Looking over the little wooden alphabet, I realized she had the makings of another triple word score. She could've pulled off *zenith*. "You would've won, Meeze," I whispered, wiping my cheeks fiercely.

From behind me, someone cleared his throat and I glanced over my shoulder, catching sight of Kian standing in the doorway. He had been at Torrent Road with Ana and Rillin, packing up the items we needed, but he must've swung back to my house for a few other items.

"Sorry," he offered. "I didn't mean to intrude, but I wanted to let you know that most of the items that Rillin and Raef specified are packed up at Christian's. I just came back for some clothes for Ana. Raef also gave me your suitcase. We're just waiting for Baz to arrive and transport everything to Faust."

"Thank God for the Moriartys," I replied quietly.

Kian scoffed. "God has nothing to do with it, Eila. Maia's sticking her neck out because you agreed to sign the club over to her entirely. She's hired muscle, so don't confuse her motivations with sainthood."

I didn't respond, knowing Kian was probably right. When I had called Maia from Torrent Road before I headed to 408 and explained what we had uncovered and James' warning, she'd gone silent on the phone.

"*You're asking me to draw a line in the sand against Lawson Waite, Walker. You're asking me to put my family – my son and all those who work for me – into Waite's line of fire. And I've seen what that bastard's Links can do. I've seen a young Mortis girl be butchered from the inside out by one of his Links. This place is a safe haven for soul thieves and their human companions. You want me to turn Faust from a safe haven into a foxhole in the middle of a coming war. You are asking for a fortress to stand against the enemy. I am highly reluctant to do so, whether you are Christian's granddaughter or not,*" she'd replied.

It took time, but Maia eventually offered us safe haven and protection when I stressed how dangerous the Gate was; that if Waite did use it and changed the timeline, Faust might never exist. SHE and her son might never exist. To seal the deal, I offered up the ownership of Faust entirely to her and she finally accepted.

I turned back to the board game, my mind tumbling with so much stress that I could barely breathe. If we failed, humanity and history could very well be rewritten. I could be responsible for the destruction of all that we'd ever known. All that HISTORY had ever known.

The weight of responsibility that rested in our hands – on me – was suffocating.

I felt, more than heard, Kian approach, finally sliding in next to me, his arm brushing against mine. "Scrabble," he muttered, looking over the board. "I suck at Scrabble. Hideous game."

I snorted, a choked laugh escaping a crack in my sadness. I glanced up at him, wiping another tear from my cheek, but smiling a bit.

Kian looked down at me, an eyebrow quirked as he mercifully ignored my tears. I was grateful for it – his ability to focus past my heartbreak and try to reroute my emotions. "That's private knowledge, Sparky. If I find out my word-forming inferiority is broadcast to the others, I'll hang your undies off Cerberus' flydeck for a week during the Fourth of July when the harbor is mobbed."

"Raef may have an issue with that," I replied, drawing a deep breath to clear the tightness in my chest. I could envision Raef trying to yank my bras from the top-most deck of the yacht, cursing Kian to Hell the whole time. That is, I could hopefully imagine it as long as there was another Fourth of July to celebrate.

Kian waved me off, "Fine, fine. I'll hang his shit up there along with yours. Tourists will be thinking it's some sort of kinky festival and hopefully be chased away."

"Or want to join in the fun," I offered.

Kian grumbled something about traffic increasing ten-fold

because the tourists could be real perverts.

I tried to laugh, but the silence in Mae's room set in like a crushing fog. Everything we were facing felt like we were about to drown – as if the room itself would fill with water, mocking my inability to save myself or my friends. Kian seemed to sense the true essence of my mood, and rather than say anything, he slid his long arm around my shoulder and tugged me against him.

"We're not gonna win," I whispered, as if I could no longer hide from what was a likely reality for us all.

"'Course we are, Sparky. Have a little faith in us – well, especially me. I always win."

I sighed, leaning against Kian. "And why is that?"

"That I win?" he asked. "Easy – I'm fabulous. Plus, I'll lie, cheat, and happily murder my way to the finish line. All excellent values if one is to save the world."

I leaned back and looked at Kian. His smile widened, his handsome face and blond hair now so familiar to me. When I first met him, he had gotten between me and Nikki, protecting me from her rage. Back then, Kian made me nervous, my body reacting subtly to his presence like my genetic code was blaring a warning signal. Now, however, I saw him as a dear friend and Ana's one true love. He and Raef even found a truce and friendship – a brotherhood even – over the past few months.

"Lie, cheat and save the world?" I asked. "Is that seriously your plan?"

"Absolutely. And don't forget murder. That's a key aspect of the plan as well."

I shook my head, chuckling as Kian released me. "Your morals may need a reboot someday, Kian. Just sayin'."

He began heading for the door, "Sparky, morals are just self-imposed roadblocks on the highway to Funville. Such a waste of time."

"I'll try to remember that," I muttered.

As he was about to leave, I remembered seeing Ana's ring from earlier in the day. I had yet to pull her aside and ask her about it, but I suspected it came from the soul thief headed out the door. "Kian," I called, totally bold, "Is it an engagement ring?"

He froze, stopping dead in his tracks just before he was about to exit the room. Kian and Ana, despite being loud and outgoing, kept their relationship close to their hearts. They didn't offer many displays of public affection, though the constant heat between them could melt your face off. And Ana once told me that some soul thieves and humans could become soul-bonded. She said it was a supernatural joining, so powerful that those linked to one another would be so forever, until death and then beyond.

I knew Kian and Ana shared that link. I felt it with Raef as well – as if our heartbeats shadowed one another.

Kian, quiet at the door for a moment, finally replied, "I'm going back to Torrent Road. Let Raef or MJ know if you think of anything else you want me to grab and pack up before Baz arrives."

He glanced over at me, his eyes flashing to the Scrabble game. "Mae lives within you, Eila – not in some board game. She's alive in every memory you carry with you, for the rest of your lifetime. Things don't matter – games, necklaces, houses, even rings. What matters is what they stand for and that's what makes them priceless inside your heart. That's what makes them a permanent piece of your soul." He flicked his head towards the game, adding, "Mae will understand if you leave it here, Sparky."

I swallowed hard and nodded as Kian left the room, refusing to directly answer my question.

I listened to his footsteps as he descended the stairs, but then I heard him pause for a moment, speaking in hushed tones to someone, then continuing on. Within seconds, Raef appeared on the threshold.

"Hey – I was looking for you," he said, coming into the room, concern etching his features as he studied my damp cheeks. "Are you alright?" He cupped my cheek, his thumb barely touching the wetness there. "Kian said you were upset."

My eyes met his. "Just missing her, you know?"

He nodded and wove me into his embrace, his dark, haunting scent surrounding my senses. Raef always smelled the same to me – this gorgeous mix of ice-cloaked wind and tumbling sea, as if he was born of the darkest storms that clattered over the bay, begging for a chance to tussle with the coastline.

I snuggled my face down into his soft shirt, his wide chest warm and solid beneath my cheek; a safe harbor, as always. "It's hard to leave, I know," he replied, stroking my hair. "But this is the right choice. This house, though protected from Mortis, is too well known to Waite. And I believe we will come back here, E. I believe we'll get the upper hand on Waite, wreck that damn Gate, and then we'll come back and we'll be free."

I rubbed my face against his shirt, drying my cheeks, and glanced up at the boy who had stolen my heart. "Ya know, Kian has a plan of attack that involves not playing fair and ditching one's morals."

Raef smiled at me as he twisted one piece of my hair over my ear, his fingers tracing my chin. "That's not a plan – that's just Kian's normal operating procedure."

I chuckled, and Raef brought his lips close to mine, kissing me carefully, slowly, and the fire he created over my skin tangled wildly with the ice I radiated at his touch. It was a twisted, addictive electricity that I never tired of, and it turned the Kill Mark on my back into a neon sign.

It had grown, my Kill Mark, with every Mortis life I'd taken. What had started out as a small, deadly brand on my lower back in October, had twisted itself upwards on my spine, flaring outwards towards my hips, like a leafless, sapling tree caught in the frigid clutch of winter. It pulsed hot against my skin whenever Raef and I became entangled with one another, a possible reaction to the fact that our kinds were designed as enemies centuries before.

He could take life by stealing a soul. I, on the other extreme, could kill by wielding the power that flowed like a river between living human souls. Some people called it telepathy. Others called it witchcraft and premonition. The truth, however, was that it all rode an invisible, powerful energy that bound all living things together. The Mortis and Lunaterra called it the Web of Souls - an infinite, dangerous energy that made Iron Man's Arc reactor look like a 60-watt light bulb.

Rillin suspected, however, that I channeled something else as well - not just the Web of Souls, but something darker. Something that allowed me to physically damage the Breakers mansion and Christian's library. Something that tangled with the Light from the Web, and allowed me to lay waste to more than the Mortis population. Something that made me more of a weapon than he'd ever seen before.

I intended to use it on Waite. Repeatedly, if need be.

Raef, oblivious of my thoughts, leaned his forehead to mine, whispering, "I love you. So damn much."

I ran my hand along the back of his neck, clearing my mind as I caught the ends of his dirty blond hair in my fingers. "Ditto, Mr. Paris," I whispered, but added with a devilish smile, "And you can be morally compromised with me whenever you like."

He growled, low, and I swear my body heated like a fever in response. I had come so close to losing him last night and the need to just be in his arms and know he was okay – alive – was like needing to breathe. I opened my mouth to tell him how badly last night scared me when our quiet moment was shattered by an irked voice from the doorway.

"Oh, for Pete's SAKE! Can I, for once, NOT walk in on you two about to play tonsil hockey? Take an anti-hormone pill or SOMETHING. Please!"

I looked behind Raef to the door where Nikki was glaring at both of us, having snuck up the stairs to Mae's room like a freakin' phantom breeze. Raef grinned, totally unapologetic, but I blushed something fierce and stepped back from his embrace.

"Ya know, you can always knock. That works too," I replied, heading over to her, mildly pissed. "You just take your hand and rap it a few times on the door and we will snap back into a G-rating so as to not wreck your prim and proper senses. Sheesh."

She narrowed her gaze at me, a snarky reply dancing on her tongue as she leaned against the wall. But then she sucked in a swear as she yanked herself away from the plaster, her face suddenly pinched in pain.

"Your arm?" asked Raef, now serious as he stepped next to me, studying Nikki.

Nikki gritted her teeth as she snapped back, "Yeah. If I accidentally put pressure on just the right spot, it feels like I'm being stabbed all over again. Sucks."

Raef flicked his brows to her shoulder. "Can I take a look?"

Nikki took a step back, less than thrilled at the idea of being poked and prodded. "Why? Leo already fixed it."

Raef raised his hands, a clear sign that he wouldn't touch her without her okay. "Because, if it was healed properly, you should be able to use it. And it shouldn't send shooting pain down your arm when you lean against a wall. Nerve damage can be tricky to fix, but . . . maybe. Maybe it can be corrected."

Nikki continued to glare at Raef, conflicted. "I'll be careful," he soothed. "I'm not going to try to fix anything or do anything right now, but I may be able to see why it's bothering you."

"And why she can't use it?" I added, 'cause currently her ability to shove someone into a goal post was limited to just her functional right hand (and I knew for a fact that doing so was a favorite pastime of hers).

He nodded, but kept looking at Nikki. "That too."

Nikki debated his offer for a moment, her lips tight. "Rillin said he thought he may be able to figure out a way for me to use my arm as well."

Raef shrugged, "That's true, but I'm assuming you'd also like to be pain-free before Thor gets his hands on you."

Nikki muttered some unsavory things about Leo's crappy skills before she finally sighed with a nod.

Raef reached up and slipped the sling from Nikki's left shoulder, careful to cradle her useless arm in one hand as he did so. He then reached up and eased the oversized t-shirt MJ had given her from her shoulder, revealing the pink, jagged line where Rillin had stabbed her when the Link was in control of him.

Raef's thumb swept over the fine bones of her arm and collarbone, as if he was tracing a poem written entirely in Braille. Nikki, her body tense, kept her eyes on the picture window near the Scrabble board, bracing herself for more pain.

Raef looked at Nikki's face, judging her reaction as he eased her arm away from her body and slowly began to raise it upwards. Just as her elbow came level with her chest, she gasped. "Stop! Shit, stop!"

Raef immediately froze and lowered her arm. "That hurts?" he asked, easing her arm back into its sling and fixing her shirt.

"God, yes!" she breathed, a thin layer of sweat having broken out on her brow. She looked pale, and I knew whatever Raef just did caused her a ton of agony. Heck, she looked like she wanted to puke.

Raef's hand slid into her sling as his Fallen Marks bloomed on his skin. They extended onto Nikki's fingers, lightly trailing under the shirt. I caught a brief glimpse of a few of Raef's healing marks up near Nik's collarbone, but they quickly bloomed and faded, almost like a single beat of a heart.

Nikki loosed a breath, the pain easing. "Damn."

Raef drew his hand away, the Fallen Marks slipping away like morning haze before the sunrise. "Nikki – I think Leo may've healed the bone wrong. I just eased your pain by calming the inflammation, but to fix it . . . I don't know. I need to talk to Kian."

Nikki let out a string or curses.

"Kian? Why Kian?" I asked.

Raef crossed his arms, thinking as he replied, "We were both wartime medics. I'd like him to take a look at Nikki as well. Together we may be able to come up with a plan to fix it. We can't do anything about it right now, but once we are settled at Faust, I'd like him to take a look." Raef's eyes met Nikki's. "It's possible that we may be able to heal you well enough that you get the use of your arm back – or some of it, at least. Hopefully."

"Whatever," muttered Nikki. "Look, I came up here in the first place because Rillin called from Christian's McMansion: he wants to know what Eila wants to do about the dead chick in Raines' bedroom. He doesn't seem too keen on being the one to deal with her, and I can't say I blame him. Carting around a corpse wouldn't be on the top of my To-Do list either."

"His reasons for being uneasy around the body have nothing to do with the dead part," Raef replied. "He knew her many years ago." Nikki looked a bit confused, but I ignored the questions in her eyes.

"We need to bring the body with us," I replied. I couldn't believe that my normal life had warped into a casual discussion about transporting a supernatural body to a nightclub for killers.

How, HOW was this my life?

"If Rillin's right," I continued, walking back to the Scrabble board as I spoke, "then the energy stored inside Elizabeth's body is still dangerous. Plus, Baz may need the body for more blood samples, but at some point, we're going to need to bury her. Or cremate her." I carefully picked up a few Scrabble tiles from Mae's side of the board and pocketed them in my jeans. Though I wouldn't play her turn, I would keep a small piece of the game we adored with me – a reminder of all that we'd once loved and all that had been stolen from us.

Too much insanity was hitting me at once and my head began to pound in response, an all-too-common headache beginning to ignite behind my eyes.

"I believe Faust has an incinerator," said Raef, watching me closely as he spoke. I swear he could see the minute changes in my face as the headache grew worse. His tone stayed level, however, and entirely serious. "I saw it in the basement when Rillin was in the holding cell. We could use it – nothing would be left of the body."

Ugh. Forget Nikki - now *I* was gonna puke. This was not the discussion I needed to be having at lunchtime. "Raef, that's a bit too much information for me, but thanks for the tip."

Nikki looked equally horrified. "You know, your life is seriously messed up, Walker. I mean, like, you make all those twisted reality TV shows look downright dull by comparison."

I finally left Scrabble behind, walking back to where she and Raef were standing. "Yeah, yeah – whatever. This coming from the chick who can probably chew on a paperclip and then spit out a fully formed Tin Man that can rap the alphabet."

Nikki grinned a bit, her red lips parting wide to show her straight, perfect teeth. "Plus backwards and in French. My Tin Man would be top of the line – don't forget that. That is, if I decided I needed to recreate an idiot from OZ, which I wouldn't. I'd rather make something more useful . . . like a key."

I narrowed my eyes, "A key to what?"

"My father's desk. In his office at my house."

I froze, my eyes locked on Nikki. "Okay . . . you wanna explain where you're going with this?"

Beside me, Raef was silent and tense. He warned, "Don't say it, Nikki. Don't even suggest it. Not now – not after last night. Not after what your father did to Rillin. You'd be walking right into their hands and we are in no position to form a raid on your – "

"I'm going back to my house," interrupted Nikki, undaunted.

"Hell, no!" I snapped, wincing as my voice jarred the pain in my head. I was beginning to wonder if I was starting to have a blood-sugar problem due to all the headaches. Maybe I wasn't eating enough, especially given that the last few days had been one big nightmare. I made a mental note to eat better.

"Not happening," Raef added, almost in a growl, then looked at me. "Are you okay?"

Not wanting to discuss my stupid health, I simply replied, "Just a headache. I'm fine. I just need food and sleep." I glared at Nikki, "And YOU are not going back to your house!"

"Screw you! What gives you the right to tell ME what I can and can't do? If I need to go back to my blasted house and grab some crap, I'm going!" Nikki's tone was sharp, but hurt and rage made her voice shake.

Her parents were making the Links for Waite, we were certain, and even worse, we knew it was her father who had restarted Rillin's Link. Mr. Shea had turned our fearless, selfless knight into a mindless assassin, bent to the will of others. He had nearly succeeded in murdering Raef and Kian, and had attempted to incinerate Nikki and MJ. And when I finally fought him, he overpowered me. Beat me.

Nikki had managed to deactivate Rillin, at great cost to herself. She'd also managed to remove the Link from our scarred comrade.

She had every right to demand this of us.

I could hear someone coming up the stairs, taking the steps two at a time as if drawn to the top floor by Nikki's fury. The angry cheerleader stood there, oblivious to whoever was coming, her one good hand clenched at her side.

"Let me tell you, Walker – if I'm right, then my father is keeping information on the Links and maybe the Gate itself in his desk.

That's where he kept the French book originally. And if I'm right, those details are a non-negotiable necessity if we have the scrawniest chance of destroying that Gate." Her glare was like iron as she took a step into the room, "You OWE me this, Walker. I earned the right to answers."

Just as Nikki stopped talking, MJ appeared behind her. He took in her clenched hand and stone-cold face and spun on Raef and me, accusation clear in his voice. "What the heck is going on? I can hear Nikki telling you two off from the first floor."

Raef flicked his chin towards Nikki. "She wants to go back to her house."

MJ's eyes nearly popped from his skull as his head snapped to face Nikki. "Are you NUTS? You took the Link out of Rillin and we sent Booth overseas. Perhaps you don't recall, but that would've pissed-off Waite. BIG TIME. We took his fancy playthings without permission and he's going to stomp all our asses if we go back to your house! For crying out loud, your folks are in on all this crap! And . . ." his face fell into concern, "you're injured."

Nikki glared at MJ, "You think I don't KNOW my folks are part of this? Damn it, just 'cause my arm is messed up, doesn't mean I can't do what needs to get done!" She glanced back at Raef and me as she added, "And I doubt Waite knows about Rillin and Booth . . . yet."

MJ looked frazzled. "Of COURSE he knows! Booth didn't bring Waite back the items on his wish list, which included Eila and Rillin!"

Nikki poked MJ in the chest hard. "Ana said that Booth was due to bring in Eila by midnight – TONIGHT. We've got ten hours before he realizes Booth failed."

"Are you kidding?" MJ demanded in a horrified laugh. "We've got NO hours if James is to be believed – his warning said that Waite has a bounty out on Eila and he blabbed the details on all of us. We're probably a blasted Wikipedia entry at this point. For God's sake, I bet our homes will be marked as points of interest on Drivequest by nightfall!"

"Nikki, aside from MJ being correct, you also shut down Rillin's Link. You deactivated him," Raef argued as MJ rubbed the spot on his chest, which probably now had a perfect indent of Nikki's forefinger. "Isn't it possible that interfering with the Link could somehow alert Waite that Rillin had been compromised?"

Good point. I nodded like a drunk, my headache mercifully starting to fade.

Nikki shook her head, insistent. "I doubt it. Rillin's Link is some old-school Feon work. Back when it was implanted in him, it was designed to control him and keep him locked to the palace. Before I went to work on removing it from him, I asked him how he believed the Link operated. He gave me what it could do, but he also said that once he was outside the palace walls, no one tracked him down."

I rubbed my thumb across my palm, thinking. "So you're saying that although Rillin's Link could control HIM, it did so by a . . . downloaded command? Like autopilot? But once it was up and working inside him, Waite couldn't track his movements?"

She shrugged with her right shoulder. "That's my best guess, yeah. Look - my ability to understand the Links is limited to what I *feel* when I touch them or make contact with them via steel. Kinda like . . . gut instinct. That's why I need access to my father's desk. You want me to help you, then I need all the information I can get."

The room fell silent for a moment, but then I spoke. "So . . . Waite may still be in the dark about our little stunt last night."

"Maybe," added Raef.

"BIG maybe," muttered MJ.

I took a long, appraising look at Nikki. "Fine. I'll send a couple of the guys back to your house to get whatever you need, but if a bird chirps funny, I'm ordering them to get the Hell outta there. And you – you're staying back. We'll send you on to Faust with Baz once he gets here with the trucks."

Nikki looked pissed, about to protest, but Raef cut her off. "That's not going to work," he said, surprising me. "Kian, Rillin, and I can't get into her house – we need to be invited by the owner and I doubt Nikki is on the deed. We can guard the outside, but we need to send someone who can get in."

MJ cursed, "Well, that's me. How fabulous."

"I'm not letting you go alone. I'm going too," said Nikki, looking right at MJ, who blushed slightly.

Oh, heck no! The town stray and the iron maiden?

Kill me now.

Nikki shuffled on her feet, trying to backtrack and clarify. "I mean, it'll be much, you know, *faster*, if I come, 'cause, well - I know where stuff is. And I'll be able to tell if my father has modified his desk – it may only be able to be opened by a Feon and for all I know, it could have a few new security features. Especially since my dad knows I nicked the French book from it. I'm sure its now a total tank."

Nikki's cheeks pinked as well.

FRAK.

MJ cleared his throat, realizing that Raef and I were staring at them like parents who had caught the two of them snogging behind the bleachers. He attempted to act unflustered by the girl next to him as he replied, "Bummer we don't have our own mind-controlled warrior – we could send him instead. Like when cops use those robot things to check for bombs and retrieve stuff. You know, he may be a pervert, but Waite is pretty slick to use the Links on immortal killers to do his dirty work. 'S'all I'm saying."

MJ was still blushing. I tried to force whatever was going on between the two of them to the back of my mind, lest I launch into Mae's notorious safe sex talk and cause my brain to implode.

Suddenly, I had an idea. "What if . . . what if I did have a robot thingie?" I asked, a small voice in my head pitching a fit that I was offering up a totally suicidal solution.

Nikki narrowed her eyes, dubious. "Walker, you do realize that MJ isn't referring to those plastic ones from the toy store that can retrieve a pencil, right?"

"I have . . . well, I have a robot. Sorta. You may be able to program it, since you're a Feon and all."

That little Voice of Sanity that I'd come to so often ignore was now in a full-on temper tantrum, screaming and writhing as it began decomposing – an obvious victim of the "use it or lose it" rule. Kian's morals had already bitten the dust; may as well kick Sanity out the door as well.

MJ and Raef looked shocked as both of them finally realized what I was thinking. Raef tried to signal to me to stop talking, but Nikki caught it. "Wait," she demanded. "You really have a robot? Like, not the Wall-E kind, but a legitimate robot?"

"Technically he's more like a suit of armor. Or, actually, a Tin Man with a ton of upgrades," I replied. "Listen, I'll let you meet him, and if you think you can handle him, I'll let you go back to your house. But you need to bring him with ya to retrieve whatever it is you think your dad has locked up in his desk."

"WHAT? No, no, NO!" demanded MJ. "That damn thing will probably twist us all into a braided rug! Rillin said it can only be shut down by your power! Not by Nikki, but by YOU."

"Technically, Rillin didn't say that a Feon couldn't turn it off," I muttered. "I mean, Christian said he watched Elizabeth take one apart."

"One that was SMASHED beyond repair!" howled MJ. "The one we have looks pretty damn pristine . . . and like it could run through a concrete wall and easily keep going!"

"This is a terrible idea," added Raef. "Rillin is never going to let Nikki use it. God help us if she loses control of it and it goes on to level half the town."

MJ nodded, "My folks will be livid if it tears through the Milk Way. We just fixed the antique freezer by the service bar. If that sucker gets wrecked, my mom will take it outta my hide."

Nikki's eyes sparkled and she looked unnervingly like a druggie desperate for a hit. "Dang! It can do all that? What is this fancy little toy you've been hiding from me, Walker? Can it come out and play?"

I nodded, Sanity offering up a weak death rattle as it shriveled and died.

CHAPTER 3
408 MAIN STREET, CENTERVILLE, MA

There was no way, and I mean NO WAY, I was letting Nikki fool around with the Mime. And part of me knew that Eila – the Eila I had grown to adore – would never make so many reckless decisions in such a short period of time.

Something was off.

Determined to uncover the truth, I snagged E by the hand, nearly dragging her with me across Mae's room as I told MJ and Nikki that we needed a minute. When we were far enough away to not be overheard, Eila yanked free of my grasp.

"What?" she demanded, hands on her jean-clad hips.

I studied her face, her freckles standing out in sharp relief against her fair skin. "Eila – what's going on with you? First you wanted to use True North's pirates and now you want to let Nikki fool around with the Mime? I feel like you're not thinking through your decisions. Like you're running head first into chaos – into Death."

She looked furious – barely holding it together – and part of me cracked. I cupped her face gently, bringing my eyes down into line with her, "Talk to me, E. Please. What's going on?"

I could feel her breath pick up, her chest rising and falling quicker as she struggled to stay in control of her emotions. "I want him dead!" she seethed. "I want it over. Now! I want him to pay!"

"I know. And I swear to you, we will nail the bastard. I swear to you that I won't ever stop until Waite is dead and the Gate is gone."

I held Eila's face tighter as her eyes pooled. I was desperate for her to feel my love over her agony and frustration. "Eila, we will get him, but we must be smart about it. We have to out-think him. Out-maneuver him. This war isn't about might – if we fight based on strength alone, I fear we will lose. But if we are smarter – sneakier – we can kill him. We can get through his defenses and lies and crucify the bastard. Nail him right to his blasted Gate."

Eila reached up and hung on to my wrists, finally nodding. "Trust me, E? Please, trust those of us who have lived in the shadows and been bred as killers. This is our type of war."

"Raef Paris, you will *not* leave me on the sidelines," she snarled. "Do you hear me? I am a weapon in my own right and I demand that I be put into play – used, as I should be. As an asset."

The idea of using Eila in a fight made my skin feel too tight, as if I was about to suffocate on dry land, strangled by my own instincts. But I knew if I denied her or tried to keep her out of the fray, that she would go off on her own – a wraith in need of vengeance.

She'd also go to Rillin rather than me, and that damn former knight would aid her, ditching whatever orders I gave him. He served her and no one else. And though I appreciated his determination to protect her, I also want to rip his throat out for being willing to do whatever she asked, no matter how dangerous. He had no ability to refuse her because he was still chasing the ghosts of the past.

"Swear it," she whispered. "Swear that I will be used to my fullest ability. Swear it now, because you believe in me."

I blinked, startled. She doubted how I saw her? "E – I always believe in you. Always. You are incredible in a fight and I am madly proud of you. But you are human."

She opened her mouth to protest, but I pressed a finger to her lips, silencing her. "I know, I know – you're Lunaterra. You've got Mortis genetics as well. I got it. But you can easily be killed, and nothing scares me more than the idea of watching you die." I stroked her face, "I wouldn't survive that. I *know* I wouldn't survive that."

E grabbed my neck, pulling my face close to hers. "You will not watch me die," she pledged fiercely. "We guard each other, remember? We keep each other safe. Always."

"Always wasn't in the Breakers," I sighed, reminding her that her heart DID stop beating once and it was because of me; because I didn't see the double-cross we were walking right into with Dalca.

"I'm not the innocent, untrained girl you knew back in October, Raef. You KNOW that," she urged.

I did know that. God, did I ever know that. The skilled, sharpened warrior that stood before me now would've made her grandmother Elizabeth proud.

Reluctantly, I swore the oath she wished to hear, "You will fight. I will make sure you are used as the brilliant, fiery weapon you were designed to be. I swear to you, Eila, that I will not leave you on the sidelines of this war."

She looked up at me, satisfied.

"Now, about that damn Mime," I continued. "Can we please just wait on that disaster in the making? Because if Nikki is right and Rillin's Link is so decrepit that Waite can't tell if it's running or not, then we have some time, but not a lot. We need to be in Faust, with all our equipment, before sundown. Any attempt to cash in on Waite's bounty by grabbing you will be made after dark – when a Mortis has a far better chance of succeeding thanks to the shadows. That doesn't leave us ten hours, like Nikki thinks."

"That leaves us only three," Eila replied, her eyebrow raised. "That's not much time." She glanced over her shoulder at Nikki and MJ, who stood waiting for us.

"Any day now!" demanded Nikki with a huff.

Eila looked back at me. "Okay – fine. No Mime, but Nikki needs a solid crew to go back to her place. I'm going with her as well."

I was about to argue – the words were literally on my tongue to tell her no, but Eila's glare kept my mouth sealed. "You promised, Mr. Paris," she said with a smooth smile. "No take-backs and no do-overs, got that?"

I suspected I'd just been played. "Eila . . ."

"Nope. Done deal," she replied, then turned and headed for Nikki, MJ, and the door they stood by. "MJ – call Rillin. Tell him we need him with the four of us to make a run over to Nikki's place. She's got stuff she needs and we're gonna retrieve it."

MJ asked, "What about Kian and Ana? And all the crap ready to go at Torrent Road?"

"Kian was heading back to Torrent Road," Eila replied. "Call him and tell him that when he gets there, to have Rillin come over here, but ONLY send him once Baz and Leo arrive. I don't want to leave them without some extra security, so Rillin doesn't come over here until help arrives from Faust. Kian may be one Hell of a fighter, but I'm not taking any chances anymore. And have Kian tell Ana that I need the two of them to help Baz load the stuff, Elizabeth included, into the truck and take it all back to Faust. We'll meet them there."

Eila, satisfied that our marching orders were clear (dead woman from the 1800s included) headed out of the room, no doubt to get ready.

Nikki smiled broadly as she turned and followed Eila from the room, but paused for a moment as she looked over her shoulder at MJ and me. "And that, *boys*, is how we *girls* get shit done," she said, then headed down the stairs after my girlfriend.

Eila called up from the stairs, "And tell Kian to pack up the Mime too!"

MJ and I looked at each other.

"Is it just me, or does it feel like a dude's manhood is thoroughly crushed whenever we're in the presence of the ladies in our group?" he asked with a groan.

"Constantly," I replied.

CHAPTER 4

408 MAIN STREET, CENTERVILLE, MA

SATURDAY, 2:30 PM

Twenty minutes later, I was sitting by the kitchen table as Rillin knelt before me, his beastly size keeping him easily at eye level with me, though I was seated. The weak afternoon light cast subtle orbs of color over his broad shoulders and floor, thanks to the stained glass window near the sink. Glowing pink and purple blots of color wobbled over the tile floor, catching the silver of the katana sword he'd removed from the sheath at his hip and laid on the floor beside him so he could kneel.

So he could do what he did best: prep me to fight.

Prep me to be a killer.

Occasionally, his eyes would glance up to mine as he worked in silence, his knee drifting against my leg now and then. He was dressed in black cargo pants that contained more pockets than I'd ever seen, many of them outfitted with a variety of weapons. Over his black t-shirt, he wore a tightly-fitted, equally dark Kevlar vest with an ebony Baretta holstered in place right over his heart, next to the spot where his Link use to reside. Strapped with leather to each tattooed bicep he'd secured small, deadly daggers. Every time he moved, I held my breath, certain their razor edges would catch on the many raised scars covering his arms, but they never did.

Rillin tugged one of my throwing gloves over my palm, his wide, scarred hands carefully fitting the silver wires against the sensitive skin of my underarm. This close to him, I couldn't help but contrast the way Rillin treated me with that of Raef.

The knight who trained me saw me as the tip of the sword. The killer who loved me, however, saw me as a precious gift that could be stolen away in the night.

I wasn't sure I was entirely one or the other anymore.

I wasn't even sure I was "Eila" anymore.

I kept MJ's phone tucked in the crook of my shoulder as I listened to Ana run down the hundred or so reasons why she and Kian should also be going with us to Nikki's. Many of her suggestions included her epic ability to blind people to her existence so she could sneak up and warp their minds.

"Ana," I sighed, adjusting the phone as I looked to the corner of the kitchen where Raef was securing his Kevlar vest, as equally dressed to kill as Rillin. MJ stood in the far corner of the room, helping Nikki carefully into her vest, her left arm proving to be a challenge. Not far from them, a selection of black and silver handguns rested on the counter right next to the coffee maker and my Jaws mug. Someone had dropped a knife in the mug, and the silver blade stuck out above the rim, just like a shark's fin.

Raef's eyes met mine for a moment, his unease with having

me go with them clear. I understood his hesitance – I was the prize Waite wanted, after all. But I was also the most dangerous weapon in our arsenal when it came to the Mortis. I could kill at a distance, shattering a soul thief into a cloud of ash with one focused hit of Light.

I was far more deadly than any gun, given the right target, and Rillin knew it.

Raef gave his Kevlar one last tug and looked at me, his eyes darting briefly to Rillin who was still focused on my glove. "I'm going to grab your Glock from your nightstand and your vest. I'll be right back, okay?"

I nodded, then turned my attention back to my pissed-off Bestie on the other end of the phone, MJ and Nikki starting to check the handgun clips for any missing bullets.

I dropped my voice lower, as if I could gain some privacy in the room, which was entirely pointless. "Ana, please. Please do this for me. For us. This isn't about whether you're an asset in a raid like this or not, trust me. Woman, you kick ass, no doubt. But right now I really, REALLY need you to make sure all of our stuff gets to Faust safely. I need you to do this. Please." Out of the corner of my eye, I saw Nikki hold an unloaded gun out with her good arm, closing one eye as if she was checking the front sight down the barrel.

Ana huffed, finally bending. "*Fine. God you owe me. And Kian is so pissed about having to bring the Mime. He says it weighs a ton and gives him the creeps. I totally agree. Feel like the damn thing is watching me! Oh, OH! - And did you know Baz isn't the only one here right now? Maia sent two trucks, no strike that, she sent two ARMORED TRUCKS, black ones. One Baz drove, the other Leo drove. And guess who rode in the back?*"

My brow furrowed. "Who?"

"Bane! And he ain't in his hunky human form!" snapped Ana. In the background, I could hear Kian protest the "hunky" comment. *"Eila, he stepped out of the back of one of the trucks and my heart nearly stopped. He's huge – far bigger than the ones on Polaris. I mean – shit! Fair warning would've been nice!"*

Bane. One of Maia's employees. A cursed shifter.

A Lesser, just like those that murdered Christian and Mae.

I swallowed, unable to reply as a cold sweat began prickling over my skin. Rillin paused, his gaze shifting from my hands to my eyes, but I was no longer in the present. Ana continued talking in my ear, Nikki and MJ still discussed clips and rounds near the far counter, but their voices were more like a distant buzzing in my brain, as if reality was fading out.

I was no longer in my kitchen on Cape Cod, but right back in the hallway of Christian's Caribbean home, two Lessers roaring at me as their talons carved into my fears with brutal efficiency. I was once again face to face with Mae, begging her to run to safety; to run to Christian and the wine cellar.

My decisions killed them both.

The memories of what happened on Polaris were flashing like a filmstrip through my mind when Rillin's deep, roughened voice drifted over my visions. He eased the phone from my shoulder, said something to Ana, then ended the call. I felt him shift to a position directly in front of me. Closer. I felt like I was in an endless fog, but his voice reached me through the pain and black memories.

"Bane is an ally, Eila. He's not one of them."

I nodded slowly, but my thoughts were still tangled on the floor alongside Mae's body.

Rillin's warm fingers eased into my clenched fist and he

carefully slid his hand into mine. "Eila?" he asked quietly. "Bane has suffered as well. He is here because he too lost people he cared about on Polaris. Look past the monster on the surface – see the good soul beneath. You did it for me. You can do it for Bane. You are strong enough to push back on the agony. Don't let it own you."

I blinked, Rillin's words drawing me fully from the past. His deep blue eyes were steady, appraising – a fighter checking on another in his squad.

"I'm sorry," I whispered, ashamed that I was so easily triggered back to the attack.

Rillin's face hardened, "You don't ever apologize to me. Not for what you went through – not for all that you've survived. Understand?"

My chest tightened as I finally nodded.

He watched me for a moment more, the sounds of Raef's footsteps coming down the stairs echoing through the house. Finally, he eased back, putting more distance between us. "Good?" he asked, flexing his broad hand in my line of sight. I raised my own, mirroring his movements to test the glove.

"Yeah, good," I replied, my voice a bit raw, as if the screaming I'd done in my mind had somehow scored my actual voice. He focused his attention back on my hands, moving on to the next glove as Raef entered the room, his leather jacket, my vest and gun, and his sweatshirt all in his hands.

"Not too tight?" asked Rillin. "Full range of motion?

"Yep," I replied, turning and twisting my hand to prove it.

Raef handed me my gun as Rillin finished the last of the laces on my second glove. "It's loaded, E, but the safety's on."

I turned the gun in my hand, a custom-made weapon that was

a gift from Rillin. The grip still fit perfectly to my palm despite the leather gloves. "Thanks," I replied.

Rillin finished securing my second glove, and I thanked him as I got up, Raef helping me into my Kevlar, checking the fit. Behind him, Rillin got to his feet and drew his sword from the floor with a metal *tang*, sheathing it back into its home not far from his hand. If he drew it on an enemy, I doubt they'd even see the blade coming before their head hit the floor.

"What about you?" I asked, tucking the gun in my back waistband, not far from my Kill Mark. I slipped into the soft shearling of Raef's leather jacket. "Don't you want a jacket?"

He just smiled. "I'm fine in my sweatshirt," he replied, tugging his gray hoodie over his head.

"So, rides . . ." said Nikki coming over to where I was, her own gun tucked in at her back as well. I noticed she also had a knife strapped to her thigh, no doubt a highly lethal weapon in her metal twisting hands. "I need to get my car. I'm not leaving my Pony behind Food Mart any longer than need be. It draws way too much attention and if I don't go get it, Jesse will just come back again, hounding us for details about what is going on. And since it's on the way to my place . . ."

"You wanna grab it," I finished. "That's fine by me. Why don't you guys ride with Rillin and he can drop you at the Mustang? We'll follow in my Jeep."

"I'd actually like to take the Nightrod, Eila," said Raef, leaning against the counter.

"Really?" I asked, surprised. "I mean – I love your bike, but I'm surprised you'd want to use it this time of year."

He shrugged, "The roads are dry. Plus, I like the fact that my bike can't get stuck in traffic like a car."

"You want a faster getaway, if needed."

Raef just looked at me and I knew that's exactly why he wanted the bike. If it came down to my safety, he'd ditch everyone else and get me outta there as fast as possible on the back of his Harley. I could argue that I wouldn't leave my friends behind in a fight, but for his peace of mind, I'd bend.

"Bike it is. Rillin's got his Chevelle and Nikki and MJ will have the 'Stang. I'd say we all have fast rides, so if we do have to haul butt outta there, we are well prepared."

Nikki glanced at MJ, "Can you drive stick?" she asked.

"I, well – yeah. 'Course I can . . . sorta." MJ winced.

Nikki's face hardened. "Dude, you better not screw up my tranny! I can't drive and shift with my stupid arm being messed up, but if you grind out the gears, I'll strangle you!"

MJ's face slowly broke into lopsided grin and he leaned in close to Nikki who was fuming, "Gotcha," he whispered, tapping her nose. "I can drive stick, no sweat. I just wanted to see ya freak out."

"You know what, Dog Boy?" hissed Nikki, half-livid, half-amused. "I think I'm gonna beat you with a big stick just for kicks. How'd ya like that, hmmm?"

MJ winked, "Oh, I just might like that."

"OKAY – we can GO, NOW," I yelled, mortified I was subject to the two of them and their semi-flirting.

Raef, fighting a smirk, looped his arm over my shoulders as he herded me around the table, Rillin already in front of us, pushing through the side door as his eyes scanned the yard for any trouble. An assortment of blades were tucked neatly into his wide belt, making him a moving arsenal.

Raef, equally armed to the teeth, stayed vigilant, but managed to whisper in my ear, "I could carve her a very nice stick, you know? For all her dog-training needs."

"Oh my God, just stop talking," I moaned.

CHAPTER 5
FOOD MART, HYANNIS, MA
SATURDAY, 3:05 PM

When Ana and I were fifteen, we spent an entire week screwing around with an old, decrepit VW Super Beetle in the dirt lot behind RC Garage. It was yellow, like the color of bile, and stank like a Frat house the day after a keg party. We even had to tie the passenger door closed with rope looped through a rotted hole in the sheet metal and around the door frame of the busted out back-side window. RC's owner, Jack, didn't care that we were messing around. The car was getting junked anyway, for metal money, and since he was fond of Ana, he let us have fun.

Thank goodness for stupid adults.

And the car was absolute crap – 100% destined for the scrap pile – BUT it still ran. Plus, it was a standard. And since no one would ever care if two kids without their licenses learned how to drive a stick in a private dirt lot, it was a great way to learn.

The only problem is, I'm not sure I learned a damn thing over those seven days because Nikki's Mustang hated my guts. I'd already stalled twice, just trying to exit the frigging grocery store parking lot, and managed to grind through first and second gear on my way to the stop sign. When I finally came to a jerking halt at a red light, Nikki's glare was boring a hole through the side of my head that rivaled the Ted Williams tunnel.

"You lied," she snarled.

I sighed, turning to her. "Okay, technically I didn't lie because I thought I could drive stick. I mean, I learned a few years back . . . sorta." I caught sight of Raef easing his beastly bike up alongside Nikki's window, his black helmet entirely obscuring his face as he rapped on the glass, Eila tucked against him.

Nikki, grumbling something that sounded like a bodily threat aimed at me, rolled down the window. Raef flipped up his visor.

"So," he asked, smiling, "I was just wondering if doing twenty all the way to Osterville was the plan, or if MJ is just having some issues driving stick? Because I thought the Mustang was about to eject a piston through its tailpipe a few times back there."

Eila's shoulders shook a bit as she sat wedged behind Raef on the bike, her matching helmet at least covering her laughter. Freakin' no loyalty . . .

"He can't drive for shit," snapped Nikki.

"I'm a very good driver, damn it! Just . . . ya know . . . not really good with the whole shifting part."

"Oh, for God's sake," hissed Nikki as she unsnapped her seat belt and began climbing into the back seat of the Mustang, a lush variety of curvy body parts brushing against my arm and seat.

"Be careful!" I demanded, trying to think of ice cold showers and elderly women. "For crying out loud, watch your arm! What are you doing?"

"Jeezus, Williams – shut up for a minute, will you?" she ordered, finally situating herself directly behind me. She scooted forward on the back bench seat, pressing her knees against my driver's seat back. She angled her torso between the front seats, placing her face right next to my shoulder as she reached between the seats, snagging the shifter in her right hand. "I'll shift, you drive and run the clutch. I say, 'shift' and you step on the clutch. Got it?"

"Uh, yeah. Got it," I replied.

I would not sweat. I would not pass out.

I would not stare at her glorious chest.

Raef looked dubious. "This should be interesting," he said, snapping the visor back into place.

The cross-road traffic was slowing and I knew we were about to get a green light. This was either gonna work, or it would fail in legendary fashion.

I ducked a bit so I could see Raef, his gloved hands throttling down on the bike's handlebar accelerator. "Hey," I yelled, catching his attention, "I say we drive by Nikki's first – make sure no one is home. If it's clear, we can go back and park at the florist near her house."

Raef nodded, now a faceless biker cloaked entirely in black. Nikki's white Mustang reflected in his helmet as he revved the bike, and it roared in response, loud enough to cause the cars around us to vibrate. An older man in a huge tank of a car gave Raef a disgusted glare, no doubt thinking some young brat was showing off. If he knew a killer sat astride the Harley next to him, he wouldn't dare even glance in our direction. No one would.

No one except Eila, that is. She snuggled in closer to Raef as the light switched to green. He pulled sharply in front of us, Rillin and his rumbling Chevelle at our back bumper.

"Shift!" demanded Nikki and I pressed down on the clutch, as she put the car into gear. I slowly eased off the clutch as I pushed down on the gas and the car lurched and stalled, causing Nikki to bounce against the seat. Cars behind us beeped. Rillin simply shook his head from the driver's seat of his car. I quickly cranked the engine over again, Nikki ordering how I should feel for some stupid "sweet spot" in the way her car purred so I knew when to release the clutch and apply the gas.

"Try again," she demanded, and I pressed down the clutch, realizing Nikki was now looking between my legs.

"What the heck are you doing?" I asked, horrified.

Not thinking about boobs. Not thinking about boobs.

"I'm watching your feet, you idiot! Now ease off the clutch and start slowly going for the gas."

I did as she instructed when suddenly she yelled, "Go!" and the pissy Mustang actually moved slowly into first gear, finally getting through the stop light at the last possible moment, leaving the poor suckers behind us, Rillin included, waiting at the red light. Nikki continued barking orders to me as she ran the stick, and I started to get a feel for that sweet spot she'd mentioned between the clutch and gas. Slowly, with her direction, I managed to get the Mustang up to 3rd gear without having it cannibalize its own engine. Pleased, I offered myself a mental high-five.

After a few more minutes of driving in tandem without killing each other, our view that of Raef's black bike swaying back and forth in front of us, Nikki cleared her throat. "So, seeing as my ass is on the line with the rest of you at this point, I have a few questions that I'd like answered."

I glanced at her, and the closeness of her face as she remained nearly wedged between the front seat startled me. I leaned away from her subtly, trying to act casual. "Uh, okay. I'll do my best to answer them."

"What really happened? In the Breakers, I mean."

The question took me by surprise. "Can I ask why you wanna know?"

Her manicured fingernail tapped on the shifter for a moment. "Well, I've seen Eila use her power - that Light shit - on Rillin when he was less than friendly last night. And I gotta tell ya, I don't see how what I saw could do the damage that was shown on the news at the Breakers. So what really happened?"

"Eila happened, with Raef's help. She caused a Core Collapse of the Light. Damn near killed her. Technically it DID kill her - stopped her heart. It would've been the end of the line for any other Lunaterra, but because she's part Mortis, she was able to heal." I shook my head, trying to forget what Eila looked like in the ICU, hooked up to so many machines and breathing devices.

I wasn't sure she was going to make it back then, Mortis genetics or not.

"Raef helped her?" asked Nik, looking dubious. "I find that hard to swallow. He's the ultimate mother hen. I mean, he was arguing with her not even an hour ago over her fighting alongside the rest of us. You're telling me *that* Raef helped her . . . die?"

I swallowed, taking a turn onto another road as I followed Raef and Eila, getting ever closer to Nikki's house. In the rearview mirror I saw Rillin follow us around the corner. "Yeah. He did. Back then, Eila really had no clue how to use her ability, but she had figured out what happened to Elizabeth. You know – the dead lady that Rillin doesn't want to be with. Anyway, Eila figured out that her grandmother knew she was going to die in the harbor by creating a Core Collapse, which would also kill Jacob Rysse, the angel dude. Eila basically did the same thing, but to do it, she needed Raef's help to trigger the reaction that would call down the Core. The destruction in the Breakers was totally Eila – she is far more dangerous than you know."

We slowed to a stop at a red light and I turned to Nikki. Her face and lips were mere inches from mine and I saw the slender column of her neck rise as she swallowed. She felt it – whatever *this* weird thing was between us.

It wasn't just me – I could see it in her face.

Dang, I wanted to kiss her.

The selfish side of me whispered that I could easily lean forward and press my lips to hers. The sane side of me, however, warned that I'd probably be punched in the nose for my efforts – a knee-jerk reaction on her part from our long-standing history of loathing one another.

Since bleeding all over her car's white interior would probably be even worse than my shitty shifting abilities, I decided to leave her lips alone and simply keep talking.

"Raef is fiercely protective of Eila because of what happened in Newport. When he first decided to guard Eila, he did so because he was seeking redemption for watching Elizabeth die in the 1850s – he was a friend of Elizabeths before he was turned, but once he was a Mortis, he didn't care. He stood by while she committed suicide. He wanted to make amends for not helping Elizabeth, so when he figured out who Eila was, Raef assigned himself as her protector. But then . . . then he fell in love with her."

Nikki finally broke eye contact with me as the light turned green, and we shifted together. The sudden silence in the car was making me insane, and like a moron, I blurted out the first thing that bubbled to my mind. "I thought you were going to die in my arms."

"What?" she asked, turning suddenly to me for a moment, before she returned her attention to the road ahead.

"When I was holding you in Raef's truck, after you'd been stabbed, I thought you were gonna die. Bleed out, right in my arms, and there was nothing I could do to save you. All I had was my ability to keep you warm and talk to you." I gripped the wheel harder, remembering how her breathing became slower and slower, as if each rise of her chest would be her last. "You were . . . in rough shape."

"I don't remember much," she replied, quietly, "but what I do remember, hazy as it is, was you. Talking to me, pressing your hand around the base of the knife, trying to keep it from moving. I remember you told me I was gonna be okay and I held onto the words, as if they could keep me from . . . leaving."

She stopped talking, the smooth curve of her jaw flexing as she wrestled for control of her emotions. I carefully placed my own hand over hers on the shifter and settled my fingers between her own.

"I shouldn't have brought it up. I'm sorry."

"No – I'm okay. It's just . . . I can't remember some parts. It's like the file that stored that part of my past was just deleted – burned up by the stress and pain and just left in ashes. So, yeah – I remember the ride in the truck to a point and the next thing I recall was waking up in Faust, my arm useless."

We turned down the oceanfront road where Nikki's house was located, and I kept my focus on the street, scanning for anything out of the ordinary. She hadn't pulled her hand away and I felt her thumb hook in with mine, startling my heart into a sprint.

She deserved to know what happened when she lost consciousness. She deserved the details of last night, rather than being left in the dark. I glanced at her, "You passed out in the truck, and for a brief moment I actually thought you stopped breathing, which scared the shit out of me. We got to the back entrance of Faust and Maia was waiting with Leo and Bane and a few other people I didn't recognize. They pushed open these massive steel doors and we drove the truck right inside. Maia went batshit when we arrived because the place was packed for the concert, but she didn't turn us away, thank God."

"They kept us well away from the crowds and took the guys upstairs, but Maia said you'd lost too much blood to move you very far, so Leo had me bring you into a room on the first floor. He set to work healing you. He asked me to leave, but I may have told him exactly where he could shove that order, because I wasn't leaving you."

Nikki chuckled for a moment, but then looked at me, her thumb stilling. "I woke up in someone else's shirt."

I flushed and looked away from her. "Uh, yeah – that belongs to Baz, just FYI."

Nikki chewed her lip, suddenly finding the view of the windshield very fascinating as she asked, "How many, uh, people were in with me when Leo fixed me up?"

"Just Leo and me," I replied, feeling the need to shield her from the ideas that were no doubt running rampant in her head about what happened in that room while she was unconscious. Trying to ease her mind, I went with honesty, "We, uh, got you on the floor and cut your shirt off as the blade was still in your shoulder. I did cover you up quickly as soon as he checked your torso for any other stab wounds. I swear it."

She simply nodded, her jaw set.

"Nikki . . ." I started, but she just shook her head.

"Keep your eyes peeled, Williams" she replied, easing her hand out from under mine. As if ignoring what I just told her would make it all a dream. "My house is just up a bit on the left."

I got that she was probably embarrassed, but I didn't understand why she was suddenly closing herself off once again. I'd seen her do it a few times over the past few weeks, and I couldn't figure out what triggered it. "Nikki, I'm sorry. I swear, all I was thinking about was making sure you were gonna make it. That you were gonna live. No matter what I saw, all I cared about was hearing you talk again . . . and probably tell someone off."

The corner of her lip turned up into a small smile, but it felt forced, "Don't worry about it, MJ," she replied. "Ain't like I haven't been naked and unconscious before."

"What's that supposed to mean?" I demanded, a nasty fear slithering up through my gut. My hand was once again strangling the Mustang's leather-bound steering wheel.

She waved a dismissive hand in my direction. "Nothing. Never mind. I'm just being stupid."

"Nuh uh - ain't ditching that conversation THAT easy," I demanded. Nikki Shea was many things, but *stupid* was not one of them. "You don't say something like that to me and then just breeze over it!"

"Jeezus, Williams! Haven't you ever partied so hard that you can't remember the night before? Don't be such a prude." The steel-hearted vixen I'd known for so long was suddenly back with a vengeance, replacing the young girl who'd slept against Marsh, mere hours earlier.

I chose my words carefully as I replied, "No, actually I've never been so blotto that I blacked out the night before. And if you *were* that drunk, then someone should've known better – should've made sure you stayed in your clothes and out of harm's way." I shook my head, "Your *friends* are jerks, Nikki, present company excluded. I would've made sure you didn't get that hammered; I would've made sure you got home safe."

She snorted, "First of all, I'm a loner at heart, Williams, so I don't really have any so-called 'friends,' despite those that follow me around at school and do what I tell them. And secondly, that home that you said would be safe for me? I'm pretty sure that was a mirage as well, don't you think?"

I wanted to pull over; to yank her into my arms and give her a shake, demanding she stop closing herself off. That she had a place where she belonged now – with US.

"You. Are. Not. Alone," I snarled, angry that she'd grown up in such a shitty situation and no one had ever stopped to help her. I was pissed at myself for never looking past her mean-girl attitude and for buying into her spoiled-little-rich-girl routine.

She flicked her good hand between us, "Look – let's just get through whatever this is," she replied. "We take out Waite, shut down the Gate, and then we go our separate ways. I've got enough stashed in my savings that I can get the Hell outta this town and float for a couple of months."

"Nikki – "

She straightened, flatly ignoring me, "Slow down. My place is up next."

"This conversation ain't over, Nik."

"Whatever," she replied, dismissing me once and for all.

Damn it - I wanted to either strangle her or kiss her until we passed out from oxygen deprivation.

Our small convoy drove by Nikki's massive brown Tudor home, but her parents' vehicles were nowhere to be seen. The lights in the house were off, and no movement was visible through any windows.

"I don't think your folks are home," I said, still studying the house.

Nikki sank back behind my seat and I glanced in the rearview mirror, watching her as she pressed one hand against the window, her breath clouding the glass as she whispered something that I didn't catch.

"What did you say?" I asked as we continued past the house to a parking lot several blocks away.

Nikki slowly wiped the glass clear of the fog she'd left there, her face torn. She swallowed hard, reining in her emotions as she replied quietly, "I said goodbye."

CHAPTER 6
TINA'S TULIPS, OSTERVILLE, MA
SATURDAY, 3:30 PM

I totally recognized the parking lot.

It was the same one where MJ and I had parked his Bronco (well, former Bronco) when we decided to ditch all sense of intelligence and break into Nikki's house. At the time, I was decidedly NOT in favor of his psycho plan to retrieve my necklace, but now I was mighty grateful that we'd ended up going through with our criminal ambitions that night, otherwise Baz may've stabbed Nikki in his doped-up haze.

How Maia Moriarty's pothead son ended up as an ally still made my head spin, but the kid was smart (save for the whole drug habit thing) and I was hopeful that he'd be able to locate a Mortis cure between my blood sample and Elizabeth's.

I gotta admit, I was a tad tweaked about bringing her body to Faust. I wasn't even sure Baz had told his mom of the existence of

Elizabeth's remains. I could just see Ana commanding where different items needed to go and then adding, "Oh yeah, about the body – it's rockin' enough energy to blow the roof off the club, so be careful will ya?"

Yeah . . . I needed to lay Elizabeth to rest.

Soon.

MJ, Nikki, Rillin, Raef and I all gathered by Rillin's Chevelle, and I rubbed my hands furiously, trying to warm up. While I loved the bike, riding in the cold weather wasn't exactly the toastiest of transportation options.

Raef had shifted to a spot near me to better block the wind as Nikki ran through what she was intending to grab at her house. In and out at top speed – that was the goal.

"So, my Dad's office is on the second floor, back of the house. There is a security system installed, but it isn't used that often."

"Why's that?" I asked, shivering a bit. Raef slid up closer and wrapped his arms around me, trying to convey some heat into my frozen bones.

"What? Not using the security system often? It turns out that closed circuit systems don't respond well to Feon proximity. Basically, between my folks and me, the system can be super glitchy. We must give off a weird sorta frequency that interrupts the cameras."

"Seriously?" asked MJ.

Nikki just nodded, "But it's intermittent. So sometimes it works, other times it's dead."

Great. "So, is there a way to make sure it's down before we try to get in?"

"Oh yeah – I can roast it from the power panel on the outside near the garage. That part is easy. It's breaking in to my dad's desk that is gonna be a project."

"Built like a tank?" I asked.

"Yes, but I think he modified the desk after I managed to swipe the French book. I don't know what countermeasures are in place in that room, but if I were to guess, knowing now what I do about his ties to Waite, I'd say the desk is rigged to blow if someone unauthorized tries to get into a drawer."

MJ's eyes widened. "Rigged to . . . blow? Like, EXPLODED?" Nikki just shrugged. "WHAT the Hell is wrong with your family?"

Nikki leaned back against the Chevelle and rubbed her damaged arm, as if working out a kink. "Like I said, I could be wrong, but my guess is that they'd rather have that info destroyed than in the hands of someone else."

I glared at Nikki. "Well that's just great. You dragged us here, and NOW you tell us your father has a possibly exploding desk? Did you have a brain fart or something and just now remember this detail or what?"

Nik snorted. "Jeez, Walker – have a little faith, will ya? I got an idea, so don't sweat it." She smiled at Rillin. "You bring what I asked you to, Big Guy?"

Rillin glanced at me, then walked around the back of his car and popped the trunk, hauling out a long length of heavy chain, the links rattling like Marley's burdens. "This enough?" he asked.

She offered a thumb's up. "Perfect. Let's go."

"Wait, wait – what IS the plan?" asked Raef, glancing at Rillin, who was easing the chains back into the trunk with a steeling *crash* and heading to the driver's seat. "And where are you going?"

Rillin paused. "Nikki informed me earlier that my vehicle would be needed. I'm to drive it over to the house, but come up through the back dirt road, behind the far side of the home."

"Start talking, woman," demanded Raef, looking at Nikki. "What's with the chains and the Chevelle?"

Nikki smiled. "Let's just say that torque and speed will be required. Oh yes – and a sturdy chain."

Though we all started asking questions of her at once, she simply held up a hand to stop our yammering. "Trust me, Freaks."

Trust me, FREAKS?

"Are you kidding me?" I demanded, but she just started walking for her house. Raef and MJ seemed too stunned to object, though Rillin seemed entirely indifferent. Watching her jean-clad butt sashay down the street away from us, I recalled why I was so fond of daydreaming about strangling Nikki from time to time.

Trust me, Freaks. HA! This "freak" was so gonna kick her ass if this went south.

MJ snapped out of his daze and went to catch up with Nikki, but Raef grabbed him by the elbow, halting him mid-stride. "MJ, where's your head at, man? We need Marsh, remember?"

"Shit," blurted MJ, backing up and shucking his jacket and shoes. He stripped down to the underwear that Collette had made him, his boy parts probably freezing, but he kept a sharp eye on Nikki who was headed down the road.

I watched, awed, as a glittering rain-like effect began tumbling from MJ's skin, falling from his body like snow. He slowly curled inward, bringing his arms in against his chest and tipping forward, as if gravity was dragging him down. But before he hit the ground, Marsh's outline took shape in a flash of brilliance, all four massive paws landing smoothly on the concrete.

MJ, now Marsh, took a moment to let out a snort and then

shook, scattering the thousands of diamond-like chips from his black fur like a burst of stardust. As they struck the ground, they winked out entirely, as if the break in contact with their creator sent them back into nothingness, like delicate snowflakes instantly melted against a flame.

Marsh looked at us and struck a show-dog pose for an instant, his head high and leg extended out behind him. His tongue lolled out of his mouth as if he was smiling at us, gloating at his ability.

"Show off," muttered Raef.

I ruffled his ears. "Go get her, Cujo. Keep her safe."

"Yeah – and try not to hump her leg either," added Raef.

Marsh sucked in his tongue and leveled an unfriendly glare in Raef's direction, then proceeded to kick gravel in our direction before sprinting after Nikki.

"Your dog needs obedience training," said Raef, walking alongside me as we began heading in the same direction as Marsh and Nikki. Rillin pulled out past us and headed down the opposite end of the street, hooking a left at the end to get around to the dirt road Nikki specified.

I grinned at Raef, "My dog doesn't need obedience training. You just need to give him a belly rub once in a while, that's all."

Raef narrowed his gaze at me. "Yeah, that's not happening. Ever."

I fiddled with my throwing gloves, scanning the road and homes for any potential trouble. Raef did the same as I asked, "I can't figure out the point of the chain and Rillin's car. What in the heck would she need those things for?"

"It sounds like she's intending to tow something."

"Yeah," I replied. "Probably her ego."

Raef snorted, tugging me close as we walked. "Eila, I don't care how much horsepower Rillin's car's got - nothing short of an eighteen wheeler is hauling that girl's ego, or the chip on her shoulder."

"Amen to that," I muttered.

CHAPTER 7

SHEA RESIDENCE, OSTERVILLE, MA

SATURDAY, 3:45 PM

Standing at the base of Nikki's grand staircase, Marsh stalking around the empty house like a dutiful guard doggie, I had an overwhelming urge to rip the ball finial off the wooden handrail and hurl it at Nikki's head.

"Are you crazy? We can't do that!" I demanded, shifting the length of chain that Rillin had handed to me over my shoulder. The steel links were digging into my skin, which enhanced my seriously pissed-off attitude that had set in the instant Nikki had revealed her grand, f-ing plan.

I dragged my boyfriend, my best friend, and my trainer to her house FOR THIS?

I was livid.

Her fat head + ball finial = Done deal.

I glared at her as she stood casually leaning against the wall near the staircase. "This is the STUPIDEST idea ever!" I snarled. "Plus, we'll alert half the neighborhood!"

"Oh, suck it up, Walker! First of all, the neighbors are older than Dumbledore. If they can hear anything at this point in their lives, it would be a miracle. Plus, it looks like most people aren't home, probably because they have NORMAL LIVES, none of which involves a time machine."

"Or ripping a desk through the second floor WINDOW!" I snapped.

Nikki cocked her hip, pointing at me. "Okay, first of all, your hearing is also crap because you obviously didn't comprehend what I just said. I *said* my dad's office has a set of French doors leading to the balcony. Everybody knows that an executive desk would never fit through a window. They're like, the size of a double wide freezer. Jeez, get with the program."

I tugged on the chain, trying to move it to a less abused area of my shoulder. "I'm sorry, but when you said that the plan was to chain the desk to the back of Rillin's bumper and have him rip it out of a second floor room with a '69 Chevelle, I figured I was . . . oh, I don't know . . . HALLUCINATING?"

Marsh padded back into the room and plopped his butt down near the stairs. He happily watched the two of us argue, his tail swishing back and forth across the polished wood floor like a black duster. His pink tongue hung out the side of his mouth as he panted, and I swear the bugger was smiling, highly amused at the absurdity of what we were about to do.

Damn dog.

"This WILL work, Walker. I know my dad – he'd have pressure rigged the area under the desk, so if we lift it slow, the sucker will blow. But if we yank it, hard, and thus get it instantly off the floor, then the explosives built into the floor won't be able to level the desk."

"But the floor is still gonna explode," I snarled. "How do you expect us to secure the chain around the desk without us triggering the floor and getting blown to bits?"

"Leave that to me – I need your arms, though, to help," she flicked her jaw to her own dead arm as it hung, unmoving, in the sling.

I flexed my jaw, thinking. Shit, we needed the crap in the desk, but it would be pretty dang pointless if we weren't alive to use it. I felt like, up until this point, our fate resided on one of those antique balancing scales; sure, it wobbled once in a while, but in general, it found its way back to level . . . until Nikki confessed her plan, and the damn thing went crashing to one side, scales flying.

"If you get me killed, Nik, I'm gonna haunt your ass for centuries. Got it?"

She waved me off. "Nonsense – if we trigger the floor the wrong way, then we'll both be kickin' it in the afterworld. You can't haunt my ass if I'm dead too."

"Yeah – that makes me feel so much better. Thanks for that."

She slapped me hard in the arm, a jarring physical pep-talk that would probably leave a bruise. "Anytime, Walker. Let's go."

We headed up the stairs, me dragging the chains, Marsh trotting ahead of us, his tail wagging. "So, what did the guys think of your grand plan?" I asked, really surprised they'd even agreed to something as nuts as this.

"I haven't told them yet."

I stumbled on the stairs, "You what?"

"Didn't tell them. Damn, girl – clean the wax from your ears once in a while."

We reached the second floor and headed down the hall to a room with a massive set of double doors, passing by the crystal doorknob that I recognized as belonging to Nikki's own bedroom. She didn't even glance in its direction, and my chest tightened for all that she had learned and all that she chose to leave behind.

Her world had imploded thanks to me.

Sometimes I wondered if the destruction and agony I brought to the Cape would eventually ensnare everyone I knew.

Nikki paused, "Look, if I told them the plan, they'd be like you – flipping out, expounding on the virtues of not sending my dad's custom desk sailing through the air and avoiding the C-4 he has layered in the floor."

My jaw dropped open. "He has C-4 in the floor? Nikki - we'll level the house! Forget the office, your WHOLE HOUSE will be GONE!"

"Well, that's why you're here, Walker. If I'm doing the math right, and if my physics teacher from Junior year wasn't the functional alcoholic that everyone said he was, then a direct hit of your Light at the same instant the floor triggers should, technically, hold the destruction to this room only."

I laughed hysterically. "Technically?"

"Well," she shrugged, "There's a little bit of gray area in whether or not the explosion will kill us first or not, but yeah – it'll be fine."

I glanced at Marsh and he no longer looked like a doggie doofus, but a seriously concerned canine. His eyes flicked between Nikki and me.

"Nikki. We need a plan B, otherwise we are *not* doing this.

Whatever is in that desk will have to wait."

"Until when? Until my folks get back here and realize that I may try to grab the information I KNOW my dad has on the Gate?" She shook her head. "No way. We do it now, otherwise we won't have another shot."

I swore, rubbing my head and trying to think. "Damn it. This plan sucks."

Nikki stepped towards me, her look like iron. "Are you, or are you not, the girl who survived the Breakers? Are you not that girl I saw handle what looked like molten white fire when she was tackled by Rillin?"

I cursed sharply, but nodded.

She placed a strong finger right between my breasts, where my scar resided. "You are either a fighter, or you're not. I'm gambling on the former, so I need *that* girl, right now, to get her shit together and stop second guessing her ability, got it?"

Hell, she was right. Screw this – I came to kick butt.

I glared at her as I began calling to my ability in a whisper only my mind could decode. I could feel it respond instantly, like the expanding sound from a guitar string once plucked. It was this *monster* that lived within me, trapped under my skin and restlessly pacing; waiting until I freed it to devastate the world.

The power began to flare in my veins as the energy from the Web of Souls poured into me, causing my vision to brighten and leech life's brilliant colors from the hallway, leaving the world in a startling black and white.

I turned my eyes to Nikki as she smiled wickedly, no doubt taking in the golden halo that now ringed the brown of my eyes. "You ain't seen nothing yet," I replied, and the Light building inside me sang in response.

"Now you're talking, Walker. Let's get this done."

CHAPTER 8
SHEA RESIDENCE, OSTERVILLE, MA

I settled against the chrome bumper of Rillin's Chevelle after making yet another sweep of the Sheas' yard and sprawling grounds. Everything was quiet and there was no sign that Waite had been alerted to our meddling with Rillin and Booth.

I glanced at the broad, tattooed knight next to me. He stood, hands clasped behind him, scanning the area, his sword catching the light from the setting sun once in a while. His close proximity still left me on edge, and while I knew that his attempt to murder Kian and me was due to the Link that had resided in his chest, I still couldn't shake the memory of him shooting me in the chest at point-blank range.

Some memories are like tar, sticking to your heart and poisoning your instincts so completely that they may never wash away entirely.

I checked the rounds in my gun, which I kept firmly glued to my hand, and then turned to Rillin. "Nikki had mentioned that you didn't seem too thrilled to have to move Elizabeth's body. She said she got the distinct impression that you were grossed out by having a dead person kicking around."

Rillin's jaw flexed, causing the scar that dragged down the side of his face to pulse. "I have no problem with the dead, Raef. And I wrapped the body in blankets and moved it into the back of the armored truck Baz was driving. Kian won't let anything happen to her."

"You do that on a regular basis, you know?"

"Do what?"

"Flip between calling Elizabeth a "her" and an "it." It's okay to honor her by still referring to her as, well, *her*, rather than just a thing." I glanced up at the back of the house, trying to see through the French doors that Nikki had told Rillin to park under. What was taking so long? We needed to make our visit here as brief as possible, and the girls had already been in there for at least ten minutes.

Rillin said nothing in reply.

"Just so you know, I corrected Nikki on the matter of you and dead people."

He glanced at me, "What, exactly, did you tell her?"

"I may've alluded to the fact that you and Elizabeth have history and that it is probably difficult to constantly be reminded that she is no longer among the living."

Rillin shifted his weight, and settled back against his car, mirroring my pose. "I am more concerned at the threat her body poses if her Light is triggered. *She* is quite deadly in the wrong hands. When I moved her, she felt as though she was buzzing with electricity.

And she glowed, like when Christian kissed her. She reacts to our kind. She's dangerous."

"Eila would agree with you. She mentioned burying her," I carefully studied Rillin out of the corner of my eye, "or cremating her." I thought back to the one time I moved Elizabeth's body when we had fled Polaris. Her skin didn't react to me at all. I was about to tell him that, but he sighed, as if a small fracture had opened in the armor he always wore over his emotions.

"It would be the wisest decision, I agree," he replied, quietly.

I knew his agony – what it felt like to be faced with such loss. When Eila's heart stopped in the Breakers, part of me snapped in two. The moment when the heart monitor picked up a weak beat was something I'd never forget. For Rillin, however, there was no monitor to tell him the girl he once loved would come back to him. She'd never smile up at him again.

I looked at Rillin, his broad shoulders ever so slightly fallen. "Eila will give you a chance to say your goodbyes, Rillin. I hope you know that."

Rillin's gaze narrowed on the glass doors above us as he pushed off the car. "I already told her goodbye once, Raef. In the woods after we escaped. I don't want to have to do it again." He flicked his head towards the French doors. "I think I see them."

I pushed off the car just as the glass doors slid open and E appeared above me. In her arms was a length of the chain, but the end of it was still located in the room.

"Here – grab this and hook it up to the back of the Chevelle," she ordered as she began slowly feeding the chain down from the second floor.

Rillin and I glanced at each other as we gathered the length of steel between us. "Why exactly are we rigging this to the bumper?" I asked, dubious of whatever half-baked plan was afoot.

"Oh, well . . ." she stuttered for a moment, which was a sure sign I wasn't going to like whatever was about to come out of her mouth. "See, for us to deactivate the, uh, countermeasures in the floor, we need to yank the sucker fast. This end of the chain up here is secured to the desk and that end of the chain – "

"Goes to the car. I got it," I replied. "You do realize that this is gonna make one Hell of a crash, right? It'll probably alert the neighbors that we are being less than helpful in regards to the Shea's belongings."

Eila glanced behind her into the room briefly, "Yeah, well – Nik says the neighbors are deaf as a doornail."

"What, exactly, are the countermeasures in the floor?" asked Rillin as he attached the chain to the undercarriage of the car.

Eila laughed, "Oh, it's just a little bit of *sherrfor* . . ."

"It's a little bit of what?" I asked, totally confused as she'd mumbled the last word.

Eila was about to reply when Nikki stepped out next to my girl. "C-4. It's just C-4, but we got it under control. You do your part, we'll do ours."

"C-4?! ARE YOU INSANE?" I yelled, Rillin shooting to his feet as well. "Get out of the house!"

Rillin was glaring at Nikki, but his words were aimed for my girl. "Eila, Raef's right – that explosive is extremely dangerous. You shouldn't be in there – none of you should."

Nikki waved us off, "Chill out, Thor. We got this – quit whining and do what you're told. Ain't like you can stop us anyway, since you can't get into the house, so I suggest you stick with the plan."

"This isn't a PLAN!" I roared, enraged that I'd been duped by a cheerleader with attitude. I wanted to rip her functional arm off and use it to knock some sense into her. Rillin, standing next to me, had turned into a live wire, anger pouring off him at the betrayal as well.

"Hurry up, Walker. Let's get this done," said Nikki, walking back into the house. If this worked, I'd need to keep away from Nikki Shea until I calmed down . . . or I might legitimately kill her.

I stepped to the balcony, looking up at my girl and noting the deadly, golden ring caressing her eyes. She was already pooling the Light within her, building it like a terrifying tsunami; a wall of raw power that grew stronger and stronger inside her until she released it like terrible, devastating curse. "E, baby – don't do it. Just come on down. We don't need the desk this badly."

"Nik thinks I can contain the explosion with my Light," she replied, flexing her gloved hands. I noticed the silver balls embedded in the palms were glowing white hot. "She thinks if I hit it at the moment the floor triggers, I can basically burn back the C-4."

I glanced back at Rillin. "Would that work?" I demanded, angry I was even forced to seek his advice, and massively pissed Eila was tempted by Nikki to do something so crazy. Desperation apparently bred recklessness and I had a sinking feeling this was just the tip of the iceberg in that regard.

Rillin, who had been like a statue, finally stepped forward from his car. "Possibly. Eila, you'll have to be exact about the timing and seek to encompass the explosion – don't throw straight. Throw in a curve, like a half bubble."

E held up her delicate hands, displaying her throwing gloves. "Will these even bend the Light in such a way?"

He nodded. "The gloves take your intention and form it to reality. If you seek a sphere, you will form a sphere. Remember your training - remember how you must see the target and the surrounding area without *seeing*." He tapped his chest, as if pointing to something within himself. "Hone your instincts, Eila. Feel the power deep within you - feel it throb like a heartbeat. It's yours alone to command, so do not hesitate or pull back when you wield it this time. The gloves will serve you well."

"I haven't exactly had much of a trial period with them, Rillin. Besides fighting with you, I haven't used them at all."

My gaze ran between the two of them as Rillin shifted his weight, obviously not thrilled with the memories of last night. "You formed a whip and a dagger with the Light last night."

Eila's brows shot up. "You remember?"

"Not really. Just bits and pieces. Some memories are very complete, others are more broken. Nikki told me. She'd asked about the gloves - how they channel and concentrate your power."

Understanding hit me. Nikki had been intending to use Eila to grab the desk, probably since late last night. That BRAT! She'd been planning this! She got us here, got E and MJ in the house, where she KNEW we couldn't enter, and now she knew she had us backed into a corner.

Furious. I was absolutely furious!

I took a running leap and grabbed the bottom of the balcony, hauling myself up and over the railing. Eila, started, stepped back, but I caught her by the arm, pulling her to me as I glared through the open doors. Nikki stood just beyond the threshold, her hand on her hip, scowling.

"What if I took Eila right now? Tossed her in the car and left you here to rot?"

Nikki smiled, "And would you leave your pal, MJ, here to rot as well? Because I doubt his chivalry will allow him to leave me so undefended."

Sure enough, Marsh, head low as if he'd been scolded, appeared from a dark corner of the office and slid in beside Nikki. Her hand rested on his wide head, her fingers sinking delicately into his thick, black fur.

I could tell he was going to stay by the cheerleader's side, no matter what I said. I knew he was *that* guy – the one who would sacrifice himself, without regret, to save another, even if she was a deceptive liar. Marsh's huge brown eyes seemed to beg me not to take sides; begged me to be forgiving no matter how angry I was at the moment.

Damn it to Hell!

I dragged in a deep breath, my hold tightening on Eila, who had wrapped her arms around me, her hand running slowly up and down my spine as if trying to ease me. "It'll work, Raef. And, if it makes you feel better, we are gonna position ourselves in Mr. Shea's massive claw foot tub."

She pointed toward the far corner of the office where a door was cracked. I could see the edge of a large tub seated in the center of the blue tile floor – an obvious connecting bathroom, probably that also led to the Master bedroom.

My jaw tightened as I looked down at E tucked in next to me, her dark hair pulled back in a loose ponytail which had allowed a few defiant curls to escape around her face. If anything happened to her in this stupid stunt . . .

"I can make the shot while in the tub and the cast iron that it's made of should protect us pretty well," she explained, running a finger along the base of my neck, the stubble once again coating my jaw and rasping against her touch. "I can do this," she whispered, smiling gently. "Plus, I love you too damn much to leave you behind. I thought you knew that already."

I held her freckled face in my hand, tilting her so she was nearly nose to nose with me. "Be. Careful. And do as Rillin told you and hit the sucker with everything you have, E. Got it?"

She nodded and I pressed my lips to hers, the taste of her strawberried tongue sliding along the seam of my lips too much to resist, audience be damned. I yanked her in tight against me, taking over the kiss with a growl.

I could sense the power inside her, as if the sweetness was backed with an electrical bite that rang through my own skin. I'd never kissed her when she was . . . lit. That's what she was: a weapon loaded and ready to fire.

Feeling the rawness of the Light throbbing inside her and snapping at my mouth and skin, as if static was rioting between us, I finally understood entirely what Rillin always had: Eila Walker was a true killer. A war machine, designed by a warrior Archangel who'd fallen to his own twisted reality and was destroyed by his own creations.

I broke from Eila, and her eyes were shining like a supernova, her skin nearly luminous, as if Mars and Venus were melded to her bones creating a true fallen star locked in the body of a young woman. I dragged my hand down the edge of her face, studying her as I always should have - not as someone who needed protection, but as someone who needed a partner. An equal.

I finally smiled at her. "You got this, E. You tell us when, and we're gonna leave half of Rillin's tires in the flower bed and send that desk to the next zip code.

"Yeah?" she asked, her eyebrow raised, but totally pleased at my sudden shift of heart.

"This is your show, E. Let's get this over and done with so we can get to Faust before Kian pisses off half the workers with his stellar personality."

She chuckled, but I looked past her to Nikki and MJ. I pointed at the Ironess who was still stroking the shifter at her feet. "If you ever lie again, however, you're out. You're on your own. No second chances. Too much is on the line for any of us to not trust you 110%, got it?"

Nik rolled her eyes. "Fine. Whatever. I need your Electric Lightshow girlfriend to face off with my father's homemade booby-trap so I can get the shit he's stashed in his gaudy-ass desk." She glared at me, "How's that for honest?"

"Much better," I replied and then glanced to the desk. "And, you're right. It's gaudy and a piece of junk. Trust me – whatever he paid for it was too much. I know my furniture; I'm a carpenter after all."

Nikki's horrified gaze swiveled to Eila, "He's a FREAKIN carpenter? Are you serious? I've been putting my life in the hands of Mr. Bookshelf?"

"Well, yes. But, lemme tell ya, Raef's bookshelves would be totally killer," said Eila with a wide smile. "Trust me, freak."

CHAPTER 9
SHEA RESIDENCE, OSTERVILLE, MA
SATURDAY, 3:30 PM

It turns out that a clawfoot tub can be surprisingly spacious, though Marsh's left hind foot was constantly slipping down the porcelain surface and digging into my leg, his furry paw and doggie claws unable to gain much traction. He kept trying to reposition himself, but after the fourth time he groaned and gave up.

I'd have an indent of a few of his toenails near my butt by the time this was over. Well, if we weren't incinerated.

"We're in place," said Nikki squeezed in next to me, her phone wedged in her shoulder, her good right hand pressed tightly against the tub wall. She was giving Rillin last minute instructions over the cell phone – a device I doubted would survive this whole debacle in one piece.

"When Eila says GO, you floor it and rip that sucker clear out the doors, got it? I'm gonna have her count down from three. So, she'll do three, two, one, and GO. Don't hesitate, Rillin, or this is all for nothing."

On the other end of the phone I could hear Rillin reply that he and Raef had it covered.

Nikki's eyes fell to me, as if assessing whether I was still here or if my soul had split, leaving the teenager she knew locked away and something else in her place.

The truth was, I ditched the fuzzy-sock-wearing, chocolate-hoarding version of myself a while back, and now I was solely focused on channeling all of Rillin's training into the next few seconds.

The Light felt as though it was streaking and skittering in icy threads under my skin, as if the Kill Mark on my back had set its glowing embers loose throughout my body.

I focused all my attention on the C-4 that was hidden somewhere in the floor below the desk. I was the warrior. The killer. The ultimate weapon, locked and loaded.

I braced my arms over the top lip of the tub, my palms open and aimed at the desk as the Light boiled in my veins. My peripheral vision had faded to an intense pinpointed area below the desk. Under my glare, forced into submission by my relentless will, my ability seemed to bend the molecules in the air. With my vision no longer that of an average human, I could see it - how reality seemed to curve towards the desk, as if a whisper thin glass wall had formed between us and Mr. Shea's booby-trapped furniture. It flexed outward and back, as if breathing as it cupped the desk.

I had never channeled, willingly, this amount of Light. I knew the only time that I was more powerful was in the Breakers and that was entirely out of my control.

This time I *owned* my destiny - I controlled the beast within.

I could feel the Light as it pulsed and writhed inside me – *around* me – as if I were the center of a deadly thunderstorm, and the tumbling black clouds were the raging Web of Souls, screaming for release as a hurricane.

"Three," I breathed as I began the countdown, and Nikki shifted, placing the phone on her lap so Rillin could hear me. She pressed her good hand against the gouge in the porcelain of the tub in front of her. She had dug through the tub's coating to access the iron underneath so she could mutate the bath into a wave of metal to shield us if necessary.

If I failed.

"Two," I whispered, and my hearing began to fade as I eased my hold on the Light, as if giving a furious kite a little bit more slack in its string. The Light raged hotter in response, like a racehorse about to break through the starting gate. "One."

I flexed my hands, and the tub wall rippled under Nikki's hand. She was ready. Waiting.

"GO!" I screamed as I ripped away my hold on the Light and it crashed through the room like a ball of white fire. The desk ripped free of the floor, the chain gasping a steely breath as it held fast.

My Light slammed against the triggered C-4, the explosion throwing the tub free of the floor and sending us sliding across the tiles, the claw feet screeching as we were sent careening.

I bellowed in determination as my Light forced the explosion backwards, my arms and chest feeling as though they were being crushed as the blast curled backwards like an ocean wave slammed into reverse, pushing against my power.

The Light poured from me, an inferno blasted in one direction, and the C-4's volatile power smashed through the outer wall of the office, catching the end of the flying desk and sending it spinning like a pinwheel as it fell. The blast tore the plaster from the ceiling and incinerated the walls and remaining furniture, rendering the glass windows and French doors to glittering shards as the impact finally blew out of the house entirely.

My power collapsed, a once deep well entirely drained, and I slumped back into the tub. I could no longer feel my arms nor my chest, as if my body had been doused in novocaine. The Light that had danced under my skin sputtered out.

And I was deaf. Like, REALLY deaf.

Couldn't hear crap except this irritating ringing.

I glanced to Nikki, then Marsh, and realized they appeared to be sans hearing as well. Dust and debris floated through the air, and all three of us were coated in a fine layer of sheet rock, making us look like ghosts. Marsh's big black nose was caked with a white film of crap, like a cow's hide, and his big brown eyes blinked madly, as if trying to clear his vision.

Next to me, Nikki was coughing, fanning her hand through the haze of sheetrock, now in fog-like form, but she had a big smile on her face. She turned to me and said something, but all I caught was her lips moving. It looked like she said *luckit lips*? That can't be right . . .

"What?" I yelled, and the ringing receded slightly. I spied her cracked phone, which had been tossed against the tub during the blast and was now probably living in the iPhone afterlife.

She yelled something over her shoulder and slowly I began to hear Raef's voice and Rillin's, calling to see if we were okay. Nikki yelled back that *we were fine* and *we were coming*, though to my ears it sounded like a whisper at the end of a tunnel.

She turned back to me. "BUCKET LIST!" she yelled and made

a check mark in the air.

"Bucket List?" I demanded. We staggered to our feet inside the tub and I heard MJ snort then sneeze hard. "Are you kidding me? THIS shit is on your bucket list?!"

Nikki nodded. "Yup – play with explosives is now officially checked off!"

"ARE YOU CRAZY?" I yelled, but Nikki just waved me off.

"Walker, you MUST have a bucket list. Everybody does – or a wish list, but I'm going with Bucket List since, ya know, we are trying to screw over the Grim Reaper by not dying anytime soon."

I stepped out of the tub, dusting myself off, but it was pointless. I needed to be hosed off. "Yes, I have a Bucket List but playing footsie with C-4 ain't on it."

"Well?" she asked as Marsh hopped out of the tub. "What's something on your list, Walker?"

"I don't know – reading all the plays from Shakespeare?"

Nikki's face fell into that of absolute horror. "Are you kidding me? That's like . . . shit, that's like English class' version of purgatory. That can't be on your list!"

"Well, what would you suggest?" I snapped.

"I don't know, but something more risky – more exciting!"

I gave her a ridiculous look. "Nikki, I'm dating a cute immortal guy who can ingest a person's soul and fade into the darkness like a shadow. I'm trained by a dude who's basically a gladiator and my two best pals can shift into a dog and read the minds of dead people. Exactly how do I enhance my 'Bucket List' when reality is so intriguing?"

Nikki opened her mouth to argue, but paused. "Okay. Point taken. Boring playwright it is." She turned to Marsh, as we began making our way carefully through the demolished room, a gaping hole where the desk used to reside now giving us a view of the first floor and the staircase. I noted that the ball finial had actually stayed on the banister.

Sure. NOW it doesn't fall off.

"I'll need to ask MJ what's on his list when he's, ya know, not a dog anymore," she said, but Marsh moved before I could warn her, leaping up on his hind legs, paws landing on her shoulders as he dragged his big, pink tongue across her face, clearing a swath of dust from her chin, lips and nose like a racing stripe.

Nik froze in place, too stunned and probably grossed out to move as Marsh dropped back to the ground and continued out the door, tail high and happily wagging as he left.

I choked back a laugh, but smiled huge at her as I made a check mark with my finger in the air. "Bucket List!" I sang.

It was a miracle she didn't hurl me through the hole in the floor, but the sound of sirens in the distance, no doubt headed our way from the explosion, had us running for the guys, all amusement gone.

Going to jail was not on my bucket list either.

CHAPTER 10
FAUST, NEW BEDFORD, MA
SATURDAY, 6:00 PM

We managed to get to Maia's nightclub an hour past sunset, and I'd never been so glad to see Kian and Ana waving us through a set of massive steel bay doors at the back of Faust.

I parked the Harley where Kian had specified, not far from two armored trucks and alongside Rillin's half-dead Chevelle and Nikki's Mustang. Amazingly, with the exception of Rillin's ride and Mr. Shea's desk, our crew was in one piece and reunited, though some of us were truly filthy.

I knew that at some point I'd need to retrieve Agent Howe from Collette's loft where he was holed up, because he most likely was a target as well. Rillin had called him the moment we got James' cell phone message and told him to stay put in Boston for now. Truthfully, saving his Irish hide wasn't on my top ten things I wanted to do, but I knew his computer tech abilities could be damn helpful, especially if he proved to be a full-on hacker.

We needed him to get through the FBI firewall and find the Soul Gear that the Feds apparently held - a nice little treasure they had found in a safe under Dalca's burned out store. He and James were the only two of our crew currently not under Maia Moriarty's guard. James, however, was in the wind and completely on his own. He'd gone AWOL with nothing more than that one warning via a cheap cell phone, and a promise to contact us when he found us a safe place to hide.

I had serious doubts that we'd ever hear from him again. He'd been one of Christian's original pirate crew and his pilot. With Christian and Collette dead, I didn't see any reason for James to stick his neck out for us anymore. He didn't really know us. He didn't really give a crap about Eila beyond what Christian had instructed him to do. I couldn't see him helping us. I just couldn't.

I cut the Harley's engine and Eila released me with a sigh as she sat back and pulled the helmet from her head, her dark hair, now tinted white, tumbling free. She flashed me a smile and I twisted in my seat to wipe my gloved hand along her ghostly cheek, smudging the sheetrock dust.

My girl.

My furious, fearless warrior.

I'd never underestimate her control or her power ever again.

I also vowed to never underestimate the weight of a gaudy desk again, as Mr. Shea's weighed a ton – a fact made unforgettable when it unfortunately ended up ON Rillin's car, rather than in the flower bed, as planned. I suspected Eila's power, which funneled the C-4 from the house like a rocket, had propelled the flying desk onto a collision course with the Chevelle. The classic car now had a partially caved-in roof, blown out back window, and completely missing trunk lid (currently wedged in the back of Nikki's Mustang). I'd never tell Eila that her power nearly murdered the Chevelle, however, and I knew Rillin wouldn't either.

She did her job. She saved lives and scored the prize.

Though we'd managed to avoid the fire department and police as we took the backroads to get off the Cape, I knew it would be all over the news at some point. Plus, I knew we were going to be interrogated instantly, police or no, with the way Kian was eyeing the damaged piece of furniture strapped to a once mint Chevelle.

"Good grief, if this is how you losers move furniture, I'm never letting you help me if I ever buy a house or renovate Cerberus," Kian chuckled as he walked over to us and gave a nod to Rillin, who was getting out of his battered car.

Ana took in our wrecked appearance and then her eyes landed on the Chevelle and her face fell. "Oh, my God! What did you do to the car? Damn it, does no one appreciate fine American Muscle anymore?"

Eila, MJ, and Nikki looked like they'd gone to war with white paintballs, and Rillin and I were lightly dusted with sheetrock, but it was the fact that the Chevelle looked like the Jolly Green Giant had sat on it that concerned Ana Lane.

She was a car fanatic to the core.

With the desk strapped to the Chevelle and looking as though it had starred in one of those stupid YouTube catapult videos, plus our demolished appearance, we were the definition of a walking disaster. The only things that escaped relatively unscathed were my bike and Nikki's Mustang, save for MJ's terrible shifting skills. Thank heavens, because Ana may've entirely lost her mind if more vehicles had been damaged.

Ana, finally giving up on her mental tally of how much work the Chevelle would require, placed her hands on her hips. "Lemme guess – the house is totally fine too, right?"

Nikki, leaning against her car with MJ standing nearby, waved her off as she looked around the cavernous room that was the lower level of Faust. Last night Rillin had been on this level somewhere, kept in a cell, but the "garage" that we were currently in seemed to be a separate area – perhaps where the original trains had been repaired. Everything was coated in rough-textured black paint and the walls were riddled with pipes, duct-work, gears, and massive turning wheels.

It was the steam-driven heart of Faust.

Nikki smiled as she replied, "Oh totally. A little paint, some curtains – ain't no one gonna know anything is missing."

"Uh huh. Right," Ana replied, walking over to me and Eila as we sat on the Nightrod. I balanced the bike as Eila climbed off slowly, her hands on my shoulders for balance. She looked physically beat, but ever so proud. She'd done what she needed to and our mission (if you could call it that) was a success because of her.

E was a total badass. A rock star.

Truth was, I was mighty damn proud of her as well. But during the ride here, I could tell she was tired and possibly sore, especially in the way she leaned against me and her grip on my waist had weakened.

She need a hot shower, decent meal, and a warm bed to get some much needed sleep. Technically we'd left Faust only a few hours ago, in the wee hours of the morning, and now, roughly fifteen hours later, we were back, seeking safety. And sleep. God, we all needed sleep, Mortis included.

I wouldn't mind hunting either, as I felt fairly run down.

"Where's Maia?" Eila asked Ana as I swung myself off the bike and rested both our helmets on the seat.

"Maia and most of the Faust workers are upstairs, dealing with some last minute club stuff before they open in a couple hours."

Eila paused. "She's still opening?"

Ana nodded, "She said if she shut down, it would draw way too much curiosity. Plus, and I quote, she said that 'some of us have to work, you know?'"

"Right," muttered Eila.

The girls began talking, Nikki joining them, and Kian tipped his chin towards the side of the two trucks, obviously needing to speak to me. MJ and Rillin caught it as well, and followed.

Before he could say anything, I asked, "Why are you and Ana still down here? Where's all our stuff?"

Kian crossed his arms, "We've been stuck here because Faust rivals the TSA in terms of screening all incoming items. And all our crap is still in the trucks because Bane wants a full run-down on everything that we brought with us."

"So? Just tell him," said MJ, looking confused. Truth was, I was confused too. Maia knew what was going on. Why block our things down here?

Kian huffed, "Yeah, well, I would've except this guy," he pointed at a darkened corner of the room, "keeps asking the same f-ing thing, which makes me concerned that Baz may not have told his mother everything."

"What guy?" I asked, but just as I said it, the massive, dinosaur-like form of a Lesser slipped out of the shadow. Though I knew it was Bane, I still stiffened. MJ swore under his breath, taking a step back.

Rillin, however, just stood there, appraising the massive shifter, from his death-gray skin and reptilian like face, to his razor sharp claws and heavy, dragon-like tail. The curved horns jutting from the back of his head had braided bits of fabric hanging from them, the ends woven with beads and feathers, like a tribal member.

Bane was bigger and broader than the Lessers we faced on Polaris and his skin contained some truly gruesome scars – as if he'd been in fights, which surprised me given the claim that Lessers were peaceful. In his cursed form, the Faust worker truly looked like a raptor, meshed with a demon-like man. His lower canine teeth jutted out from his jaw, like a bull dog, and as he stepped forward into the dull light of the room, he looked towards where Eila was talking with Nikki and Ana. He kept himself hidden from Eila's view, however. He did it for her benefit, I was sure, and for that, I was grateful.

"What's the question?" asked Rillin.

Kian gestured dramatically to Bane, who opened his monstrous mouth and asked, "What's in the blanket?"

"HOLY crap! You can talk?" demanded MJ. I had to admit, I was equally surprised, mainly because I never heard Bane talk, even in human form. The dude was basically the embodiment of silence.

Bane's broad forehead fell slightly as he looked at MJ. "Of course," he replied, his gray lips managing to form the words despite the massive teeth that slid along his mouth as he spoke.

MJ stuttered for a moment, "But . . . but . . . you're shifted! Into . . . well, THAT. How does *that* speak? The ones on Polaris sure as shit didn't!"

"Lessers can speak, even when shifted into our cursed form. And I suspect that those who attacked you on Polaris could not speak because of the Links. No doubt they were forbidden to do so and their entire freewill taken from them."

MJ sobered at the memory of those we had killed on Polaris while defending ourselves. They had been slaves to Waite, unable to stop themselves from turning into murderers.

Kian, however, seemed unaffected by the mention of Polaris. "Hear that, Fido?" he demanded, grinning at MJ. "When are you gonna cut the doggie charades and just start talking?"

"I can't talk as a DOG!"

"Oh yeah? If Godzilla here can do it, why can't you?"

"Jeezus Kian! Have some tact, for God's sake!" I snapped, horrified. Kian was not one to pull his punches, but I'd never heard him be so callous. I glanced at Bane, "Sorry, man. We are running on fumes at this point. Our patience is fairly shot."

Kian, unapologetic, glared at me. "Look, my girl and I have been stuck for hours in this crappy, dirty, soot-covered basement, so excuse me if my tolerance has hit an all-time low. Ana is tired and hungry and all I want is to get her out of here. I'm pissed that my ability to give her those simple things has been foiled by this guy," Kian pointed at Bane. "PLUS, if he asks me one more bloody time what's in the blanket, I may just try to suck his soul out, cursed shifter be damned."

Bane let out a low growl.

I stepped quickly between Kian and Bane, who towered an easy couple of feet above the two of us. "Okay, well, let's just take a breath and I'm sure we can get this settled. I say – "

"Lessers can smell death, correct?" questioned Rillin, looking at Bane and cutting me off.

Bane offered Kian one last hard glare and stepped back, answering Rillin. "Yes, we can scent the loss of life in any living thing."

"But you don't know what's in the blanket?" demanded Rillin, almost forcefully. Almost . . . desperately.

Bane cocked his head. "Are you saying whatever is in the blanket is deceased? A person?"

Rillin didn't answer and I knew both Kian and I were trying to gauge where this line of questioning was going. We stayed silent, deferring to Rillin and his far greater understanding of Lessers.

"That's not possible," continued Bane. "If a corpse was in the blanket, I'd know it. Whatever is in the blanket has no scent of death."

"What?" MJ asked, floored. "What do you mean it doesn't smell like a dead person?"

Rillin turned to me. "We need to speak with Baz. Now. If Bane can't scent her, then something is off."

"Could it be that the Light in her body overrides the laws of normal death? She is preserved after all, and let's face it – she doesn't smell, period." *Thankfully.*

Bane, listening in, stepped forward. "Her?"

"The blanket contains the body of a deceased female," confirmed Eila, standing at the far end of the truck, Nikki and Ana on either side of her. None of us had even heard her approach, too wrapped up in our own shocking revelations. She swallowed hard, looking at Bane's massive size and finger-long claws, no doubt remembering how violent her last encounter with Lessers had been. No doubt remembering the loss of Mae and Christian.

She cleared her throat, her voice dry as she spoke, "Bane, if you'd be so kind as to go find Baz and Maia for us. We need to speak with them. She is free to inspect all the contents of our truck, but I believe her son may've neglected to mention to her that we are in possession of a historic, and rare, relic."

Eila took a careful step forward, then another, finally coming up to Bane, who lowered his head slightly to her level. The width of his forehead seemed to match the expanse of E's shoulders.

"Please tell her," she whispered, nearly face to face with the shifter, "that we've brought the remains of my fourth great grandmother with us and her body maintains the power from her own Core Collapse."

Bane, stunned for a moment as he knew the history of Elizabeth Walker, finally bowed low to Eila, then slipped back into the darkness to do as instructed. In his absence, our group relaxed slightly and began talking about what to do next, but out of the corner of my eye, I watched Rillin.

He stared after Bane long after he'd disappeared and I wondered, suspiciously, what thoughts had suddenly consumed the knight.

CHAPTER 11

FAUST, NEW BEDFORD, MA

SATURDAY, 6:30 PM

Maia was not a happy camper.

She paced the length of Elizabeth's body, silently studying my grandmother's still form in Baz's lab, and occasionally pelting her son with questions about what he'd learned from her blood and its potential for a cure. Baz answered honestly (usually with 'I don't know yet'), but acted like a scolded child. He hadn't told his mom of the body's existence, and I could tell he felt guilt ridden about it. Parental rule number 1: thou shall not drag around a dead chick and neglect to inform your mom.

I don't think Baz did it on purpose, but rather simply forgot to pull his mom aside and tell her, his scientific brain too wrapped up (or too stoned) in trying to utilize Elizabeth's silvery blood to find a cure for the Mortis.

And mine – he took samples of my blood as well.

Maia, however, was rocking her pissed-off momittude to maximum effect, continuously spinning a large ring on her forefinger as she studied my young grandmother. If she turned the jewel anymore, she'd unscrew her knuckle. For someone who lived and breathed soul thieves, I was kinda shocked she was so freaked out by a dead body.

Only twenty minutes earlier, Rillin had carried Elizabeth up from the armored truck, her body well hidden in the blanket until we reached Baz's lab. He had laid her gently on the cold steel table, which had been the same place where Maia had dug the bullets from Raef's body not even twenty-four hours before. As Rillin unwrapped her, revealing her young face and dark, wild hair, I could tell that even Maia was stunned by how beautiful Elizabeth still looked, as if she was a napping 20-year-old, and not a nearly two-century-old remnant of a murder-suicide with an Archangel.

Rillin had carefully rearranged her gossamer blue gown, smoothing the skirt and making sure her legs were well covered. Occasionally his hand would graze her calf or bare foot, and her body glowed fiercely in response. The bloom of blue light would flash through her skin from their contact point and race over her body in a tidal wave effect, only to sink into nothingness when he pulled away, like sea water disappearing into the sand.

While my memory wasn't perfect, the reaction seemed far more intense than when Christian had kissed her, and I wondered if it was possible that Elizabeth had, at one time, loved someone other than Christian. Perhaps loved someone even more . . .

I eyed the way Rillin tended to her now, and if I had any doubts about how much he adored her, they were all washed away. Her Monster. Her Trial. Even death couldn't dull his feelings for her.

The look on Rillin's face every time he was in Elizabeth's presence was a mixture of devastation and steely resolve, and I knew, *knew*, his heart was entirely hers. He loved her as Kian loved Ana; as Raef loved me. What I didn't know was the secrets held within the heart of my Grandmother. Had Christian been the love of her life? Or had Rillin? Did it even matter anymore? The fate of her remains was soon to be decided inside Baz's elaborate (though seriously disorganized) lab, and the decision to get rid of her once and for all was no longer mine alone.

Maia finally paused beside Elizabeth, her fingers drumming a steady rhythm on the metal table.

She turned her attention to me. "So, Christian had kept Elizabeth, here, in his underground vault since her run-in with Jacob Rysse, or rather Therophel, in 1851?"

"Yeah," I replied. "But after the first Polaris attack, we took her with us because Rillin told us about how dangerous she is right now. You know, with the stored up energy from her Core Collapse."

Maia turned to Rillin, an eyebrow raised. "Why do you think she is storing the Core Collapse's energy?"

He moved closer to the body. "Well, it would explain why she is so well preserved. The Lunaterra did keep the bodies of those who died in their own Core Collapse and reused them as IEDs."

Maia crossed her arms. "Did they stock pile these lovely IED bodies for nearly two centuries and, if they did, did those body stay as flawless as Elizabeth's?"

"I couldn't say. The Lunaterra reused the bodies so frequently that they wouldn't have needed to . . . store them."

"And this reaction she has – the glow of energy under her skin when you touch her – does that occur when other Mortis make contact with her skin as well?"

"It happened with Christian as well, Ma'am," Rillin replied.

"But not me, nor Kian," Raef clarified.

"I didn't think so," Maia replied. She looked at me. "And, according to this whole IED theory, if Eila throws her own Light at Elizabeth, then it will cause Elizabeth to release a secondary Core Collapse that can wipe out every Mortis in the building, save for Kian and Raef who are immune. Is that right?"

"Yes, that's what Rillin believes. I didn't want to test the theory, though, for obvious reasons," I replied, shuffling under Maia's scrutinizing gaze.

"Jeezus . . . what a circus," muttered Maia. She looked at Ana, "And let me guess – you tried to Reload her, because she's dead, but it doesn't work too well, does it?"

Ana crossed her arms as she stood next to me, Raef and Kian on either side of us. MJ and Nikki were on the other side of the room, listening intently.

"HEY! I DID manage to read her – once," snapped Ana, defensive, pointing her finger at the angry Gypsy. The blue gemstone in the ring Kian had given her sparked like fire and flint in the light of the room, just as pissed-off as its owner, apparently. "I did it on Polaris. Since Christian's death, however, she's been . . . silent."

Ana looked at our knight, "I was sure it had to do with Christian's death, but I gotta admit that the blue effect that just happened when Rillin touched her – I don't know. Maybe I can read her now? Maybe she's been . . . reactivated?" Ana's face twisted on the last word, as if it was total insanity to discuss a dead body in such a way. She muttered something under her breath about needing a long vacation.

Maia crossed her arms. "Well, two things. Number one is that she's not an IED. The energy you see flowing inside her when Rillin touches her is actually the bond. Their *soul bond*."

Rillin blushed. "I'm not her . . . but we never . . . I was HER TRIAL! "

"Oh, just shut it, Blackwood. You still look at her like she owns your entire existence. For her to react so strongly to your touch means that she felt the same way. At least . . . she did when she nearly leveled the harbor square. The fact that it happened with Christian as well . . . it was possible she was bonded to both of you, though one must take precedence over the other."

"Her reaction with Rillin is way stronger than that of Christian," offered Ana.

Rillin looked as though he wanted to melt into the floor.

"So, does that mean that I can't, ya know, set her off?" I asked.

Maia shook her head. "No, you can't."

Thank God! "So what's the second thing? You said there were two things."

The corner of Maia's mouth curved into a devilish grin. "The second thing is that Christian, unfortunately, never told me of her existence. If he had, I would've told him that he shouldn't keep her in his vault."

"Why's that?" asked Rillin, concern etching his face.

"Because Elizabeth is not dead. She's *asleep*."

CHAPTER 12

FAUST, NEW BEDFORD, MA

I blinked. Like, ten times.

"I'm sorry, but can you run that by me again?" I croaked.

"What do you mean SHE'S ASLEEP?" snapped Rillin, hope twisting with disbelief and anger. "She has no heartbeat! How can she be asleep?"

Maia played with a few of her necklaces as she replied, "Perhaps *asleep* is too simple a term. She is suspended, though I've never seen such a state last for so many years. While a soul bond itself cannot cheat Death, I believe that Elizabeth accidentally took some of Therophel's immortality when she killed him in the Harbor square. Between Therophel's dose of invincibility, and the fact that her soul-bonded mate was still alive when the fight occurred, I believe she was knocked into this state of . . . sleep. Suspension. Whatever you wish to call it. She's only *mostly* dead. There's a big difference between mostly dead and all dead."

"You're saying she's . . . Sleeping Beauty?" asked MJ, a stunned look on his face.

Maia rested one hand on her hip, her eyes still drifting over the body. "In the loosest, non-fairytale comparison, yes."

I studied Elizabeth's form lying on the table. She looked so young. Heck, she looked like a college kid. "Can . . . can she be . . . awoken?" I asked, nearly holding my breath.

"Possibly. I can try a few things, but the fact that she did not wake for Christian in all these years leads me to believe that the one she was truly bonded to was not Mr. Raines. It was not his love that kept her bound to this life, but someone else's." Maia's gaze drifted to Rillin. "Because of this, I suspect the ability to revive her does not lie in my hands, but in Mr. Blackwood's."

"I was her Trial," he replied quietly. "She did not care for me in such a way. A bond between us . . . it's not possible."

"The bond is possible if she did, in fact, love you," countered Maia. "And I don't mean in some simple, passing affection, but in the truest sense of the word. Her body, even in this suspended form, reacts to your touch, Mr. Blackwood. What more proof do you need of her love for you?"

"What if you're *wrong*? What if I can't wake her?" asked Rillin, desperation and doubt now clear in his voice.

"Then she remains as she is, not dead, but not living either. And she cannot be passed off endlessly from place to place and person to person, as some piece of property. If she can't be *revived*, then she should be laid to rest."

"You just said she's NOT dead!" I snapped, horrified at the idea of burying someone who could potentially return to life.

Maia turned and opened a few drawers, looking for something as she spoke. "She's not dead, but she's as good as gone if Mr. Blackwood cannot wake her. I am certain that your Blacklist dealer is the one who is soul bonded to Elizabeth Walker."

"Mum – what are you looking for?" asked Baz, watching his mother ransack his drawers.

"A knife, Basil . . . how do you NOT have one?"

Rillin stepped forward, pulling a small dagger from his arm strap. He weighed it in his hand looking at Maia's back. "I have one, but before I give it to you, I need to know what you intend to do with it."

Maia turned, slamming a drawer shut with her hip, one jeweled hand landing on the granite countertop. A selection of glass vials and jars, super-charged chemistry sets and bunsen burners lined the tile wall behind her. "I intend to mark both Elizabeth and YOU with bonding sigils. My hope is that it will tighten the soul bond between you both. She will draw from your strength, if the bond is true. It should slowly rouse her." She held out her hand, "Hopefully, anyway."

Rillin flipped the dagger in his hand, handing Maia the weapon, handle first. She stepped over to the table and picked up my grandmother's hand, turning it palm up as she eased open Elizabeth's delicate fingers. Maia edged the sharp tip of the knife into Elizabeth's palm, cutting an elegant design of soft curves and slashes. I was shocked to see that Elizabeth's blood welled up from the wound, red, not silver. "Baz," I asked, pointing to Elizabeth's hand. "Her blood is red! When the heck did it turn to red? I saw you draw her blood earlier and it was as silver as the chrome on Ana's Trans Am!"

Baz blinked, looking shocked. "I . . . I don't know."

"It is most likely the soul bond," Maia replied, her focus on Elizabeth's palm. "Her proximity to Mr. Blackwood, and the fact that he touched her when he carried her up to the lab, has already started the process."

"The change happens that fast?" demanded Rillin.

Maia nodded, "If the bond is true and strong, yes. I've seen it happen that fast, but never in a soul who has been in this type of suspended sleep for so long." She placed the knife on the counter and pulled a roll of gauze from a first aid cabinet, using it to bandage Elizabeth's hand. She then turned, picking up the knife once again and running it quickly under the small faucet built into the counter. Rillin, at Elizabeth's side, held my grandmother's small hand, examining the bandage. When the knife was clean, Maia turned to Rillin. He eased Elizabeth's hand back onto her stomach, ready for Maia's handiwork to score his own skin, but I stepped in front of her quickly, forcing Baz's mom to halt.

"Are you sure this is safe? For Rillin?" I asked, glancing towards my trainer.

Maia turned the knife slowly in her hand and the lamp's glow bounced off the steel blade like a ribbon of sunlight. "I've never done this between a Lunaterra and Mortis, Eila. There are always unknowns in waking those who have been viewed as dead, but that is especially true in this instance due to the supernatural factors running between Mr. Blackwood and Elizabeth. I do not know the risks, and once she wakes, if she wakes, she may not remember her past."

"It's okay, Eila," said Rillin, carefully easing me out of of the way. He held his hand out to Maia, palm open. "Do it. I accept the risks."

Baz threw his hands in the air, flustered. "MUM! Faust opens in a few hours! You can't try this now," he demanded, eyes wide. "What if it works and she wakes up and fries the place!"

Maia took a breath, leveling a hard glare at her son. "Basil, are you questioning me?

"MA! God help us if she wakes up during a full house – she could kill every Mortis in the building. It would be pure carnage. You said yourself there are unknowns in doing this type of thing – what if she wakes up, like, PMSing?"

"You did *not* just say that! PMSing? Are you kidding me?" snapped Nikki.

Baz pointed at her. "YOU! Don't even start! You're ALWAYS in a raging mood, ready to kick me in the balls!"

"That's not PMS," she smiled evilly. "I just don't like you."

I raised my hands, signaling a time-out. "Okay, OKAY! Baz - you have a good point . . . for once."

"HEY!"

I sighed. "As much as I want Elizabeth awake and answering questions, the safety of Faust is important as well," I turned to Maia, "If you want us to wait, we wait. The call is yours, Maia."

Maia turned the knife in her hand, then stepped closer to Rillin. "I appreciate your concerns, Eila, but the truth is the club fell into danger the moment you walked through my door last night. I will do whatever it takes to protect Faust, and that includes waking a young woman who is our best shot at destroying the Gabriel Gate. Time is no longer on our side, but if it makes you and Baz feel better, we can separate Rillin and Elizabeth for the evening. I'll add the sigil to his palm, but keeping them physically apart should temper the reaction. After the club closes, however, Mr. Blackwood will need to do all he can to stay close to Elizabeth and hopefully she will wake to a friendly face." Maia held out her hand and Rillin placed his wide palm in hers, watching as she began adding yet another scar to the many he already had. He didn't so much as flinch under the cut of the blade.

As she worked, Raef's gaze seemed to narrow on her - as if he was seeing her for the first time. When Maia was finally done, he spoke up, his voice hard, "Are you a priestess . . . or a bokor?"

Maia eyed Raef as she handed Rillin a rag. He pressed it into his palm, staunching the blood as he was aware that it could be toxic to me. I knew he'd heal quickly, but he was being careful for my sake. "I see you've spent time in New Orleans, Mr. Paris," she replied cooly.

"And Africa," Raef replied. "Which are you?"

Maia's voice seemed laced with the promise of darkness, sending chills over my skin. "I am what I am, Mr. Paris," she said. "Be thankful my sister, Dalca, could never grasp the nuances of true black magic. But I have no such problem."

Ana snorted, "Yeah, well, she grasped the nuances of a sparkly witch ball pretty damn well, lemme tell ya."

Raef cursed under his breath, then turned to me. "Eila, Maia is a bokor. Dark curses, black magic - you name it. There are enemies of the Mortis who also practice in the dark arts. If she does as well, she could be allied with them . . ."

"Mr. Paris!" snapped Maia. "I practice many forms of magic. I do not run around casually creating zombies nor aligning myself with questionable . . . clans. Just because I am a bokor, does not bar me from also being a priestess. I am what I am - a mix of the dangerous and the elegant. Piss me off, however, and you will get a taste of my darker side."

"Did she just say *zombies?!*" whispered MJ urgently.

"I did not sign up for this level of crazy," muttered Nikki through her teeth.

Ana raised her hand, as if back in school. "Okay, so, since we're apparently tempting fate with this whole wake-the-potentially-pissed-grandma plan, is there also somewhere we can set up all our gear that we've brought, ya know, in case this whole idea takes us down a seriously unsavory path? 'Cause we have weapons and information on the Gate, and even a Mime . . . if Elizabeth gets really testy."

"Yeah," I muttered, "I'd feel better about having my hands back on my stuff, especially my weapons." I glanced quickly at Rillin, but his gaze remained focused on Elizabeth. "I'd also be willing to sell a kidney for a hot shower, so I'm hoping you've got one of those somewhere as well, Baz."

"And eat?" added MJ, hopefully. "I require food more than oxygen at this point."

"And sleep for a few dozen days?" added Nikki.

Maia rinsed the knife and returned it to Rillin who sheathed it back on his well-muscled arm. She nodded to Baz, "My son will show you to your room up here among the catwalks. I can only spare *one* of the recovery rooms – the one Kian and Raef were placed in after the attack." She cleared her throat, "Elizabeth stays here, in the lab, but the rest of your equipment can be stored on the lower engine level. I'm sure you'll find the space suitable for your needs. Bane does live here at Faust, down on that level, so don't be surprised to see him. And try not to get in his way."

"And don't get freaked out by his eyes," added Baz.

"What about his eyes?" asked Ana, narrowing her own.

"They glow the color of amber at night, so don't piss yourself if you see him watching you in the dark."

"Great," she muttered. "There goes a few MORE decades off my life."

Kian just smiled and gave her a squeeze.

"You know, the whole Sleeping Beauty thing would explain why Bane was unable to scent Elizabeth," MJ said to Maia, scratching his head absently. "Like, her . . . deadness. Is that even a word? *Deadness?*" He shook his head.

Maia was about to reply when a knock on the door interrupted her. Leo, covered as always in his Fallen Marks, entered the room. He was dressed in dark slacks and a white button down shirt, just like when we first met him. In his hands were more clothes in the same white and black palate of color.

"I have their uniforms," he said, looking at Maia.

Kian looked warily at the clothing. "Uniforms for who?"

Maia pulled the clothes from Leo's hands, offering a set each to Raef and Kian, who looked stunned. "For you two, though Rillin will have to make do with what he has – I don't have a uniform that will fit him. If you're hiding out here, I expect you to also help guard Faust." She walked past me, heading back to Leo, "Plus, I'm down a few of my best bouncers. They've been assigned elsewhere for now."

"I can help. Put me to work," I said, stepping forward. If Maia wanted to defend Faust, then placing her biggest gun into rotation made sense.

She sized me up, crossing her arms as she studied me. "Fine. You and Rillin can be on the roof, since he needs to stay away from Elizabeth for now. I normally don't place guards up there, but it affords a clear view of the surrounding area. Considering the circumstances, it makes sense to have a better view of the city. There's a bounty on your head, Ms. Walker - once our world finds out you've fled your home, they'll start turning over other rocks to find you."

I swallowed hard. Maia was right - it was only a matter of time until we were located at Faust.

"What about me?" asked MJ.

"AND ME!" demanded Ana, Nikki nodding in agreement.

"I can't have liabilities running around Faust. Ana was sheared last night by Kian. If that happened to her again tonight, it could kill her. And Nikki is in no shape to be useful either, thus both girls will remain confined to the lab, with Mr. Williams. You three," she pointed at Ana, Nikki, MJ, "are to stay here with Baz and Elizabeth. If she so much as twitches, I want to know."

Ana snorted, "This should be a thrill a minute."

Nikki was livid. "This is stupid! Since when do I get relegated to babysitting duty! I can still control metal despite the fact that Leo totally screwed up my arm." Leo took a sudden step towards Nik, and MJ immediately put himself in front of her.

"First of all, YOU were going to bleed to death," growled Leo. "Saving your life seemed to be more critical than your arm in that moment!"

Nikki snarled in his face, "Yeah, well, Raef and Kian are going to fix it, no thanks to you!"

Kian leaned behind Ana and me, whispering to Raef, "Uh, since when are we fixing Mistress Iron Heart over there?"

"I'll explain later," muttered Raef, turning his attention back to Baz's mom. "Maia – I'm entirely willing to help maintain the safety of Faust, but I must be honest: Kian and I are run down from last night. We need to hunt."

Kian gave a tight nod. "I did shear Ana, but I could use a more complete hit." Ana looked a bit put-out by that remark.

Maia tossed a hand at her unsmiling bouncer. "Leo will see to your needs. Doors open at 10pm tonight. You have less than four hours to get fed, cleaned up, and recharged. I run a night club, not a bloody Bed and Breakfast, and I'm low on workers tonight because of the nonsense that you dragged to my door *last* night."

"What's that mean?" asked Raef, his brow falling. "Did something happen to some of your workers after we left?"

Maia just glared at us, replying, "Four hours. Be ready."

Leo glanced to Elizabeth's still form, then to Maia. "The crew is gathered on the dance floor, as you requested."

"Thank you, Leo. I'm on my way," she replied, heading for the door, her patchwork skirts and numerous bangles making her every movement a hushed symphony of sound. "See to it that Mr. Paris and Mr. O'Reilly are shown where to hunt. I believe Mr. Blackwood has already been taken care of this morning with a Blacklisted soul, correct?"

"Yes, Ma'am," replied Rillin. "I do not need to hunt at this time. I'll stay here, with Eila and the others." Beside me, Raef shifted, and I knew that leaving me with Rillin, despite the presence of MJ, Nikki, and Ana, was not something he'd be easy with.

"We don't have time to hunt off the Blacklist before the club opens," argued Kian. "What exactly are we going after? Alley cats? Dumpster rats?"

Leo rested against the doorframe as he answered, "The harbor is frozen, so we have an abundance of seals on the ice floats at the moment. They'll serve us well, for the time being."

Kian cursed, "I hate seals. Damn things bite."

Across the room, MJ tried to hide his grin, but Kian saw it and flipped him off. I, however, was more curious as to what Baz's mom was doing with the Faust crew. "Why have the workers gathered?" I asked, and Maia turned back to us, her dark eyes boring into me.

"This club is my whole life, Ms. Walker. I do not hide the details of what is happening from the workers - every last one, including the four Lessers that were taken from us - are MY family. They deserve to know that I have placed Faust in the crosshairs of Lawson Waite's rage. They deserve a chance to leave, now, and I will hold no ill will against them."

I reached out and grasped Maia's forearm, the lace and beads of her elaborate blouse digging into my palm. "I'll go with you."

She shook her head. "This is a discussion I need to have with those closest to my heart and no one else. If they wish it, I will come back and get you."

Unable to argue, I simply nodded, dropping my hand.

She turned to leave, but paused. "This fight isn't just about you, Walker. This is about all of us, but I will sacrifice you and your crew before I sacrifice my people."

"I expect nothing less, Ma'am," I replied, and she headed out the door, Leo giving me a hard glare before following her and closing the door after them both.

Maia Moriarty would offer us shelter, protection, and even attempt to wake Elizabeth, but she'd not sacrifice her own crew to save mine. So far, we'd been a liability. Starting now, we'd become an asset. In that moment, I knew we'd protect the club as one of our own, whether Moriarty saw us as part of her crew or not.

I leveled my eyes on Baz, who was pulling what looked like a glass case of golden thumb tacks from one of the cabinets behind him. "Did something happen here after we left late last night?" I demanded, sensing Maia was hiding something.

Baz sighed, his hands pausing on what he was doing. "My mom isn't one to sit and wait for fate to take hold. She prefers to play offense, not defense, whenever possible."

"Which means what exactly?" I ground out.

"My mom, Leo, Bane, and a few other workers went hunting after you guys left. They went to the address in Boston that Ana had gotten from Sara Booth. You know, the place where Rillin was supposed to take Eila once he had her?"

I blinked. "Holy crap – seriously?"

"What did they find?" demanded Rillin. I noticed he'd shifted closer to Elizabeth's side, his fingertips resting on the steel table. I wasn't sure he even realized he'd done it.

"Mostly equipment and parts used to install Limiting Links, which they brought back here," Baz replied, entirely absorbed it what he was doing at the counter. "Bane said it was basically a bust, since Nikki's father wasn't there. The goal was to kill him."

We all froze, stunned into silence.

Baz paused, realizing what he'd just said aloud. He turned slowly, a weak laugh falling from his lips as he was probably judging how fast he could make it out the door if Nikki turned psycho on his butt. He swallowed roughly, continuing his nervous chuckle.

"It's uh, kinda amusing that he's disappeared, but Nikki is here. I gotta admit we didn't plan on seeing you guys back so soon. But, it's all good, 'cause, you know – my mom didn't kill him after all."

Looking as though he might puke from fear in about ten seconds, Baz glanced warily at Nikki who was staring daggers in his direction. "And, uh, since we're all friends now and whatnot, I should probably mention that the plan was for me to dope him up with a concoction of my own when they got him back here, drill him for answers, then dump his dead body in the harbor. But, instead, all we have is just his crap - stashed in my Mom's office."

He looked nervously at all of us, shuffling a little closer to the door, weighing the need to bolt. "So, vaccines . . ." he said as he held up the little golden injectors. "Do I have a volunteer or do we rock, paper, scissors who goes first?"

CHAPTER 13
FAUST, NEW BEDFORD, MA

Nikki moved mighty damn fast for someone who was damaged. One second she was glaring at Baz, the next his vaccines were sailing through the air as she body-checked him into a metal cabinet. I swear the entire thing vibrated in reaction to her rage.

"YOU WERE GONNA KILL MY DAD?" she screamed, her good hand latching on to Baz's throat like a boa constrictor. I bolted forward and tried to pry her off him as Baz also struggled against her, his face turning red as the air was cut from his lungs.

I gripped her wrist, trying not to hurt her but still squeezing in an attempt to get her to let him go. Our friends moved to help, but Nikki was like concrete, unyielding. "Nikki!" I begged. "Let him go! Stop!"

As his fight or flight response kicking in full throttle, Baz gave up on trying to pry her hand free of his neck and suddenly punched

Nikki's injured arm. His fist connected with her shoulder and she cried out, instantly releasing him. She staggered backwards, gasping for air as I swore at him, grabbing Nikki against me as she crumpled in pain. I eased her to the floor with me, the sound of her choked gasps echoing in my ears as she rested her head back against my shoulder.

"Jeezus, Moriarty – was that really necessary?" demanded Kian, kneeling down in front of Nikki, Raef joining him.

"Yes!" he coughed, "She was trying to kill me, damn it!"

"You just told her that you planned to drug and kill her father," muttered Eila, checking Baz's throat. "I'd say you deserved what you got, dumb ass."

Nikki leaned back into me harder, as if trying to push herself away from Raef and Kian, but they didn't back away. She was breathing through clenched teeth and shaking hard, no doubt from the pain. *Stupid Basil Moriarty!* I should've bitten him when I had a chance.

"I just want to take a look, Nikki," soothed Kian extending a cautious hand to the clammy Ironess in my arms. "You look like you're about to pass out there, Girlie, and I can hear your heart pounding. You're obviously in agony, so let me see if I can help, alright? Just, you know – don't kick me in the balls suddenly, okay? 'Cause that would really be the icing on this craptastic day that I don't need right now."

Nikki coughed out a small laugh, but then drew a shaky breath, her eyes turned to Raef. He gave an encouraging smile.

I slid my hand into her right palm and she dipped her head in consent. Her fingers tightened around mine as Kian touched her shoulder, towing the shirt down her arm and she let out a small groan. I watched him as Nikki closed her eyes, her grip turning brutal, as if she was trying to realign the bones in my hand every time Kian touched her.

Finally, he sat back, readjusting her shirt, and looked at Raef. "You're right – I think we can fix it. Gotta re-break it though, and be damn precise in healing it."

"No way," breathed Nikki. "I can't . . ."

"Don't worry, Nik – we'd never do it with you awake," Raef replied, resting a hand on her shin as if to ease her fears. He looked up to Baz, "What did you intend to drug her dad with?"

"A modified form of Valium. Basically Twilight Sleep, but my version," Baz replied, easing himself down to the floor to pick up the vaccinations. His throat looked red and sore. At eye level with Raef, he added, "It would knock her out so you could fix her arm, but you need to be careful with the dose. It can make her breathing touchy if you give her too much." He looked over at Nikki, who had a fine sheen of sweat dotting her brow. "I'm sorry Nikki – I thought you were gonna kill me."

Forget Nik - I WAS gonna kill him.

"I wanna see my dad's stuff," she replied weakly. "I need answers too."

Baz looked grim, "I gotta ask my mom first, but I'm sure she'll let you see what they grabbed last night. She's gonna want to go over the stuff with you though, that's for sure. She's gonna be busy right now, with club stuff, but I'll ask her when she has a moment."

"What about Nik's mom? Maia didn't see any sign of her when she raided the Boston address?" asked Ana, standing near Rillin, his hand still clenched around the rag Maia had given him. I noticed his eyes kept trailing over to Elizabeth, but his face had turned into an unreadable mask.

"According to Bane, there was no sign of either Nik's mom or dad," Baz replied. Having collected all the gold vaccines, he stood and slid the glass case onto the counter.

I gave Nikki's hand a squeeze and looked at Raef and Kian. "Well, if Maia is up to her eyeballs in club stuff at the moment, is there any chance Nikki's arm can be repaired now? You know, before Faust opens for the night?" Nikki turned to me, her eyes wide. I replied quietly, "It's gonna be okay. I'll stay with ya."

"WAIT a second!" protested Baz. "I don't want to be left with Semi-Dead Sally over here! My mom said that Nik and Ana were gonna stay in here WITH ME."

Raef and Kian looked at one another, totally ignoring Baz's panicked tone. Kian replied, "Yeah. We can work on her now as long as Baz can provide us with his Twilight Sleep."

"And as long as Nikki is willing, obviously," added Raef.

Baz flung his hands out, exasperated. "DUDE! HELLO? I don't wanna be stuck here with ELIZABETH!"

Nikki, also ignoring Baz, studied my face, seeming to look for guidance, so I just smiled gently. "I've seen Kian heal Ana – he knows his shit. I wouldn't compliment the guy in any other instance, but I know he and Raef can fix ya."

"Thanks, Hairball," muttered Kian. "Way to offer praise with a slap."

"Anytime," I replied happily.

Raef stood. "Nikki will need to shower and we need some supplies and a place where we can work on her. A place where she can sleep off the drug would be helpful as well."

Kian nodded, getting to his feet and wrapping one long arm

around Ana's waist and tugging her against him. While he joked in response to my praise over his healing of Ana, I knew those moments were hard for them both, and for me as well. Kian had healed Ana multiple times after her father's beatings.

I watched as Ana hooked one finger in Kian's belt loop by his hip, and her ring shone against the denim of his jeans.

I knew *that* ring. I knew exactly where Kian must've bought it, because I remembered him looking at it nearly two summers ago when he was searching for birthday gifts for Ana. He had high hopes for that day – plans to throw her a little birthday party on Cerberus. Instead we found her beaten and freezing in the rain, and I, at the lowest point in my life, asked Kian O'Reilly to kill Ana's abusive father. Thinking back on it now, I'm grateful fate intervened and a heart attack, not Kian, claimed the life of Harold Lane. I wasn't proud of that moment – of how I let my rage take over my sanity.

The blue round diamond in the ring fit Ana perfectly, and I was grateful Kian had found his way back to her. Sure, we beat on one another once in a while, but Kian and I actually got along (sorta) and I knew he was her soulmate.

Baz was finally soothed by Ana, who said she would stay with him while Kian was with Nikki. Finally calm, he began discussing options for the 'surgery' spot with the guys. He shrugged, "Eh, heck with it – just use my bedroom. There's an attached bathroom with a shower."

"No way I'm sleeping with you," muttered Nikki.

Baz snorted. "Please – I like my boy parts in one piece. Sleeping with you is not the way to keep them intact, that's for damn sure. You'll only be there for a couple hours, then you can go crash in your own room . . . with the rest of your friends."

Nikki looked at all of us and she seemed to realize, for the first time, that the title "friends" actually fit. We *were* her friends, though I knew deep down my heart was hoping for more. I prayed she actually saw *me*, the tall kid with a small family ice cream shop, and not just Marsh the dog.

She studied Kian and Raef, as if debating what she was willing to risk, and how much she truly trusted the two soul thieves who'd become like brothers to me.

Finally, she asked, "When can you start?"

"As soon as you're showered," Raef replied.

Proud of her bravery, I wrapped one arm around her waist and gave her a squeeze.

She didn't pull away.

CHAPTER 14
FAUST, NEW BEDFORD, MA
SATURDAY, 7:30 PM

"We haven't done this in a while," muttered Kian as he walked beside me, carrying the IV bags and equipment we would need to put Nikki into a semi-conscious state. Thanks to Faust's thriving human-Mortis business, the club kept a huge stash of medical equipment for humans who found themselves a bit overzealous in their shearing highs with the Mortis.

"No we haven't, but I'm confident we can fix the bone quickly. I can't believe Leo fused it wrong."

"He said she was bleeding out. Badly."

"That's no excuse," I replied.

It had taken only a half hour to get the room set up for us and the supplies gathered. According to Baz, Maia had been appraised of all that was going on, including the fact that Nikki was aware of her prior intention to murder her father the night before – all information relayed to Maia via her pothead spawn.

I was impressed that Nikki was willing to let us work on her, though she had shown her fearless side relentlessly over the past 24 hours. All the girls had displayed the warrior that lived within, and I knew such acts of bravery should no longer shock me.

A few minutes ago, I had boiled razor blades to disinfect them, and rather than walk into the room with them on display, I tucked them carefully into the clean linens. Nikki didn't need to see the instruments we would use to open up her shoulder.

Further down the catwalk, the door to Maia's office was being guarded by two Mortis I didn't recognize, Nikki's father's enslaving equipment somewhere inside. I couldn't believe Moriarty had actually gone after him at the address in Boston, given the risks involved. Like Eila, Maia seemed to be able to shut down any doubts and fears she had. I intended to never get on her bad side, especially with the undeniable knowledge that the woman was a bokor.

I might dance with the devil on occasion, but playing chess against a woman who commands Voodoo's flip-side? I'll pass.

"What do you think of Maia's theory about Elizabeth?" Kian asked me as we walked along the catwalk above the club. I tucked the towel closer to my chest, ensuring the blades didn't peek out and give Nikki a hint of what was coming.

"I'll let you know what I think as soon as Elizabeth wakes up, IF she wakes up. How's that for an opinion?" I replied.

Kian slid me a sidelong glance. "Impressively sarcastic, especially for you."

Below us, the Faust's crew was busy cleaning and organizing the tables and dance floor. The bar was being restocked for humans, and voices of several dozen workers, mostly Mortis, filled the space as they talked. Baz said that not a single one left after Maia told them what was going on and who was staying at Faust, though she did leave out the details about Elizabeth. He said that *that* was Faust – a true family, who had one another's backs.

"What can I say?" I replied. "My experience with the dead rising from the grave is thankfully nonexistent, so I'm leaning on snark as a coping mechanism. It's a talent I learned from you."

"Har har," replied Kian, unamused.

We finally approached Baz's bedroom and I paused before knocking. "You ready?" I asked.

Kian nodded.

I struck the engraved wood door with my knuckles and immediately heard footsteps approach the other side. The door eased open, revealing Eila.

My girl gave me a weak smile as she said, "Nikki's all set up. She showered and I braided her hair to the side, as you asked. And I stripped down the bed and layered it with clean towels." Eila glanced over her shoulder and my eyes followed where she looked.

Nikki was stepping out from the bathroom, a white sheet wrapped around her. She glanced at Kian and me, her face paler than normal as she headed for the iron bed. MJ appeared out of the corner of the room and walked over with her. She sat on the mattress, her back towards us as she spoke to MJ. Next to her, there was a stack of clean clothes folded on Baz's bureau, waiting for her once our work was done.

Eila turned back to me, dropping her voice low. "She's really nervous. I know you want the minimal amount of people in here, but she's got a connection with MJ. I think she won't be so scared if he stays."

"He can stay," I replied.

"As long as he doesn't pass out," added Kian.

Eila fidgeted in front of me for a moment.

"Hey – don't worry, E. She's gonna be fine," I urged, offering her a gentle smile.

"She won't feel anything?"

I shook my head, "No – we'll put her in Twilight sleep. She won't be totally out, but it will handle most of the pain and she won't remember a damn thing. It's kind of like a trance – she can talk to us, do as we ask, but she'll not ever remember doing so."

Eila rubbed her neck, "Jeez, that's creepy."

"It's a standard sedative. It works really well."

Eila nodded, "Right – well, I'll get out of your way."

She smiled at me and I leaned down, stealing a brief kiss on her lips before she left the room, shutting the door quietly behind her.

Nikki glanced over her shoulder, her wet braid causing the sheet to dampen, tension sharp throughout her body. Determined to try and ease her, Kian and I walked casually over to where she sat, her eyes watching us carefully. Nervous didn't even cover it. She was downright terrified. I set down the folded linens that concealed the blades on the end of the bed, then knelt before Nikki. Kian stood behind her on the opposite side of the bed, waiting.

She swallowed hard. "Will I feel it?" she asked, her voice dry.

I shook my head, resting a hand on her knee. "No. We'll make sure you are very comfortable. You won't remember anything."

She glanced up at MJ and he eased himself down next to her, weaving his fingers into her limp left arm as it rested beside her on the bed, useless. She clutched the sheet tight to her chest with her one working arm, both of her pale shoulders exposed and speckled with goosebumps. I could hear her heart-rate hammer in her chest.

I squeezed her knee, “MJ can stay too, okay?”

She nodded, drawing a quaking breath as she turned her eyes to him.

MJ smiled warmly, “Hey, you’re gonna be fine. These two are actually really good at this stuff. And I’ll stay right next to ya. I’ll talk to ya and hold your hand, even if you can’t hear me. Even if you can’t feel me. I’ll be right here and I’ll make sure you’re not in pain, okay?”

Nikki swallowed, her nerves getting the better of her. “I don’t like others being in control of me. I don’t like being unable to defend myself,” she replied, a broken sound to her voice.

MJ slid closer to her and wrapped his arm around her shoulders. “I’ve got your back," he said quietly, his face tucked close to hers. "Hand over the reins for a bit – let us take care of you. I know life can suck. I know you feel like you're on your own, but you're not. You got us. Ya got me and, heck, I'm a two for one deal: hot guy and cool dog."

She cracked a small smile as MJ threaded his fingers in hers. "I swear, nothing will happen to you while I’m watching over you. Ever.”

She took a breath and looked back at me.

“Okay?” I asked.

She nodded and slid herself back on the bed with MJ’s help and the use of her legs. He eased her down so her head rested on the pillow and her eyes met Kian’s. “So, feisty pants, are you allergic to anything?” he asked, trying to make her smile.

Nikki, however, simply shook her head.

Kian’s face maintained a smile, but it softened. “You got nothing to worry about, kiddo. We’ve got ya, okay?”

She swallowed and Kian glanced at MJ, who seemed to understand that he needed to distract Nikki. He knelt next to the bed and started talking to her, drawing her attention away from Kian who started an IV line in her arm. He rigged the bag against the headboard as I leaned over Nikki, easing her hand from the death grip she had on the sheet.

I said to her, "I just need to tuck the sheet tight around you – need to make you a human burrito, but leave your arms out."

She watched me, her body tense as I tucked the sheet tight to her body, keeping the edge of the sheet low on her chest to expose much of her shoulder and collarbone, but maintaining her modesty.

"How you doing?" I asked, knowing Kian was starting to inject the drug into the IV line. My goal was to keep her focused on me so her body wouldn't fight the sedation. MJ kept a close eye on all that was going on.

"I'm majorly freaked to be honest," she replied, but the edge of her words began to slur. Kian gently touched her neck, feeling her pulse as the drug began to take hold, but Nikki didn't even notice his fingers. "I don't like . . . any . . . AnNnYyy."

Her head lolled to one side, her eyes drifting shut.

We watched her for a moment, Kian feeling her pulse relax and her heartbeat slow to a drowsy rhythm. We followed Baz's instructions for the dose, though giving her a bit less than he recommended. Neither of us were willing to risk the possibility of stopping her heart if Baz's calculations were off. Genius or not, the kid smoked weed daily, which made us both question his math skills.

"Is she alright? Is she out?" asked MJ, glancing to both of us.

I nodded, "Yeah, she's out. Semi-out at least. If you talk to her, she may respond. Don't ask her anything you don't want a blunt, dead-honest answer to, though – sometimes this stuff can act like a truth serum."

Kian smiled, coming around my side of the bed where I was laying out the gauze and blades. He looked at MJ, "Yeah, so don't ask her if she thinks you're hot, 'cause your doggie dreams will be dashed when she tells you that you're ugly as sin."

"Ha ha – jerk. I'm not prying into her mind when she's like this," he responded, stroking her hair.

I touched her clavicle, running my hand over the area of bone that had fused wrong. "It's more towards her shoulder," I told Kian, no longer willing to joke.

Kian felt over the same area as MJ watched us both in silence, his hand resting on Nikki's head. "Yeah, I feel it."

"I'm going to open a four-inch incision right over it and re-break the area precisely, then heal her properly."

I chose a blade and glanced at MJ, assessing whether he would pass out at the first sight of blood. He looked good however, and I set the blade to her collarbone near her shoulder, pressing it through her skin and muscle. Nikki took a deeper breath as I did so, her blood welling up and running over her shoulder to the towels under her. Kian touched her pulse again, ensuring that if she was in pain, it was minimal.

"You're okay," whispered MJ to Nik. "Think of something you like."

"Music," she breathed in a heady, intoxicated voice.

I glanced at Kian and he gave a tight nod. I drew the blade through Nikki's skin in a perfect line and her blood flowed freely over her shoulder and down onto the white sheet that covered her chest. Her heartbeat spiked for a moment then relaxed.

MJ swallowed, whispering to me, "She can't feel this, right?"

I set down the bloody knife, easing open the wound I had caused to get a good look at what Leo had screwed up. "She might feel some of it, but she won't remember," I advised.

Carefully, I examined the bone, figuring out where I would snap it. I finally turned to MJ, "Keep talking to her. I'm gonna break the bone now so I can reset it properly."

MJ turned his attention back to Nikki, asking her about a band they both liked as Kian moved his hands to Nikki's opposite shoulder and chest, his fingertips sliding through the blood that ran across her fair skin. He needed to keep her from moving if the drug wasn't strong enough to compensate for her body's reaction to what I was about to do.

He looked at me, determination in his face as MJ's voice echoed softly in the background. I eased my fingers against the deformed bone and pushed. It gave a clean *crack* as it snapped, and Nikki drew a sharp breath. Her heart rate jumped quickly and she let out a small moan, her body stiffening.

"Damn it, she really felt that!" protested MJ, cupping her face.

"She won't remember," I stated sharply, intent on repairing the bone and closing the wound before she lost too much blood. The Fallen Marks bloomed onto my skin as I lined up the broken bone and began to heal her.

"Slowly," said Kian, watching me work.

"I know, I know," I snapped. I didn't want to ever have to do this to her again, so getting it right the first time was critical. The slim bone seemed so delicate under my touch, and I set my healing ability sliding over the break like the ebb and flow of the tide, until the bone was perfectly fused. I then set to closing the layers of skin and muscle, noting several nerves that had been damaged before.

Though my goal was to heal them properly, I was unsure if she'd regain feeling in her arm. Some parts of the human body were like the universe - secretive and temperamental, and repairing them was like wishing on a star, the results hit or miss.

I could feel myself weakening as I healed her, the events of the night before having taken their toll on my strength. I glanced to Kian. "We need to swap," I said, knowing he needed to take over.

He didn't argue, and we switched places, Kian's Marks flaring to life on his hands as he finished closing the wound, leaving Nikki's skin virtually scar-free.

Once done, we cleaned the blood from her body the best we could, and I pulled the pile of clean linens from the end of the bed. "We need to wrap her arm tight to her body," I said. "The bone's weak and she could very easily snap it again. It needs time to harden and fully recover. We can take turns treating it, so the process will be accelerated, but she still needs to be bound, for a day at least."

We both glanced at MJ. "Ya gotta leave, man," said Kian.

"I'm not leaving. I promised her I'd watch over her, and I'm not breaking that promise."

"She won't remember," Kian argued.

MJ's face hardened, "Would you promise Ana to stay by her side, but sneak out when you didn't think she'd know?"

"MJ, man, just turn around for a second," I said, unraveling the long pieces of fabric.

"Uh, hell no - you guys turn around. I've already helped her before. How the heck do you think she got into a change of clothes when Leo first healed her?"

I raised a stunned eyebrow, glancing at Kian.

"Trust me, I've gotten an eyeful and she knows it. You two are on the no fly list with regards to this, understand?" MJ glared at us, the angle of his body placing him in a protective stance over Nikki's unconscious form. Her chest rose and fell slowly, the drug working well. I don't think I ever respected MJ Williams as much as I did in that one instant.

I nodded and Kian just shrugged. "I'll make a deal with you, MJ. I'll tell you how to get it started so that she's covered up, and then Kian and I will take over, because this is a fairly precise science. I need to bind her arm to her body in such a way that her circulation is fine, but she can't move it at all."

"That works for me," he replied. "Now face the wall and start telling me what to do."

I smiled as Kian rolled his eyes, but we did as we were told because one fact had become abundantly clear: No one disobeyed Nikki Shea's guard dog.

CHAPTER 15
FAUST, NEW BEDFORD, MA

After leaving Nikki in the care of the guys, I went in search of Rillin. I knew he was struggling with his own guilt about Nikki – about the fact that she needed what was basically supernatural surgery to fix the damage he had done to her outside Torrent Road. Nikki seemed to have forgiven him for what he'd done, but I knew that the knight Rillin once was still resided within the soul thief, and he was not the type to so easily forgive himself.

Even more pressing, however, was the revelation about my grandmother, Elizabeth.

If Maia was right, and she could be brought back from the supernatural coma she was in, would she be an ally or an enemy? Would she remember Rillin and recall how she defended the Mortis race? And how could we ever break the tragic news about Christian? Would she even want to be revived, now that her own son was long since dead and her world had entirely changed? Even worse, what if she wanted nothing to do with any of us? What if she took Rillin away from us? Away from me?

With my head and heart pounding, I headed back to Baz's lab, hoping to find Rillin nearby, but no such luck. Instead, I found Baz, readying a supply of vaccines for Faust's human patrons who didn't want to *really* walk the wild side and be sheared in a few hours when the doors opened. Ana was there as well, attempting to once again read Elizabeth. By the number of curses spilling from her mouth, I knew she was having no luck whatsoever. Apparently the light show that my 4th great grandmother had offered under Rillin's touch did not break her silent streak.

"I can whip us up some dinner in just a few," said Baz. "I just need to get these vaccines set for tonight first, then we can chow. We can put some aside for Nikki when she's awake."

"That works for me." I glanced at Ana who had pulled up a stool next to Elizabeth, her hands placed on my grandmother's arm and forehead. "You starving as well?"

"Yeah, but not for food poisoning," she replied, shooting an accusing look in Baz's direction.

He paused in his sorting task to defend himself. "Hey, my cooking isn't that bad!"

"Leo said you once left ziti in a pot of hot water after cooking it to keep it warm," said Ana, shifting her hands on the body, as if trying to find the on switch. "He said by the time your mom came home to eat, the ziti were the size of bangles!"

"Pfft - Leo exaggerates. They were not that big. Hoop earrings, maybe, but bangles? Uh, no."

I laughed, "Food in a bit sounds good, Baz. Thanks." I knew his food was crap, but at this point, I was so blasted hungry that burnt mac and cheese would probably taste like 4-star cuisine to my rumbling stomach.

"Yeah, well, I hope you like barfing, E," muttered Ana, closing her eyes to concentrate in a more focused manner. Baz made a face in her direction, though she didn't see it. Ana spoke to the room, her eyes still shut, "If your Grams doesn't start talking in the next sixty seconds, E, I'm gonna go see if Maia has any books on my kind. Lord knows, she's got a big enough library in that office of hers, and I wouldn't mind learning more about fine tuning my Swayness." She frowned, "Huh. Maybe I can't read Elizabeth 'cause she's like, brain-suspended. Maybe, in this state, she's like a Lesser - can't read those buggers either, so maybe when she's zombie-grams, she's like them."

"Uh, I wouldn't tell Bane you compared him and his kind to zombie-brains, just FYI."

Baz nodded. "Yeah. Don't tell Bane that. That's like, real anti-friendship territory if you say that. Plus, I know my mom has many journals and some borrowed grimoires, so she probably does have stuff about your weirdness, Ana. She should be up in her office shortly. She's just going over what needs to be done with Leo right now, per her usual."

"Just be careful, Ana," I urged. "We don't know what Mr. Shea's stuff can do . . . or if there are poisons and nastiness tangled in with his crap."

She waved me off, opening her eyes once again. "Please, girl. I'm not planning on touching any of the stuff Maia recovered from Boston. That's Nik's department, not mine. I've got no desire to peek at her dad's toys."

Yeah, right. Hello, Liar. "Hey, do you know where Rillin is?" I asked, knowing that arguing with Ana would be pointless.

Baz pointed towards the ceiling. "Rooftop. He said he wanted to check out the surrounding area before his guard shift with you started. The stairs to get up there are at the end of the catwalk. Small door on the left. Stairs lead to the trapdoor on the roof."

"Thanks," I replied, offering Ana a thumbs up. She returned the gesture with a different finger.

I chuckled and left, shutting the door to the lab and crossing the intricate patchwork of catwalks that hung high above Faust's massive dance hall. The steel planks and railings wove between the massive chandeliers and blown glass lamps that dripped from the ceiling, like a bewitched, black forest. Below me, workers hustled and laughed, and I could see Maia standing with a purple-haired girl at the center of the dance floor, pointing to the stage and talking to her.

I loved it up here, feeling as though I'd slipped into a Grimm's fairytale treehouse, where dragons slept and roses bloomed into crystals. I trailed my fingers along the twisted, black banister, noting the intricate thorny vine that was inlaid in the ironwork.

Faust, though having some major moral shortcomings, was breathtaking.

I found the door that led to the roof and the narrow set of stairs that spun upward to a trap door. I pushed through the door and the frozen tang of the ocean's wind hit me, licking across my cheeks in a frosty kiss. I drew breath, the chilled oxygen feeling like an icy charge of energy to my exhausted mind.

Pushing upwards on the door, it thunked against a stone half-wall, and I climbed through the hatch, taking in the glittering, frozen city that surrounded us. I dragged in another deep breath and felt, for just a moment, like I was back on Cape Cod. As if I were standing on the balcony of Torrent Road or the Widow's Walk of 408, listening to the purr of the ocean.

The rooftop of Faust was home to at least a dozen large stone creatures, clutching the corners and outer walls, no doubt guarding against enemies unknown. While some (re: normal) people collect shot-glasses from theme parks, Maia Moriarty apparently collected gargoyles.

I moved toward the edge of the roof, easing next to a winged, dragon-like thing with loads of wrinkles and a pig nose. It was clutching the very edge of the ledge and all I could think of was a Frankenstein version of a Muppet, but cast in granite. I just shook my head at its weirdness as I rubbed my arms furiously, cursing my stupidity for not grabbing a jacket before coming up here.

I looked down to the street below, noting how plain Faust looked on the outside. To any passerby, it was a mere warehouse, bricked over and forgotten – a central artery for the once bustling railways of an age gone by.

But then I caught sight of not one, but *three* shadows, moving along the side of the building. They were tough to see in the nightfall, but I knew what a Mortis wearing a cloak of shadows looked like, and those three were *not* tooth faeries.

"Shit," I whispered. "Oh, please be friendly."

"They are," rumbled Rillin's deep voice directly behind me, causing me to jump.

I spun and whacked him in the arm, his biceps basically stone under my frozen fist. "Jeezus, you gave me a heart attack!"

He shrugged out of his leather jacket and came close to me, tossing the bomber-style coat around my shoulders. "I saw you come up and figured you might be looking for me. You shouldn't be out here without a sweater." He shook his head, "You can't get sick. Not now. We need you."

"Thanks. For the jacket and the confidence," I replied, shivering as I pulled my arms through the heavy jacket. Rillin's body heat still clung to the soft inside and I snuggled my face down in the collar, grateful to be able to defrost the icicles from my torso and boobs.

"You didn't notice me," he accused, taking a step back as if he realized our intimate closeness. "I was standing by the gargoyle over there and you didn't even see me. What's the point of training you to be vigilant if you just enter some unknown rooftop and walk over to the side without checking the area for predators?"

I crossed my arms and raised an eyebrow, a bit pissed. "Um, okay, for one thing I knew you were up here, which means that if a bad guy HAD been up here, he would've been snapped into kindling. And second of all, I didn't see you, so I'm assuming you had super glued the shadows to your bod like the three down there," I stated sharply, pointing a finger down to the alley.

A voice from below us demanded that I stop whining like a baby, and I leaned over the ledge, glaring into the darkness. "Excuse me, but I've had a real lousy day, so can you not be a prick?"

One of the Mortis moved into the alley and the shadows fell away from his skin like dust in the wind. I instantly recognized Leo's accusing glare under the small hallow of light, thrown by the mason jar attached to the building.

"Did you just call me a prick?" he asked slowly, looking up at me. His entire body was covered in Fallen Marks and in the darkness, he'd let his eyes bleed to black as well.

Crap. "Oh. Sorry, Leo. I didn't realize it was you. I thought you were inside with Maia."

"I was. Now be quiet or you'll draw attention to the building. Your voice carries in the alleyways like a howling cat."

"Fine. Okay, jeez," I whispered back, giving him an ugly smile and a thumbs-up.

Leo just glared at me, pulling the darkness back over him like a second skin as he disappeared back into the edge of the building, but as he did so, I noticed a shadowy hand stick out from one of his buddies, offering a small wave.

I gave a quick wave in return and stepped back from the ledge, turning to Rillin. I stopped dead as I watched him cup a flame in his hand and light a cigarette in his mouth. "You . . . smoke?" I asked, floored. And horrified. "That stuff is so bad for you. It'll cause lung cancer!"

Rillin took a deep drag, turning his head to blow the haze away from my face, his dark eyes never leaving mine. The smoke curled slowly in the frozen air, like a witch's boney fingers casting a curse unto the night. "I'm a Mortis, Eila. Cancer is not on my list of worries and, if we are talking technicalities, I am dead."

"You're not dead," I protested.

"VOICES, damn it!" snapped Leo.

I said some choice words under my breath about Leo's control issues as Rillin led us back towards one of the huge, round smoke stacks at the center of Faust's rooftop. "Yes, I am. All Mortis are, to some extent. We feed off the living to prolong our own lives. Without the essence of a life force, or soul, we slowly decay into ash."

I frowned, not liking this line of thinking. "Raef doesn't feel dead to me. Nor does Kian. Or you. Christian didn't either. And, if we're getting real technical, and somewhat maudlin, then I'm dying too – slowly. We all are, every second of every day. Well, except . . . except

Elizabeth, if Maia is to be believed."

Rillin didn't reply as he took another drag on the cigarette. The scent seemed to be different than that of tobacco and Baz's pot. "What exactly are you smoking?" I asked, coming closer.

Rillin looked down at me for a moment, then offered me the hand-rolled cigarette. "Passion flower, kava, and lavender. And a little bit of hops."

"You're smoking potpourri? What are you, a repressed hippie or something?"

The edge of Rillin's mouth curved into a small grin. "It's not potpourri. It's a custom blend we Mortis call Tantalus. Or, Talus, as it's mostly known."

"It's potpourri, Thor, and I'll pass, thanks." I wrinkled my nose.

He brought the cigarette back to his lips and took a drag, blowing it out slowly. It was hypnotic to watch. "Why are you smoking? I've never seen you do it before."

He tapped the end of the cigarette, sending burning bits drifting in the light breeze. "I don't do it often. I haven't done it in, well, decades. It helps calm the stolen essence of life, which my body stores. I only do it when I know I'm riding a thin line with control."

I swallowed. "Control of what?" I asked, quietly.

His gaze finally left mine and he focused on the blackened harbor in the distance, as if hoping for the dawn. "The rage. The . . . anger. One does not take life without paying a price, Eila. One does not live for centuries as I have - as a killer - and not collect the burdens of the past, like a thousand pennies in a jar."

"And your jar has become too full?" I asked, sadly. It really hadn't hit me until just then – how hard this must be for Rillin, to be in constant contact with Elizabeth. To know all that had happened to her after he left her in the woods, and how much he probably regretted not staying with her that night. Of how he would've wanted to be at her side and possibly stopped her from entering the Harbor and facing Rysse. Of how deeply he cared for her, yet never had a chance to tell her. And now, with the knowledge that she was doomed to a supernatural sleep for all eternity if he couldn't wake her, it seemed as though he was about to lose her all over again.

He turned his head slightly, blowing away the smoke once again, his jaw flexing. "Something like that," he replied quietly. He drew a breath, "How can I be of service? You sought me out, so how can I help?"

I studied his face in the darkness, the angle of his stubble-covered jaw and broad neck; the line of the scar along the side of his cheek and the edges of his tattoos peeking out of his shirt collar. Despite the abuse his body had endured as Trial over the decades, despite the scars running like road maps over his skin, Rillin Blackwood was a handsome man. He wasn't polished and refined like Christian, or youthful and stunning like Raef and Kian. No, Rillin was the essence of hard-honed masculinity, rough-cut and dangerous — like a fine sword that had seen too many battlefields, or handcrafted pistol that resided in the worn leather pack of a gunslinger.

Immortality as a Mortis had frozen him at the age of twenty-seven, and his choices as a Templar knight had removed any chance of creating a family of his own. As a Blacklist dealer, friendships were a liability, thus he peddled the names of those who deserved to die from the shadows, never fully revealing himself to anyone. I couldn't fathom such an existence of solitude; of loneliness and heartbreak. And now he was *my* knight, *my* Trial, *my* Blacklist dealer. But even among us, he still seemed alone, never fully escaping his past, yet unable to move forward without the woman he once loved. Without Elizabeth.

Guilt hit me so hard that I thought my chest would cave in. My cursed life had no doubt become many pennies in the jars of those I cared for and loved; a demanding toll dragging them all through Hell. I watched as Rillin flicked the remaining stub of cigarette away, his eyes still on the distant harbor. "I'm a penny in your jar," I said quietly, my throat tightening.

Rillin turned to me, his hard gaze locked on mine. "No, you're not."

In my mind, I saw Mae and Christian's bodies on the pool table, draped in white. I saw Nikki on the ground outside Torrent Road, bleeding and turning a terrifying shade of pale. I saw Ana at the bottom of the stairs, Kian trying to heal her, and I saw the guys, their bodies peppered with bullet holes. And I saw Rillin the night he came to Torrent Road for the first time, touching the Link that had resided under his skin, deeming him a slave and explaining who he truly was.

"Rillin, I'm not worth this madness. If I'm the key to the Gate, then the simplest thing is to get rid of the key. All of this stops if I no longer exist." As hard as it was to admit, the truth was that I was a critical component in our war with Waite. If I was removed from the equation, then the Gate would be as well. No key, no time jump.

He leaned down to meet my eyes, "You are worth the fight, Eila. I swear it."

"I'm not!" I begged. "All of this loss. All of this pain and brutality - one girl is never worth this. One life is never worth this. You KNOW I'm right! You were a Templar knight, for Pete's sake! You understand war! I am no longer the path to peace. I'm the cause of continued violence! And now, with the possibility of Elizabeth waking? You could have a life with her. You could have her back, to love her and to be with her! With me in the equation, there will never be peace for anyone, Elizabeth included!"

Rillin grabbed me by the arms, giving me a solid shake. "You listen to me, damn it! You are here for a reason, not simply to be some sacrificial lamb. You will not reject the warrior you are for an easy way out simply because you have collected too many burdens and they weigh you down. You will not abandon this fight because guilt is whispering in your ear that you can escape the pain by suicide. Do you understand me? Elizabeth CHOSE to die. A twist of fate placed her as she is now, but she thought she would die that night. She chose to leave Christian and their son!"

I heard it, the agony in his voice, and the fear and anger. I placed my hands over his as they held my face. "You're angry with her," I replied quietly, shocked. "You're angry because she chose to leave everyone, which included you. I'm right, aren't I?"

He sighed, his hands dropping, "I taught her to fight. I taught her to hold fast to every last shred of determination. To never sacrifice herself, even if all she had left was a single breath left in her lungs. The night of her fifteenth birthday she fought her suitor because of me. Because of all I had taught her. But the harbor . . . she just threw her life away."

I reached out and gripped his hand. "Elizabeth fought her suitor because she loved you. Because she wanted you, even at fifteen."

His jaw clenched as he looked past me into the steadily falling snow. "I left her in the forest. Alone. Why would she ever forgive me?"

"You got her out of the palace before she could be executed. You came back to the woods for her, but she was gone. You couldn't have known Christian would find her. She loved you, I'm certain!"

"That was a long time ago," he replied sadly. "I fear that this world, without Christian, without her son, will not be a world she wishes to live in. I'm torn between letting her sleep, unaware of the losses and changes since her death, but also selfishly wanting her to open her eyes and speak to me again."

I sighed, "True love is endless, Rillin. It can be beautiful and joyous, or total, epic crapdom, but it's always worth entering the ring and testing your nerve. It's worth the agony."

Rillin smiled weakly, his eyes dropping to mine. "What if Maia is wrong and I am not her true soul bound mate? What if I have cherished a memory, only to find out that such love was one-sided and that I am not who she would want to see again?"

I placed my hand against Rillin's chest, over his heart, and his wide hand covered mine, clutching it tightly. "You assume the worst, but what if Elizabeth has longed to find you since that day in the woods? What if this, THIS, is your chance at happiness, Rillin? What if she's always wanted you?"

Rillin leaned closer to me, his smoky scent wrapping around me as he whispered, "You are so much like her, Eila. Your fierceness, your passion and devotion. This, THIS, is why you stole Raef's heart." Rillin's thumb grazed my jaw, tracing the angle of my bones gently. "I hope he understands the exquisite gift it is to love someone as rare as you. I hope he knows what a privilege it is to be allowed into your bed and into your heart."

I let out a shaky breath, my insides starting to do backflips.

This felt *dangerous* . . . as if we were flirting too close to an invisible line I flatly refused to cross.

Rillin took a deep breath and eased back from me. "He is a lucky man. I envy him."

I swallowed. "Rillin, I think you confuse me with the young woman you truly love. What I have with Raef waits for you inside Baz's lab. I suspect she's waited for you her entire life."

"I am not confused," he whispered, but made no move to close the distance he'd placed between us.

I went to argue, but he simple raised a palm, silencing me. "It's okay, Eila. I know where your heart lies. I would never . . ." He cleared his throat. "I am grateful our paths crossed that night you went riding at Blackstone Acres," he replied, easing back into his formal knight persona. "You have been a true friend and a very patient student of mine . . . though you do have a tendency to curse while training. It is most unladylike."

I laughed, but it felt sad and twisted in my heart. "You will always be my friend and my trainer, Thor. Always."

He smiled at me, "I'm sorry if I – "

Rillin's words were cut off by a low, brief rumble under our feet. The roof shuddered slightly, bits of granite sliding off the gargoyle near us, and scattering across the roof tiles.

"What was that?" I breathed, terrified I already knew the answer.

"An explosion," said Rillin, yanking a gun from his hip holster and grabbing my hand as we ran for the ledge. "Call the Light. Be ready!" he commanded, and we halted at the edge of the roof. Leo and his guys were already gone, no doubt racing back into the building.

We bolted for the trapdoor, Rillin yanking it open. "Do you think we're under attack?" I demanded, as I focused my mind on calling the Light. I could feel it respond, like a shark hooked on a line and slowly being reeled in. It flared inside me, forcing my vision into a glorious black and white.

"We could be. I don't know," he replied, heading into the stairwell, the sound of people yelling drifting up from inside. He glanced up at me and offered his hand.

"It was an explosion," I said, pausing.

"I know!" he snapped.

I grasped his hand and squeezed. "Rillin, what if Maia is entirely wrong. What if it is . . . Elizabeth."

Rillin paused, his eyes distant and devastated for a moment as he replied in a ghostly quiet, "I know."

CHAPTER 16
FAUST, NEW BEDFORD, MA
SATURDAY, 8:10 PM

I clapped Kian on the shoulder, proud at what we'd hopefully accomplished for Nikki. "I think she's going to get her arm back, don't you?"

He smiled, a true honest-to-god smile. "Yeah. I do. Good work, man. And thanks."

"For what?" I asked, turning a corner onto another catwalk. Below us, workers were milling around, readying the stage in deep blue and silver drapes. We were headed for Baz's lab to find the girls.

"For, you know, having confidence that I could do it. That you trusted me to help."

I stopped walking and Kian halted next to me. I studied him for a minute as he leaned back and crossed his arms, watching me with a quirked smile. "What?"

I shook my head and laughed. "I'm just thinking back to when we used to really hate each other."

"Hate may be a tad strong. 'Gag-worthy dislike' would be a more accurate description."

I chuckled, rubbing my neck and studying the massive chandeliers and the ornate, gothic beauty that was Faust. "Can you imagine our lives if you'd never walked into that bar in Miami and screwed with my billiard game?"

"You looked bored. I saved your sanity that night, just admit it," he replied, smiling, but then it slowly fell. "In all seriousness, Raef. I'm grateful our paths crossed again that night. I'm glad you came up here with me. If it wasn't for you, I may've never found my way back to Ana. It was you that wanted to check on the new owner of Elizabeth's house, not me." He stood up, resting one hand on my shoulder. "Fate doesn't get much right in our lives, Raef, but that night in Miami brought us here, with our girls, and I call that damn fine luck."

I rested my hand on his shoulder as well, the closest the two of us were ever going to get to a bonding moment. "Just to be clear, though – you still irritate the shit out of me on a regular basis, Kian."

He shrugged. "Yeah, well – perfection as brilliant as mine can chafe those around me. You'll get used to it."

I laughed, and gave him a shove. "You are such a – "

Suddenly the far end of the parallel catwalk slammed outward from Maia's office, a massive explosion shattering her door and crashing into one of the center chandeliers. Easily the size of a car, it exploded into a riot of iron and glass, sending hundreds of deadly pieces raining down on the workers below. They were instantly yelling in alarm. Kian and I had been thrown to our knees, and in the onslaught of smoke I fought to be able to see as I heard the screams of the injured echoing throughout the building.

"Raef! You alright?" called Kian through the cloud of ash. The scent of blood and burning flesh was intense and became stronger with every second as the smoke poured from Maia's office, filling the nightclub.

I coughed, "Yeah! You good?"

"Yes! What the hell just happened?"

"Explosion, I think!" I called back, finally finding Kian's ash-covered face through the haze. If I hadn't seen the blast come from Moriarty's office, I would have thought it might have been Elizabeth, Maia's opinions on her safety-factor be damned.

I heard Leo's voice, shouting from the lower level and I called down to him. "Up here! It was Maia's office!"

"WHAT?!" screamed Leo, racing up the spiral staircase near the bar that lead to the shattered catwalk. He jumped onto the damaged metal and it groaned, dropping a few inches with a bone-chilling *bang*, but Leo was undaunted.

"Fire extinguishers!" he shouted to some other Mortis racing across the dance hall below. "Vent the club! NOW!"

Kian started moving on the catwalk, feeling his way towards the lab. "We gotta get the girls!"

"Christ, that sounded like the Shea's house all over again," I replied as I moved with him, squinting through the smoke as Leo, not far from us, worked his way carefully to Maia's office.

"Let's pray no one was in there," Kian replied, coughing as he glanced back at me. Somewhere below us I heard people yelling about the venting system. Within seconds, the roar of powerful fans filled the club, forcing the smoke up through the ceiling's elaborate network of vents and out into the city.

We reached the lab door and pushed it open to find Baz on the floor, trying to rise as blood streamed from a gash in his forehead. Vials and liquids were strewn all over the tile floor. Elizabeth, though jarred by the explosion, remained on the table, but her arms now hung limply off the edges. I stepped quickly to her, placing my fingers to her neck in the off-chance her heart had been jolted into beating again. I felt nothing. I eased her hands back onto her stomach as Kian pulled Baz slowly to his feet.

"What the Hell just happened?" coughed Baz, waving a hand in front of his face as Kian steadied him against the counter. I quickly scanned the room and my heart bottomed out as one thing became undeniably clear: the girls weren't anywhere in the lab.

"Where are the girls?" I demanded, my voice a near growl. Kian, beside me, became still as death as if every cell in his body had frozen solid as he realized Ana was not in the room.

Baz coughed again, pressing his palm to the cut near his hairline as he slumped back against the cabinets. "Eila went looking for Rillin. She's probably on the roof. And Ana – she went to my mom's office. She wanted to get her hands on my mother's books on Sways. My mom should be with her." He glanced up at us, "Was that an explosion or did something malfunction?"

All the color bled out of Kian's face as my heart fell entirely through the floor.

He bolted from the lab and I followed hot on his heels, Baz's voice still demanding answers as we raced to the end of the catwalk. Across Faust's cavernous expanse, Leo was balancing precariously on the slowly crumbling catwalk that led to Maia's office.

"PIX!" screamed Kian, but I swung myself over the railing and eyed the mangled chandelier that hung between Leo and us. By some miracle, it was still attached to the ceiling, the roar of the venting fans working hard above it.

I glanced back at Kian, who was still calling Ana's name, desperate for her voice to answer. With Maia's catwalk barely clinging to the walls and ceiling, we had no way to access her office unless we could use the ornate light as a hanging island. "We can jump!" I yelled to Kian. "Come on, man! We can use the chandelier!"

He realized what I was going to try, and so did Leo. I looked across at the bouncer, the smoke still thick in the air despite the roaring fans. I pointed to the light, "We're gonna get it swinging and we'll have to jump for the office, got it?"

Leo nodded, easing his way over the twisted metal of his catwalk so he could make the leap at the right moment. But just as I was about to jump, the door that led to the roof swung open behind Leo.

Rillin appeared.

Kian and I shouted a warning, but we were too late as Rillin leapt down, landing hard on the damaged catwalk. It jolted in response, ripping free from the ceiling. Leo swore, spinning fast and vaulting into the air, his desperate reach barely making it to the chandelier as he managed to catch the bottom light with one hand.

Rillin instantly spun, reaching for the bottom of the stairwell door, his body slamming against the brick wall as the catwalk gave way under him. It crashed down onto the dance floor, metal rods and pipes twisting like vines from the wall and ceiling and clinging to remnants of the catwalk.

His feet kicking free, Rillin roared a warning to someone in the stairwell. To my horror, it was Eila who appeared.

"GET BACK!" I screamed.

My world slowed as she tumbled free of the stairwell, realizing too late that the catwalk was gone. She screamed, but Rillin snagged her roughly by the arm, and she crashed hard against the bricks. She twisted in his grasp, trying to gain purchase with her sneakers against the wall.

"I've got you!" Rillin yelled, "Don't let go!"

Gasping, she hung on with all her might as he hauled her up to his chest with one arm, the other holding them both from a fatal fall to the tables and shattered glass far below.

"Eila!" I yelled, and she turned to see me across the expanse of the club, the broken chandelier turning slowly between us.

"RAEF!" she called back, "Oh my God! What happened?" She held tight to Rillin, and he clung to the doorframe with one arm, their bodies dangling together against the stonewall, dozens of feet above certain death.

"Are you okay?" I demanded, as Rillin pushed her above him and back into the stairwell. She called back she was okay as Rillin, certain she was safe, finally hauled himself up next to her.

"Stay with her!" I demanded. Rillin nodded, but then he yelled back a question, desperate to know if it was Elizabeth.

"No," I called back. "She's okay." In the back of my mind, I realized that 'okay' and 'Elizabeth' really didn't exactly go together. The woman had been in a suspended supernatural coma for more than a century.

Kian demanded we get to the office. Standing shoulder to shoulder with me, he gave a nod and together we leapt to the twisted chandelier, Leo having pulled himself up to the outer branches of the ironwork. It swung in Rillin's direction and the three of us began urging the ornate light to rock back and forth. Between our combined momentum, the huge chandelier started to finally swing towards

Moriarty's office.

"Get ready!" I yelled to Kian.

"I am!"

We all leaned one way then another and by the third pass, Kian went for it, managing to grab onto the burned doorframe and haul himself inside. Leo quickly followed, nearly missing the door, but scrambling inside. I pulled myself to standing and leaned back on the chandelier, forcing it to swing hard again as I repeated a constant prayer that Ana was alive. Finally, I managed the jump as well, and landed hard on the charred edge of the door, pulling myself inside.

The carnage was astounding. Choked in smoke, the area looked as though someone had lit a fire bomb inside the office.

All the decadence, all the beauty, had been ripped from Moriarty's once ornate office, as if someone had painted the room in an oily black and shredded it with a buzzsaw. Kian and Leo were calling over and over for Maia and Ana, but I snarled at them to be quiet. "Be silent! Listen for a heartbeat!"

The guys instantly stopped moving, all three of us pulling upon every ounce of our Mortis side in a desperate attempt to further enhance our hearing.

A few seconds passed when Kian suddenly started moving, running for the desk that was overturned near the bookcases. He yanked it from the corner to reveal the two guards that had been outside the door. They were crumpled in a heap, one's lifeless eyes staring at the ceiling, most of his chest burned down to the bone, the other slumped over his friend's legs. But beneath them were two more bodies.

And both had heartbeats.

We pulled the two dead guards off of Maia and Ana, but neither moved as we dropped to the floor next to them. Leo eased Maia into his arms, talking to her as he pushed her dark hair from her face. She didn't respond, but though her heartbeat was slow, she was alive.

Kian ran his hand down Ana's back. "Oh, God, please . . ." he sobbed as he bent forward and eased her carefully onto her back. She was like a rag doll, her small body limp as Kian ran his hands down her torso and face, searching for an injury. I could hear her heartbeat as well, thankfully sounding strong. She was bloodied, but much of it seemed to have come from Maia and the two guards.

"Pix?" Kian whispered, his voice broken, but she didn't respond. "Come on baby, wake up."

I touched her forehead and glanced to Kian. Tears streaked his ash-covered face. "I think she's just knocked out, Kian. And probably blew her eardrums, but her heart is strong. Let's get her out of here – both of them. I'm sure they have smoke inhalation, but we can clear their lungs." Leo nodded, pulling Maia into his arms, her dress in tatters, the once vibrant colors muted by blood and soot.

Kian gathered Ana into his arms, pressing a shaking kiss to her forehead. I'd never seen him so totally lose it before.

"How are we going to get them down?" I asked, just as the sprinkler system kicked in and doused us in water. "Shit."

"We're gonna need a ladder. Or Bane. He can scale the ceiling as a Lesser. He may be able to carry the girls to . . ." Leo paused, the sound of banging steel echoing inside the building. "Oh, shit, what now?"

I heard it too, as did Kian. It sounded like metal moaning and iron tapping against itself. We looked out the ruined doorframe and slowly, as if rising from the dead, the catwalk began to appear through the smoke. Piece by piece, it wove itself back together, metal bending and twisting together like live vines, forming a mutated form of the catwalk that had fallen from under Rillin not minutes before. It continued to move and groan until it finally settled into stillness – a black path to sanctuary that had risen from the rubble.

I heard the pounding of feet and Eila and Rillin appeared in the doorway, E nearly tripping at the site of Ana. "NO!" she screamed and I caught her before she crashed into Kian, as he was holding her friend.

"She's okay, E. I think she got knocked out."

Eila fell into my embrace, relief hitting her hard. Rillin came over and knelt by Maia, discussing what healing she'd need with Leo, but then glanced around the room. "This was deliberate, no question," he said, his face cut in a hard, angry profile. "I'd be willing to wager that this was also C-4, like Nikita's house."

Ana coughed and Kian snapped his gaze back to her, "Pix?"

"Key?" she asked, her voice like gravel. She coughed loudly, but Kian laughed, a huge smile lighting his face. "Yeah, baby. It's me."

"Is Maia?" she asked, blinking.

"She's gonna be okay too. What happened?"

"Nikki's dad's stuff. It just . . . exploded," she replied, confirming Rillin's theories.

I looked over to Rillin. "The catwalk?"

Rillin's jaw hardened. "Nikki. She's awake, but I'm not sure how long she can stay alert and hold the catwalk together."

I glanced at Eila, who swallowed hard. "Jesus, Nikki could've died," she whispered. "Her father had to know she's been with us. He had to know the equipment could potentially injure or kill her. How are we ever going to tell her?"

"I'll tell her," said a male voice from behind us.

We turned to see MJ standing in the doorway, looking over the devastation in the room. His eyes met Ana's as she lay in Kian's embrace, "You okay?"

"Yeah," she rasped, and her lips turned down in sadness. "But what about Nikki?"

MJ just rubbed his arm, leaving a streak of ash on his skin and t-shirt. "She's at the other end of the catwalk, holding your escape route together. She wanted me to tell you all that you need to 'move your asses' and get out while you can. She doesn't know how long the fire-damaged metal will hold out and she's keeping the structure together on pure stubborn will. Plus, she's still a bit doped-up."

He stepped back from the door, looking at all of us. "And, uh, give me some time alone with her. We'll find you when she's ready. After I tell her." He turned and sadly walked away, the sound of his footsteps on the re-made metal fading.

Leo got to his feet with Maia, Rillin beside him. "That kid's your shifter, right?" he asked.

"Yeah," I replied, rubbing Eila's back, trying to ease her.

"So, he and your Ironess are a thing?"

My gaze once again drifted to the door. "Yeah, I guess they are."

CHAPTER 17
FAUST, NEW BEDFORD, MA

I couldn't feel Marsh anymore.

His constant presence, like a phantom limb that manifested to real as needed, was gone. Just . . . missing. Entirely.

I was about to lose my shit.

I braced my hands on the porcelain sink, staring hard at my hazy reflection in the fogged-over mirror. I felt as though I'd been dropped into a different body. And a different, seriously messed up reality.

Half an hour before, I'd sunk down next to Nikki on the mutated catwalk she'd managed to bring back to life, her eyes searching mine. "Was it . . . my Dad's stuff? Was it a bomb?" she'd questioned in a painful whisper as she kept her right hand clutched tightly to the iron railing, making sure the catwalk held as Maia and Ana were carried out of the office, followed by Raef and Leo. Her eyes slipped past my shoulder to our friends walking to the safety of the spiral staircase at the other end of the catwalk. I didn't turn to follow her gaze.

I didn't even need to answer her. Didn't need to confirm that her father was a total heartless bastard. There was no way her father didn't know she was hanging with us, and yet he tucked a bomb in with his bounty. He could've killed us ALL.

When she finally looked back at me, her eyes were filled with pain, and I knew that I didn't need to say it out loud. I knew, in the way her breath had a slight catch to it, and how her jaw tightened and her lip trembled, that Nikki knew her father didn't give a crap about her. That he was willing to potentially end the life of his only child, and for what? Money? Fame? A sick belief?

In that one moment, the father Nikki thought she knew was also consumed in the blast. I could see it in her eyes – the knowledge that there was no coming back from such a betrayal. No forgiveness to be given. And though he was a crappy parent, probably seeing Nik as an accessory in life rather than the reason for existing, he was still her dad. Yet he was willing to kill her, even if she was just collateral damage.

I had eased myself against her and slipped one arm around her waist, her chilled torso wrapped with the fabric strips I'd applied after Raef and Kian repaired her shoulder. Still wrapped in the bed sheet from Baz's room, I gave her a gentle pull and though she remained rigid at first, she eventually leaned against me. I felt her chest and back tremble as she continued to breathe, fighting for emotional control.

I don't know if she really won the battle or not, because she didn't cry, but she also hadn't said a word since. And somehow her patchwork catwalk was still standing, defying everyone's prediction that it would collapse once she released her hold.

As for me? I'd blown through every emotion in the book in the past 24 hours, probably twice, including denial. But as I stood in the large, communal shower room that the Faust workers used, all I had left was numbness.

And a lack of Marsh, which was really starting to rattle me.

After the explosion and ensuing chaos of making sure everyone wasn't fatally injured (except for the poor guards, who apparently saved Ana and Maia's life), Baz had told everyone to get cleaned up and to meet on the rooftop. They were currently venting the dance hall area through a state-of-the-art system that was part of their anti-fire protocols, but it was taking forever. Whatever Ken Shea had tucked in with his goodies produced a doozy of a blast and enough smoke to rival New York during the Industrial Revolution.

Thankfully, Maia had been thorough when she renovated the roundhouse that became Faust, and I was sure she'd be pleased to know that her club and its workers were trying hard to pull themselves together. Last I heard, she was still unconscious and Leo wouldn't leave her side.

Baz was now in charge of Faust until his mom recovered.

Baz. In charge of Faust. Talk about terrifying.

We'd waited until the workers had used the showers, getting rid of the ash and grime from the explosion before Kian, Rillin, and I dragged our sorry butts into the bathroom and showered. The girls were in an adjacent one with Raef, who didn't want them without a guard. I knew Nikki, however, couldn't get her bandages wet. I'd offered to change them for her if they were too filthy, but she refused. I was worried that the scent of burnt Mortis flesh and fire was branded to the fabric.

I wanted to phase for Nikki's sake – she seemed to seek out my furrier form whenever life was just too hellish, but FRAK! I couldn't seem to shift! It was as if the black Shuk I'd known for so long had finally had it with my crazy life and resigned.

Exhaustion. Stress. That had to be it.

I was just too dog-tired to shift into, well . . . a dog.

"MJ, get your shit together," I muttered into the mirror.

I heard the water shut off in the nearest shower. "I tell you that all the time," called Kian from the stall, the sound echoing off the tiles.

"I've, uh, got a bit of a problem," I called back, realizing that we all were in deep seagull poop if I couldn't phase. Marsh was a damn fine fighter in a rumble, and we couldn't be down a protective asset right now. I was man enough to admit that my dog form could even kick *my* human butt . . . theoretically speaking, obviously.

"Ha! Get in line, MJ," said Kian, walking out and grabbing a towel from a nearby hook. Fallen Marks covered his body, an apparent reaction to the extreme stress we were under. Though he seemed balanced and irritatingly sarcastic as usual, his body hadn't caught up with his attitude yet. When he thought Ana had died in the blast, his body reacted so strongly that the Marks appeared on their own, entirely out of his control. He had yet to be able to rein them in.

He came up next to me, sweeping his blond hair back from his face with his fingers. "The list of problems we've got now is so long, it could outlive an immortal."

Rillin, dressed in just his black cargo pants, his body still damp from the showers, came up next to me on the other side, making me feel like I was the width of a toothpick. He wiped away the fog on the mirror in front of his station, his huge body showing off far more tattoos and scars than I ever knew he had. He literally looked like a heavyweight, cage-fighting champion who went ten rounds with a deranged grizzly bear. And won.

Kian paused, glancing at the former knight. "Work out much?" he asked, eyebrow raised.

Rillin's eyes met his in the mirror. "Genetics, actually, both human and Mortis." The massive owl on his back flexed, as if in flight, with every move he made. "What's your problem, MJ?" he asked, never one to joke.

"I can't seem to phase."

All of Kian's cocky amusement fell. "Are you serious?" I nodded, and Ana's boy-toy looked flustered. "Well . . . try harder, damn it!"

"HEY! Piss off!" I snapped, "I've been trying and it's just not there! Marsh is like, GONE, and I'm, like, having a wee bit of a heart attack. So you yelling at me ain't too freakin' helpful right now!"

Kian put his hands up, as if seeking a truce, and I realized I'd gotten right in his face. Though he could snap my neck in my human form, we were the same height, making a nose-to-nose confrontation totally possible. "Alright, alright – I'm sorry. I'm just . . . shit, man. We NEED Marsh." He stopped talking abruptly, then rubbed his face hard. "I can't believe I just said that out loud. Oh my God, I'm actually dead and this is my version of Hell – stuck for eternity with you two in a basement bathroom."

Rillin glared at him for a second, then turned back to me. "MJ, it is probably severe stress. We all need to decompress. Baz has some hand-rolled Tantalus. He gave me some earlier – I'm sure he'd be willing to offer you some." He looked at Kian, "In fact, it may be useful for everyone, especially Nikita."

"Weed Boy has Talus? I haven't smoked that in over a century." Kian raised an eyebrow, "Is it high quality?"

"Very," replied Rillin, and Kian looked hopeful.

"What's Talus?" I asked, suspicious.

Rillin rubbed his hand down the beard that was starting to show on his face, as if debating whether or not to shave. "It's a combination of herbs and flowers that Mortis are known to smoke to calm the *soul rage* that can build up over time. It . . . mellows the anger."

"IT'S WEED!" I accused.

Kian rolled his eyes, "Oh for cripes sakes, it's not weed. It's like . . . well, it's like tea, but you smoke it."

I glanced between the two killers flanking me, trying to judge if I was being screwed with or not. "You smoke TEA? What the heck? Why not just drink it?"

"First of all, it's not REAL tea and secondly, we don't eat, moron," Kian replied with a sigh. "You know, I really prefer Marsh. Get him back. Soon."

"It's tea, Shark Boy. And I'm working on it."

Rillin dropped his hand from his face for a moment, briefly studying the sigil carved in his hand. "You know, there may be another reason you can't form the Black Shuk anymore."

Kian and I looked at the scarred dude next to us. "Which is?" I asked.

"Maybe you can't form the dog because the dog doesn't form to you anymore."

"Speak English," I sighed.

"Perhaps, you are attempting to feel for Marsh's form, when Marsh has evolved into something else within you."

"Like what? An ulcer?" asked Kian, but I knew what Rillin was getting at.

I stilled, my mother's words ringing through my ears. "You mean my alpha form? You think I'm starting to make the shift to something . . . else?"

Rillin simply looked at me, his dark eyes trailing over my body as if seeking a shadow that wasn't human; trying to find a hint of what was to come.

Suddenly, I didn't want to know what else lived under my skin, biding its time. I could control Marsh. What if my Alpha form, however, had no desire to be tamed? What if I was like a Lesser or a thousand pound tarantula? I hate spiders!

"I may puke," I whispered, making my way quickly to one of the toilet stalls. I slammed through the steel door and braced my hands against the wall, trying to control the nausea.

Kian called from his spot near the sink, "Puke and rally, puppy dog, and be quick about it. We're needed on the rooftop."

"Screw off," I gasped, and then proceeded to drop to the floor and dry heave until my body felt as though it would break.

As I wretched, something stirred under my senses, and it wasn't Marsh, but something darker . . . and far more dangerous.

I prayed I could control it.

CHAPTER 18

FAUST, NEW BEDFORD, MA

SATURDAY, 9:30 PM

Maia's crew had already gathered on the rooftop by the time Ana, Nikki, Raef, and I managed to join them.

A little while ago, Ana and I had showered and changed, and Nikki did her best to clean up with some hand towels, Bane having loaned her a heavy sweatshirt big enough to fit her wrapped arm underneath.

Raef had shared the shower with me, running his hands down my body as we stood under the warm spray. His kisses were soft and worshipful, his touch gentle yet fierce, as if his mind warred between relief and rage. He'd refused to stray from my side after what was obviously an attempt on all our lives, and I had no desire to lose sight of the boy I adored. Once showered, he had stood watch outside the bathroom, making sure neither we, nor Kian, Rillin, and MJ were bothered.

I looked over at Kian, who was now seated on the rooftop deck near us. Ana was wedged between his legs with her own knees tucked in under her chin. Kian had wrapped her in a huge coat, his long arms curled around her, their hands entwined. He spoke quietly in her ear, his voice turning to vapor in the winter air as we waited for Baz to arrive. On the other side of the roof, the Faust crew had formed their own group. Away from us.

Not far from us, Nikki sat in the cold night air next to MJ at the base of a huge stone lion-like beast, its mouth wide in a frozen roar, fangs hanging low, raven wings spread wide. In the falling snow, Nik looked even paler than she had in the showers. Even cocooned in the heavy blanket MJ had wrapped around her, she didn't look good. Raef, standing next to me, had whispered that her body was toeing the line with shock. That we needed to keep a close eye on her.

As I watched MJ, I knew he wouldn't leave Nik's side. Though they didn't say anything to one another, I noticed that their bodies were in total contact as they sat side by side, as if MJ's warmth could ease Nikki's chilled soul.

Her parents had apparently flown the coop – left their teenaged daughter on her own, like a pet tossed to the side of the road. On top of her traitorous folks, she also basically lost her home, as blowing up Mr. Shea's home office sorta sealed the deal . . . especially since Baz had mentioned the explosion had been featured on the evening news, and the cops were now looking for the Sheas, Nik included.

I bet anything that Jesse Vale, the football captain who for some insane reason liked me, was losing his mind over the explosion. After all, he'd shown up at Torrent Road with his dad, the FIRE

CHIEF, demanding answers as to why MJ's Bronco had been torched in the driveway, and where-the-heck Nikki was. Ana had managed to mess with Chief Vale's memories, and Nikki showed her face and told Jesse we'd all gotten hammered at a Thai restaurant the night before, but I'm not entirely sure Jesse bought it. I knew there was no way he'd let the explosion thing slide.

Quite frankly, I was becoming a favorite source of gossip for the Cape.

The icing on the cake, however, was the fact that poor Nikki still looked a little drunk from the Twilight Sleep the guys used to put her out for her surgery.

She needed sleep. Food. She needed a new life and a chance to change her fate. And maybe, like me, she was running on vengeance. She was powering past the pain, both physical and emotional, for the sake of survival. Rillin said that he collected bits of pain and penance like pennies in a jar. Nikki Shea was also banking a heavy count at this rate, and I prayed she would be able to shoulder the weight . . . at least until we could take down Lawson Waite.

I'd sent Rillin to stand guard over Elizabeth because I didn't fully trust the safety-factor of Faust anymore, given the fact that Maia's office had been forcibly redecorated. Of course, the other reason I wanted him to hang with my Gram's was that she needed to WAKE UP! If she could tell us what she knew of the Gate from her time in the palace, life would probably be a whole lot more bliss-freakin-full.

I knew that Rillin had major reservations about Elizabeth - about whether Maia was right in the first place, and whether he was her true, soul-bound mate. I could tell that Rillin hadn't wanted to go to the lab. He wanted to stay with me, guard me, but he did as I instructed, never questioning my decision. He was, as always, my loyal knight.

And then there was my bodyguard, the love of my life, with whom I could argue endlessly and who was currently trying to block the winter wind for me. Two hard heads, that's what we were, each one damn sure we knew better than the other. At the end of the day, though, those arguments made us perfect for one another. It forced us both to see life through the eyes of one another, rather than just ourselves. And that restless, addictive bond that seemed to snap and writhe between us only existed when I was with Raef. He said it was our own soul bond, heady and intoxicating, especially when the need to be in each other's arms became all consuming. I wondered if that was what Elizabeth and Rillin had kept buried. I wondered if it would be downright explosive if she was ever able to open her eyes again and see her Trial standing at her side.

My mind a tumultuous mess, I rested my head on Raef's shoulder, studying the faces of the Faust workers, eighteen in all including Bane, who had maintained his cursed form since we'd arrived. Rillin had mentioned that, for a Lesser, maintaining a human form was sometimes a challenge, whereas allowing their demonic form to take hold was like a relaxed sigh – effortless and comfortable.

I felt bad for Maia's crew. They looked worn out. Emotionally spent. Standing across from us, I knew they were a mix of humans and soul thieves – a varied family that Maia had sheltered and served for God knows how many years. Their minds were all with their feisty matron, praying she'd be alright. Praying she'd wake up. Several Mortis had set to work on her as soon as she was pulled from the office. Broken bones and some deep cuts were the easy things to repair, as well as reversing the smoke damage to her lungs. Fixing her brain, however, was not so simple. Leo said she had a bad concussion.

He said he believed she would rouse from it soon, but it had been an hour since the explosion, and Maia hadn't come around.

And Leo hadn't left her side.

I sighed just as the trap door at the center of the roof finally banged open and a very exhausted, very sober looking Baz pulled himself through the hatch and stepped onto the roof. The Faust workers, who had eyed me and *my crew* warily when we'd arrived on the roof, immediately surrounded Baz, offering hugs and peppering him with questions. He finally calmed them down and simply stated that his mom was still unconscious.

The workers stilled, but Bane moved silently towards Maia's son, his gray tail slashing back and forth as he approached. "What do we know, Baz? About . . ." he looked quickly in Nikki's direction, "about the bomb?"

"Not much. I'm hoping Ana can shed some light on what the Hell happened," he looked directly at Ana and all the workers swung their attention to her.

"Me?" she asked, slowly getting to her feet, and no doubt horrified she was now in the spotlight. Kian followed her lead, one muscled arm tightening around her hip, his glare downright dangerous. I pitied any moron who came near Ana Lane in that one moment.

Ana rubbed her arms, "Well, when I got to the office with Maia, she started talking to me about the few books she had that mentioned Sways. We were looking through the bookshelf behind her desk, and the boxes of stuff they'd snagged from the address in Boston were on the other side of the room. I was able to see what was in some of the boxes - tools, books . . ." she looked at Rillin, "and Limiting Links. I saw an entire box full of Limiting Links."

Maia's crew murmured their unease, but Ana continued. "Anyway, Maia and I were just talking, and she asked me if I was able to like, do the whole mental disappearing thing. I said I could and I'd done it down in Polaris. She said that some of the books she had mentioned the Sway being able to hide other people that way. She said it was theorized that the Sway also hid Aztael castle from passersby in the same way. But then Maia's guards ran into the room. They were screaming . . ." Ana paused, her eyes sliding over to Nikki, who had gone entirely still. "Nik – I don't have to talk about this right now. I can do this somewhere else."

"Keep talking," said Nikki, her face hard.

"You don't have to do this Nik. You don't need to hear this. No one will think less of you," said MJ.

She turned her face towards his and they were so close, their noses almost touched. She quickly looked back at Ana, "Keep going. I need to . . . know." The last word broke slightly, her lips sealing tight. MJ placed a hand on her knee and gave Ana a nod.

She glanced to Kian, seeking assurance, and he gave her shoulders a squeeze. Taking a deep breath, she forged ahead, "The guards were yelling. Screaming. Freaking out. Telling us to *get down*. They grabbed Maia and me and, well . . . the next thing I knew, I was in Kian's arms."

"They sensed the bomb," said Bane. "Right before it triggered, they must've heard it activate just before it blew."

Baz approached Ana, Kian still watching him and the crowd carefully. "Did you see anything else in the boxes that may tip us off to where Waite is? About the Gate?" he asked.

Ana blinked. "I already know where Waite lives. I know his house. He lives on Martha's Vineyard - in Lower Makinokey."

"How do you know that?" demanded one of the Mortis in the crowd.

Ana paused, realizing some things were not entirely known to the Faust crew yet. "I used to work on his cars at his private garage that was part of his estate on the island. He used them to . . . to move drugs."

"Cocaine," added Kian. "He moved cocaine."

"You worked for this man?" demanded the purple-haired girl I'd seen earlier with Maia. She pushed her way to the front of the Faust pack, her attitude a match to Ana's. I recalled her from the very first time I'd set foot in Faust. Her Fallen marks were a blazing contrast to the snow drifting in the air.

Ana flexed her fingers, as if feeling her mechanic's tools in her hands. "Yes. I was one of his mechanics, but I didn't work for him that often. And I rarely saw him, but yes, I knew him." Ana paused, as if thinking. "Actually, come to think of it, when I was reading Sara Booth, Waite looked a little . . . different. In her mind, he looked different."

"Different how?" I asked.

"Well, when I knew him he was kinda skinny and geeky, I guess. He had guards on him all the time, because he looked like a kindergartener could probably take him in a fight. But in Booth's memories, he looked healthier. More fit. It was definitely him, but it was as if . . . as if he got in way more time at the gym. When I was reading Booth, I was just focused on getting the information about what happened to Rillin, but thinking back . . . He looked different"

"Plastic surgery?" asked Raef.

"I don't think so. The change isn't that drastic."

"Could he have been turned? Into a Mortis?" I asked, looking at my best friend.

Ana frowned, frustrated. "I just don't know."

One of Maia's employees, a tall, willowy woman with a voice like a thee-year-old piped up, "Screw this - I say we go raid Waite's place. The Sway knows where he lives on the Vineyard. I say we head to his turf, on the Island, and rip his house down around him and bury him in pieces inside."

A blood-thirsty cheer went up from the Faust crew and I could feel Raef slowly move in front of me, sensing a shift in the tension in the air.

Baz began walking around us, "Yes . . . yes, and we could bring the war to his doorstep. We could rain hell down on his life. We could go and demand his blood."

The crew roared, fists driving into the air. Baz continued his slow trek around the Faust crew, his face hard. Dark.

"And why stop there?" he shouted. "After all, aren't we the ones that are paying the price to protect her?" He spun, pointing right at me, and the Faust workers turned their gaze on me, some agreeing in a low growl while other's seemed surprised.

Around me, Nik and MJ were now on their feet, Kian pushing Ana behind him, Raef doing the same as he placed himself between me and the unchecked malice rising in Maia's crew.

Baz continued to rally his crew, words like *blame* and *suffering* tangling with my name and that of my ancestors. With each proclamation, the crowd grew more ravenous. He had flipped from being our ally, to being a nightmare, demanding we pay. Demanding blood for blood.

"Basil," Raef snarled, his arm holding me to his back. "What are you doing?"

Baz, however, seemed to be fueled by anger, his ability to think clearly replaced by a desire to enter the warpath. Our names were being tossed in with others as targets for the crew's rage and for the blame of everything that had happened.

Kian urged, "We need to get out of here. This is turning into a lynch mob. Stupid pothead – MJ should've killed him in Nikki's house the first time they met." He tugged Ana closer to his broad back.

"I can't believe he's doing this," I whispered as I watched the chaos unfold across from us. It was as if Basil Moriarty was a completely different person, and worse, he had suddenly decided we were worthy of the same fate as Waite. "I can stop this," I urged Raef, but he only held me tighter.

He looked over his shoulder at me, "By doing what, E? Displaying your power? Forcing them to change their minds and listen to reason? You show off the Light and threaten them to back down and we confirm everything Baz is saying."

I was about to argue that I could talk some sense into Moriarty's crew when I noticed Bane. He was wandering around the outside of the crowd, but he wasn't reacting to Baz's words. Instead, he was watching all the workers as they cheered and roared for Baz's traitorous lies. He carefully stalked the perimeter, his long limbs and gray skin fading in and out of the gargoyles' shadows. He appeared to be looking for something within the virulent crowd.

Baz took a breath, the Faust workers now in a near frenzy, all of them watching my crew. We'd closed ranks, ready to defend ourselves. I looked over at MJ and was shocked to see he hadn't phased into Marsh.

Baz looked at me and paused, "Of course, there is one

problem with demanding such brutal payment of Walker. I mean, technically she hasn't ever lied to us. Been ignorant? Maybe. But lie? Knowingly act as a traitor? No. She hasn't."

The crowd began to argue, but Baz held up his hand. "I, however, have found out there IS a traitor here on this roof tonight. One who planted THIS in my mother's office."

The crowd went still as Baz held up a small blackened device. "This is a detonator. It is remotely activated but has a very short range. Short enough, in fact, that the person triggering it would have to be within the building when the bomb went off." Baz's gaze swung carefully to Nikki. Like the rest of us, confusion was slowly giving way to understanding. "Though your father's equipment contained well-disguised explosives, they still needed to be triggered by someone here."

Dear, God.

The Faust crew had gone entirely silent, looking around at one another nervously.

Baz looked past Kian to my best friend. "I could use your help, Ana. I need you to find the liar in my mother's crew." He hissed the word *liar*, as if it scorched his lungs to even say it.

Behind him, Bane had pulled several workers out of the crowd, pushing them forward with his taloned hands. "These three," he said, his huge canine teeth sliding along his jaw as he spoke. "Their reaction was subdued when there was talk of raiding Waite, but they became bloodthirsty at the mention of Eila's punishment."

The rail-thin girl with the purple hair who had advocated the raid, gave a hard nod, her face angry.

That's when it hit me.

Baz's speech had been a set-up for HIS friends, and Bane and the purple-haired girl had been in on it.

Ana blinked and we all looked at her, every one of us realizing that this was a trap to nail one of Maia's employees. She eased around Kian, who kept an eagle eye on all the Faust workers. "Well, I can't read the memories of a soul thief, but I can usually read whether they are telling the truth or not. If I ask them a question, and their answer is a lie, I can sense it. I'll know."

"Works for me," Baz replied, fury crossing his face.

She walked slowly to Baz, Kian following closely as the rest of us spread out a bit, ready to jump in if the Faust crew suddenly revolted and went after any of us . . . or Moriarty's bold-ass son.

"What do you need them to do?" asked Baz, turning to the three Mortis standing nervously behind him. Bane's glare was keeping them from bolting.

"I, uh, need to make contact. Touching their hands would do it."

Baz ordered the workers to extend their hands and Kian snarled a warning that if any one of them flinched wrong, they'd be dead before they even drew their next breath.

The first Mortis, a shorter and older male, with brown hair and a petrified look on his face, extended his arm. Ana, with Kian by her side, laid her hand in the Mortis' and closed her eyes. "Did you trigger the explosion in Maia Moriarty's office?" she breathed, the question designed to draw the truth from Maia's employee.

The rooftop fell silent as we all waited, but Ana slowly shook her head. "He's innocent," she said, opening her eyes. The soul thief nearly crumbled in relief, muttering a thank you over and over as he scurried back into the crowd. Raef's iron glare traced over the man's face, no doubt committing his features to memory as the pardoned soul thief disappeared into the pack of Faust workers. Mere moments ago the man had cheered for my demise. My killer boyfriend wasn't going to ever forget it.

Neither was I.

The second soul thief extended his hand confidently, his dark skin contrasting sharply with Ana's. But just as she was about to touch him, Ana paused, and her gaze slid slowly to the third Mortis, a black-haired female, waiting to be read. The Mortis looked . . . oddly confused. As if slowly coming out of a daze.

Kian must have sensed Ana's focus shift, and he suddenly lunged just as the Mortis female attempted to bolt. Baz yanked Ana out of the way as Kian slammed into the woman, forcing her to the ground as she fought back. Kian, however, was unyielding.

Chaos erupted in the crowd, shouts of alarm tangling with a woman's voice in the crowd screaming about her sister. Seeing her chance as Kian pinned the Mortis to the ground, Ana scrambled from Baz's arms and grabbed the struggling soul thief's hand, demanding, "Did you plant the bomb in Maia Moriarty's office!"

The woman screamed to let her go, but Ana simply released her and rocked back on her heels, looking over her shoulder at Raef and I. "I can't . . . I can't get a read off her. It's like I'm blocked."

"I don't know what's going on!" wailed the soul thief, pulling hard in Kian's grip. She struggled to her knees, as if bowing before her executioner. "What . . . why are we on the roof?" she demanded. Baz glared at her, nothing but rage in his heart, but her reaction – her confusion – seemed genuine.

A terrible sinking feeling began to stir in my gut. I pushed my way towards the soul thief on the ground. "Did you cause the explosion? In Maia's office? Was that you?"

Her forehead wrinkled, her breathing fast as she rubbed her chest. "I . . . I can't remember."

Another female Mortis, who looked a lot like the accused in Kian's iron grip, finally shoved her way through the crowd. "NO! Eris, no!"

She fell to her knees in front of Baz, "Please, PLEASE show my sister mercy. She traded herself for her girlfriend. She traded herself for her human love!"

What the HECK was going on? I was about to demand an answer, but then Eris shook her head, as if whatever fog she'd been in lifted. "Oh, God. I think I did it . . ," she coughed, beginning to wheeze. Her skin had begun to pale.

Baz pulled back sharply, glaring at the begging worker, his fury clear as he seethed. "Imogen, your sister attempted to kill my mother and Ana Lane! Your sister's actions murdered Lance and Tristan." He paused, then suddenly grabbed the woman roughly by her arm. "DID YOU KNOW WHAT SHE WAS PLANNING?"

Imogen, still sobbing for her sister, shook her head.

Eris wheezed, "I had . . . no control. I'm sorry. So sorry. Did it for my love . . ." Her fingers dug into her shirt, as if trying to claw through the fabric to get to her heart.

"Kian, what's going on?" I asked, pointing at Eris, who suddenly didn't look so good. Kian's gaze narrowed on the soul thief, studying her carefully, but he didn't let her go.

The condemned Mortis gasped hard, as if she was struggling to catch her breath; as if she'd run for miles. As she spoke, her voice grew brittle and chafed, like a smoker's rasp. "Needed smoke . . ." she choked, drawing a ragged breath as her eyes began to water.

Ana looked confused. "Smoke?"

Eris nodded weakly, looking at Ana. "I'm so sorry," she whispered, then turned to Baz. "So, so sorry."

Suddenly Eris screamed, her eyes wide as she arched backwards, acting as though a knife had punched through her spine. The crowd shouted as Kian caught her before she crumpled to the ground.

Baz shook Imogen, "Does Eris have a Limiting Link!" he demanded.

"I don't know!" she cried. "PLEASE! Help her!"

Kian eased Eris onto her back as she convulsed, her body jerking as if she was being electrocuted. Blood began to leak from her mouth as she screamed again and again. In that instant, I recalled what Baz had said about Embry – that she'd been shredded from the inside out by a Link, in seconds, right on the dance floor.

Kian ripped Eris shirt down the middle, revealing a pulsing Limiting Link just under her skin near her heart and partially hidden by a simple white camisole.

"Damn it! She's got a Link!" he yelled, trying to brace her on the roof tiles. Raef moved quickly, dropping down next to the screaming worker.

"Nikki! Can you stop it?" demanded Raef.

Nikki, frozen in place, her eyes locked on the Mortis in agony, seemed too stunned to answer. "NIKKI!" yelled Kian, and she finally snapped out of her daze.

She blinked, then ran to where Kian, Raef and Eris were, dropping to her knees. "I need a knife!"

The purple-haired Mortis seemed a bit shell shocked about what she was witnessing, but finally pulled a switchblade from her back pocket, handing it to Nikki. She drew a shaky breath, whispering to the soul thief to "hang on" as she quickly felt over the Link under her skin.

The switchblade in her hand, Nikki ordered Kian to hold Eris steady. He braced the young woman against the roof tiles as Nik slipped the knife into Eris' skin, forcing the steel blade to connect with the gear. Metal to metal, her fingers grazing the blade, Nikki's face hardened in concentration, but Eris had begun to bleed from her ears.

Baz, realizing Eris might only have moments left, let Imogen go. She crawled over to her sister, sobbing as she grasped her hand, whispering calming words to her dying kin. Nikki's eyes opened and she looked over her shoulder at me, shaking her head ever so slightly, and I knew Eris was doomed. Nikki couldn't stop the Link.

Raef's eyes caught mine. "Look away," he said, but I refused.

"Just . . . help her," I urged. "Don't let her suffer any longer."

MJ stepped up behind Nikki and guided her to her feet, one hand at her elbow. He carefully pulled the useless knife from Eris' skin and dropped it to the ground.

Refusing to let go of Nik, MJ turned her into his chest, holding her tightly. She gripped his jacket like a lifeline with her good hand, refusing to look at what my boyfriend was about to do, but I saw the tears in Nik's eyes, threatening to spill.

Raef's jaw tightened as his focus shifted back to Eris. He moved carefully to her head, gently cupping her jaw with one hand, and the back of her neck with his other. Eris, still in agony, choked out a broken message to her sister. "I was right, Imogen. I was . . . right. Must . . . tell them."

Imogen stilled, as if stunned by whatever was said, but I was more focused on Kian and Raef.

Kian grasped Eris' hand tightly in his own and leaned down to her ear. "Godspeed, sister. May the shadows welcome you home," he told her, then nodded to Raef.

In one swift move, Raef snapped the tortured soul thief's neck, ending her agony, and her gasping instantly stopped. Her body, once twisted under the brutality of the Link, went limp, as if she was in a deep, peaceful sleep.

Silence fell across the lot of us.

Through the falling snow, the lights of New Bedford danced and twinkled, oblivious to the sadness cloaking Faust's rooftop. Like a hesitant ripple in the crowd, each of Faust's workers slowly raised a fist towards the stars, and then, as one, softly opened their palm to the night sky.

It was haunting to witness, a heartbreaking farewell to one of their own – a woman born of the shadows, now returned to the endless night.

Imogen's soft crying trickled though the stone gargoyles as she eased herself down over her sister, protecting her from the snowflakes and cold breeze that tumbled across the rooftop.

Raef sat there for a moment, Eris's head still resting in his lap, and Kian gave his shoulder a squeeze, slowly rising from his spot near the body to retreat to his girl. "Unto the night," Raef whispered to Eris, his jaw pulsing as he brushed his hand down Eris' forehead, closing her eyes. In that moment, I was struck by the harsh reality that mercy sometimes comes at great cost to one's own heart.

I knelt down next to Imogen, unsure how to help her, and carefully placed a hand on her back – a Lunaterra trying to comfort a Mortis. "I'm so sorry," I whispered. "I swear to you, I will find Lawson Waite and kill him for all that he has done to so many."

Imogen dragged in a deep breath. Raef focused on how close she was to me, wary of my safety in the presence of Eris' shattered sister.

She sniffed, wiping her tear-streaked face. "He's not a man," she replied, her voice trembling.

"What . . . what do you mean he's not a man?" I asked, a thousand terrifying ideas spinning through my head at once. "Of course he's a man. He's a drug dealer. He's a billionaire. Ana knows who he is, Imogen."

She shook her head, the snow starting to catch in her hair. "No, he is Therophel. He walks among us in the skin of a human host, but he is Therophel," she urged in a gasping sob. "That's what Eris said to me. The last thing she said. She whispered to me that she was right. Only days ago, she had told me that she believed Waite to actually be possessed, possibly by The Fallen One himself. I thought she was crazy, but she must've confirmed her suspicions. Therophel is in possession of Lawson Waite's body."

I grasped Imogen's hand. "Are you sure?"

Imogen nodded. "We are doomed, Ms. Walker," she whispered. "Not even someone like you can stop a fallen Archangel."

I swallowed and looked up at my friends, all too floored to respond. Everything we thought we knew about Elizabeth and her murder-suicide with Jacob Rysse in 1851 was obliterated in a single deathbed confession on the rooftop of Maia Moriarty's nightclub.

Jacob Rysse, aka Therophel – angelic creator of the Mortis race – was still *alive* and now hiding out in the body of Lawson Waite.

I took an icy breath and gave voice to what everyone in that moment suddenly knew with horrifying clarity. "Elizabeth . . . *failed.*"

CHAPTER 19
FAUST, NEW BEDFORD, MA
SATURDAY, CLOSE TO MIDNIGHT

I couldn't sleep.

I'd been lying across the two beds Ana and I had pushed together in the recovery room, effectively creating a king mattress out of two twins, but my mind wouldn't shut off. I was more exhausted than I'd ever been before, but I just couldn't stop. Stop thinking. Stop worrying. Stop replaying the past day. All of it was racing through my mind, over and over, an endless loop that kept sleep far from me.

For the first time since Mae's death, I felt truly helpless. It was one thing to face off against a man with a militia of Linked Mortis, but to face off against a creature of biblical strength . . .

We were entirely screwed.

And what the heck did Eris mean about *needing smoke*. What the frak was that all about?

Therophel must've hidden in the body of Jacob Rysse for

years, systematically killing the Lunaterra after the fall of the empire. Once he'd decimated the European Lunaterra, he'd hopped the pond to America, probably in pursuit of Elizabeth.

According to what Raef told me months ago, Rysse had created a fun little anti-boyscout troupe in the form of his very own cheering section, called The Rysse Clan. He even tracked those who were my grandma's friends, and turned Raef and Kian into the soul thieves they were now - a fact we only recently figured out thanks to Kian and Raef's more unusual Fallen Marks. Leo said they were the marks of those turned by the creator, Therophel, himself. He said Kian and Raef were First Army – more powerful than other Mortis.

Leo's revelation was the first time we realized Therophel had been Jacob Rysse . . . only we thought Elizabeth fried the pervert in the harbor square. Instead, somehow, Therophel had managed to survive Elizabeth's attack . . . and to go on to inhabit the body of Lawson Waite.

What the FRAK EVER?

I shook my head, my brain cramping at the math and physics involved. How would we ever, *ever*, get the upper hand against an archangel that survived and conquered so much? Could we even win against such a creature?

I forced myself to shove all thoughts of Therophel to the back of my mind. I would solve nothing while lying in Maia's garishly decorated recovery room and silently flipping out.

Kian was right – the room did resemble a hooker's pad.

I turned my head carefully, studying Nikki's profile, her chest rising and falling slowly, her eyes closed and face calm. I'd heard that people in extreme situations could turn off their emotions for the sake of survival.

Sleeping next to me, I was sure that was what Nikki did – shut herself down and refuse to even recognize all the stuff being thrown our way for the time being, especially what happened on the rooftop. I'd seen people die before, but Eris's tortured death had probably been a first for Nik.

Lying next to her was MJ, and like Nikki, he slept in a weird sort of stiff manner. The relaxed, floppy kid I had seen sleeping on Cerberus, happily snoring with the blankets twisted around his body, was gone. It was as if, even in his sleep and in his human form, he was still on guard.

I swiveled my head to my left, where Ana was squashed against me, shoulder to shoulder. Her colored dark hair had grown since I first met her, and though she still couldn't get it in a ponytail, it now curled around her ears. She basically went from looking like Tinker Bell to the spitting image of a Lost Boy over the past couple months. Kian, however, would always call her *Pix*. He also continued to have a hungriness to his eye whenever he was near his short-statured girlfriend, probably 'cause he wanted to inhale her lips.

I stared at the floral wallpaper and crown molding, ready to lose my mind. I couldn't stay in bed any longer. I was going to start fiddling and wake everyone up. I'd been in the room for the past hour and a half, waiting for Kian and Raef to return from hunting, fearful for their safety but also in a desperate need for them to simply be with us.

After we'd left the roof to digest the terrifying realization that Therophel was in fact using Waite's body like a cheap onesie, Baz had sent out teams of Faust guards to patrol the surrounding city blocks, in case we should be visited by unfriendly patrons. Our crew and Maia's also decided to hunt from Faust's Blacklist. They went in teams, so that Faust was always well protected, with Kian, Raef, and a protesting Leo, being sent out first.

Though the original plan had been to hunt the harbor seals, everyone agreed that human lives would be best when facing an archangel with a score to settle. Those of us non-soul thieves were not allowed to see the Mortis choose from the List, a rule which I suspect was quickly instituted by Kian and Raef. Though they shared much with us about how their kind operated, some things were just tougher to talk about. Killing people, even bad people, for their souls was one thing the guys just couldn't share with Ana and me. I respected that. I had to.

I stole another quick glance at my sleeping friends and slowly, carefully, slid my way out from my blanket and down off the bed, trying not to jostle anyone as I emulated a Slinky. Once free, I tiptoed across the room and eased the door open, slipping out onto the catwalk and shutting the door behind me with a soft *click*.

Below me, the dance hall was full of activity, all the workers attempting to clean up and get the nightclub back in order. On the flatscreen TVs above the bar, the news played, and I knew that the media was all over the explosion at Nikki's house. Keeping her off the police radar was something I couldn't even deal with yet. One day at a time, one fight at a time, and we might just make it out of this life . . . alive.

Across from our room, on the other side of Faust, I could see Maia's office. It had been boarded up for the time being, and the main chandelier had been re-secured to the ceiling with new chains, though the shattered glass orbs made by Teddy Bencourt's family would have to be replaced. I seriously hoped that Jesse wouldn't get it into his head to start searching for Nikki or me. That's all I needed –

for him and his buddy, Teddy, to start sniffing around in my messed up world.

As I watched the activity below me, I noticed that a few workers were also painting small symbols on the walls of the nightclub, using brushes dipped in what looked like burnt red paint. As they worked, the art seemed to bleed slowly into the steel and stone of the wall as it dried, turning into a powdery texture. I didn't ever recall seeing the marks before, and I suspected the Faust crew was doing more than simply fixing broken tables and catwalks. I suspected they were also fortifying their security systems against the winged badass.

Well, if he had wings, that is . . .

I sighed, leaning against the railing, my eyes landing on Bane who was standing at one end of the dance hall. He looked up at me and gave a small wave with his taloned hand, then continued on his way, patrolling the area, his heavy tail dragging behind him like a cape.

For the first time in her history, Faust was closed on a Saturday night. Baz made the call to shut down as his mother was still unconscious, and an encoded message was placed on one of the Mortis community's online sites. Humans would never understand all that was passed through the soul thief world via the Internet, but those who hunted souls or frequented Faust knew exactly where to look for information.

Baz was also able to locate the bounty that had been listed by Waite, the one for me and my crew, but he was unable to remove the listing. I was hoping Howe, who was due to join us at Faust in the morning, would be able to hack his way in and pull it down since James had obviously failed to do so.

James. We'd heard nothing from him.

I had told Howe what was going on and what had happened at the club. The dude seemed more shocked about the fact that New Bedford had a secret nightclub for killers than about an explosion in Moriarty's office. How that man ever made it through the FBI academy was often a mystery to me. He said he could get himself to New Bedford - that he didn't need an escort, which was good, because I really couldn't spare any of the guys anyway.

I sighed, a headache once again playing behind my eyes. I went to massage my neck, hoping to halt the pain, but stumbled backwards, stunned at the state of my arms. Starting at my palms and extending down to my elbows were dozens of deep gashes. Blood welled up from the wounds, as if I'd just thrown the Light without wearing my gloves.

I was frozen. Confused. My arms were shredded and I had no clue how I didn't notice it before. I had no clue how it even *happened.* Realizing I needed to wake Ana for help, I pressed my arms tightly to my chest, trying to stem the blood dripping everywhere.

As I turned to run back into our room, I heard the door to the lab open. Baz stepped out onto the catwalk, only a few doors down from me. He yawned, stretching his hands above his head, and then spotted me. "Girl, you're supposed to be getting some sleep. This ain't sleeping."

"BAZ!" Baz, can you help me?" I begged, holding out my arms to display the damage. "I don't know how it happened, but . . ." I glanced down at my arms. The wounds were gone.

Baz looked at me as though I really had lost my marbles. "Uh . . . Maybe? What do you need help with?"

I ran my fingers over my skin, trying to feel the cuts I had just seen, but my skin was perfect. Smooth. Unharmed.

"Uh, never mind," I mumbled, fairly freaked out. Fatigue. It had to be fatigue. I looked back up at Baz, finally dropping my hands. "God, I need sleep, but my mind won't stop running. I think I'm starting to see shit."

Baz nodded. "Yeah. That can happen. It's like your brain goes, '*Okay? You don't wanna sleep? Fine. We'll send your nightmares out to get you when you're awake.*' Yeah, trust me. Been there, done that."

I studied him and he looked as beat as me. "Why ARE you still up?"

He raised an eyebrow, walking over to me. "You mean besides the whole nightmarish revelation about Therophel coming to kick our asses?" He hooked his thumb over his shoulder in the direction of the lab. "I'm up because of Elizabeth."

"But Rillin is with her. He'll let you know if she wakes up."

He yawned again, shaking his head hard. "The way I see it is that IF she wakes, she may not want me testing her blood anymore, so I need every second I can get with her non-objecting body. I've still got goals. I'm still seeking a cure, although now I'm thinking that it's more important to keep everyone who is a Mortis, AS a Mortis, if Eris is to be believed. Although having your broody Blacklist dealer watching my every move around his zombie girlfriend is getting on my nerves."

"So, you're not convinced Therophel is alive?" I asked, a bit surprised and ignoring the *zombie girlfriend* comment.

"I'm more of a 'see it and believe it' type dude, but, given all the crazy crap you've dropped into my life recently, I'm gonna play it safe and trust Eris' word. For now, anyway."

"Yeah, you do that." I replied, rolling my eyes. "So, find

anything useful? In Elizabeth, I mean."

"Not really. Not yet anyway, but I'll keep trying."

Something occurred to me that hadn't before. "So, not that I'm complaining about your continued search for a cure, but, uh . . . the cure was Christian's dream. Now that he's gone, why are you still pursuing it?"

Baz rested one hand on the iron railing, glancing down at the workers below us. "Christian may've been the one to first believe in the possibility of a cure, and yeah – it was his unicorn of sorts to pursue. But, I don't know, once I realized how *frozen* the Mortis are," he flicked his chin towards the workers, "I knew that so much more than just Christian's dreams were on the line. This is it for them. I mean, our human workers – they can change. Evolve. Grow old, get married, have kids; all that stuff. They have seasons to their lives. But Mortis? It's like Groundhog Day for them. Yes, they can do different things, pursue different dreams and fall in love, but after a while, you want more. You want those things humans take for granted."

"Like the flu and food poisoning?" I asked, a bit sarcastic and unable to deal with what truly was at stake in Baz's work.

He chuckled. "Yeah. I guess so," he replied, but then he looked at me and his amusement slid away. "You get what I'm saying though, right? Though you and Raef are, ya know, the 'it' couple so to speak, where's your future? Your real future? Because let's be honest – you two don't have one, even if Therophel doesn't exist."

"That is NONE of your business," I snapped, scared that what Baz was saying was toeing the line way too close to the truth. Raef once said that he wanted more for me than he could ever offer, but I convinced him that we could defy the odds and that our love was worth protecting. Having Baz throw his opinions in my face, valid or not, was not what I needed.

"Hey," he bumped shoulders with me. "If I can find a cure, you two can have a very human happily ever after . . . I mean, assuming he wants to be human and, well, we're not obliterated by one of heaven's rejects."

I felt mentally cooked. "Thanks, Baz. For what it's worth, I have faith in you despite your poor choice of recreational drug use." I yawned, unable to control myself.

"Ya know, I have some stuff that would help you relax."

"Dude, I'm not smoking your stupid weed. I don't care how badly my life sucks."

He held up a hand. "Nope, not marijuana. In fact, I gave some to the big guy earlier in the evening."

"You mean Talus?" I never thought of humans smoking that, but if the list of ingredients from Rillin was correct . . .

Baz blinked, looking a bit shocked. "Wow. I didn't think you'd know about that stuff. You seem so . . . so . . ."

"Smart?" I offered.

"I was gonna say prudish. Controlling. Possibly high maintenance."

"What?" I demanded. "I am not prudish or controlling! Or high maintenance!"

Baz smirked, leaning against the railing. "I've seen you boss more people around than my mom. And you don't drink or get stoned or run around nude, sadly. I call that prudish."

"Run around nude? How did that even enter the conversation!"

Baz shrugged, "Just threw it in there in case I could plant the idea. Was hoping you'd get all high and mighty and, just to prove me wrong, you'd flash the dance floor."

"Good grief. No wonder your mother homeschooled you. She was probably worried you'd go to jail as a pervert by the time you were twelve."

"Ten, actually. I think she was worried by the time I hit ten."

I finally cracked, chuckling at the absurdity that was Basil Moriarty. But as he stood there facing me, his devilish grin slowly faded. I could see it on his face - the worry for his mom, who was still unconscious.

"She's gonna be okay, Baz." I said quietly. He simply nodded. "And I'll do it."

His eyes widened, "You'll streak the dance floor?"

Oh my, God. "NO, you idiot! I'll try the Talus!"

The sadness that descended over Baz briefly lifted. "Dang. I got really hopeful there for a second, but, ya know – baby steps for peeps like you. I get it. But I'm glad you'll try the Talus – it will help ya sleep."

"What are we trying?" asked Ana, coming up behind me, Nik and MJ following.

"Not streaking, but smoking. I'll go get the Talus," said Baz, heading back to his lab.

Ana stared after Baz, asking, "Did he say *streaking*? What in the heck did I miss in the five minutes you've been out here?"

"How do you know how long I've been out here?"

She turned her attention back to me, MJ and Nikki by her side, "'Cause you suck at sneaking out of bed. I swear it felt like an earthquake as you slid like an eel down to the floor."

I snorted, smiling as I looked over my bedmates. "Why are you two up?"

MJ shrugged, "Besides the bouncing bed, I really wasn't sleeping either. None of us were. I suspect we're all up for the same reasons you are." He scratched the back of his neck. "I just can't, like, *let go* enough to nod off. Sucks." He looked in the direction of Baz's lab, "So we're smoking Tantalus? This should be interesting . . ."

My brow fell, eyes narrowing on MJ. "How do you know about Talus?" I asked.

MJ stretched, "The guys were talking about it in the bathroom after we took showers. I guess Rillin already smoked it and Kian knew what it was. He said he hadn't used it in over a century."

Ana smiled, "That's 'cause I'm his best drug. He just needs me to – "

MJ quickly held up a hand, "Oh, please don't. I have enough nightmares without thinking about you and Frat Boy and . . . *that*."

Ana glared at her pal, "I was gonna say SMILE, you jerk."

"Sure you were," MJ muttered, making a gagging sound. The two of them began teasing one another, Ana offering relationship tidbits while MJ claimed his ears were bleeding. Nikki just stood there, emotionless, the oversized t-shirt she wore containing the huge bulge that was her arm strapped to her body.

I tipped my chin to her. "You want some too?" I asked quietly as Ana and MJ argued.

"Whatever. I'm down for whatever," she replied, stepping over to the railing and watching the workers. I moved over to stand next to her and saw two workers toss a silk tablecloth over an ebony table, letting it drift down between them slowly. We watched in silence as they smoothed the wrinkles from the fabric, talking to one another as they worked, their mood subdued.

"Sometimes I feel like I'm two people," said Nikki quietly.

"Sometimes I think that the cheerleader and field hockey captain were always the falsehoods. They were the lies, and with them went all the others - my childhood, my home, my parents. All of it." She trailed off, and I dared a glance in her direction. She bit her bottom lip. "And it makes me wonder who I really am. Did I even exist at all? Like, what was the point of all those years, of all the bullshit, if I only ended up with none of it in the end."

She went silent and I stepped closer to her, glancing over my shoulder to make sure Ana and MJ were still deep in horrified conversation.

I cleared my throat, offering what advice I could, "I really thought that the girl I was when I came to the Cape, didn't exist anymore. All the things I was raised to believe, all the lies I thought were truths, just sorta . . . imploded. I thought that suddenly my entire life had been deleted and this new one booted up to take its place. Sucked."

Nikki's eyes drifted to mine as she listened.

"And then, one day, I realized that everything I came from and every step I'd taken through my whole life, somehow got me to *this* one place in time. Nik, all that stuff you were raised to believe and all the things you did throughout your life? They still count. That stuff made you who you are now. Our history, no matter how embedded in lies or untruths, is still OUR history. And each little piece of that history is who you are, right now, and I sure as shit am grateful that all that past crap got you here. Standing next to me. As a friend." I glanced around, "Though I probably would've chosen a different venue for the here and now part, rather than a nightclub that looks like a pimped out house for harlots."

Nikki's eyes pooled and she wiped at them roughly with her

good arm. "I swear, Walker, if you make me cry like a girl, I'll beat the snot outta ya, friend or not."

I offered her a crooked smile, "Nikki, you *are* a girl. We both are."

"Screw that. We're warriors."

I placed my hand on hers and squeezed, "Damn straight we are, but we also bleed. We also feel. And when you are ready to talk about what happened tonight, I am here for you. Girl to girl, warrior to warrior."

Nikki swallowed and gripped my hand hard, a silent pledge to take my offer seriously.

I heard the lab door open and we glanced over at Baz who was carrying a small bag in his hands, and a lighter. Ana and MJ stopped arguing, turning to Maia's only son.

"Okay," he announced, shaking the bag. "Who's least likely to gag?"

CHAPTER 20
FAUST, NEW BEDFORD, MA
SUNDAY, HALF-PAST MIDNIGHT

I pushed my way through the exterior doors of Faust, walking down a long narrow hallway that would lead us to the night club's main floor, Kian at my side. Several heavily armed Mortis guards gave us a nod as we made our way through the metal-walled corridor, none of it looking like the elaborate interior of the nightclub that resided inside. Though we didn't want to leave the girls, the other Mortis in the club had assured us that hunting would be brief since Fall River targets tended to be predictable and easy to find. And quite frankly, Kian and I had been running dangerously low on stolen life essence and that was *before* we healed Nikki. But after her surgery, hunting became critical for us. We had to go, and we both knew it.

Thankfully, our time away from Faust had been brief and everything seemed fine at the nightclub upon our return.

We'd spent an hour and a half hunting with Leo, our Blacklist targets easy to locate and feed from as promised. Though Leo didn't want to leave Maia's side, Baz had kicked him out, demanding he feed or be the "weakest link." That had pissed Leo off enough to go hunting with us and then bolt for Maia's room the instant we got back. I was certain that Moriarty was romantically involved with Faust's fierce bouncer, probably for years.

The night, however, wasn't entirely a normal hunt, for we had noticed a homeless man. He was curled near the heat vent from an apartment building, clearly in the late stages of what appeared to be sclerosis of the liver - death by alcohol, basically. His remainder of his life had been whittled down to mere hours.

He was suffering. We all knew it.

Kian, taking mercy on the dying man, had knelt beside him and asked him if he wished to go - to be released from this world.

At the end stages of his life, the man seemed to understand we were some sort of courier for Death. He had smiled, said he was ready, and Kian let the Fallen Marks flare to life on his skin, not bothering to hide them. The man actually looked relieved despite Kian's sudden change in appearance. It was as if he knew that peace was only moments away. Kian placed his hands on the man's, easing his pain while softly calling the life from his abused body.

There was no funeral or mourners, save for us. We became the final witnesses to a life lived on the fringe, sleeping under bridges and begging in shadows; a soul discarded and unimportant in the eyes of proper society.

When death had claimed the man, we closed his eyes and wrapped him in his faded plaid blanket, carrying his body to the front of the alley so someone would find him. He was yet another anonymous soul, lost to the city and forgotten.

While I'd taken the lives of those suffering on the battlefields of war, something about the man's death seemed to haunt Kian. Since that moment in the alley, he'd been pensively silent.

Now, walking alongside him under the sputtering overhead lights, I started to wonder what was haunting my friend. He finally cracked when we neared the door to Faust.

"Do me a favor," he said, stepping in front of me and forcing me to halt before we reached the ornately carved door. "Don't tell Ana about what I did in the alley."

I paused, studying Kian's face. He looked dead serious. "Okay," I replied slowly.

He released me with a sigh, "Look, if she finds out I killed in the name of mercy, she'll encourage me to start doing that rather than hunting off the Blacklist. And then she'll want to come with me because she'll think she can help."

Now I was confused. "Help? I don't get wh – "

"She's ANA. She'll want to read the dying. She'll think she can ease the living by communicating the thoughts of those who are dying to those they are about to leave behind."

He rubbed his forehead, the strain of the night really starting to show on his face. "I just . . . I don't want her to be tangled up in that part of my life; the part where I kill to survive. Yes, she knows about it, but seeing it happen in front of you, without the filter of your imagination, is just something I refuse to show her. She doesn't let me stand in her way about many things, and I don't try to wrangle her in very often, but this? The Lists? The murders? How we pull the life-force from a person? I won't share that with her. She's seen me kill a deer, and that was tough enough for me to reveal to her. But the human kills? No way - that shit is my own to carry. I get to protect her from that."

I simply gave him a sharp nod and we continued across Faust's dance floor, heading for the staircase that led to the catwalk rooms. I was desperate to crawl in bed with Eila. Or at the very least, crash in the same room with her.

Unfortunately, in the confined space of Maia's recovery room, wedged in with the rest of our team, I couldn't exactly lose myself in Eila's gentle curves and breathy voice. I made a silent promise to myself that I would steal her away once this whole nightmare was over. I'd whisk her off to some beautiful, secluded paradise where just the two of us could enjoy one another, endlessly. *Thoroughly.*

The few times we'd been together intimately, we weren't entirely alone; fear and loss always haunted us from the shadows like a taunting voyeur, whispering that we couldn't outrun the damnation that Fate had carved out for us. But someday I'd make love to E and we would worry for nothing. We'd be unburdened by those who now hunted us. We'd only know peace and joy and how our hearts raced in tandem with one another, each of us a perfect fit for the other.

That knowledge – that Eila was truly my soulmate – was something I had battled against initially. I thought that I could close off my heart, thereby protecting her as only a bodyguard. But it was Eila who showed me that I could be the killer who loved her, the soul thief who'd fight to protect her, and the man who would battle alongside her.

I wanted her in my arms. Now.

Determined to get back to our shared room, I started walking faster, nearly outpacing Kian, but I slowed when I noticed several workers painting some sort of graffiti on the walls of the club, though it did not look like vodou veve symbols. I flicked my chin to a set near us. "What do you make of those?"

"My guess is they are some sort of protective charm," Kian replied, slowing as well. "Possibly some sort of rune, though they're way more elaborate."

"Wiccan?" I asked, strongly suspecting Maia was flirting with the occult - a bokor that really walked the wild side.

"Maybe," Kian replied.

We walked next to one another, watching the activity in the dance hall, and I could feel the flow of stolen life force throbbing through my body. It made me feel as though I was invincible. As if I might even have a shot at facing off with Therophel and coming away in one piece.

Leo said Kian and I were First Army – born from Therophel himself. He said we were the most dangerous of our kind, yet he doubted we'd tapped our full potential yet. If there was ever a time for Kian and me to pull our "A" game, now was it. Elizabeth had given her all in the harbor, and I needed to do the same.

My mind had turned frequently to Elizabeth lately, memories of what she was like before she died flickering through my mind unbidden. I even began remembering bits and pieces of the night she died. I suspected it was Ana's attempts at reading me that may've triggered them.

"I've been thinking about the night Elizabeth killed herself. Or rather, almost killed herself," I admitted to Kian. "I think I remember a man. I think someone else was in the harbor that night."

Kian stopped short, looking at me. "You're beginning to remember?"

I jammed my hands in my jacket. "Some. Bits and pieces. I think the memories may've been caused by Ana practicing her ability on me these past months."

"Ana said she couldn't get a read on either of us – nothing clear," argued Kian. He almost looked panicked, as if he feared what Ana might be able to see as reflected in his memories.

"I know, but I think she's getting much better and I may have her try to read me again. But I'm telling you, I think there was a man in the harbor square with us. Possibly that drunk. Aarons? Afrens?"

"Adams?" asked Kian, his face shocked. "Benjamin Adams? He couldn't walk a straight line half the time!"

I nodded. "I know, but I swear I have this . . . broken memory of him in one of the alleyways that led to the harbor." I looked right at Kian, "Actually, now that I think about it, I remember walking with YOU. We passed Adams. He was seated on the ground outside the Black Whale tavern, mumbling something incoherent. He was definitely intoxicated."

"I don't remember any of that," said Kian, looking stunned. "I never knew how I even got to the harbor. You're saying I came with you?"

"Yeah. Not sure what compelled us to be there, but being that we were part of Rysse's clan back then, I'm assuming he told us to be there."

Kian rubbed his jaw, thinking. "Okay, well we know that the dude Elizabeth cooked in the harbor was actually Therophel in the body of a man we knew as Jacob Rysse. And Rysse WAS a Mortis, that part I'm certain of. I remember watching him take the life of humans. I SAW him do it."

I did recall seeing Rysse kill people, drawing out their life-forces. "But there was nothing left of him after Elizabeth's core collapse. And I remember being hit with what I think was Elizabeth's

Light. Hurt like a bastard."

Kian rubbed his chest, as if remembering the pain that had slammed into us that night when Elizabeth and Rysse were consumed by her Core Collapse. "Thanks for the reminder, Raef. Is there a point to this trip down memory lane?"

"I didn't see an angry Archangel pop out of Jacob Rysse, did you?"

"What are you? Dense? I just told you: I DON'T REMEMBER that night. I recall the pain, but nothing else!"

I held up a hand, trying to calm Kian who was looking fairly pissed off. "Look, the Cape Cod legend about Elizabeth Walker being killed by lightning had to come from somewhere. What if Adams witnessed the whole thing and he told the town? What if that is where the urban legend came from?"

Kian's brow dropped. "Well, if that's the truth, why didn't he mention the two of us? Why didn't he mention Jacob Rysse? And for that matter, if Therophel did leave Rysse's body during the Core Collapse, why the heck didn't little drunken Benjamin spew those details, hmm?"

"Because I think Therophel changed bodies that night."

Kian paused. "Wait . . . You think Therophel jumped from Rysse to Adams? Raef, I don't know about that one . . ."

"Think about it. If Adams was in fact a witness that night, then why didn't he say what really happened? Why say that Elizabeth Walker – a sea captain's wife - was killed by lightning? The only answer I can think of is that he didn't want people to know the real details."

"Dude, he probably did tell everyone the truth and they assumed that he was drunk off his ass and babbling nonsense."

I pointed at Kian, taking a step towards him. "And THERE is another problem. Adams, from what I can recall, was never drunk again after Elizabeth was killed. And he didn't stick around the Cape very long after that night - maybe a few weeks at most - but I never heard about him being drunk again. And he was the town joke, stumbling around wasted on a regular basis. He went from being the town jester to being gone. Where'd he go?"

Kian crossed his arms, thinking. "So, you're saying a Fallen Archangel went from the body of a powerful Mortis into that of the town drunk? Why?"

I shrugged, "I don't know. Maybe he had to. Maybe Maia's right and Elizabeth *did* hurt him in the harbor and maybe he could only escape using Adam's body. I mean, if we were there, why not jump into one of us?"

Kian swallowed, "Shit, that's one hell of a nightmare. Thank God that didn't happen." He looked at me. "You think Elizabeth may've taken a bite out of Therophel? You're saying he may be . . . injured."

I nodded. "Think about it. If he really is an Archangel, then why does he hitch a ride in different bodies? Why is he hiding out in Lawson Waite? Why not just come right at us from the get go? I mean, you're talking about a dude that is so far above us in terms of strength, he could easily take whatever he wanted."

I turned to Kian, who seemed lost in thought over Therophel. His fingers absently played with the sea glass pendant hanging around his neck. It had been a gift from Ana, who made it for him when we had sailed the Caribbean on Cerberus.

Putting the questions about Therophel to the back of my mind for a moment, I cleared my throat, knowing I was about to cross into one of those secretive sides of Kian O'Reilly that he rarely shared with anyone, save for Ana. "I need to ask you something and I need a straight answer," I started. Kian eyed me warily.

"Okay," he replied slowly, walking once again, heading past more workers. "Your needs, however, may not line up with my obligations, Raef. Just FYI."

I didn't move to follow him. "I heard Eila ask you about the ring Ana's been wearing. I overheard it, at 408, before we left."

Kian stopped in his tracks, pausing for a moment before he finally turned to look at me.

"She's right, isn't she? It's an engagement ring."

Kian stuffed his hands in his pockets, clearly debating whether to answer or not. He finally came back to where I was, lowering his voice. "Yeah. It is. I've had it since the summer I met her. I saw it in a gift store when I was shopping for a birthday gift for her. At the time, I didn't buy it, but after her father's death, I went back to the store and purchased it. It reminded me of her and how she loved the ocean and loved to surf. It was like a piece of her I could keep with me. I've had it ever since."

"You asked her . . ?"

"I asked her last night. Or rather, technically, early this morning. After all the crap that went down with Rillin, I never wanted to regret not asking her to marry me ever again. There's a catch, however, to our engagement, and that's why we haven't come out and said anything."

I paused, asking in a low voice. "Is she pregnant?"

Kian's face wrinkled. "No, you idiot. Haven't you ever been near a pregnant woman before? You can hear the fetal heartbeat if you pay attention. It's like a faster little shadow to the woman's. Ana doesn't have that. She's not pregnant – she even took tests to confirm it after the whole nightmare debacle at the hospital."

"So, what's the catch then?"

"A cure. I want to marry Ana, don't get me wrong, but I want to do so *only* if Baz can find a cure."

Shit. I wanted this for my friend and Ana, but a cure? "Kian, man. That's a mighty big catch. What if Baz never uncovers one?"

"Then the engagement is off. I won't wreck her life no matter how much I love her. Someday she may want to be pregnant. She may want kids. I can't give her that and I don't age. I don't eat, I rarely sleep, and I murder others to survive. Yes, I want to be her husband. I want to be legally bound to her in every way, body and soul, but only if I can be human." Kian rubbed the back of his neck, suddenly looking a bit uneasy. "Plus, I, uh, may've installed a small tracking chip under the diamond."

"You had a *WHAT* installed?"

"Tracking chip. I did it when she was recovering from her broken leg after the Breakers with the hope that someday I could propose. Given the crap we went through, I never wanted to not know where she was."

I starred at Kian for a moment. "Oh my God, you outfitted your fiancé with LoJack? Does Ana know this?"

He shrugged. "About the tracking chip? Not so much. About the deal with me being human for us to get married? Yeah, she knows all that and she believes that Baz will find a cure. She has faith."

"Do you?" I asked.

"In a cure? Maybe. In Baz Moriarty? I'm not so sure . . . especially since he seems to be showing the girls and MJ how to smoke a roach."

"WHAT?" I demanded, and Kian pointed over my head at one of the catwalks. Sure enough, it appeared that Basil Moriarty was showing my girlfriend how to light a joint, Ana, Nikki, and MJ looking on as they clustered together just outside our room.

"That moronic, half-baked stoner!" I snarled. "That kid is fish chum."

"Ya know," said Kian, a smirk growing on his face. "I always knew Sparky had a flip side. Let's just pray she doesn't light this place up like the Fourth of July once she's high as a kite and hallucinating Sponge Bob."

I cursed under my breath about Rillin being the worst babysitter on the face of the planet as I headed up the staircase to join our gang. "You do realize Ana's up there too, right? Aren't you pissed?"

Kian shrugged. "While I don't think drugs prior to bedtime is the best course of action, I don't dictate my fiancé's freewill."

"Right. You just track her every move," I retorted.

He rolled his eyes. "Fine. If it ever happens again, I'll help you feed Baz Moriarty to the sharks, alright?"

"Much better," I replied under my breath as Eila finally saw me and waved. I waved back, then whispered to Kian, "I can't believe I didn't think of installing one of those tracking chips in Eila's bracelet. Damn."

Kian smiled wide at me, gloating. "Stalkerhood is reserved only for the finest of us killers, my friend. Someday, I may let you join the club. If you ask nicely."

I shook my head. "See, this, *THIS* is why I still want to choke you at least once a day."

CHAPTER 21
FAUST, NEW BEDFORD, MA
SUNDAY, 10 AM

I slid my sweatpant-clad butt onto Faust's massive bar, enjoying the very, *very* fine sight of my shirtless immortal boyfriend as he crouched behind the bar, repairing some of the damage to the ornate woodwork.

Sometimes I had trouble believing that Raef was mine – that he chose to be with me over all others. That he loved ME, the girl who could channel the Web of Souls like a lightning rod, but also had the luck of a blind, one-legged chicken who tries to cross a freeway during rush hour. Repeatedly.

Last night, Raef had leaned over me, brushing a kiss against my jaw as he wished me sweet dreams before crawling onto the floor, leaving the bed for just Nikki and me. I'd wanted, so *badly*, to yank Raef down to me and press his body to mine, forgetting everything but how he touched me and brought my girl parts into a riot of epic awesomeness.

Unfortunately, I couldn't entertain my desires because Nikki had been lying not far from me, giving me the evil eye. It was as if she knew what R-rated ideas were running through my head. Plus, our entire crew was bunked in the room with us, with the exception of Rillin, who chose to stay in the lab with Elizabeth.

I had no clue what to do if she failed to wake up and Rillin was forced to watch her fade away all over again. I wasn't sure my trainer would survive the loss for a second time. I wasn't sure he'd want to.

Ana, smart woman that she was, had claimed the couch with Kian last night, so they could sleep wrapped up in one another's arms. Raef and MJ had slept on the floor. I was left to be bunkmates with the girl I creamed with a milkshake a few months back, and was having trouble nodding off, despite the Talus. To be honest, I wasn't entirely sure that Nikki wouldn't try to suffocate me with her pillow the second I closed my eyes.

But then the memory of Maia's shattered office hit me, and I realized that Nikki had sadly joined the ranks of Ana and me, the only requirement being coming from a family that no longer existed. I'd lost Mae and Christian to the Lessers; Ana had lost her mom, Sula, to a gunman; and Nikki had basically lost her mom and dad to a supernatural slave trade. All of them, despite their differences, had one thing in common, however: Lawson Waite, aka Therophel the Psychopath Angel.

And while we couldn't, with absolute certainty, link Sula's death to Therophel, we did know that she'd been drawing the symbol for the Links and the Gate in her case files. To me, that was pretty damning evidence that the fallen angel had a hand in her murder, and that of her partner, whoever the heck he was.

Now, sitting on the bar and quietly contemplating our probable doom, I watched Raef's muscled back flex as he dragged a sharp blade over the wings of a serpent that he was carving into one of the bar's many wood panels. The original creature, a griffin, had sustained heavy damage when the chandelier shattered. My boyfriend, being madly talented, was doing a breathtaking job of bringing it back to life as a new animal as he sculpted the wood.

I smiled a little, despite our craptastic situation, because I knew I'd lost my heart to Raef Paris. I'd known it for some time now. I loved him in a way I'd never loved another, even Mae. It was this heady mix of trust and passion, free-falling thrills and warm, snugly comfort. He fit me – my soul, my dreams – my *everything*.

I smiled wider, watching as he tried to fix Maia's beautiful bar. It was a simple act by a talented craftsman, despite the difficult fight ahead of us. It was a moment of peace in the eye of a deadly storm, and I knew going back to his trade eased him. It had after Polaris, and now, after last night, he was doing it again - finding peace in the sawdust and steady rhythm of his lathe. In watching him, I somehow felt at ease as well.

Unable to keep silent any longer, I simply mumbled, "Mornin'," as I lifted my hands upward in a delicious stretch.

Raef turned from his work, offering me a heart-hiccuping smile when his eyes met mine. He set the silver chisel on the bar's polished surface and braced his hands on the bar top, leaning across to me. "Good morning," he whispered, pressing a soft kiss to my lips and causing the Kill Mark on my back to tingle.

One of his wide hands snaked around my waist and he dragged me back across the bar towards him, nuzzling the freckles along my neck. "You looked so warm and relaxed this morning," he breathed in my ear, "I didn't want to wake you. I made sure no one else did either. Did you sleep well?"

"Mmmhmm," I replied, the only scrap of intelligence I could muster as his fingers tiptoed under the hem of my shirt and over my tummy in a madly distracting way.

I ran one hand through his hair, causing his dirty blond locks to scramble as I kissed him again. "I would've rather woken up next to you than alone in Maia's spare room."

Raef ran his fingers along the curve of my jaw. "When this is over, I will live in bed with you for weeks if you want."

"Promise?" I asked boldly, though I could feel my face blush hot.

"Absolutely," he replied, kissing me again, harder this time. He pulled away when an echoing *bang* from one of the far doors rang out through Faust. We turned, spying Bane, in his human form once again, marching across the dance hall towards us, his eyes boring into our heads.

"Uh oh . . ." I muttered. "What'd we do now?"

Raef slid his arms around my hips as I sat on the bar. "Hello, Bane. What can I get for you?"

He glared at us, ignoring Raef's poor bartender humor. "There is some short, round, red-headed man wandering around the outside of the building, as if looking for the entrance. He would've been picked him off by Leo's team, except I heard him calling for Eila. Constantly." Bane glared at me. "Apparently stealth is not his strong suit."

Calling my name, red hair, a bit of a beer belly, and looking a bit lost? I knew only one person that fit that description. I sighed, "If he looks like a Hobbit, then it's gotta be Agent Howe. You can let him in. He's with us."

"Agent?" asked Leo, an eyebrow raised. "What type of agent?"

Raef planted his palms on the bar and vaulted easily over the bar top, landing on the floor like a cat, not far from me. "He was FBI, but now he helps us out," Raef replied. "I saved his life when the . . ." Raef paused, his good mood falling slightly. He cleared his throat, "When we were attacked on Polaris. He was nearly killed, but I healed him. He's aware of all that is going on. Mostly."

"And WHY does he needed to come *here*?" demanded Bane. "We don't allow just anyone to enter Faust, especially people who work for government agencies that would probably frown on our kind! I'm sorry he was nearly killed, but he can't come in here."

Raef leaned back against the bar, curling one arm behind my butt and tugging me closer. "Howe can probably hack the FBI firewall. We need to know where they are keeping the Aztael gear that was discovered at Dalca Anescu's place."

Bane paused. "You mean . . . the Soul Gear? The FBI has the Soul Gear? The one that is required to make the Gabriel Gate work?"

I nodded, resting my arm around Raef's broad shoulders. "Wanna let him in now, or would you like Therophel to figure out that the Feds have the Gear first?"

While I knew we didn't have much going for us when facing Therophel, we did hold one Ace in the Hole card if we could steal it back from the FBI – the Soul Gear. A gear built from the bone of Aztael himself when he was killed by his own creations, the Lunaterra. Supposedly the Soul Gear was like a keystone for the Gabriel Gate. No Soul Gear, no working Gate, or so it was written in the Iron Scrolls . . . which could be a total fairy tale.

Kian's plan to lie, cheat and murder his way to victory sounded better by the minute.

I slid down off the bar, "Look, Bane – I'm sure that Waite, er, Therophel, is looking for the Soul Gear. He may very well have no clue that the FBI snagged it. The only reason we know they have it is because Howe came by my house just after Thanksgiving and he showed me a picture of it. He said the FBI had confiscated it after Dalca's place was burned down – it was under the floorboards, in a safe."

Bane shook his head, "Basil is going to be in serious trouble when Maia finds out."

"Why would Baz be in trouble?"

"Because Maia sent him to burn down her sister's shop. She wanted to make sure any links back to Faust were incinerated. But Baz apparently didn't sort through the burnt-out Crimson Moon the way he was supposed to, and now the FBI have the Gear. He should've found that, if he'd taken the time to do what he was supposed to."

Oh. Yeah, Baz was a dead dude the instant Maia woke up.

Raef rubbed his hand across his mouth trying to hide a grin, no doubt gloating that Baz was gonna be in deep dog doo.

"So, can you please let Marcus Howe into the building?" I urged. "This isn't the best area of town, and we really do need him."

"Fine," growled Bane, fully aware that he was about to do something that Maia would undoubtedly loathe. He strode away across the dance floor to fetch Howe before the agent was mugged, all the while muttering some foul things about Basil Moriarty.

"Ya know, when he loosens up, he acts less like a creepy dragon-dude, and more like a pissed off uncle," I said, rubbing one hand over Raef's back.

My boyfriend snorted. "Please. He's far more palatable when he's uptight with talons and a tail."

CHAPTER 22
FAUST, NEW BEDFORD, MA

If I ever saw another freakin' wood screw, it'd be too soon.

Mr. Shea's desk must've had, like, four-thousand of those little twisted bastards holding it together and I was actively cultivating calluses as I worked to unscrew all of them. Granted, Rillin was helping as well, but given the fact that his hands were basically twice the size of mine, he seemed to have no problem using the Philips screwdriver over and over. AND OVER. And despite Maia having the coolest nightclub on the planet with a crap-ton of fancy toys, she had the CHEAPEST bloody tools.

"I am so tempted to run down to the hardware store and drop every dollar I have on a cordless drill at this point," I muttered to Rillin who didn't even look up from his diligent unscrewing on the opposite side of the desk. I swear, the Blacklist dealer almost looked like he found the task RELAXING.

He simply replied, “We’re almost done.”

I tossed my aching hands in the air. “Seriously? DUDE - you said that two hours ago! Don’t you want to spend your time more wisely? Like, with Elizabeth?”

If I hadn’t seen his hand pause ever so briefly on the screwdriver, I would’ve assumed he didn’t care about Elizabeth, but I saw it - the one frozen instant when my words struck true. He moved casually on to yet another screw, “I will admit that I underestimated how many screws held Mr. Shea’s desk together. It is surprising that such an architecturally inferior piece of furniture requires so much hardware.” He looked up at me briefly, “As for Elizabeth, I spent the night with her and nothing has changed. Opening this desk is a necessity so that Nikita may access her father’s paperwork. Once we have it open, I will return to Elizabeth.”

I glanced at Nik as she sat cross-legged on the floor of the cavernous garage-like space, a roaring fire in a massive brick hearth keeping the area quite toasty despite the ever-worsening storm outside. Dressed in faded jeans and a sweatshirt about five sizes too big, she looked soft and innocent. Months ago, I would’ve said that there was no way that Nikita Shea was either of those things, but now, after all we’d been through in such a short amount of time, I knew she was so much more that just an iron heart and sharp tongue.

I was mesmerized by her as she worked diligently over some small device, her right hand trailing over the detailed silver rod, forcing it to bend like water at her command. The fingers on her left arm peeked out from under the sweatshirt, the rest of her arm still bound to her body and hidden under the shirt. From a distance, I could see those delicate fingers flex every once in a while – a sign that Raef and Kian’s hard work was paying off.

We'd set up "shop" in the lower garage of Faust, where Baz had told us we could spread out our crap. Piled over many tables were all of Christian's books, Elizabeth's diary and necklace, Nikki's French book, a few laptops, and numerous items from True North.

Even the Mime was set up not far from one of the tables. It looked like a blackened mannequin made entirely of steel and, quite honestly, freaked me out.

I swear it was watching over all of us, despite its lack of any facial features. Even worse, Nikki had been drawn to the damn thing like a moth to a flame. She drilled Rillin with a thousand questions about it, but thankfully the knight wouldn't let her play with the fancy suit of skull-crushing armor. Instead, she was relegated to sorting through the old Feon technology that had come from True North, while Rillin worked at disassembling her father's desk.

Her *crappy* father, that is. No one had a clue where he'd gone, nor her mother, and the news was featuring her house like a bad rerun, over and over.

What a shit show.

I drew my attention back to the desk as I asked Rillin, "What will you say to her? Elizabeth? When, she wakes up?"

"If she wakes up, you mean," Rillin replied.

"No, I mean WHEN," I replied, but then my gaze narrowed on the huge former knight across from me. I stopped working on the screws for a moment, a startling revelation hitting me. I leaned a bit closer to his side, "Unless . . . Unless you don't want her to wake because your heart has shifted to someone else. Perhaps someone who drives my old Jeep Wrangler and likes to blow up mansions and piss-off Gypsies. 'Cause if it's THAT someone, I gotta tell ya - she seems totally smitten by her soul-sucking bodyguard."

Rillin's eyes slid to mine. He had this chilling, terrifying look to him that made me want to shrivel into one of the screw holes. "YOU don't get to question my heart, nor do I answer such tactless inquiries. You have no idea what Elizabeth and I lived through together. What we endured."

His wide hand tightened on the desk, causing the wood to pop and crack underneath his punishing grip. "How dare you demand answers of me, when it is obvious you feel for Nikita and have yet to tell her so. She suffers from the weight of all that she's come to know over the past few days. Over the past few months." Rillin's voice had taken on an low seething tone that could only be heard by the two of us. "I nearly killed her Friday night. She suffers, in her heart and her head – even her body – and yet you do nothing to tell her how you feel. So don't ever, EVER question my heart when you are too much of a coward to express your own to a young woman who has clearly become important to you."

I pointed a sharp finger at Rillin, about to tell him where to shove his psychobabble, but something hard bounced off my shoulder. I shot a look behind me and saw Ana standing near one of the tables, a huge grin on her face.

"Did you just fling something at me?" I demanded, now scanning the floor for whatever attacked me. I spied one of Baz's concrete blueberry muffins rolling away from me. Breakfast an hour ago had been . . . interesting cuisine.

"Thor! Can I borrow MJ for a second? I need his help," she called, another muffin in her hand, ready to give me a concussion.

"Absolutely." Rillin's glare met mine before he snatched the screwdriver from my hand. "Go help Ana."

In my head I cursed the knight thoroughly as I got to my feet and wandered across the cavernous room towards Ana, the muffin still in my hand. Truth was, Blackwood didn't miss much and, on some level, he was right - I was a coward. I was afraid to tell Nikki how I felt about her because if she shot me down, it would be a hundred levels of awkward since she'd still be part of our crew. On the other hand, I suspected Nikki might have feelings for me as well, so maybe the gamble was worth it.

Last night, after we smoked Soul Sucker Tea and before we finally crashed, Raef made another subtle, healing pass on her arm – an attempt to speed along the bone-hardening process. Afterward, he left me alone with Nikki so I could rewrap her bandage. She seemed entirely unconcerned with me getting to see so much of her as she sat on the counter of the bathroom, my hands grazing her body as I worked.

I don't know whether she just pretended I didn't see certain forbidden, *fabulous,* assets as I re-wrapped her arm to her body, or if she was still too shell-shocked from the explosion and Eris' death to give a damn, but it took everything I had not to start stuttering like a fool as I wove the gauze around her torso. And as wrong as it was, given how much crap we'd gone through, I couldn't help but ache, painfully, to kiss her. To touch her, as only a boyfriend would.

I forced my mind back to the present, lest my body replay the previous night with a tad too much detail.

Ana. Ana needed my help.

I tossed the muffin in the air, catching it easily as I headed over to my friend, stealing a quick glance at Nikki who was entirely focused on whatever she was doing with the pieces of metal. "Ya know," I started, "I bet if I hurled this sucker at the desk hard enough, I might actually put a hole right through that nasty veneer side. God knows, they're hard enough to be baseballs." I smiled at Ana as I got to her, "Thank you for releasing me from my screw prison, fair lady!"

Behind me, Rillin sighed.

"Taking apart a desk can't be THAT bad," Ana chuckled.

I stopped right next to her, dropping the rock-hard pastry onto the table in front of us. "HA! You go try it for a couple hours and see how much you like it! I'm all for letting Thor just smash the sucker with his BARE HANDS!"

I called the last part loudly back at Rillin, who simply shook his head. Rillin's theory was that there could be other booby traps tucked inside the desk, so even though we'd sent it flying like a Russian spy satellite yesterday, we needed to cautiously, painfully, take the sucker fully apart screw by screw, lest we trigger some other disaster that would wreck the papers we needed. Papers that could shed light on the Gate.

Truth was, I couldn't help but fear what would happen if we didn't destroy the Gabriel Gate. Last night, as I laid curled on the floor like a true dog (and even worse, not far from Raef), I couldn't stop thinking about what would happen if we failed. Would all of us cease to exist? Is history so delicate that a single pull on one of its threads will unravel everything ever known?

And how was it even possible that Mother Nature or, like, the universe, didn't realize some mental-case Fallen Archangel was running around and causing mayhem? I mean, Therophel was probably downright orgasmic over the fact he was ready to flip the switch on his doomsday Gate, yet the world kept moving along as normal. Why weren't the creatures of the forest rebelling and coming to our aid? Why wasn't an army of angels raining down from the heavens to kick his ass? Maybe Kian was right and I *did* watch too many movies. Either that or Mother Nature was just an ignorant slob sucking down a few brews on a dilapidated corner of the earth.

I must've zoned, because Ana hip-checked me, snarling as she struggled to roll out True North's Iron Scroll on a set of long tables. "MJ! Jeez, can you, like, turn your brain on and help me spread this stupid thing out?"

"Right. Sorry," I mumbled, pulling my eyes away from Nikki as I helped hold down one end of the scroll so Ana could roll out the rest.

"I thought Raef and Rillin had already read this," I said, glancing to the other side of the room where Kian was pouring over the blueprints to Waite's home, looking for a weakness - a way in - so we could hopefully kill Waite, or rather, *Therophel.*

Out of all of us, only Ana, Kian, and I had ever been inside Waite's compound. And between Kian and me, we'd only actually been inside three times total, for Waite's stupid parties. But it was Ana that really knew the layout of the buildings and grounds, although interiors of the house were still an unknown to us as even Ana had rarely gone into the main house, her work keeping her to the huge garage instead.

"They read most of it," she replied, smoothing out the antique paper on which the Lunaterra's religion was written. "But they want to go over it again with Maia as soon as she's awake and see if she can pick out anything they may've missed. Plus, I know Key wants my brilliance to look over Waite's blueprints when he's done HOGGING THEM." She gave a stern glare at Kian, who just offered her a crooked smile.

"If I see a possible way in, I'll ask for your eyes, Pix," he replied.

Ana jammed her hands on her hips, "Well, if you had me HELP you, then maybe *I* could show *you* where the weaknesses are, rather than you taking ten hours to decode the blueprints."

He smiled wider, a sure way to piss off Ana. "First of all, I've only been looking at them for a half hour. Secondly, if you are so desperate to be next to me, why don't you just admit it? Hmm?"

She bit back a smile. "You ain't that hot," she replied.

They began their damn banter-flirting from across the room, and I quickly muttered an excuse to go hang out near Nikki – a necessity to spare me from barfing.

As I walked towards Nikki, I noted that she seemed weirdly herself. Well, not *herself* as in the "Nikki" I used to know, who was a raging bitch, but rather then new version of Nikki who seemed totally normal. It was as if she didn't even acknowledge what had happened in Maia's office. While one part of me wanted her to grieve – to give herself that chance to mourn what was basically the loss of her folks – the other part said she wasn't ready; that she was a girl who'd existed for years by closing herself off, living within many distinct roles and narrow view points.

The truth was, Nikki Shea was multiple people, all hiding in one fabulously curvy body that kept running naked through my dreams.

Last night, after Raef and Kian had returned from hunting (and we'd quickly explained that we weren't smoking weed), Raef had shocked everyone by taking the Talus from Baz and lighting up. Rather than making us non-puffers choke to death by attempting to smoke, Baz and Raef did the physical smoking, then would direct the Tantalus vapor towards Nikki, Eila, and me.

At one point Raef was nearly kissing Eila as he shared the smoke between them, his lips blowing a paper-thin wisp towards her. She'd part her lips, ever so slightly, and the delicate slip of smoke would disappear into her mouth.

Kian, however, took only a brief drag, then refused any more. He didn't allow Ana near it either. He said that her lungs, while healed after the smoke she inhaled from the explosion, needed a break from any more irritants. I may've responded that if that was the case, then perhaps HE should leave her alone for a while. While it earned a laugh from our friends, Kian didn't seem amused. The two of them left us, heading back into our shared room with strict instructions not to wake them if they were asleep.

Baz had been right – the Tantulus didn't make anyone loopy or high, and it did help all of us feel more relaxed. Unfortunately, the aftertaste it had left in the back of my mouth was probably identical to licking a Sumo wrestler's armpit, so there was no way I'd ever go near the crap again.

We stayed on the catwalk for another hour or so, the clock ticking towards midnight as we passed around the hand-rolled anti-weed, semi-smoking with the help of Raef and Baz. We'd discussed how Baz's vaccines worked and what he thought about his chances for finding a cure. We'd also talked about Maia. We all knew she was a fighter, and though our crew needed her, it was her Faust family and her son who were truly lost without her. Leo's promises that Faust's matriarch would wake up had quickly become less certain with each passing hour, and as of this morning, she was still unconscious.

We needed Maia Moriarty to wake up and offer her insight, her guidance. And Baz . . . he just plain needed his mom.

Watching him fight to control his heartbreak and fears as he stood on the catwalk last night, I was reminded once again how grateful I was that my own parents had gone abroad to visit family in China. They might drive me crazy and my mother might demand the best from me, but I loved them and never wanted anything to happen to them.

As the Tantalus kicked in, talk had eventually turned to Lawson Waite and what might be required to kill the bugger, or rather the Archangel that was hitchhiking in his body. That conversation had been mighty depressing, since none of us had a clue how to replicate what the Lunaterra did back in the day to kill the other Archangel, Aztael. Raef did mention that he and Kian thought that Therophel might be injured thanks to Elizabeth. Their argument seemed valid: I mean, why ride around in a crappy human body if you were basically a fallen star with biblical powers?

What we really needed were instructions, 'cause shit this complicated should always come with clearly labeled instructions.

Eventually we had all crashed in our makeshift dorm room, tossing blankets and pillows on the floor for comfort. Nikki and Eila took the bed and we guys took the floor, though Kian and Ana were cocooned around one another on a couch that was situated at one end of the room. I heard that even Rillin caught some Zs last night as well, though according to Baz, the knight had chosen to lie in front of the lab door, acting as a lethal deadbolt if anyone tried to visit Elizabeth without permission.

I gotta say that if someone ever told me that I'd be smoking herbal tea in a Mortis nightclub in New Bedford on a Saturday night, and then having a co-ed sleepover with a crew of supernatural wackos, I'd have told them that not even a fiction writer was crazy enough to pen such an outrageous scene. Obviously, reality had a perverse sense of humor.

Pushing last night's insanity to the back of my mind, I stopped in front of Nikki, her scuffed sneakers tapping together as she worked, as if the rhythm of her ability needed an outlet. Not far from us, Rillin spared me a quick, knowing glance from his spot near the demolished desk. I knelt down, picking up a random piece of metal from her collected pile. Turning the penny-sized piece of iron in my hand, I asked, "How's it going?"

She looked up at me and blinked, as if I'd appeared out of thin air. "Oh, hey - Um, it's going fine. Need something?"

I set the piece of metal back in her stash and tucked my hands in my jean pockets, nervous. "No – just wanted to know if you needed some help with making that, uh . . . whatever that is."

She smiled a little, flicking her chin to the spot on the floor beside her. "Sure. Have a seat."

I slid down the wall onto my butt next to her, the heat of the fireplace coating my left side in bone-cooking heat. She handed me some steel do-dad.

"What's this?" I asked, turning it over in my hand. It was a small, silver cylinder with what looked like a solid piece of glass inside. Copper and chrome wires wrapped around the outer surface, like metal vines. "It's really very pretty."

She smiled, "It's an idea for a Light-channeling device for Eila. I got the idea when Rillin told me that she likes to train with a katana sword. I thought she'd like something that can wield the Light like a blade."

"So, this is basically the hilt and when Eila calls the Light, her power becomes the blade?"

Nikki nodded, "Exactly."

My gaze met hers. Sitting shoulder to shoulder, I could see all the varied bits of colors in her green eyes. "It's a great idea, Nik. She'll love it."

She smiled, but it seemed less bright than before. Her focus turned back to the device in my hand, and I offered it back to her. She took it as I asked, "How's . . . How's your arm?"

"Better, actually. I mean - check it out. Look what I can do now," she replied, and then proceeded to flip me off with her left hand. A smile tugged back onto her face.

It took me a second to realize that she wasn't actually flipping ME off, per se, but rather showing off her hand's functionality. "You can flip the bird! That's awesome! Maybe you'll be out of your bandages soon."

She nudged me with her shoulder. "Thought you'd be impressed."

I smiled at her, "Nik – I'm always impressed around you, even if the star of the moment is your middle finger."

Her sneakered feet began their bouncing rhythm once again as she said, "I heard the workers talking this morning. They said my house is still all over the news. That the cops are looking for me and my folks. According to the news, we're all wanted for questioning. I guess the Feds are in on it now too, because they think it was C-4 which is, like, terrorist stuff."

I sighed and eased one arm around her shoulders. She leaned her head back against the wall, using my arm as a pillow as she studied the ductwork and black pipes crisscrossing the garage ceiling. Her words were laced in defeat as she continued, "Even if we are able to destroy the Gate, even if we murder Therophel and Elizabeth wakes up, I will never get off the Feds' radar. They are going to be looking for me, non-stop. It was a stupid idea, going for the desk. I'm an idiot for doing it."

I gave her a squeeze, "Hey, hey - you are NOT stupid and you said the desk probably contained what we need to wreck the Gate. That is necessary crap, okay? It's not your fault your dad has a thing for explosives."

"It feels like it's my fault that Maia is unconscious and Ana was nearly killed," whispered Nik. "It feels like I should've known, should've thought of that the second I found out his stuff was here!"

I tucked my hand in hers. "Listen to me," I replied quietly, both of us watching as Rillin worked on the desk and Kian and Ana argued over Waite's blueprints. "You can't blame yourself for the choices of others. You can't blame yourself for a history you had no say in. All of this crap, this war, was started way before us, yet we are tangled up in it because it was never fully ended. You are paying the price for your own parents' screw-ups. But no one, NO ONE, blames you. Got it?"

She nodded, her lips pressed together in a thin line. She turned, tucking her face into my neck as she tried to calm her emotions.

Her warm breath rolled over the skin on my neck as she breathed, but then something inside me . . . *purred*. FREAKIN purred.

And it wasn't like some little, fluffy kitty purr (thank God, because that would have ended any manliness I'd ever had), but something deeper, heavier. It felt as though my very bones vibrated with the sound of it. I was so startled, that I stiffened sharply, causing Nikki to sit up.

"Uh, you're not looking so great," she said, eyeing me from

her spot right next to me. I just shook my head, pulling myself back together, but listening carefully for what I had heard deep inside me.

"Did you hear anything?" I asked, focusing once again on her face, but she gave me a weird look.

"Like what?"

I croaked, "Never mind."

Just then, a bunch of screws clattered to the floor near us. We both looked over to see Rillin standing beside the desk, clutching his hand. His face was drawn, as if in pain.

"I told you those screws suck after a while," I replied, sure his hand was just cramping up from using the screwdriver endlessly. But then he slowly turned, opening his palm slowly for us to see, and my heart nearly stopped.

"Holy crap," whispered Nikki.

The sigil that Maia had engraved in his palm was glowing a brilliant, fiery blue. Pulsing, like a heartbeat.

I scrambled to my feet, pulling Nikki up with me, and yelled to Kian as I kept my eyes glued on Rillin. He looked as though he was growing weaker by the minute. The blue light bled upward from his palm, moving with each pulse, and his Fallen Marks flickered to life, one by one, no longer black but the same spectacular blue.

"What the hell?" muttered Kian as he and Ana ran over to where we were. "What is that?"

Rillin seemed to be in a trance as he watched the light weave through his body, but as it reached his chest, he suddenly gasped, staggering sharply forward. Kian moved fast, grabbing onto Rillin before the knight hit the ground. The huge blacklist dealer was clutching his chest, growling in pain. It was as if the Limiting Link was back in his chest, torturing him all over again.

I ran over to help Kian. "What's happening to him?" I demanded.

Kian's stunned eyes met mine, "I think . . . I think he's having some kind of heart attack."

I looped one of Rillin's massive arms over my shoulders, Kian doing the same. "How's that possible?" I demanded, wincing at Rillin's sheer weight, thoughts of my internal purr long forgotten for the moment. Memories of Christian's death flashed through my mind and panic wove in with my confusion. We couldn't lose Rillin. "He's a MORTIS! He can't have a heart attack!"

"I KNOW!" Kian snarled at me, but then Ana yelled, "The sigil! Maia said it would allow Elizabeth to draw strength from Rillin through the bond! What if she's drawing his strength? What if this means she's waking?"

Rillin managed to get his feet under him, his whole body like granite due to the pain he was in, but raw determination driving him.

"Get me to Elizabeth," he wheezed. "Quickly."

EILA

CHAPTER 23

FAUST, NEW BEDFORD, MA

Howe fidgeted nervously in the corner booth, his eyes taking in the dark (somewhat demolished) decadence of Faust as Raef and I sat across from him. In retrospect, mentioning the whole "shearing" thing was probably a bad move on my part, because the FBI agent was now convinced he couldn't even go pee without having his soul sucked out his –

"I think I should get a vaccine, ya know – just to be safe," Howe said again, his fingers tapping out a nervous rhythm on the table. At this rate, it was probably an SOS via Morse code in the hopes that someone would come save him from Maia's nightclub.

"Agent Howe. MARCUS. As I told you before, no one is going to bother you," sighed Raef, growing impatient. "The club is closed – only the workers are here right now and they are running off a skeleton crew at the moment."

"There are probably real skeletons literally working here," muttered Howe, finally focusing on me. "Eila, what you are asking me to do – breach the FBI firewall – is basically an act of treason against the US government. That's not something the Feds take lightly, and I'd really rather not go to jail for the rest of my life."

I slid my spoon back and forth through my hot cocoa, the sound of it hitting the cup reminding me of Mae. Of how she used to take forever to stir the sugar into her coffee every morning, the sound like a delicate little bell that rang through our house. I would not let her death, nor that of all the other people Waite had killed, be in vain.

I stopped stirring, trying to figure out how to motivate Howe into being the hacker I knew he could be. "Marcus, look – this man, Lawson Waite, is not human. If we're correct, he's a relic of the original war between the Lunaterra and the Mortis. He's very – "

"He's a Fallen Archangel," interrupted Raef, causing Howe's eyes to grow as huge as platters. "He has the potential to rewrite history, and in doing so, basically end the world. In the grand scheme of things, I really don't care about you going to jail. If you don't do this, I'll super-glue one of the red bracelets to your arm and dump you in the middle of the dance floor when Faust opens, so that every soul thief thinks you are up for being sheared."

Well, that wasn't quite the motivation I was looking for, but . . .

Howe, wide-eyed, sat like a statue for a moment. I'd never threatened the FBI agent with Raef or Kian or even Rillin. I never forced him to do anything for us, believing that he was most loyal when he made decisions on his own. He seemed truly shocked, but then his eyes narrowed, anger sliding across his face.

"Fine," he snapped. "Fine, I'll hack the firewall and find your damn gear, BUT I have some non-negotiable terms of my own." Raef and I exchanged a surprised look, both of us stunned Howe apparently had balls. I took a sip of my cocoa, gesturing for the former agent to proceed.

Howe's jaw flexed as he replied, "I want Ana Lane to erase you – all of you – from my memories."

I nearly dropped the cup, the chocolate dribbling over the lip and onto the table. "You want her to . . . alter your mind? WILLINGLY?"

Raef sat back in his chair, studying Howe. "Why?" he asked, suspicious.

"Because I'm DONE! I don't want to know about this, this . . ," he tossed his hands around frantically, "this STUFF. Okay? I have nightmares, all the time. Before you all, I used to have great dreams. Awesome dreams. Dreams of babes in string bikinis, Tony Stark as my wingman, and shootin' bad guys. Now? Now all I dream of is fake agents that transform into half-human lizards, girls that can fry a hole in the roof of a bloody huge mansion, and big-ass dudes with tattoos that wanna suck my soul out through my nostrils!"

I sighed, "Marcus, correct me if I'm wrong, but you seem to enjoy living in Collette's million-dollar loft in Chinatown, not to mention driving her Corvette. I thought you wanted justice for being wrongly fired from the FBI and for being attacked. What happened to your goals?"

"Screw my goals. I don't want to know this version of reality. And if I am grabbed by the FBI for crossing their firewall, then I don't want to have any memory of doing it, so when they strap me to a lie detector, I'll PASS!"

"So much for the way of the warrior," I muttered. Howe shot me a dirty look.

Raef turned to me, "Ana was able to alter Sarah Booth's

memories, and those of Jesse Vale's father. I think she can do this, don't you?"

I nodded, but then looked back at Howe. "Marcus, even if Ana can do this for you, you still won't have a job. Whether she alters your memories or not, history won't change. Your partner will still be dead and you'll still be fired from the FBI."

Howe banged his palm on the table, causing my mug to rattle. "So give me a new life! God knows you've got the money and probably the connections. Heck, I'm happy to be an onion farmer in the middle of nowhere, I just want out."

Raef and I starred at Howe, shocked by the outburst. Finally, the agent's shoulders slumped as he added, "Please. This can't be my life. If I hadn't ended up with the Breaker's case, I'd still be with the FBI and Agent Sollen, my partner, would still be alive. And you're right, I can't go back, but I'm also stuck – I can't go forward either because of all the things I've seen and learned about you guys and this world." He looked around Faust's massive interior, his face a combination of frustration and defeat. "I need to start over. I need to be someone else."

I ran my finger along the edge of my warm mug, thinking. "I haven't looked through Christian's files on what he owns for property, and I have yet to access his money, but if I can, I'll set you up. Some place where no one will bother you. I can give you enough money so you can live comfortably for several years until you figure out what you want to do, onion farming included." Howe gave a weak, relieved laugh. "As to your memories, that is something I can ask Ana to do for you, but I can't force her. The decision lies with her."

Howe sobered quickly, "I understand."

"But you have to hold up your end of the deal," added Raef, resting one long arm on the back of my chair as he reclined. "You need to hack the FBI firewall and tell us exactly where they are keeping the gear from Dalca Anescu's shop. We need to know the quickest, most effective way for us to steal it back."

Howe swallowed, "Yeah. Yeah, I think I can do that. I'll need to cover my tracks, rerouting some computer markers and whatnot, but I should be able to do it. I gotta tell ya though, breaking into the FBI will not be easy. I'm not even sure it can be done."

"We're not human thieves, Agent Howe," Raef replied. "Our talents are a bit more advanced than the average cat burglar. I think we'll be fine."

We got down to discussing the basic overview of the main FBI office in Boston, when my phone rang. Surprised anyone was calling me, I pulled it from my pocket, glancing at the screen to see Baz's number. What the heck?

Raef glanced at me and I mouthed, *it's Baz*, and he rolled his eyes, turning back to Howe.

I stood, stepping away from the table so as not to bother the guys. I looked up through the catwalks towards the lab as I answered, "Dude – are you seriously too lazy to walk down here?"

"*Am I on speakerphone?*" asked Baz, dead serious.

I frowned, "Uh, no. Do you want to be?"

"No, no! I'd rather not broadcast this to any of the Faust employees that may be in earshot. Plus . . . Is that FBI guy here yet?"

"Yeah, he's here. What's going on?"

"I think it's . . . working," Baz whispered through the phone, though he sounded kinda tweaked. *"This shit is way too creepy for me, I'm just saying."*

Oh my God, I did not understand potheads to save my life. I paced back towards the bar, leaving Howe and Raef in the far corner. "Baz, I swear, if I could strangle you through the phone, I would. YOU are making no sense. What the heck are you talking about?"

"Elizabeth!" he hissed, *"I think your gram's got a pulse, and I swear, if she suddenly sits up like some black and white horror flick, I'm gonna piss myself! So can you please get up here!?"*

I froze, feeling as though my brain just splatted against a brick wall. I tried to reply to Baz, my voice cracking and squeaking. "I'm sorry, can, uh – can you say that again?" I croaked.

"Eila," he replied, *"I'm pretty damn sure your great grams may be doing the whole 'rise from the dead like a zombie' thing right now!"*

Just as I was about to reply, I heard a door slam open on the far side of the dance hall. Kian's panicked voice cut through the building as he called for help. I spun to see Rillin, barely able to walk, being helped by MJ and Kian.

"We got to get him up to the lab!" MJ yelled, as Raef knocked over his chair, bolting for the guys. Howe, equally startled, jumped to his feet, unsure of what was going on.

I hung up on Baz and ran to Rillin's side, but my trainer barely acknowledged me. He seemed . . . weak and in pain, unable to focus on my words. "What's happening to him?" I demanded, my hands immediately going to Rillin's chest, where his Limiting Link use to reside, terrified it had somehow regrown inside him.

Kian and Raef shifted Rillin's weight between them, trying to take more of the burden. "He was acting like he was having a heart attack," explained Kian. "But then Pix said that she remembered Maia saying the soul bond would allow Elizabeth to pull strength from Rillin. If that ain't what's going on, Sparky, then I've got no clue what is, but he's in rough shape. It came on fast - one second he was fine, the next . . . "

Raef watched as I placed my hands on Rillin's stubbled cheeks, guiding his eyes to mine. He was in agony – I could see it written in the stress across his face, and even worse, he looked deathly pale. Weaker than I'd ever seen him before.

I couldn't lose him. He'd become this connection to my past - this wonderful, steady presence in my life. He believed in me, never questioned my ability to defend myself.

The truth was, I loved him.

It wasn't the same as Raef, but Rillin held a piece of my heart and I refused to let him go.

"It's working, Rillin," I urged, my voice a near sob, terrified he was truly dying in front of me. "You listen to me. You hang in there and we will get you up to Elizabeth. You fight to hang on, you hear me? Because it's working, Rillin. Baz told me so. Your Elizabeth . . . has a heartbeat."

Rillin's eyes flared briefly with hope, but then he let out a terrifyingly thin sigh as he collapsed entirely and his Fallen Marks flickering out like dying embers in the rain.

RAEF

CHAPTER 24

FAUST, NEW BEDFORD, MA

Kian and I managed to hang onto Rillin's unconscious form, despite his massive size, Eila shouting commands to get him up to Elizabeth. As I watched her, tears streaking her face as she too attempted to help move her trainer, I realized that Rillin's affection for Eila wasn't a one-way street.

I realized that my girl - my E - had feelings for Rillin as well.

A small part of me felt as though I'd been smashed into a thousand pieces - a heartbreaking knowledge that I'd been blind to all these months. But another part of me knew, without question or reservation, that E and I were matched. That our love was the type that could burn a city to the ground and that spanned centuries. We were unbreakable as a couple, unless I let my jealousy get in the way of what my girl needed in that instant.

"I've got him, E," I urged. Her sweet, sad face was so close to mine as she struggled with Rillin's weight. "We can move him faster if you just get up the stairs ahead of us. Have Baz move Elizabeth into our room. Put her on the bed. That way we can put Rillin down next to her. I'm hoping that placing him close to her may allow them to share strength from each other." It was nothing more than a guess on my part, but with Rillin fading fast, I had no other ideas on how to possibly save the former Trial.

Eila nodded rapidly, terror clear in her eyes.

He's gonna be okay, E. I won't let anything happen to him." I said, another possible lie.

Rubbing her face to dry her tears, she drew a deep steadying breath and turned to flee up the stairs to do as I instructed. But at the last second, she paused. Turning quickly back to me, she grasped my face in her hands and kissed me desperately on the lips.

I knew this girl. I loved this girl. I loved how her lips fit so perfectly to mine and how she'd bounce her foot when she was thinking. I loved how she snuggled deeply into the pillows at night, one leg flung over the covers, her arm wrapped across my chest as if my breathing lulled her to sleep. I loved how she fought, for everyone. I loved how she saw the good in people, no matter who they were.

I loved this girl with everything I had.

Eila pulled back from me, but I snagged her arm and pulled her back, kissing her softly. "I know how much he means to you, E. I'll do everything I can to get him back to you, understand?"

She sniffed. "I love you, Raef Paris," she whispered, then bolted up the stairs, Ana hot on her heels.

I glanced at Kian who'd been watching our exchange closely. "You're a bigger man than I, my friend," he said.

"She loves him," I replied.

Kian hoisted Rillin's weight to better support him between us. He snorted, "She may love Rillin, but you, my friend, have stolen her heart for eternity. I know that type of love. I HAVE that type of love, but I've also got enough selfish balls to admit that I'd be pissed if Ana cried her eyes out for anyone other than me."

"HEY!" snapped MJ from his spot behind us. "She gets to be hysterical if anything happened to ME, got it?"

"Fine. Dog Boy is an exception," Kian muttered.

Damn straight I am," MJ replied, as Kian and I started hauling Rillin up the twisted metal staircase, Nikki at our backs.

* * * *

It took until nightfall for Rillin to finally come around. We'd placed him alongside Elizabeth on our bed, and the moment they'd been put in contact with one another, both of them became covered with a network of blue markings; a combining of Rillin's Fallen Marks and Elizabeth's Kill Mark that we'd never witnessed before. With every fragile beat of Elizabeth's heart, the blue marks flowed back and forth between them - two bodies, one shared life force. The soul bond reminded me of the ebb and flow of the tide - how the moon pulls the ocean one way, yet gravity steals her waves back in an endless tug of war.

Eila remained at Rillin's side, watching over her trainer - counting his breaths and the rhythm of the soul bond. I, too, stayed in the room, giving E space but also letting her know that I was there for her should she need anything.

Our friends had come and gone throughout the day, the mood similar to a sitting vigil, praying for a friend to recover, but not entirely sure of the outcome. They kept busy disassembling the desk and going through the paperwork, Nikki tasked with reading through all the diagrams and information related to the Gate.

Outside Faust, the wind had kicked up to a fearsome roar as day bled into early night, the snow now coming in waves that blinded the streetlights from view. The club remained closed to patrons, only her crew working and continuing repairs. Though they kept busy, I knew they were desperate for Maia to wake up. It had been nearly 24 hours since the blast.

It was close to dinnertime by the time Rillin first began to move, and Eila, who had nodded off next to me, startled awake at the sound of his rough voice.

"What happened?" he asked, dragging his hand slowly over his chest, apparently unaware that Elizabeth was next to him.

Eila scrambled off the couch next to me and I slowly followed her. She stepped over to the bed, smiling, but I could tell it was merely a front. She was worried. "How you feeling?"

"Weak," Rillin replied, his voice dry. "I feel like . . . like I've been ill. Or I've been drugged." Rillin leaned to his side, trying to rise, but both Eila and I moved to steady him.

"Slowly, my friend," I urged. "The soul bond really did a number on you. We weren't sure if you were gonna make it for a little while. It was touch and go."

Rillin's forehead wrinkled. "Soul bond?" he asked, but then awareness swept over his face and he turned sharply, glancing to the bed behind him. Elizabeth, still in the position we placed her in hours ago, rested on the bed behind him. "Oh my God," he breathed. "Did it work?" He reached over, feeling her face.

Beside me, Eila swallowed. "Well, she had a heartbeat for

quite a while. But in the past hour, the beats spaced out again, then just . . . sorta stopped."

Rillin's shoulder's sank, "No . . . I can feel her. Her life force - it still lingers within me." He opened his palm and dragged his fingers over the sigil carved into his skin. "It was working. There has to be a way to get it to work again."

"Rillin, maybe you just need to recover. You're weak. You need a stolen soul to build back your strength," urged Eila.

"Eila's right," I replied, though the truth was I had no clue if we could ever get Elizabeth to fully return to us. I had no clue whether the past few hours represented the full extent of the soul bond's abilities, or if it was just the beginning. I rested a hand at Eila's back as I continued, trying to focus on the positives. "This was a good sign, Rillin. Maia said it could take time, but we now know that Elizabeth's heart still works. We know the bond between you worked."

Rillin, ignoring both of us, eased open Elizabeth's delicate fingers to examine her sigil. His rough hand ran over her cuts and slowly he brought her palm to his lips, placing a gentle kiss over her lifeline. Eila seemed almost surprised by the intimate act, no doubt shocked Rillin had done so before witnesses. Whatever arguments he had made about Elizabeth being just his charge were swept away in that moment.

"Come back to me," he whispered, sadly. "Please, fight to come back to me. I am right here, waiting for you."

Beside me, Eila's arm slipped around my waist and she leaned her head against my shoulder. "We should leave them alone," I whispered into her hair, as Rillin begged his beloved princess to return to him. Eila nodded and together we headed out of the room, shutting the door quietly behind us.

Eila sighed, "God, what if she doesn't wake up, Raef? What if this is all Rillin gets? This horrible tease. That would be so awful."

I rubbed her shoulders, trying to loosen the tension in her body, "I'm going to stay positive. I'm going to believe that the bond will work. I'm going to – "

I was interrupted by Leo, who suddenly swung open the door to Maia's bedroom, which was located not far from us, Baz emerging as well. They paused in the doorway the second they saw us, both of them looking as worn out as the rest of us.

Leo's gaze drifted over the two of us, before landing squarely on Eila. "Maia is awake and she's asking for you." His eyes slid over to me, "All of you. And you better have a bloody good plan, because she wants to hear it."

Eila, stunned for a second, finally nodded, "I'm so glad she's awake! Uh, yeah. Sure. Give me an hour and we'll have all the details she needs."

I offered Eila a sideways glance, but kept my mouth shut. She either had something up her sleeve, or was bluffing her way into a spare hour.

"Fine," replied Leo, turning to head back into the room. Baz pulled the door shut behind the bouncer, leaving himself standing alone with us on the catwalk. He rubbed the back of his head, then finally stepped over to us.

"So, this plan of yours . . . It better be a good one, because my mom is pretty much nuclear that the club got trashed."

E tossed her hand casually, "Oh yeah - it's an awesome plan. Best one ever."

CHAPTER 25
FAUST, NEW BEDFORD, MA
SUNDAY, 9PM

"You told Weed Boy WE HAVE A PLAN?" demanded MJ, horrified. "Like, a hard and fast, 'here are the steps to kill an archangel' type plan? Are you crazy? Your quahog is totally cracked if you think we've got any clue at all!" He paced restlessly near one of the armored trucks in the lower level of Faust, which continued to be our designated hangout. It was feeling more and more like purgatory, however, in downtown New Bedford. "Good grief, Eila. We've only been studying this gibberish for a couple hours. We got nothing."

"Well, think faster, because I suspect if we don't have a plan, we may be getting the boot from Faust, deal or no deal," I replied, shifting the papers on the table and trying to figure out the maze of numbers and letters and drawings, all of which came out of Mr. Shea's desk.

MJ rubbed his arms, flustered, "Eila, next time you lie, can you like, LOWER the bar rather than telling a pissed-off zombie-maker that we are geniuses with an epic plan! Because at this rate, I'm gonna chew off every last fingernail I have by bedtime." He finally stopped pacing and flopped against the truck's iron side, the sound echoing in the cavernous room. "I love you, woman, but you seriously suck at lying."

MJ was right. We were the definition of clueless at this point.

And yeah - I totally sucked at spouting untruths.

I glanced across the table to Howe, who was tucked into the driver's seat of the armored truck, one leg dangling out the open door, the other supporting a laptop in his lap. He offered us a furtive glance once in a while as he attempted to hack the FBI firewall, a process that was taking hours. Maia's brilliant son had affixed a sticker over the glowing white apple logo on the laptop's lid. It read *Can't we all just get a bong?*

We were so gonna die.

Our crew consisted of basically every social reject (supernatural and otherwise) in the tri-state area, plus a pretty lady corpse, who might or might not remember her Trial, and who might or might not want to incinerate everyone, and who was taking her sweet time rising from the dead.

Hello, Hell. It's just terrific to be here once again.

Nikki, seated at the table, tapped a little silver cylinder restlessly on the edge of her seat, studying the papers that had finally been extracted from her father's desk. It had been in her hand since I arrived on the lower level, almost like a trinket that kept her grounded.

I looked up at Kian and Ana, who were standing side by side not far from me, the blueprints to Waite's home on the Vineyard rolled up in Kian's grasp. I nodded at his hand, "And the blueprints didn't help at all?"

Ana shook her head. "Not really. Kian and I searched for a space within the grounds that could house the Gate, but given the size that Nikki says it is, there is nothing here that can fit it and keep it hidden."

"How big are we talking?" I asked, looking at Nikki.

She finally stopped fidgeting with her toy and shoved the item in her back pocket as she replied, "Big. Roughly 25 feet in diameter. At least, according to what information we managed to pull from my dad's paperwork and my French book." She tapped her finger on the pile of papers in front of her. "This stuff from my Dad's desk – I think this is basically the 'operators manual' for the Gate, but it's not easy to understand."

"Wait a second – you said 'diameter' – you mean it's a circle?" I asked.

Nikki nodded, shuffling the papers until she showed a drawing of what looked like a platform inside several hula hoops. She shoved it across the table to Raef and me. "Yeah. Basically it kinda looks like an atom, or rather, a globe. There's the base and three rings seated around the base. When it goes into operation, those rings not only spin around the base, they flip over one another as well, kinda like a gyroscope. I think. Again . . . not the clearest of instructions."

Nikki shifted in her seat, rubbing her eyes as if she could use a pair of glasses, "I'm a little sketchy on the exact details, but if I'm understanding some of these drawings, I believe that each ring stands for something – one for a location on earth as dictated by some sort of energy that runs through the earth, one for date as founded by the destruction of something called Etemenanki, whatever the heck that is, and a third ring which channels the power of a Lunaterra's Core Collapse. There also appears to be an iron band around the outside that doesn't move."

"Etemenanki was the Tower of Babel," offered Kian from his spot near the table. "While its date of construction is not truly known, the entire city was destroyed in 689 BC . . . supposedly."

"How do you know this stuff?" asked MJ, suspicious.

Kian simply shrugged, "I'm nosey and like to read. One has a lot of downtime when one ain't gonna die anytime soon. I've got a library card for just about every library up and down the East Coast, plus a few universities. I even have one for an all-female college in Pennsylvania."

Nikki eyed him from her seat at the table. "How in the heck did you get a library card for Bryn Mawr?"

Kian smiled, "I'm charming, lest you forget. Ana couldn't resist me from the day she met me."

Ana laughed hard, "Oh, yeah right. Don't listen to him Nik - the boy lives in Fantasy Land."

MJ raised his hand, clearly more focused than Kian. "So, I already asked Nikki this when you and Raef were upstairs, but we couldn't figure out how the Gate sat on the ground if the rings have to pass under it. I know it sounds stupid, but wouldn't it just . . . roll away. Like a giant wheel?"

Nikki pointed at MJ and nodded, "Yeah – I haven't figured that part out yet."

"Maybe it needs to be suspended?" asked Raef, rubbing his jaw as he stood next to me, studying what looked like gobbledegook on the papers. "Maybe that's what the outer ring is for – maybe that's how it is held aloft."

Ana braced her hands on the table. "What if it doesn't operate on land? What if it's designed to operate in water?"

MJ snorted, "Okay – out of all this crap here on the table, how do you come up with it needing water to operate?"

Ana's gaze met mine, as if seeking permission to go on. I blinked, "Girl, if you got something to say, by all means spill. We're flying semi-blind right now, so I'll take any and all ideas."

She shifted as if her shoulders were stiff. "Well, I was just thinking of the old water wheels that were used on the Cape to grind the grain into flour. And the windmills, which did the same thing but with wind. What if the rings need to be powered by wind . . . or water? I mean, if this thing is steel or stone, and it's 25 feet in diameter, these rings are gonna be heavy. Anything in here reference water, Nik?"

"Yeah, actually. In the Iron Scrolls there is a reference to a river running under Aztael palace. It's possible that the Gabriel Gate in the palace utilized the underground river. Did Rillin ever say he saw the Gate?"

"No - he never saw it, but we could run the theory by him. See what he thinks," I replied, then added slowly, "or Elizabeth. She would know."

"If she wakes the frick up, you mean," added Ana. "God, I can't believe she had a heartbeat for a while and then it just stopped."

"Elizabeth will have a heartbeat once again if the sigils continue to strengthen the bond, Ms. Lane! I, however, nearly didn't have a heartbeat at all thanks to Eris and Nikita's damn father nearly blowing me and my office to bits!!" Maia's voice cracked like a whip over the expansive garage, and we all swiveled sharply towards her voice, stunned by her ability to slip into the room so unnoticed.

She looked majorly pissed.

Couldn't say I really blamed her though . . .

She stood in the massive arched doorway, her arm resting in the crook of Leo's, using him for extra support. Though she looked paler than usual, her make-up and hair were once again polished and bejeweled, transforming her into a queen within her realm. Leo's glare was harder than ice as he looked around the room. "If I ever find Ken Shea," Maia snarled, "I will carve his heart from his chest and replace it with one of his own damn gears." She looked right at Nik, "I pray you are not nearly as greedy as your parents, for your future will not be long if you are."

Nikki glared at Maia. "I am nothing like my parents," she replied angrily, then pushed sharply out of her seat, toppling the chair as she quickly left the room. As she fled, her broken breathing was clear to us all.

"My God, have a freakin' scrap of mercy!" snapped MJ, pissed. "What's wrong with you, saying such crap?!"

"This is war, Mr. Williams, and her father is a treacherous man with a selfish agenda who enslaved FIVE of my crew, as well as one of yours," she replied, her temper hardening like frostbite across her face. "My enemies will find no mercy harbored in me, and that includes their children should they prove to be enemies as well."

MJ muttered several obscenities as he ran after Nikki, disappearing out the same door she had fled through near the back of the garage. As the door slammed shut behind him, the sound ricocheted like thunder as steel bolt and striker slammed together in his wake.

I turned my attention back to Maia, my glare hard. MJ was right. That shit was uncalled for.

I wanted to go after Nikki, but I knew that she was in good hands with MJ. I also knew that I needed to focus on the task at hand, even if it meant I had to leave Nikki in the care of my shifting pal . . . which made me feel a bit grossed out, but whatever.

"And to be clear," Maia continued, "the walls of Faust are now painted with *Vindícamus ser múrí*, an enchantment born of those with demon blood, and one which I am well versed in using."

"Typical bokor excuse," muttered Kian. "Draw power from Hell itself, but it's totally okay if used for the right reasons. Total bullshit. YOU are playing with the type of fire that does far more than simply bite back, Moriarty. It can consume, entirely, those who attempt to use it. You know it."

"I will draw from Satan himself and gladly pay the penalty, if it protects my family. This is my house and I will do as I damn well please."

"*Vindícamus ser múrí*," muttered Raef, repeating Maia's words as he studied her. "While Kian is right in that it's decidedly not something a saner bokor would use and blatantly risky to Maia, it's ingenious. I'm impressed, although I've never seen the markings done in such a pattern. It's . . . interesting." Raef eyed Maia, as if trying to piece together a puzzle. Kian seemed to be doing the same.

"What's it mean?" asked Ana, glancing back and forth between Raef and Maia. "Stupid Spanish has obviously been a bust."

"Roughly translated, it means *We claim the lock to the wall*," Raef replied. "It basically wards against anyone coming in without permission, humans included. Some say it blocks souls from entering the afterlife . . . in either direction."

Maia eased slowly into a seat at the head of the table, where Nikki had been, Leo helping her. "My hope is that in using such a potent ward, I will be able to defend Faust against Therophel. I've never had to test these particular wards before, but they are part of our defensive protocols. All the workers know this, hence why they were able to immediately begin applying them to the building." She glanced at Raef, "My crew is well trained. Battle-ready."

"So, you've obviously been told that Lawson Waite is Therophel," I replied, the rest of us on our feet, surrounding the table piled with paperwork.

"I was made aware of our new reality the moment I awoke, thanks to Leo." She drummed her fingers along the table. "I must say, I was fairly disappointed that Elizabeth hadn't killed the bastard in 1851."

"HA!" snorted Ana. "There's the understatement of the century."

Maia offered her a withering look, but then her gaze slid past Leo to Howe, who had stopped typing on the laptop – a total deer in headlights. "And you are?"

"Agent, uh, Howe. Ma'am," he replied, his voice breaking with nerves. "I was, uh, asked to come. By Eila."

"Agent? You are the Fed that Bane was complaining about?"

"Yes, Ma'am."

Maia paused, "Aren't you a tad short for an FBI agent?"

"I, uh . . . no Ma'am. There aren't any height requirements to work for the Bureau."

Maia snorted, turning back to the table. "Pity. Probably no IQ requirements either." She hooked her finger toward Leo. On command, he leaned down to her, his face close to hers. "He will need to be taken care of."

Leo nodded, but I quickly intervened, seeing Howe's murder

being clearly planned out. "Maia, Agent Howe is no longer with the FBI and he is currently attempting to hack the Bureau's firewall so he can locate where they are storing the Soul Gear. He and James are the ones who noticed that Christian's computer system, Halee, may've been hacked. They rebooted the system, but I think it was Waite who was the hacker. I'd bet anything he was looking for the Soul Gear."

Maia went absolutely still, her gaze like molten fire aimed at me. She spoke slowly, venom in her words. "Why, exactly, would you think the FBI has the Soul Gear?"

I shifted on my feet, "Well, uh – Agent Howe here showed me a white gear that was recovered from a safe buried in the floor of your sister's shop. The Feds found it after the fire. It had the atom markings on it."

Maia slowly rose from her seat as I continued talking, though my insides were squirming. "While it sucks the Feds have the Gear, you seem, uh . . . alarmingly pissed about this information."

"I am going to bloody well STRANGLE Midas Fagan!" seethed Maia. "That self-centered, ego-maniac has no business running his family's legacy! He was entrusted with the Gear and he GAVE IT TO MY SISTER?" Maia let fly a string of profanity that could make even Kian blush. "When I get my hands on that skinny, two-timing, greedy little snake I'm gonna strip the scales from his tail and use 'em for BINGO CHIPS!"

Tail? BINGO CHIPS? "Who the heck are we talking about?" I asked.

Before Maia could answer, Raef's voice cut her off, "Wait a minute. Fagan? As in THE Fagan clan of New Orleans? Why in the HELL would the Wreckers be in possession of the Soul Gear?"

Maia slammed her hand on the table, causing the pens and

pencils to flee in opposite directions. "Because their vault is unbreakable. Because the Soul Gear is the rarest item on the face of the planet. BECAUSE HE'D NEVER GET RID OF IT! Dalca must've won the damn thing, probably at Mayhem. She must've put up something HUGE as collateral for Midas to have been willing to gamble losing it . . . WHICH HE DID, THE IDIOT!"

Kian's eyes narrowed on Maia, "That's how I recognize the wards on the wall! Your version of *vindícamus ser múri* is in the Wrecker's language! You're using enchantments from those freaks? Are you kidding me?"

"WHO THE HELL ARE THE WRECKERS?" I howled, sick of being in the dark.

"Mermaids," Raef replied.

"Assholes," added Kian.

M.J.

CHAPTER 26
FAUST, NEW BEDFORD, MA

I had followed Nikki through the door she had escaped through, thinking it would lead me to a small room. Instead, I found myself in an equally huge garage, the same as the one I'd just came from, but with one startling difference: the trains.

At least a dozen massive steam engines stood lined up in the darkness, towering over the space like sleeping iron beasts. They formed a wall of ash-covered horsepower, splendid in their craftsmanship and various angles and smooth edges. Rivets the size of my fist lined the front engine barrels and faded brass tags attached to the sides declared each engine's number.

I had no clue they were so huge. Never knew the smoky beasts I'd only seen in pictures and in westerns would easily dwarf my family's ice cream shop. Awed, I stepped up to the nearest engine, running my hand slowly over the rough surface of a rust-caked wheel easily the same height as me. "Damn," I breathed.

"Impressive, aren't they?" asked Nikki, appearing from between two other engines. Her fingers trailed over the iron hide of Engine 626, as if caressing a friend for the first time in years. "I found this place by accident when we were here with Rillin. When we removed his link. While you were busy with Leo, I came down looking for tools, and stumbled in here. I think this was the original mechanic's shop where they were repaired."

She came to a stop next to me, looking up at the engine I was admiring. In the darkness, her profile seemed to be cut from the essence of beauty itself, her long hair hanging in a loose braid down her back. "It's a shame the world has moved on from engines like this. I get that they spew coal smoke and aren't exactly earth-friendly, but they are magnificent. They shouldn't be hidden down here, away from the world. They need to be appreciated, maybe in a museum somewhere, so people can remember how steel and iron really did form America."

"Basically, they need to be on display so we don't forget our history, eh?" I asked, and Nikki turned to me. I realized then that she had tear stains on her face. My anger at Maia surfaced again. "I'm sorry about Maia – she shouldn't have said what she did. Are you alright?"

Nikki just shrugged, wiping her face roughly with her hand to remove any sign of her sadness. While the move did scatter her tears, it left behind streaks of dirt and coal ash. "She's not really wrong though, is she?" asked Nikki, oblivious to her face. "I mean, my parents are just . . . shit. They're just crappy people."

"I'm really sorry, Nik. We don't get to pick our parents."

Nikki looked back at the train, her jaw hard. "No. I guess we don't."

We stood in silence for a moment, but then she finally turned back to me, her voice having lost its sharpness. For once, she actually looked scared. "What am I gonna do, MJ?" she asked, her voice a whisper. "I don't have a home to go back to. I have some savings, but . . . I'm freakin' eighteen! I've got no job, no clue if I got into any of the colleges I applied to and, hell, I'm not sure I can even afford to go anymore. How do I explain my situation to ANYONE? And now the police are looking for me?" She started breathing faster, her hand trembling as she spoke, panic starting to choke her. "What do I do? Jeezus, do I hide for the rest of my life so the Feds don't know that I'm a bloody mutant? Do I leave the country? WHAT AM I GONNA DO?"

Heartbroken for her, I moved without thinking and grabbed her in a bear hug, holding her tightly against me. "We will figure it out and I sure as shit am not letting you fall through the cracks. No matter what, YOU are going to be okay. We all are," I rested my chin on the top of her head. I felt her eventually nod.

"Trust us?" I asked, and she shifted, tilting her head so she could look up at me.

"I trusted my parents and look where that got me," she replied quietly, her sweet face in a devastated frown.

I swallowed hard, my heart and head warring between need and caution. "Then just trust *me*," I whispered and proceeded to do the dumbest thing humanly possible: I kissed Nikki Shea. I kissed her like her lips were my own personal vaccine against all the crap that was going on in our lives.

For just a fraction of a second, she didn't respond.

But then she suddenly gripped the back of my shirt so tightly I thought it would rip in two. With her injured arm pinned between our bodies, Nikki Shea kissed me like the epic goddess I knew she was.

I stepped back with her body fused to mine, my spine colliding with the train's front platform, just above the cowcatcher. Every breath shared between us seemed to amplify the desire running through my veins, and I thought I was literally burning up from the inside out – as if my body was funneling an electric buzz that I wanted louder and wilder. But then she pulled back, breathing hard, her eyes wide and her lips lush.

I blinked, unsure if she suddenly realized I was MJ Williams – the ice cream worker and goof-ball sidekick to Ana Lane. I was an extra in life. The one nobody really gave notice to, until Eila Walker crashed into my corner of the world.

I thought Nik had come to her senses and realized that making out with the school dweeb was NOT what she wanted, but then she started pulling the massive sweatshirt over her head, the slow slide of gray cotton over her body like a dangerous tease that called to the vibrating in my bones. Distantly, I thought I heard that same *purr*, but it was deeper, rougher . . . as if lust had evolved into its own being within my skin, pacing restlessly and hungrily for the steel-wielding vixen in front of me.

Free of the sweatshirt, she tossed it onto the lip of the cowcatcher and began trying to unwrap her arm. My skin felt as though it was too tight for my body, but I tried desperately to focus on Nikki. "What are you doing?" I demanded, but my voice had grown rough, almost unrecognizable.

Nikki's gaze darkened as she smiled, pushing against me once again as she delicately drew her lips across mine. In that moment, I knew my entire existence would've happily been sacrificed in her name, over and over, should she demand it.

"Help me get out of this sling, Williams, so I can touch you," she whispered against my lips.

Oh my *GOD*, if I was dreaming nobody better wake me up or I'd *KILL* em!

CHAPTER 27
FAUST, NEW BEDFORD, MA

Supernatural hearing has its perks, but listening to MJ and Nikki partake in a make-out session was not one of them. Though I'd kept my focus on the heated conversation going on between Maia and Eila, I had also kept one ear tuned to Nikki and MJ. I stopped paying attention, however, when I detected their first gasps and lip-smacking mania.

Some things I just don't need to know. Ever.

"Look, I knew Fagan's crew to be in possession of the Soul Gear because Sula Lane told me that her FBI partner had seen it there. And I figured that Midas, being the greedy little turd he is, would keep it safe. Wreckers are like aquatic Leprechauns - they love their treasures and they don't give up on such trinkets easily. If you think Christian's vault was built like a fortress, it pales in comparison to the vault at Mayhem."

"My . . . my mom knew these mermaid people?" asked Ana, her voice small.

"She did . . . because of me. I introduced her to a young man named Kai Marlowe. He was a Wrecker who worked for Midas as a bootlegger. A transporter, if you will, of high-end whiskey moonshine. Bane worked with him."

Ana paled. "Wait - WHAT?"

"You introduced Sula Lane to a Mayhem bootlegger?" demanded Kian, glancing at Ana a bit sideways. "Are you crazy?"

Maia muttered a few curses, "Oh, for God's sake, we don't have time for this. I used to buy River Whiskey from Midas Fagan for years and years. It was delivered to me by Kai Marlowe and Bane, both of them transporters for Midas' thriving booze business. Mind you - we're talking nearly twenty years ago. It was when Faust first opened to the Mortis. Nights were long, the work endless. My crew and I were stuck here at all hours, determined to make this nightclub a success. I'd order the whiskey for us - for the Lessers and the humans. It was a way for us all to celebrate our successes and unwind after a long night. Plus, if you drank it and were sheared by any of the Mortis workers, the soul thieves would get a buzz as well." Her eyes darted to Leo for a fraction of a second, but he kept his poker face well in place.

I couldn't believe this insanity.

The Mortis and the Wreckers couldn't stand one another, and Faust was in business with them? "So you do business . . . with . . . with . . . THE WRECKERS?"

"I *did* business with the Wreckers, past tense. I stopped a few years back."

"Why?" asked Kian, eyes narrowed.

Maia crossed her arms, defiant. "We started stocking River Whiskey for the human patrons when we opened the club to them, roughly three and a half years ago."

"Good Lord, you are insane!" snapped Kian. "That stuff is potent. Drink too much of it and you are six feet under in the blink of an eye!"

Maia nodded, "Yes, but the humans loved it. Let's face it, Wrecker moonshine is like nothing out there on the human markets. But two summers ago, we had five human patrons nearly die after drinking the whiskey. We were able to save them all, but two sisters had to be turned into Mortis to save them - Eris and Imogen. After the change, they were unable to blend back in with the human world, so I gave them jobs here. They were wonderful employees. They were family, until . . ."

Maia took a breath, calming her anger. She had no doubt been told what had happened to Eris. Last I'd heard, Imogen had left the building last night, with the body of her sister, devastated. "Anyway, I cut ties with Midas after a decade and a half of doing business. He was furious about it. He said it wasn't his fault and that his cocaine supplier had dumped him out of the blue. He said he went with someone else's stock, which obviously wasn't as pure as the coca leaves he'd been getting. He told me it wouldn't happen again, but I still wouldn't buy his whiskey anymore."

Eila blinked. "Did you say . . . cocaine?"

Maia nodded, "River Whiskey made by Wreckers is like nothing else."

"Damn," muttered E.

Ana pointed at Maia. "YOU are going to tell me everything you know about my mother. NOW," she demanded. "I am OWED that much."

Maia laughed, "You are owed *nothing* - you think you've suffered alone? We've all suffered. We all carry war wounds, on the surface and in our minds. Just because you suffered, doesn't entitle you to a sliver of respect."

Kian's skin bled with his Fallen Marks as he stepped in front of Ana. "You will give Ana the information you have. Now. Sula Lane is dead. Her partner is dead. Any promises that you made or didn't make to Ana's mother are pointless now. Ana's been dragged into her mother's world, so hiding secrets protects no one."

Leo, having moved into a defensive position in front of Maia, glanced to his boss to see what she wanted to do. Maia watched us silently for a moment before muttering something unintelligible under her breath, her fingers creeping toward her neck to disentangle one of the delicate chains that remained tucked in her bustier. She finally pulled it free of her cleavage, revealing an aged skeleton key dangling from the length. It twisted slowly back and forth for a moment before she yanked it hard, breaking the clasp and freeing the delicate key from her body.

"Ana. Eila. Follow me," she demanded, shoving out of her seat and moving past the table. "The rest of you stay here."

Kian and Raef started to protest, but Maia halted, her glare like fire. "These terms are non-negotiable. STAY HERE." Her look traveled to Leo, who seemed concerned that Maia was going without him. "I'll be fine," she said quietly.

He reached out and grasped her hand briefly, then Maia left the room, Ana and Eila in tow.

Howe looked over Baz's laptop at Leo, Kian, and me. "Can I just say that I'm really not comfortable being down here with you three." His eyes landed back on me, "And I'd like to opt for that vaccine thing right about now."

CHAPTER 28

FAUST, NEW BEDFORD, MA

We trailed after Maia, following her back up to the catwalks that towered over the dance floor, the small glass beads embroidered into her skirt's edge skipping over the spiderwebbed steel like dented jingle bells. The sound seemed excessively loud in the cavernous space, yet too delicate for the killer club. Across from us was Nikki's twisted catwalk, and Maia's boarded-up office, the smell of smoke and ash still floating in the air despite the vents working like mad.

Maia suddenly turned onto an adjoining catwalk and pushed into another room, barely waiting for us to keep up. I quickly grabbed the edge of the door before it slammed shut behind her, my fingers digging into the tangle of skulls and roses engraved in its ebony surface. Decadence and darkness were the hallmarks of Faust. Even the doors were no exception, all of them a perfect reflection of her brazen, twisted beauty.

I blinked rapidly, trying to adjust my eyes to the dark room, and Ana nearly slammed into me from behind. "Jeez, where's the lights?"

"We don't need a light," said Maia, and I realized she was yanking back a rug from the floor. My eyes finally accepted the blackness of the space and I could make out a trapdoor in the floor.

Maia inserted the key into a lock embedded in the floor and whispered words I couldn't recognize as she turned the key. I stiffened as a delicate web of firelight swept outward from the door, like a ring of ripples in a pool. It faded away as it seeped further from the lock.

"What the hell was that?" Ana demanded, eyeing the floorboards beneath our feet warily, as if the red stuff could reappear on our sneakers.

"A very old curse, designed to protect the lock," she replied, easing open the trapdoor. It groaned, the old hinges protesting the movement, as if they hadn't seen use in many years. Maia set the door down and glanced up at me, "It is similar to the curse that protects your home, Eila. It draws from the same principals that bar all Mortis from entering a human's home without the owner's permission."

"That's . . . kinda creepy," I replied, but I also knew the protective curse on 408 had been deactivated once, allowing a dangerous Mortis to slip into my home. "Ya know, just FYI, I wouldn't hold too much faith in those protective curse doohickies, 'cause my house was royally screwed over by Dalca's enchanted witch ball."

"Dalca practiced witchcraft, sometimes good, sometimes bad. She was quite accomplished when she was alive, but, well, let's just say that I am far better versed in the casting of curses and the use of talismans."

"You use witchcraft as a bokor? That's the black magic Raef was talking about?" I asked, unnerved by the smile she offered.

"No. I don't practice the witchcraft that my sister did."

Ana crossed her arms, "Oh yeah? Well you dabble in something seriously questionable, 'cause I sure as shit didn't hallucinate the red oil slick that just oozed outta your lock and then did a total Houdini."

"I'm a *vodouisant*." she replied, dipping her hands into the hole in the floor and producing a small box.

"Vodoo? You practice Vodoo?" I asked, sorta horrified. All I could think of was those dolls that people stabbed with needles. Actually, that would be awesome for Waite . . .

Maia got to her feet and came over to Ana and me. "I practice the purest form of the religion, so you'd be wise to ditch the idea of dolls and pins and animal sacrifice."

"I didn't say anything!" I protested, but Maia just glared at me.

She handed Ana the box. "This is for me?" my pal asked.

Maia nodded and Ana opened the box. In it was a gold ring and a worn leather wallet. Ana eased the leather apart and sucked in a breath as a golden badge was revealed alongside Sula Lane's FBI credentials. "My mom's stuff. Her badge and . . . her wedding band."

"Where'd you get this?" I demanded.

Maia rubbed her brow, the edge of her finger catching the ring in her eyebrow for a moment. "Sula was a talented Reloader. A brilliant Sway. Initially, I'd sometimes run into her when a human murder was tied to a Mortis. Sula knew she was working in a gray area of the Bureau, especially given her ability. It didn't take long for her to realize that she couldn't bring a Mortis to the Feds, so she started coming to me and Leo and well . . . we'd intervene. It was best for all parties to keep our worlds from becoming public knowledge to the humans. Sula made me promise I'd never let any of this knowledge reach you or your father. She made me swear to keep her life as an FBI detective hidden, even if she was killed in the line of duty. She wanted you safe – she wanted you to never know this type of life."

Ana rubbed her thumb over the badge, tracing the engraved eagle perched at the top. "Whose idea was it to spin the story that she left Dad and me? That she was an addict? Who dreamt up that lie?"

"Sula," Maia replied. "She believed it would ensure that you would never come looking for her should anything happen to her. She believed that such a betrayal – to love an addiction more than a daughter – would hurt enough that you'd not try to find her. Ever."

"How ironic," whispered Ana. It hit me then that Ana lived that exact life with her alcoholic father, a man who loved the bottle more than he loved his daughter. Ana took a slow, deep breath and finally nodded. "Thank you. For giving them back to me."

I cleared my throat. "Just so I fully understand all of this, you're saying that Sula thinned the Mortis killers from the human ones . . . and then gave you their names?"

Maia began to pace the room. "Yes. We were judge, jury and executioner as needed for the Mortis who found themselves trapped by Sula's ability. To be honest, most were warned to simply keep their kills off the radar. We only executed those who were becoming true serial killers."

Ana looked down at her mother's belongings and lifted the wedding ring from the box. She slipped it onto her index finger, not far from Kian's ring. "So why didn't you just give these things to me when we first came to Faust? Or even after the fight with Booth?"

Maia shifted her weight, looking tense. "What I am about to tell both of you is known to very, VERY few people. This information must be guarded – it cannot leave your circle of fighters, Eila."

"Okay," I replied slowly. "What is it?"

"As I said before, I'd been a loyal buyer of Midas' whiskey from the very beginnings of Faust. He'd send up Kai and Bane from his stills in Louisiana to deliver my order. The very first time I met Kai, I knew he was unique, even among the Wreckers. I could feel the density of his magic, as if time itself paused at his presence. It took me a while to figure out what he was and when I did, I knew Sula could use him. He could be so much more than a delivery boy for supernatural booze. He could be so much more than a mere bootlegger."

"He wasn't a Wrecker?" Ana asked, clutching her mom's badge.

"He was, and so much more. He was what our world refers to as a Forsythe. He could see the future in a narrow scope. Such ability can be present in any person of supernatural descent, but it is incredibly rare. So rare that most of us will never meet a Forsythe in all our lifetime."

My eyes widened. "You're saying Kai could see the actual future? He could literally see what was going to happen fifty years from now?"

Maia shook her head. "No, not that far ahead. More like a snapshot of what was about to come for the person he was in contact with. Sometimes he had a longer lead time, a couple hours or days. Other times it was more limited – a matter of seconds. I set up a time for them to meet and they just . . . clicked. Immediately. They liked each other, they were well matched. Kai agreed to leave Midas as long as Bane was able to also leave the Wreckers and come work for me. Midas was pissed, but I paid him well for the inconvenience of losing Kai and Bane. And because Sula's record on the homicide squad was so flawless, she was able to appoint Kai to work for her. But, as I said, no one can ever know that her partner was a Forsythe. If people ever found out, his genetic line would be worth a fortune if they showed even a trace of his ability."

Ana stared at Maia, stunned. "He had a kid?"

Maia finally stopped pacing. "I believe he did."

I rubbed my forehead, "So, you matched them up to work with one another to solve crimes?"

"More for Sula's benefit and safety, actually," Maia replied. "Understand that Sula had been working with Leo and me for a year at that point, but I felt that she needed protection because of her ability. If killers knew that their dead victims could speak to a homicide detective past the grave, then that detective would be hunted. Constantly. Kai had the ability to see danger coming. He became her eyes forward, while Sula became the eyes of the past. Together they were an incredible team. At least, until they were both murdered."

I raised a hand, "Wait, wait. If Kai could see the future, how did he not see their murderer coming?" I glanced at Ana, judging how well she was taking this info. While Ana didn't really remember much of her mother, Sula having been murdered when Ana was only two years old, this was still tough to hear. "How'd they end up executed?"

"Up until tonight, I could never figure it out. But now, with the knowledge of Therophel, it is fairly obvious that he, most likely, killed Sula and Kai. I doubt even a Forsythe could've seen an archangel's intentions," Maia replied. She looked at Ana. "I'm giving you these items because if your mother was still alive, she would want you to have them. And, with any luck, they will show you, once and for all, your mother's life . . . and her death."

"I don't understand how her badge and wedding ring can show me such things," Ana replied.

"These items were on Sula during peaks of emotion, both good and bad. As such, they carry an imprint of those moments, like snapshots, crafted from the most vivid parts of her life, her death included. It can be felt by those of Wrecker blood. It is why they are such talented thieves - why they plunder and destroy so many ships. Wreckers can actually read the treasures they find, as if the gold whispers secrets to them. Your mother was a Sway, Ana. You were looking for answers about your ability. I believe that seeing the past through your mother's memories may help you. These items may help you understand who you truly are."

"So these . . . these are my mom, basically," Ana asked, her voice small. Maia nodded.

I shifted beside my friend. "Do you have a Wrecker on staff now? That could, like, read these items?"

"I suspect I'm looking at one."

"What are you talking about?" whispered Ana.

Maia smiled a bit as she crossed her arms, eyeing my friend. "You look very much like your mother, Ana, but you also look exactly like Kai Marlowe."

I just stared at Ana, my mouth hanging open.

CHAPTER 29
FAUST, NEW BEDFORD, MA

I pressed a kiss against Nikki's lips once again, that strange electrical buzz nearly deafening in my mind as I started helping her out of the wrap. Each strip of fabric slowly revealed her creamy skin and fabulous cherry-red bra as it tumbled free from her lush curves and pooled like ribbons of soft serve ice cream on the concrete floor.

Man, if I thought the collector's edition of *Close Encounters* I'd gotten for my last birthday was the best gift ever, I was woefully misguided. Because heaven, I'd discovered, was Nikki Shea, in a bra the color of Kool-Aid and a pair of low-riding Levi's, her hair like a rope of auburn fire swaying between her shoulder blades.

Amen – and I mean *A-FREAKIN-MEN* – for curvy high school girls.

I eased the final knot from the end of the fabric, freeing Nik of her bandages once and for all. Carefully, I ran my hand down her formerly injured arm, the incision near her collarbone now nothing more than a light pink line. I swallowed, trying to keep my brain functioning as I asked, "How's it feel?"

"Okay," she replied, glancing at her arm.

"Can you lift it?"

She slowly raised her arms, sliding them over my shoulders and behind my neck as she drew herself to me once again. I studied her face, noting how the very edge of her top lip tilted down, and how the end of her nose had the smallest uplift to it. Carefully, I placed my hands just above her waistband, drawing my palms slowly up the soft curves of her body and along the valley of her spine. Under my scrutiny, Nikki's cockiness slipped away and she looked uncertain.

The girl who dominated the school - who never showed weakness - was suddenly less confident in my arms. I settled my hands around her back, letting my fingers make lazy circles on her skin. "What's wrong?" I asked, my voice slowly coming back to normal.

She twisted her lips, as if thinking, "You're not like anybody else I know."

I raised an eyebrow. "Because my alter ego is a dog, you mean."

She shook her head. "No. I mean, well, yeah, but . . . I meant, somehow you just . . . you see *me*, but you don't care about all the flaws."

My amusement fell. "Nobody's perfect, but I don't see flaws, Nik. I see a map of survival. We all have them, these things you call flaws, but they only become flaws if we allow them to wreck us. Or worse, if we ignore how they got there in the first place. Your parents - they chose to never acknowledge their own flaws, and now . . ."

Nikki's lip trembled and she tucked it between her teeth, trying to maintain control.

I sighed, drawing my thumb across her mouth. "It's okay to have flaws. We're supposed to have 'em – they make us *better* people. And you don't have to hide your heartbreak from me. You don't have to carry all the bad stuff on your own. If you'll trust me, if you'll let me, I'll carry some of it for you." I drew my hand along her cheek, whispering, "But know that you are perfect to me."

I kissed her then, softly, gently, forming both a promise and an offering - my heart laid out for her to take. "Let me in, Nik. I swear you won't regret it."

Her hand slid from my shoulder, curving around my jaw as she kissed me back, just as sweetly. "Don't break my heart, MJ Williams."

"Never," I replied, my hands returning to their roving, the buzzing building again in my head, and the burn radiating through my body. I could feel her skin pebble with goosebumps, and I realized that without the sweatshirt, she was probably freezing. I kissed her one more time, then eased her away from me. She looked confused.

"You're cold," I explained, pulling my own Metallica sweatshirt over my head, leaving me in just a t-shirt.

She smiled a little. "I'm okay."

"You're cold. And *my* girl gets *my* sweatshirt if she's cold. Whatever she needs, whatever she wants, I can provide . . . especially ice cream," I replied, tugging the sweatshirt over her head. She snuggled into the fabric, smiling wide.

"It's warm," she sniffed it, "and doesn't smell like dog! I'm shocked!"

"Listen, Little Miss Snarky Pants - I only smell like dog when I AM a dog, sheesh."

She giggled - actually GIGGLED - but then the cavernous space plunged into darkness.

I could feel Nikki shift away from me, her focus no longer on our prior kissfest. “Maybe it’s the storm. Maybe it knocked out the power,” she whispered beside me, her voice a disembodied spirit in the absolute blackness of the garage. I couldn’t even see the train towering in front of me anymore, the lack of light was so absolute.

“Probably,” I replied, though a small part of me had a terrible feeling that something was just . . . off. Though I knew the blizzard raged over New Bedford, railing and howling against the buildings, the wind could barely be heard inside Faust, her sturdy, century-old brick and mortar easily withstanding the worst that nature could yield. But that same burn that had ignited in my bones when Nikki was in my arms started all over again – stronger, hotter. Something within my skin seemed to flex and stretch, as if sensing the “offness” of the room – how the darkness seemed too absolute.

“Nik . . .” I growled, my voice once again having transformed into something unrecognizable to my own ears. “Nikki, we need to get back with Eila. I . . . *shit!*”

Pain slammed through my back, as if all my muscles were tightening against my will. My skin warred between fire and ice, between pain and ecstasy. I was shifting, but the phase was entirely out of my control . . . and whatever was breaking free of my soul wasn’t Marsh. The simple, familiar Shuk form was nowhere in this transformation, and Rillin’s theories of my Alpha form coming forward made me fight back against the shift.

“MJ? What’s wrong?” demanded Nikki, and I could hear her move in my direction, my hearing far more advanced, no doubt due to the *thing* inside me that was trying to override my human body.

“STOP! Don’t . . don’t come near me,” I begged. My voice cut through the darkness, coming out angry, yet desperate. Pain tore down my arms as muscle and bone began to shift, and I said a small prayer that I would maintain control of the creature that was demanding to break free.

I fought the shift, focusing on pulling back against the thing inside me, but my humanity was sliding away from me like the outgoing tide. I was terrified of what would be revealed once my human side was entirely gone. I was terrified I'd hurt Nikki. That she'd finally see me for the true freak of nature that I was.

I could hear her, still speaking to me, desperate for me to answer. I could hear her hand trailing along the edge of the train, trying to navigate her way to me through the darkness. I tried to yell at her, to force her away, but my voice had disappeared, replaced by a snarling sound that chilled me to the bone.

But then, between my ragged breathing and Nikki's voice, I heard something *else* in the room.

Something that sounded like sand pouring down the concrete . . . sliding along the walls.

Nikki stopped speaking, as if she too heard it. I could sense her shifting on her feet, not far from me, the sound of metal and rust rubbing against one another, a sure signal that Nik was arming herself, probably with a piece of the train itself.

I could hear Nikki swallow as she asked the darkness, "Eila? Is that you?"

In reply, the sound of a man's low chuckle traveled through the darkness like a poisoned breeze. The shift inside me seemed to pause, as if my Alpha form was also listening. Waiting.

I didn't recognize the voice.

Nikki stopped moving as well, as if she, too, realized that whoever was with us was a stranger. The sound of sand running across the floor started again, and I swear the room felt as though the temperature dropped twenty degrees in a matter of seconds. Next to me, Nikki took a trembling breath, and in that moment I *knew*.

I could feel *him* – his pure, unearthly power flexing and pulsing in the blackness.

"RUN!" I roared to Nikki, and she scrambled for the door as I threw myself into the shift, my Alpha form crashing over me like a furious wave.

CHAPTER 30

FAUST, NEW BEDFORD, MA

"As I was saying," continued Kian, trying to keep his mind busy in the absence of his fiancée, "the second attack on Polaris makes far more sense with Nikki's belief that that Gate needs water."

I crossed my arms, rubbing the slight stubble on my chin. The three of us had been dissecting Nikki's water theory since the girls disappeared with Maia, trying to figure out where Therophel may've stashed the Gate. At first it seemed an impossible task since the face of the earth is mighty damn big, until Kian and I came up with the idea of the second Polaris raid and the possible reasons for it.

"So you think Therophel's Linked fighters came after Polaris to seize Christian's vault? You think they want the space in which this ship you speak of, *True North*, is housed?" asked Leo.

Kian and I nodded, but Leo was a hard sell on the theory. "If that's true, then how did Therophel even know about the vault to begin with?"

I stepped up to the table, resting my hand on the French book. I knew exactly how Therophel knew about the vault, and I knew who had let the cat out of the bag. "It had to be Rillin," I replied. "He'd been inside the vault with us. When he was taken by Sara Booth, and Nikki's father reactivated his Link, Rillin would've been at their mercy. I guarantee that they squeezed every last ounce of knowledge from him, thanks to Sara Booth's Sway ability, before they sent him back to attack us. That's why the second attack on the island happened *after* Rillin was taken – they learned about the vault from him."

Leo raised an eyebrow, starting to buy the theory, but then his face fell. "Maia told me that Elizabeth had been housed in Christian's vault. If Therophel knows about the vault from Rillin, then he knows about Elizabeth as well."

Shit. I didn't think of that.

The room fell silent, the knowledge that we were seriously in over our heads an undeniable truth. "We've got to get out of here," I warned. "If Maia is right, and Elizabeth is storing some of Therophel's power, then he may try to somehow reclaim it. He must know by now that the body is no longer in the vault."

Kian swore sharply, "What if Eris happened to see Elizabeth's body here? What if she reported back to Therophel before the explosion? Before she died?"

Fury laced my words, "Good grief, we've been just . . . sitting here. Like targets."

"ENOUGH!" demanded Leo. "Maia's had the club warded against the supernatural. The club will hold!"

Kian spun on Leo, "Oh yeah? Does that supernatural category

included fallen archangels, 'cause I'm thinking you don't get too many of them hawking cookies at the front door!"

Howe cleared his throat from his spot in the truck, "Uh, guys. Not that this whole conversation isn't perfect for ensuring that I will have nightmares for the next fifty years, but I've got information on the Gear thing, if you're interested."

"We have bigger problems at the moment, Marcus," snapped Kian.

Howe, however, sat up straighter, irritated at Kian's tone. "Well, O'Reilly, you'll be happy to know that I don't think the gear is a problem at all, 'cause according to forensics, it's made outta china. Possibly manufactured in India."

"It's not *real* bone?" I demanded.

Howe shrugged. "Hey, I'm just reporting what's here in the file. It's a combination of a few different things, but it's porcelain . . . just not the crappy kind found at discount stores, mind you, but it's basically dish-ware for the wealthy."

Leo blinked. "Where the HELL is the real Soul Gear?" he demanded.

"Maybe Therophel already has it? He'd hired Dalca after all. Maybe he swapped it at some point. Maybe he didn't entirely trust her and used the fake gear as a way to tempt her and test her allegiance," offered Kian.

"Or Dalca did barter for the Soul Gear with the Wreckers, but they screwed her over and gave her a fake," I replied.

"That makes way more sense. Damn Wreckers don't exactly believe in honesty, but they are brilliant at the whole bait-and-switch thing," Leo said. "For once in my life, I'm glad they are shady little shits."

"Do you think Maia can negotiate a deal with the Wreckers to get the Soul Gear?" asked Kian.

I shook my head. "The Soul Gear, made of Aztael's essence, is one of a kind. A piece of angelic power so rare that nothing would be worth the trade. Dalca was just too stupid to realize that."

"Yeah, well - I can think of another item that is one of a kind; Sparky herself," Kian replied with a snarky grin.

While I knew he was kidding, there was no way trading Eila for the Gear was going to happen.

Howe, listening from the armored truck, dared to weigh in, "I'm, uh, just thinking out loud here, and really quite horrified that I'm now theorizing on shit that should really be kept to Stephen King books, but isn't it a good thing that this critical Gear is guarded so well? And for that matter, wouldn't these Wreckers, God help me, be equally interested in destroying this Gate if it meant their own history was also on the line? Would they hand it over to us, if it meant their survival? Maybe even help fight Therophel?"

"That's . . . well, not such a totally rotten idea," replied Kian, as he and I exchanged a surprised look. Howe, it seemed, could be a bit insightful on rare occasion. But there was one big obstacle that went along with his idea: the Mortis and the Wreckers HATED one another.

Leo was definitely not of the same mind, however. He laughed, "Mortis and Wreckers working together? Please - the fact that you are even debating the idea as feasible just goes to reaffirm that your decision-making process leaves something to be desired."

"We came here, didn't we?" demanded Kian.

"And the police are currently searching for Nikita because her HOUSE exploded and a desk was ripped out the second floor balcony!" retorted Leo.

"He's got a point," muttered Howe.

Kian pointed a sharp finger at Howe. "YOU stay out of this!" he ordered, his attention swinging back to Leo. "That Gear is a critical part of the Gate. Therophel is going to want it, which means we need to grab it first!"

"And what if Therophel gets the upper hand and steals the Soul Gear from us? What if he is able to restart the Gabriel Gate with Eila's power, and jump back in time?" Leo shook her head, "No, I'm for leaving the Soul Gear with the Wreckers. Maia's right - their vault can't be cracked. You can't steal from the ultimate thieves."

"I swear, Elizabeth better have a step-by-step plan for killing Therophel the second she wakes up," muttered Kian.

"If she wakes," snapped Leo.

"There has to be another – " Kian's voice cut short as the power died, causing the room to plunge into darkness. Above us, on the dance hall level, the sounds of the fans powering down echoed through the building, as did the voices of the workers, calling out to one another in the dark.

I sighed. "Terrific. Can anything else go wrong?"

"Gotta be the storm," Leo replied. "I'll go check the breakers - see if something tripped." He walked off, no doubt to check the power panels somewhere in Faust. Howe, still in the truck, opened the laptop wider and swiveled it in the direction of the table, offering us a weak halo of light.

Beside me, Kian was muttering something about his renewed hatred of New England winters, but I was only half listening. Instead, I'd turned my focus back to the room Nik and MJ had escaped to, noting that they'd gone quiet. Actually, the room was entirely silent, as if they weren't even in there anymore.

"Hey - can you hear MJ and Nikki?" I asked Kian.

He eyed me over the table. "Do I have to? I checked out the second Dog Boy dropped the whole 'trust me' line and I heard the first kiss. All SET on that nightmare, thanks."

"I'm serious, damn it! I can't hear them. At all."

Kian rolled his eyes, but reluctantly focused his attention on the wall near us. At first he seemed bored, but then he stiffened. "Are you sure they are still in there? Is there another way out of that room?" he asked, clearly unable to hear anything either.

I shook my head, starting for the room, "I don't think so. The only staircase out of here is the one we came down. Something's up."

"Yeah, well it better not be MJ's – "

A brutal roar shattered the quiet of the garage, a roar so deafening it was like a knife through my skull. Kian, stunned by the sound, doubled over trying to cover his ears, just as the door to the room exploded off its hinges.

The massive door slammed into the armored truck, sending the vehicle smashing into the far wall with Howe inside. It left a gaping hole in the side of the building, wind and snow howling across the crumpled edge of the truck. I couldn't even see Howe in the driver's seat anymore. The window and cab were crushed like a tin can.

"MJ!" I yelled as another roar filled the building. I went to run for the room, but stopped short as one of Maia's massive gargoyles, very alive and very furry, burst through the doorway, Nikki Shea right by its side.

And behind them both was a creature made of smoke and fury.

CHAPTER 31

FAUST, NEW BEDFORD, MA

Ana remained frozen in place for a moment, until reality kicked in. She looked at Maia, incredulous. "Are you shitting me right now? This is a joke, right?"

Maia shook her head.

"You're saying my mom got knocked up by a mermaid?!"

Maia was about to say something else, but then she startled, stepping back from Ana quickly as if she'd been zapped by static electricity.

"Uh, Maia? You okay? I asked, but instead of answering me, she seemed to fall into a weird sorta trance. Slowly, as she backed up into the room, she raised her hands in front of her, as if she was feeling the air – as if she was feeling an invisible wall in front of her.

"Maia? What's going on?" I asked, but sucked in a tight breath when the air around us slowly began to glow, as if a thousand small fireflies came to life in the air, drifting softly around us. Ana let out a squeak as one slid past her face, but Maia was moving her hands slowly, like a conductor taking on a symphony that had yet to be defined. The little lights pulsed a few times, slowly turning from white to crimson. But then Maia gasped and the fireflies fell to the floor in a glittering explosion, leaving red dust scattered across the floor.

"WHAT the HELL?" Ana cursed, jumping back, but Maia was already on the move. She spun hard towards the door, grabbing us both by our arms and dragging us with her. "What the heck was THAT? Where are we going?" my friend demanded, while I tried not to trip and fall on my face.

Maia shoved us onto the catwalk, and I felt as though I'd fallen into a black abyss as every light in Faust went out. "Did we lose power?" I asked, trying to feel for the railing.

"GO. HURRY! Tell Rillin and Baz to hide Elizabeth!"

"What? Why?" I pressed, feeling Ana's hand finally clutch mine in the darkness.

"We've been breached," hissed Maia. "Something powerful - inhuman - has entered the building. I can hear the wards speaking to one another. I can sense the dark magic that flows between them and holds Faust safe against the outside world. It's like a spider's web, but I can *feel* it . . . and something powerful just caused the entire web to tremble. We've been breached. I'm sure of it."

"Breached? What do you mean breached? I thought Faust was like a freakin' fortress! You said nothing could get through the wards!"

I could sense Maia looking at me in the darkness, and her voice turned quiet, chilling in its lack of emotion. "I underestimated his power."

I swallowed, "You mean *Therophel*? Therophel is HERE?"

"I can't allow him to succeed," she whispered, a freaky tone to her voice that set my nerves on edge. I could hear the bells of her skirt slide along the catwalk, the sound coming closer to me as she moved. "You cannot be taken alive. The Gate cannot become operational."

"What are you talking about?" I asked, my instincts stirring and the fighter inside me beginning to rise. At the sound of steel sliding against leather, I knew I was in trouble.

Quickly, I called the Light to my veins. The glow of my ability filled the small space between us on the catwalk with a haunting white haze. A few feet from me, and entirely tinted in the strange aura of my Light stood Maia, a curved dagger gripped in her hand, her gaze locked on me.

"Maia . . . what the Hell are you doing?" asked Ana, but I used my arm to push my pal behind me. I would not lose Ana, nor would I fail Kian in protecting his girl.

"It's not personal, Eila," said Maia, darkly, "but I can't risk you being captured. I realize now that this is the only way to ensure that time is not altered. He's somehow breached the best wards I have - magic so dark that few would ever dare touch it. He is inside, somewhere, and if my finest wards cannot stop him, then killing him may be impossible. You, however? You can be removed from the equation, as can your grandmother, ensuring the Gate is never started."

I pooled the Light into my palms, wishing I had my throwing gloves with me, knowing the skin of my hands would split under the fury of the Light. Unfortunately, they were stashed in the lower level with all our other equipment. Rillin had told me to never be without them, but I never thought that Faust would be invaded by a fallen angel . . . or that Maia Moriarty would turn on me. "I have no intention of being taken by Therophel. My only intent is to kill him. Have faith in my ability, Maia. Give me a chance to take him out."

The dagger turned in Maia's hand, and she took a careful step towards me. I mirrored her by taking a larger step back. Ana, slightly behind me, looked horrified. "And if you fail?" Maia whispered, "If you can't kill him? There are no second chances this time, Eila. Therophel is the end game for us all if you fail. I already warned you when you came here. I will sacrifice you before I sacrifice my people."

The Light arched and tumbled inside me, begging for release. "Then I go to my death as a warrior, not as some cowardly sacrifice at the hands of a club owner who's lost her courage."

"Never doubt my courage, nor the depths to which I'm willing to go to save my family," Maia replied, taking another slow step towards me, and I backed up, my heel hitting the brick wall.

"If my death could stop him, then I'd gladly fall on my dagger, right here, right now. But I hold no power over the Gabriel Gate. But you do, Eila. You are the key."

"Maia – think about this. You don't want to do this!" begged Ana.

I sensed Maia lunge a fraction of a second before she actually moved.

I threw hard, the Light ripping from my hands and cracking against the brick ceiling above her, causing bits of stone to rain down over us. She screamed at me, moving fast as she lashed out again, her blade slicing me in the forearm. I swore sharply at the bite of pain, but I threw again as she moved. The Light crashed against the edge of the catwalk, slamming it outward and snapping part of the railing off. It fell to the dance floor below, Ana's gasp telling me that she nearly went with it.

I kept dodging and sparring with Faust's determined owner, trying to stop her without hurting her. Ana scrambled to keep behind me so she wasn't crushed or stabbed. I threw the Light again and again, my palms streaking with pain as the Light split my skin from the power I wielded. The catwalk trembled under my fury, causing Maia to lose balance for an instant.

I took my chance to focus briefly on Ana. "RUN!" I screamed at her. "Warn the others of the breach!"

"I'm not leaving you!" she begged, but Ana couldn't help me in this fight. She could, however, give our friends and the boy she loved a fighting chance.

"GO! Help them! Warn them! Protect Elizabeth!" I screamed at her, breaking my focus from Maia for an instant to shove Ana away from me. She fell to her knees, but quickly scrambled to her feet. Mercifully, she ran, racing a handful of steps before she disappeared from sight, whether swallowed by the darkness or her own ability, I couldn't tell.

I swung back to Maia just in time for her blade to slice through Raef's sweatshirt, not far from my neck. Rage lit to life inside me, the Light rushing through me in a thunderous wave. "You want ME DEAD?" I yelled, fury hot and bitter pouring through me. "I'm not one to die so easily, nor am I one to leave this life in the name of fear. I'm worth more than the curve of your dagger, Moriarty!"

I threw hard and the wall near us exploded, brick and dried mortar stinging across both our faces like century-old shrapnel. "I DIE, YOU DIE!" I screamed.

Maia swung at me again, her moves that of a well-trained assassin who'd lived as a queen among killers for decades. "You shall be praised for your sacrifice," she yelled, getting more and more frustrated that I was not yet gasping my last breath. "You'll be revered for the blood you shed in the name of all."

"SCREW THAT!" I screeched, throwing hard once again, the catwalk starting to list away from the wall as bolts and rivets were sheared from their moorings by my fury. Sweat ran down between my breasts as I called the Light again and again.

Rillin had told me I was not some sacrificial lamb. He had told me I was needed, by Raef, by my friends – by all those in the path of Therophel's devastating quest. And whether she believed in me or not, Maia Moriarty needed me, as did Faust. "I'm the tip of the blasted sword," I snarled as Maia sliced towards me again.

This time, however, I grabbed the blade in my already mangled hand. The razor sharp edge dug into my palm as my arm ran red with the blood that flowed between my fingers. Stunned by the ballsy move, Maia froze for a moment.

I yanked her to me, pinning her dagger between us, my hand numb from the adrenaline coursing through my veins despite the blade embedded in my palm. "I'm not about to let you kill me because you're afraid," I snarled, breathing hard, with her face nearly nose-to-nose with mine. "If I'm gonna fucking die, it'll be because I was brave enough, crazy enough, to run head first into the fucking fire. GOT IT?"

CHAPTER 32
FAUST, NEW BEDFORD, MA

Raef's muscled arm suddenly appeared out of the darkness and jerked Maia back from me, slamming her against the wall. He'd snuck up on Faust's owner, using the shadows to his advantage, and now he had managed to pin Maia to the crumbling brick, fury clear in his tone, "One reason," he snarled, "Just one, why I shouldn't kill you right NOW!"

Maia, unafraid, stared Raef down. "The Gate is bigger than one life. You KNOW this. Your love for her has blinded you to what must be done. I will not allow the Gate to be restarted, even if the only way to ensure it is never utilized is to kill Eila and Elizabeth."

"Raef," I urged, dropping Maia's knife from my mangled palm, blood running warm and fast from my hand. "Raef, her intentions, while desperate, were in the name of saving her crew. We can't be divided. Our only shot at stopping Therophel is to work together. And we've been breached! We don't have time for this crap!"

I hissed at the throbbing pain in my hands and grabbed the edge of my sweatshirt, trying to press it to my palms and stem the bleeding. "We gotta go!"

Raef looked back at me, suddenly realizing that the pool of blood by my feet was coming from me. "Jeezus, what happened to your hands? Your throwing gloves - are they still with our equipment? Did you throw the Light without them?" he demanded, but before I could answer, his attention swiveled sharply back to Maia. His grip tightened on her throat, "To me, you are a liability. To me, you are weak," he snarled as Maia choked. "She had to defend herself against YOU! You are supposed to be on OUR side!"

"RAEF! Let her go!" I demanded. "Did you hear me? We've been breached! Someone is inside Faust without clearance!"

"I'm aware. I saw it," he growled, his fingers flexing on Maia's pale neck.

"RAEF!" I demanded, but then I froze as the sound of an animal's roar echoed somewhere outside the nightclub. "What is *that*?" I breathed.

"MJ . . . he and Nikki ended up outside," replied Raef, suddenly letting Maia go. She slumped onto the catwalk, gasping, her hand pressed to her neck.

"That didn't sound like Marsh . . ."

Raef glanced at me, "He's . . . upgraded."

"Come again?" I demanded, but Ana's voice called to me from somewhere in the darkness.

"Eila!" I shifted my focus over the darkened nightclub, my eyes trying to find the door to Baz's lab in the darkness. I finally caught sight of her, waving wildly near the lab, a flashlight in her hand, Kian alongside her. "What do you want us to do?" Behind her, Rillin held Elizabeth's glowing form, her dark hair fanned out over his arm as her head rested on his shoulder.

Raef called over the darkness to his semi-brother. "Kian! Meet where we agreed. Get them out! And watch the ductwork. It's in here somewhere!"

"What's in the ductwork?" I demanded, but Raef didn't reply, instead lowering himself down to Maia, his eyes linked with hers. "You get ONE pass from me, Moriarty. I don't care if Eila says your intentions were in the name of saving others. Grow a pair, or get the Hell out of our way."

Maia's gaze darkened as she dragged in a ragged breath. "What is it?" she asked.

"It's something I've never seen before – almost like a sandstorm unto itself, but blacker than a moonless night. As if it has no end. No beginning."

He took a slow breath, "I think it killed Howe. Crushed him inside of the truck he was sitting in. And it threw MJ and Nikki right through the garage doors and into the snow, as if they were nothing more than dried petals. I saw MJ get up, however, and run for the other side of the building with Nikki."

"Howe . . . Howe is DEAD?" I gasped, horrified. Anger and pain warred inside me. I should never have dragged him into our world. Never brought him to Faust.

"Tell me how to kill it," demanded Raef, looking at Maia.

She swallowed "We have to assume the worst. We must assume this thing is Therophel. If it is, it's possible that the same things that injure a Mortis may injure their creator. It may buy us time to get everyone out."

Raef nodded and got to his feet, grabbing Maia by the arm to haul her up and bring her with us. She yanked out of his grasp, however, shaking her head. "No. I'm staying."

"Maia – it could kill you," I urged, the screams and yells of Faust's crew starting to fill the darkened club as they ran into the dancehall from other levels and rooms, no doubt now aware of the breach. Leo's thunderous voice rang out over them all, tangling with Baz's, both calling for Maia.

"I'm here, Leo! Baz!" she called. But then she swiveled sharply to Raef and me. "Go. Get out. I'll buy you whatever time I can, but you MUST take my son with you." Raef didn't react, and Maia's plea caught in her throat, "Please. Please take Basil with you. Protect him, I beg you."

I shouldered past Raef. "If he's willing, we will take him with us," I promised, but then I heard the strangest sound – as if sand was sliding through the vents that ran up the walls of the club. Silence, heavy and thick, fell across the club, as if the workers heard it as well.

Leo finally appeared out of the darkness, Baz hot on his heels, and relief hit him hard the moment he saw Maia, unharmed, standing near us. "Thank God you're alright," Leo breathed, grabbing her into a hug and pressing a solid kiss against her cheek, our presence be damned. He pulled back from her. "It's in the vents," he whispered.

Baz also hugged his Mom, but then his eyes landed on me. I looked like a bloodied horror flick. "Good God, what happened to you?"

"Your mom and I had a difference of opinion on how to handle the current situation," I hissed as Raef took my hand, pressing the sweatshirt tighter to my palm.

Leo looked on, stunned, as Raef tried to slow the bleeding. "I thought a Lunaterra's blood is toxic?" Leo whispered.

"Not to me," Raef replied, "Kian and I are immune to both her Light and her blood."

An idea hit me all at once. "My blood. Can my blood be used against Therophel?" I demanded.

Maia looked briefly hopeful. "Possibly! Or at least keep him at a distance!"

I turned to Raef. "Do you have your gun?"

Raef looked at me, wary, but he pulled his Beretta from his back waistband, showing it to me. "I just need the bullets," I whispered, easing my injured hands away from Raef's and peeling away the sweatshirt, allowing the blood to well in my palms.

Raef, realizing what I was up to, quickly emptied then gun's clip and his spare rounds into my palm, and I rolled my bloodied fingers over each pointed cylinder, coating them in Mortis poison. He looked back at Maia, Baz and Leo. "Are you armed? If so, I need your bullets," he said quickly, the sound coming from the vents becoming louder, as if *IT* was slowly snaking its way towards our side of the club. Therophel or not, whatever was inside Faust was staying well hidden and apparently searching for something. I feared that when it finally reached our side of Faust, it would find what it sought. Mainly . . . me.

Leo and Baz quickly pulled three guns and two knives from their clothing, Maia offering up a freakin' Colt 45 that she'd stashed somewhere in her many skirts. Even Raef looked surprised by the massive revolver as Maia emptied the chamber, the copper-toned bullets clattering together into her hand. She glanced up at us, realizing we were all staring. "Size matters, boys. Don't look so surprised."

Leo's lips fought a smile, but Baz caught it and looked like he wanted to ralph all over the floor. She handed me the bullets and knives, and I coated them in my blood, handing them all back to her. Raef flicked his hand to the blood dipped weapons as Maia's bouncer pulled on leather gloves that he had tucked in his back pocket. "Be careful, Leo. Her blood has killed a Mortis before."

"Hence the gloves, brother," Leo replied.

As everyone around us finished reloading bullets and discussing exit strategies, I looked across the nightclub and was relieved to see that Ana, Kian, Rillin and Elizabeth were already gone. I touched my bleeding hands to my face, drawing the blood down my cheeks and over my torso and arms.

The sounds of those around me halted, and I looked up, realizing they were watching me. Slowly I stepped over to Baz, raising my hand and waiting. "War paint," I explained, "but the type that bites back. The type that is a deadly armor against those that may want to kill you." He slowly nodded and I set to sweeping my blood over his fair skin, then moved on to Maia.

Leo I couldn't help, but when I returned to where Raef was standing, I raised my hand and waited. He softly clutched my wrist and then brought my palm to his forehead, sweeping streaks of scarlet across his beautiful face.

The sound in the vents had stopped, halting not far from us, and Raef clutched my hand. "You are fierce," he whispered in my ear. "Let's show this bastard what true vengeance feels like."

The Light lit to life inside me just as the vent ripped apart at the other end of the catwalk, and slowly a creature poured from the vents like molten ash. Spider-like, with what seemed like a dozen thin, skeletal arms, the blackness morphed and flexed, never collecting into a fully defined body as it eased its way from the steel ductwork, dropping onto the catwalk.

The mass of darkness seemed to swallow the catwalk, blocking our only escape route, and eliminating all hopes that we were being raided by a mere stupid blob. As the last trails of ashy sand slid from the ceiling and added to the blackness, the once formless mass began to fold in on itself and harden, slowly forming a human shape that towered easily ten feet.

"Eila Walker," the darkness purred, as the facial features of strikingly beautiful man became evident. It was as if he'd been carved of black granite and every feature maintained the same ebony tone. He smiled in a chilling, dominating manner and the Light inside me thrashed, as if aware of the inhuman danger in front of us. "We have not been properly introduced."

His voice was deep and musical – almost a muse to my mind, both tempting and dangerous. Though scraps of smoke still slid about the edges of his body, clinging like cobwebs to his massive form, *He* had become real. Solid. "I am The Darkness. The First," he continued, taking a step forward. The steel below his feet groaned at his weight.

Raef moved closer to my side.

Leo, Baz, and Maia stepped carefully beside me.

Slowly, like dawn breaking, wings unfurled from his back, their clawed tips scraping along the ceiling of Faust. They weren't the elegant wings I'd seen painted on angels in church, but rather those of a dragon. Of a devil. And they were marred – shredded and in tatters, as if he had burned too close to the sun. As if he'd been branded by Hell itself; an Archangel, now stripped to the marrow and reborn as a demon. "You may call me Therophel, as my children have done for centuries. Leave with me, now, and I shall spare those here. Attempt to fight, and I will kill everyone in your name. The choice is yours, but I shall still collect you, all the same."

Rage, fearless and unfettered, boiled inside me. The creature in front of me was responsible for Christian and Mae's deaths. It had condemned the Lessers, murdered Howe. It had acquired thousands of deaths over the centuries and banished souls to exist on the fringes of life as Mortis.

"It seems you have covered all my options, but I'll pass on both," I hissed, taking a daring step towards Therophel and shocking the heck out of Maia, Baz, and Leo. Raef, however, moved with me, the Fallen Marks covering his skin and his eyes as black as Therophel.

Therophel slowly cocked his head, "You are quite arrogant."

"Takes one to know one," I snarled. "Question: your wings appeared to be made by a two-year old who'd snorted a bit too much glue. Are such pitiful additions reserved only for losers like you?"

Therophel's gaze narrowed slightly, as if stunned by my brazen defiance. "I am sensing sarcasm; that it is your nature to be rebellious. I assure you, such behavior is irrelevant to me. My terms stand." The smoke stirred around his feet, as if it were simply dried leaves kicked up during a walk in the Fall.

The Light pooled in my hand, glittering and beautiful like a ball of electricity entangled with really pissed pixie dust. "Your terms blow."

Therophel prowled forward again and I heard the click of guns near me. While I wouldn't pull my gaze from him, I was sure that three guns were now aimed at Therophel, thanks to Maia, Baz, and Leo. "I cannot be injured," he stated, like a total condescending turd. "Your weapons are pointless."

"Then I guess you should pay them no attention, though Maia tells me size is everything and your wings are, well, lacking in that department."

"Your English leaves much to be desired," Therophel replied. "Elizabeth was far more poised and . . . refined. I am aware her body was taken from the Polaris vault, and given that you and your legion are encamped here, I must conclude her body is here as well. Give her to me."

"Grams ain't here," I replied, "But if she was, I'm sure she'd be happy to drop-kick your smoky ass again. How'd it feel to be fried by a twenty-year old girl? Is she the one that shredded your wings, eh? Maybe stole a bit of your almighty power? Is that why you've been riding around in the bodies of people since the harbor?"

Therophel had visibly straightened, his wings snapping against the ceiling. Sarcasm might not bug him, but the memory of Elizabeth beating the tar out of him in 1851 definitely struck a nerve.

"Check your tongue, Miss Walker. I will not tolerate disrespect."

I snorted, "That's funny, 'cause I have no intention of tolerating you at all."

Therophel growled, taking another step towards me and causing the catwalk to rattle. Below us, the Faust crew had remained silent, but the sound of steel sliding and guns cocking assured me that Maia's workers weren't the type to tuck and run.

"Lawson Waite tried to resist me as well, but his attempts were futile," warned Therophel. "I devoured his soul and took his body. And when the ruse of his human form became useless to my cause, I left his rotted husk of skin and bones along the northern beach for the wolves."

"They're COYwolves, dumbass! Ya know, for a FORMER angel, you sure ain't too bright about the All God's Creatures thing. You must've skipped the whole chapter on Noah and his Ark."

"I am an ANGEL!" roared Therophel, apparently harboring one hell of a grudge about the whole "Fallen" thing. He lashed out, one of his smoky ribbons flashing towards me, but I pivoted fast and threw sharply with my hand, sending the Light racing from my palm like a lightning strike.

It slammed into Therophel and he fell to his knees, the catwalk jarring hard as my Light skittered and snapped over his body. I smiled angrily, my confidence rising that I could actually kill the Fallen Angel in front of me. Below us, the crowd roared their approval.

But then Therophel began to chuckle. Slowly he rose back to his feet as his wings expanded to balance him. The Light that had so viciously attacked him seemed to slow its onslaught and softly sink into Therophel's smoky form, as if being absorbed. The blackness of his body eased, and a white glow settled into his chest like a transplanted heart come to life. It pulsed there, for only a moment, but with every shuddering beat, a white halo of light flowed over Therophel's body.

For an instant his tattered devil wings returned to their former glory – white as snow, and gilded in a thousand silvery feathers. For an instant, I was facing down a true Archangel, no longer cursed and Fallen, but pure and powerful, etched with the glory of Heaven itself.

"No," I breathed, "It's not possible."

"Yesss," he hissed with a chuckle, drinking in the last drops of the Light that skated over his body. His blackened form, tattered wings and all, slid back into place as the heart of Light died out. I realized with absolute horror that he inhaled my Light . . . and he *liked* it. He *wanted* it. My Light somehow reversed his burnt, demon shape. Somehow I gave him a brief ticket back to true Glory.

Raef swore next to me, no doubt realizing quickly that the creature in front of us probably wanted me for *himself*.

Therophel leveled his black gaze at me. "Such a fearless fool," he purred, power and confidence rolling off him in waves. "You are a half-breed, girl. A perfect abomination whose power was gifted by the trappings of pointless love between enemies. One piece of you is a remnant from me, the other from Aztael. Thus, you don't simply channel the Web of Souls of the living. You also channel the energy of the dead. Of the *stolen*. You throw the icy shadows of the world and I feel your winter, your darkness. It caresses the Light you channel. You cannot kill me, fearless little one, for you are part *of me*."

I was too stunned to react, but Raef screamed to the others to open fire as he slammed into me, pushing me towards the edge of the catwalk. "Hang on to me!" he demanded as an endless volley of bullets burned through the air, striking Therophel.

Raef pulled me down, covering my head with his wide hand, trying to protect me from being hit by an errant bullet in the onslaught. Too horrified to even think straight, I managed to watch as Therophel was struck over and over again by gunfire, but he began plowing towards us on the catwalk, enraged.

"We gotta go" urged Raef.

"We can't leave them!" I demanded, but Raef easily

overpowered me, hauling me to my feet and pulling me with him over the side of the catwalk, our feet barely fitting on the slim outer edge of the steel railings.

"We have no choice! If he gets a hold of you, then we are ALL dead. We MUST leave!"

"They won't make it!" I screamed, but then gasped as I eyed the staggering drop to the dance floor below us. Raef pulled my face to his, the sound of the Fallen angel behind us roaring in rage.

"Trust me?" shouted Raef. "I swear I will keep you safe, E! I need you to live to fight another day!"

I swallowed hard, nodding.

Therophel must've noticed Raef and I were about to jump, because he roared my name, but then I saw Bane, forcing his way through the crowd. Gunfire whizzed past us, so close that I could feel the heat of the bullets from Faust's crew, all of them fueled by Maia's rage and her own volley of bullets.

"Bane!" shouted Raef, and the Lesser looked up, his monstrous form looking more like a savior than ever before. Raef grabbed my face, focusing my attention. "I'm going to throw you to Bane, understand? If we get separated in the chaos, get outside, stay with him. Find MJ and Nikki. We are to meet at the old ice house on the harbor."

"No! I'm not leaving you!" I snarled, but Therophel's smoky ribbons suddenly shot from his body and tangled around the catwalk's suspension equipment. The catwalk jarred hard and my feet slipped, Raef managing to grab me by the wrist before I fell. Behind us, Therophel was ripping the catwalk apart. Maia, Baz, and Leo started losing their footing as the catwalk tilted sharply. They slammed into the railings near us, and I turned to look at the three people who had become part of our crew. They were caught in this Hell because of us.

Because of me.

"Get her out of here!" screamed Maia, as Leo managed to grab her by the waist. Below her, the workers were scrambling to make sure they could catch her if she fell. "Take Baz! You promised!"

Baz looked stunned. He was about to argue with his mother, but the catwalk suddenly dropped sharply. Leo lunged for Baz, managing to snag his wrist as the two of them slammed into the catwalk, saving Baz from a neck-breaking drop.

Behind us, Therophel was roaring, lashing out and shredding the steel. Though he was determined to get to me, his body didn't seem to be following orders, possibly from the blood on the bullets. While they didn't kill him, they did seem to mess with his control, transforming him into a raging drunk.

"We will find you, Basil! You MUST go!" demanded Leo, nodding to Bane who was now standing below us, his tail lashing back and forth. The dragon-like Lesser gave a nod and Leo looked back at Baz. "Do as your mother says! I swear I will protect her, but I can't protect you both!"

Baz opened his mouth to yell, but instead screamed as Leo dropped him. He fell thirty feet into the waiting arms of Bane, who quickly pushed him into the safety of two Faust workers who dragged him from the dance hall. His screams for his mother echoed among the gunfire and shouts of workers.

Raef pressed a kiss to my lips. "I love you. Get to the ice house. I swear I will be there. I swear we are not over and I will find you, always."

I choked on a sob as I kissed him back, Therophel's form

getting closer by the second. Raef squeezed me one last time and then let go. The sudden grab of gravity caused me to gasp as I fell through the air into Bane's arms.

I scrambled out of his hold, looking back up to the mangled catwalk as Leo and Maia managed to get back to their feet, bracing against the steel and brick alongside Raef. Together they all began firing relentlessly as those beside me did as well.

"We gotta GO!" snarled Bane, dragging me through the crowd. Someone shoved a dark cloak at me, and I flung it over my shoulders as I disappeared into the crowd. Above me, Therophel screamed my name again, but I was already exiting the hall and being shoved down the outer corridor as Bane raced me along towards the outer doors.

He slammed though the steel exit and the raging blizzard hit me immediately in the face, nearly ripping the cloak from my body. The sound of yelling and fighting cut through the wind in bits and pieces. I tried to shield my face from the flying snow, but just as I turned to Bane, a raven-haired Mortis slammed into him, driving him into an alley. The two raged at each other and it was then that I realized that fighting was happening *everywhere* – Linked Mortis, no doubt planted by Therophel, were fighting hand to hand with Maia's guards.

I hesitated for a moment, torn by the knowledge that those Mortis who were Linked had no choice in the battle, forced into servitude by the Fallen Angel currently shredding Faust from the inside out.

But then I remembered Eris on the rooftop of Faust, the agony she endured while being butchered by the Link, and the mercy Raef showed her when he took her life.

These Linked Mortis were already dead. They would suffer a horrible fate under the Link should they even attempt to break free of Therophel's orders. And there was no way Nikki, if I could find Nikki, could save them all.

I called the Light to my damaged hands, shutting out the pain in my arms and palms just as a familiar roar cut the night. To my absolute shock, a black winged lion burst from behind a parked car, landing on the hood with a sickening crunch. With his wings spread wide and the ash of dead Mortis covering his muzzle and feather-tipped mane, he looked like a big, fluffy psychopath kitty.

Which could only mean one thing: MJ had found his alpha form.

As if to confirm my suspicions, Nikki Shea suddenly came tearing around past the car, fury in her eyes and screaming some sort of screwed up war cry as if she was an Amazonian fighter. And though the world around us had fallen into the apocalypse, Nik seemed in her element, her auburn hair caked in snow and ice, and her face flushed crimson.

She carried two daggers as she bolted down the street, both arms apparently working well. MJ jumped from the car, following her as they threw themselves into the fray alongside the Faust fighters. I ran for my friends, hurling the Light, some of it slamming into windows and cars and setting off alarms. It was total mayhem.

As I threw, my understanding of what I felt inside me when I volleyed the Light changed. I didn't just channel the living. I channeled the dead. I channeled the hopes of those alive, looking toward the future, but I also threw down in the name of those whose existence had been stolen by the Mortis. By killers like Raef and Kian and Rillin . . . Some were saints, others were destined for Hell. I wielded them all.

I was hope and vengeance combined, and the Light responded to my knowledge, hotter and brighter and more precise than ever before.

I burned through the crowds, feeling strong and confident, as if the Light was endless. As if I could fight forever. I spun to throw again when a Mortis smashed into my side, sending me crashing into trashcans near a dumpster. He launched at me, blonde ponytail snapping in the breeze as he grabbed me by the throat, but then hissed out a curse, yanking his hand back from my skin. He snarled, flexing his palm as the top edge of skin sizzled, and I realized I was still covered in blood. I got to my feet, kicking one of the toppled cans out of my way. "Yeah, that's right. You don't wanna be touching me. Bummer for you," I snapped, thinking I had the upper hand.

But then he yanked a gun from his pocket and I dove for the ground as I threw the Light, the same moment he fired. The bullet smacked into the wall behind me, and when I looked back to my attacker, all that was left was a pile of gray ash, his Limiting Link still sputtering on the ground alongside his silver gun, my Light having found its mark.

I scrambled to my feet and snatched the gun from the ground, giving the Link a hard kick and sending it sliding like a hockey puck under the dumpster. Determined to get to MJ and Nikki, I raced out of the alley and immediately spied Bane, his glowing amber eyes like two beacons in the darkness. He'd ripped the door off a brand new Prius and was using it as both a shield and weapon, swinging it back and forth like a scythe against the Linked Mortis.

"EILA!" Nikki's voice cut through the blowing wind and snow, and I turned to spy her running at me. "Here!" she breathed, finally catching up with me and shoving the small silver cylinder she'd fiddled with earlier into my hand.

"What's this?" I yelled over the fray.

"Call the Light and see!" she demanded, a huge, deranged grin on her face.

I did as instructed, focusing my power to my painful hand that clutched the item. To my absolute shock, a long blade of light flashed to life from the hilt.

"You made me . . . a LIGHT SABER?"

Nik nodded. "Use the Force, woman! Call the freakin' Dark Side if ya have to! The worst of the fighting is two blocks over - Maia's crew needs help!"

Gripping the snazzy new weapon in my hand, I turned back to Bane. "Dude! Let's GO!" I yelled, and together Nik and I ran down the road, Bane and his glowing eyeballs at our heels, and the Toyota's front door in his taloned hand.

CHAPTER 33
FAUST, NEW BEDFORD, MA

I kept a sharp eye on Therophel as I hauled myself back up onto the barely functional catwalk, Eila being escorted quickly out of the building by Bane. Choosing to send her from my side was brutally difficult, but entirely necessary.

Eila told me to trust her as a fighter. Believe in her ability to be a finely crafted weapon, capable of greatness in the darkest shadows of war. The instant I dropped her from my grasp, I had to accept that the Lunaterrian assassin that burned within my beautiful girlfriend was strong enough to protect herself *and* our friends. I had to accept that she was a fearless, unstoppable force of nature. I threw my heart into believing in her ability to stand on her own. Fight on her own. Kill on her own.

Not far from me, flailing in rage and possibly pain, Therophel continued to destroy the catwalk, now beyond furious that he'd lost sight of Eila as Bane had finally shoved her from the hall and through a side door. My creator began to slide his strange, mutating form over the side of the shattered railing, as if intending to pursue E, but I would not let him leave the building. No matter what it cost me, Therophel would not be allowed to pursue the young woman I loved.

"Do you remember me?" I called, my voice rising above the din of bullets which seemed to go straight through Therophel's smokey form, sinking into the wall behind him. Though they didn't result in actual wounds, the blood-tipped rounds definitely appeared to hurt him, possibly acting as a poison in his phantom-like body.

The fallen angel snapped his attention in my direction, his black lips pulled back in a rabid snarl.

"I am Raef Paris," I yelled, "You created me, a year before Elizabeth died in the harbor. Do you remember me?" I took a step forward, making a slow show of setting the safety on my gun and tucking it back in my waistband. Behind me, Leo whispered a warning about not letting my guard down, but I knew what I was doing. Hopefully.

Therophel's multiple spider-like arms latched onto the twisted side of the catwalk as he hoisted himself back onto the precarious steel, the iron bolts and rods starting to buckle under his abuse. He was solid, somehow, beneath his fog-like exterior, for the protesting steel of the catwalk didn't lie.

"Yesss," he hissed. "I remember you. You are the farm boy, the carpenter of Elizabeth's decrepit house. I turned you in your barn, after you had returned from her home." He slid towards me, and I carefully waved my hand behind my back, signaling Maia and Leo to escape while Therophel was focused on me.

"That house was NOT decrepit. I take offense to that remark."

Therophel's gaze narrowed, "You mock me? A foolish move by one soon to die."

"I'm First Army, by your own hand. I'm not your average Mortis, and by the looks of you, I'd say you're not exactly in top form. I bet I can finish disassembling those *decrepit* wings of yours," I laughed, mainly to make sure he was irritated enough to stay focused on me, though I was certain that this "piss him off" plan was gonna hurt like hell at some point. "Why did you choose me? Why did you . . . create me?" I asked, not really giving two shits about the answer, but figuring if I could keep him occupied, Bane could get Eila far from here.

"She trusted you, fool that she was," he snarled, trying to pull himself back into his black angel form. His attempts, however, seemed futile, for just as he formed a wing, it seemed to melt away, like quicksand, pouring in a thin stream onto the catwalk with an eerie *hiss*.

"You seem to be having some problems there, buddy," I teased, daring a fast glance behind me. Leo and Maia had disappeared. Someday, Maia and I were going to have a serious chat about her knife wielding and Eila, but for now, I needed Faust's matriarch alive. "Lunaterrian blood doesn't do a body as good as the Light does, now does it?"

Therophel, ignoring my taunts, managed to rise to his feet, his human shape beginning to stabilize as he smiled hatefully in my direction. "I knew she would follow you, and I was right," he chuckled, his wings beginning to form.

I paused. "She?"

"Elizabeth," Therophel snarled, his tone like the sand that dragged along with him as he moved closer to me. "She trusted you, and you told her to go to the harbor. To meet me. To die."

I felt as though I'd been sliced clear through the belly. I convinced Elizabeth to go to the harbor? I had no memory of that. I felt gutted for an instant, but I pulled back, hard, on my guilt. Now was not the time for remorse.

I shrugged in mirrored response. "Not my problem if people are dumb enough to fall for my charms."

Therophel looked pissed that I wasn't sobbing on the catwalk, guilt-ridden. He sniffed, "You still smell new. A true killer, replete with a newly stolen soul, yet covered in the blood of your bedmate."

I bristled internally.

"Tell me, do you sleep with Eila Walker so you feel in control? So you feel . . . invincible? Powerful? Is she a mere pawn to your own needs until you somehow feel human once again? That's what you seek, do you not? Your *humanity*?" he spat the last word, as if it were some disgusting plague.

"You know nothing," I growled, flexing on my feet as I realized Therophel had closed to striking distance. "And you will die knowing even less."

"I know every inch of humanity and none of it deserves to survive. The world must be purged of the weak, of the sick. We shall rise and devour the bones of the Lunaterrian empire and go on to command the humans. They need structure. They need a ruler."

"You mean they need a slave master," I replied.

"Perhaps. This future is a foregone conclusion, Raef Paris, for I command the past."

"RAEF!" howled Baz from below us.

Therophel and I both swiveled to look at the disheveled teen standing alone in the dance hall, a stuffed superhero backpack slung over his shoulder. I was stunned to realize all the workers had disappeared. "Smash it!"

He whipped what appeared to be a golfball in my direction, and for an instant I thought he'd finally lost his mind entirely. But as the ball sailed towards me, I realized it was actually a small glass ball containing silver and red liquid, somehow separated inside the sphere – like a yin yang symbol.

Therophel sprang forward, attempting to reach the ball first, but I was faster. Yanking my gun from my back waistband, I took fast aim at the flying ball, prayed Baz knew what he was talking about, and pulled the trigger. The resulting explosion of Light from the ball slammed me entirely off the catwalk, as if a black hole had blown to life inside of Faust. I heard Therophel roar just as I hit the dance floor, back first, my teeth rattling at the impact.

"Jeezus! That worked way better than I thought it would! Hot DAMN!" panted Baz, wide-eyed as he scrambled to help me to my feet. "We gotta go, though – it's pure chaos outside. Therophel must've brought fifty Linked Mortis with him and they are basically reenacting World War Z in the street. I came back for you . . . and the blood bombs."

On the quickly crumbling catwalk above us, Theophel looked like an electrical storm, slashing and writhing, his body once again back to a spidery cloud of ash, unable to pull his form together. While he was able to ingest Eila's Light, whatever was in Baz's glass baseball didn't settle too well with the bitter angel.

"Blood bombs?" I demanded.

"Eila and Elizabeth's blood, sealed into two separate chambers inside a glass ball. It's like a really mean version of a Pokeball, but when it evolves, it's basically a dwarf freakin' star going supernova!" Baz smiled broadly, "Epic, right?"

"Right. Epic," I glanced up again at Theophel still slashing around, but then looked past him to the ceiling. A huge crack was quickly spreading across the ceiling of Faust and I realized that the building wasn't going to stay standing much longer. "We gotta go!" I grabbed Baz by the arm and yanked him into a run, bolting for the door, "Is everyone outside?"

"Yes! Shit man, don't run so damn fast! I have a dozen of those Pokebombs in my backpack. I'd rather not crack one and blow my butt off!"

"The building is about to collapse!"

"WHAT?" Baz glanced up and the crack was now spidering across the entire ceiling, the chandeliers beginning to shudder as Therophel continued to roar and writhe. "Oh, God no," he gasped as I dragged him along. I could feel his pain. His agony. The home he'd known all his life was about to come crashing down, but there was nothing that could be done to save Faust in that moment.

The building shuddered and I yanked Baz over my shoulder, like an injured comrade, running at top speed for the far door, the kid's screams for his home echoing behind us and tangling with Theophel's rage. Just as I reached the door to one of the outer halls, I heard the ceiling give way and the entire building rumbled as it began to collapse, wall after wall, catwalk on catwalk, all falling and smashing; a thousand carefully carved and cared for dominos destined to be obliterated in a matter of seconds.

I slammed through the outer door, and was hit instantly by the flying snow and blowing wind carrying the sound of fighting everywhere. I heard Maia's voice, yelling for her son, and I ran for her, screaming for everyone to get back from the building. Some heard me. Others did not.

Gargoyles toppled from the stone facades, crashing onto the ground and splintering like granite shrapnel in the darkened streets, a few landing on unfortunate Mortis.

Maia and Leo yanked Baz from me, and Maia hugged her son hard. "Mom – the club!" he gasped, but she just held him tighter.

"We've gotta go!" demanded Leo.

I looked back at the falling building and the bloodied, ash-strewn streets where Mortis continued to slaughter one another. "Eila? Bane?" I demanded.

"We saw them," nodded Leo, rushing Maia and Bane farther away from the building, Faust guards surrounding them and me, acting as shields against the Linked Mortis in the area. "They were headed down the street that leads to the east end of the harbor. One of our workers saw Eila too - said she was with Nikki and what looked like a lion with wings. I'm thinking that's gotta be your shifter pal. Our whole crew is out here, helping us duke it out with Theophel's fighters. We're getting the upper hand, but the police will be here soon. We've gotta go!"

I gripped Leo's hand and shook hard. "Be safe. I've got to go find Eila at the ice house."

Leo nodded, but Maia grabbed my hand. "Contact us. As soon as you locate the Gate, you call us and we'll be there!"

Baz shook his head. "Mum – no way Theophel is surviving that!" he nodded towards Faust, which was slowly leaning in on itself, the bricks raining down from the sides.

Maia glared at her beloved building as her world died in pieces. "He's a Fallen Angel. A building collapse won't kill him."

I nodded, hearing the sounds of sirens in the distance. We could NOT be found, especially the Mortis or Bane. "Go! Get out of here!"

She nodded and Baz shucked his backpack, handing it to me. "Take it – you've seen what the glass orbs can do. These are all I have, so be wise about using them."

I squeezed Baz's shoulders. "I will."

He nodded, tears in his eyes as he looked one last time at Faust, and then Maia and her group were off, running down an alley until they disappeared into the darkness of New Bedford. I turned, eyeing the Linked Fighters being systematically killed by the remaining Faust guards. In another life, I would've stayed and fought, but not now. Not when so much was riding on our ability to kill Therophel and destroy the Gate. And so I turned, Superman backpack hiked on my shoulder, and ran for the harbor and my E.

CHAPTER 34
NEW BEDFORD, MA

We'd been battling our way through the fighting Mortis for what seemed like hours, when in reality it had been mere minutes. At first, we realized it wasn't so easy to pick out the Linked Mortis from Maia's crew. But then Nikki got it in her head to scream out Eila's location (much to Eila's horror), and the Linked Mortis all paused in their fighting for an instant, turning as one towards Nikki's voice.

It was like sounding the lunch bell at the high school.

That one fleeting pause in the fighting allowed us to see who were the good guys (relatively speaking, of course) and who were the bad guys. It was only then that I realized that Nikki had used the Limiting Link's design against their owners. Because that was the thing about Limiting Links – they made you mindless, programmed to one mission and one mission alone. We saw it with Rillin. We saw it with Eris. We saw it with the Lessers from Polaris.

And once the Linked Mortis spotted Eila, they stupidly stopped fighting against Moriarty's clan and began trying to get to Eila. From that point on, the fighting turned into a systematic extermination of the Linked Mortis, all of whom doggedly tried to get to my pal.

At one point, I managed to steal a glance at Eila. She stood in the middle of the main road leading to where Faust had once stood, the wind and snow howling around her, sending her dark cloak flying outward in the wind. Light Sword clutched in her hand, ash and blood caking her hands and face, she looked like a true killer, honed by Fate and some seriously bad luck into one badass supernatural assassin. Bane, glowing eyeballs and all, acted as her brutal partner, his tail lashing over the asphalt and ice as he protected her from behind, picking off stragglers that managed to break through Faust's crew.

Eila was both the bait and the weapon, and it worked brilliantly.

I kept myself close to Nikki, trying to protect her without her knowing (lest she kick MY ass). Any Linked freaks that tried to gang up on her on their way to Eila found themselves hurled into buildings and light poles, thanks to my new massive size and heavy wings. My mouth tasted of bitter death and burning ash as I sunk my teeth into the necks of Linked Mortis, one after another, snapping bones with brutal efficiency. Nikki was equally relentless as she let her rage loose with a chrome sword she'd formed from the bumper of a car, her fiery hair entirely caked in ice.

I watched her out of the corner of my eye as she swung the blade like a ninja, slicing the edge though necks and driving the tip home through the Limiting Links. Like Eila, she was covered with the remnants of war, ash and blood dusting her like a second skin. At one point, I saw tears streaking her face, cutting clean lines through the ash of the Mortis she'd killed. I wanted nothing more that to hit *pause* and freeze the world so I could go to her and banish the darkness that I knew was haunting her mind. I knew, angrily, that these few days she'd been with us would become the type of memories that could drown you slowly. When Therophel was dead, when the fighting was all over, I'd make sure she wouldn't suffocate in these terrible moments we were experiencing together.

I'd be the guy who'd be at her side through all that life threw at us.

I'd be hers, heart and soul, if she'd have me.

I prayed that what we'd shared in the engine room of Faust wasn't just desperation and loneliness on her part. I prayed she felt as deeply as I did. I prayed I wasn't just a warm (and furry) body that she needed to lean on only until this crap was all over.

I slammed another Mortis against a car, causing the theft alarm to begin screaming into the night, the sound mixing with the fighting and howling wind. But then, out of the corner of my eye, I spotted another Mortis just standing in the road not far from me. He caught my attention because, for a moment, I thought I recognized him.

For an instant, I thought it was *James*.

But then the wind and snow kicked up once again and he was gone, like a phantom stolen away by the blizzard.

I turned back to finish off the soul thief I'd pinned against the car, but just as I turned, he punched me hard in the shoulder, sending a flash of pure pain through me. I roared in rage, the sound vibrating against the buildings, and swiftly decapitated the Mortis in front of me, sending his head sliding into a nearby pile of garbage. I stepped back off the car, causing it to bounce roughly as the alarm continued to blare, and glanced at my shoulder. I was lucky - he could've done far worse damage than just striking me. The bastard could've stabbed me.

I needed to keep my head in the game.

"MJ! Are you alright?" called Nikki from far behind me. I could hear her footsteps echoing down the road as she headed for me. Not wanting to alarm her, I tried to rub away the ache in my shoulder, pushing my body back and forth against the protesting car. It seemed to work . . . to a point, at least.

"MJ," breathed Nikki, finally running up to me and throwing her arms around my thick mane. Her grime-covered sword clattered to the ground. "I heard you roar, like you were in pain. Are you okay?"

I leaned my huge head against hers, loving her delicate smell. She pulled back, running her cold hands over my head and around my ears, examining me. "Well, you look okay. You are, right?"

I offered a snort and the closest I could manage to a nod, though the movement caused my injury to bite back. I hid my pain well, however, and Nik let out a sigh of relief just as Eila and Bane ran up to us.

"I heard sirens! The cops are on their way," announced Bane, glancing at the carnage around us. Faust Mortis were grabbing bodies and chucking them into a minivan, which even had an Honor Student sticker on the back. Some poor soccer mom was gonna be pissed when she found her mommy-mobile missing in the morning. "We've got to get out of here," Bane urged. "Raef is at the ice house on the harbor, correct?"

Eila nodded, "Yeah – we'll head there. It looks like we got all of Therophel's fighters."

Bane and I both looked around, and it was true – somehow we managed to get the upper hand, taking out all the Linked Mortis save for a couple that were being finished off by Maia's crew. Bane turned back to Eila. "Can you get to the harbor yourself? I need to help get this under control before the cops arrive. We can't risk being discovered by the human world. We can't leave any evidence of the fighting."

"We'll be fine," said Eila, reaching out to rest a hand on my good shoulder. "I've got Nik and MJ, and the roads look clear. You do what you need to, Bane, then meet up with us at the ice house."

Bane nodded. "Be safe, Eila. I'll see you soon." He then ran down the road to join the Faust crew, his leathery skin and dragon-like shape disappearing into the swirling blizzard of the night.

"Alright, let's go," said Eila, and we all turned, running down the streets, all the while trying to avoid being seen and dodging the wail of police sirens. We turned down one road and nearly crashed into one another as we stumbled to a stop. At the other end of the street was a police cruiser, a spotlight hooked on the driver's side, its beam of light sweeping over the dark corners and doorways, searching.

"Damn it!" hissed Eila. "Now what?"

"In here!" whispered Nikki quickly, pointing to a side alley.

We all darted into the alley just as the cruiser's spotlight swept the area we'd been standing in seconds before. We ran down the side alley, but soon realized that the end of the alley was blocked by a brick wall and a white box truck with a picture of a donut on the side.

"Shit!" snapped Nikki, turning back to Eila and me. "We're trapped! Stupid dead ends! I hate this city!"

Eila turned to me, jamming her little silver light sword device in her boot for safe keeping. "MJ, can you fly? Can you get us outta here? Maybe get a running – OUCH!"

Eila grabbed the back of her neck, as if something had stung her.

"What the . . ." she slurred, but then swayed sharply, as if drunk. I took a step towards her, unsure of what was going on. Just as I got to her, however, Eila's eyes rolled back and her knees suddenly gave way under her.

Shocked, I moved fast, trying to catch her with my body before she slammed into the ground, but as she slumped against me, I felt a sharp sting as well, in my flank. I turned fast, and the alley seemed to instantly sway, like the deck of a ship. I staggered to the right, trying to focus on moving my paws, but my hind legs gave out under my massive weight. I felt as though I'd drunk a few gallons of whiskey and was entirely skunked off my lion butt.

"MJ! Eila!" yelled Nikki, realizing something had happened to us. Through my slurred haze, I realized, slowly, that Eila and I had somehow been drugged. Shot with something designed to knock us out.

I looked at Nikki, and she seemed to be wavering in and out of my vision, another shadow behind her. I opened my mouth to warn her. To tell her to run. But all I could form was a strangled groan as Nikki spun at the last minute and was tackled by the shadow from the darkness.

I heard her scream my name just as the world went black.

CHAPTER 35
WHALER ICE, NEW BEDFORD, MA

By the time I made it to the abandoned ice house tucked into the furthest reach of the frozen harbor, my heart was in my throat. I hadn't seen Eila anywhere among the fighting, but she'd asked me to trust her, so I was hanging on to her request by my fingernails. I shoved my way through the wooden door at the back of the building and found myself slammed to the ground by Kian, who was channeling his honed killer instincts to maximum effect.

"Jeezus, man," he demanded, releasing me from his grasp now that I was flattened to the floor. "I thought you were one of Therophel's Linked thugs. For cripes sake, KNOCK next time – I could've snapped your neck like a toothpick."

I shoved him off, about to demand if Eila was there, but then I caught sight of Rillin. He was kneeling in the center of the room, not far from the uncrushed armored truck, which they must've taken from Faust before the collapse. In his arms was Elizabeth, her body covered in Rillin's jacket and Kian's. Ana sat beside the two of them, her hand resting on Elizabeth's arm, as if trying to read her, but that's not what got my attention.

It was what I was hearing. A heartbeat. Elizabeth's heartbeat, clear in my ears, and from what I could tell, steady.

Her breathing, however, was more hit or miss, which was not so promising. Rillin, his broad arms and wide hands carefully keeping Elizabeth against his chest, was watching her closely. I was about to tell him she hadn't taken a breath for longer than normal when he gently lifted her torso higher with one arm, cupping the curve of her jaw in his scarred left hand.

His touch was delicate, as if he feared his roughened, war-damaged hands would tarnish her fair skin. I knew the feeling well. I was always vigilant of my strength over Eila despite her abilities, and Rillin's fears seemed all the more intense. As if the girl in his arms was nothing more that a teasing phantom; a dream he could never truly have.

I watch as Rillin dipped his head and pressed his lips to Elizabeth's, causing her body to glow brilliantly in response. The blue tone radiated from her skin and cast Rillin's face in a haunting halo, as if their kiss was in a spotlight despite the darkened building. I realized that he was actually breathing for her – not constantly, but every once in a while. As if her body had yet to fully seize onto the rhythm of drawing air to stay alive.

"What happened?" I asked quietly, watching the scene unfold in front of me. Ana kept one hand on Elizabeth's bare arm, her eyes tightly closed.

"Elizabeth had some sort of seizure as soon as we got here," Kian replied, yanking me to my feet. "Scared the crap out of Rillin, but it was almost as if it jump-started her heart. We performed CPR on her until her heart pulled into a steady rhythm. Her breathing is touchy though. It's as if her body forgets that she needs to inhale."

"As if she's coming out of anesthesia," I replied.

Kian nodded, "Basically, yeah. And since this craptastic hideout has exactly zero medical supplies, Rillin is acting as an oxygen boost when needed. Not that he's complaining." Kian looked at his fiancée, "Ana's been trying to link with Elizabeth's mind and wake her. So far, however, that's a dead-end."

I crossed my arms, finally looking around. "Is E here yet?"

Kian looked surprised. "No. Isn't she with YOU?"

I shook my head, "No. We had to separate – she went with Bane while I distracted Therophel. One of Maia's workers said she was with Nikki and MJ, moving south – in this direction."

Kian nodded, "If she's with Bane, Nik, and Hairball, she'll be okay. This time, the fight favored us, Raef. Theophel may've brought a crap-ton of Linked Mortis, but we had an army of our own, and the Moriarty clan to boot. And Sparky is one badass when she wants to rock her light show, so don't panic. I'm sure she'll be here soon."

"I should go look for her. What if she ends up on the wrong side of the harbor? We need to get her off the streets quickly. Though Faust was collapsing, I seriously doubt Therophel was killed in the rubble."

Kian blinked. "Faust . . . is *gone?* Holy crap, what'd you DO?"

"Let's just say that Baz is a closet pyromaniac," I replied, finally retrieving the middle schooler backpack from where I had sent it sliding for safety when Kian jumped me. I unzipped the bag and fished out a blood bomb, handing it to Kian as my eyes drifted to the door, hoping Eila would walk through it any minute.

"What's this? A Magic 8 Ball?" Kian asked, turning the glass ball in his hand, the liquid inside swirling like a lava lamp.

"It's E's blood and Elizabeth's, but separated. When the glass barrier between them is cracked, it creates this massive burst of energy. Like a portable core collapse. Baz had tossed me one and I shot it and, well . . ."

"*Boom,*" Kian replied, holding the glass orb far more delicately.

"Yeah, massive *boom.*"

"How many of these did Weed Boy make?"

I glanced down into the bag, "Maybe twelve?"

"Did they hurt Therophel?" asked Kian, hopeful.

"He seemed seriously pissed off by the one we used. And before you ask, I don't know if unloading the whole arsenal at him can kill him." Suddenly, Ana gave a sharp whistle. Kian and I turned, stunned to see Elizabeth *moving*, her hand weakly traveling up her chest. Ana quickly scrambled to her feet, stepping away.

With a deep breath, Elizabeth's eyes slowly opened, her long lashes framing a golden ring that etched the edge of her deep brown eyes – a golden ring far brighter and more intense that E's ever was. It was unchained Lunaterrian power, gifted only to those of pure bloodlines.

Rillin, still holding her in his arms, was suddenly frozen, as if he was afraid that any movement would shattered the dream or startle the young woman whose eyes he hadn't seen in nearly 200 years.

Elizabeth drew her hand slowly up his broad chest, her strength a mere whisper of sheer willpower, but determined to touch his face. When her fingers finally grazed the edge of Rillin's stubbled jaw, the knight finally broke. Tears began to trace his face, many following the deep scar that ran along the side of his cheek.

"Hello," he whispered in a rough, emotion-choked voice. I could see actual joy on the face of our Blacklist dealer, as if the armor he'd worn around his heart for so long was finally shredding to pieces.

Elizabeth seemed too disoriented to smile. Instead, she kept touching Rillin, as if she couldn't believe he was in front of her. She blinked frequently, as if her vision wasn't yet perfect. Finally she whispered, "Monster?" The sound of her voice, nearly forgotten to me from the years that had passed, brought back a rush of memories in my mind.

Rillin laughed in disbelief, "Yes. Yes, it's me." He ran his hand down her cheek, feeling her warm skin.

Slowly Elizabeth smiled, her own tears sliding down the curve of her face and into Rillin's hand. And though her voice was brittle and dry, the girl who had resided in a tomb since 1851, who had willingly gone to her death to protect those she loved, finally whispered back, "I thought you dead. I thought . . . you had been killed."

Rillin shook his head, "No. I'm right here. I've been right here, missing you, for a very long time."

Ana glanced between Elizabeth and Rillin on the floor, and Kian and me. Elizabeth had yet to realize where she was – or that she and her Trial were not alone. Not wanting to panic her, Ana simply cleared her throat, catching Rillin's attention. Elizabeth frowned and slowly turned her wobbling head towards the sound, catching sight of Kian and me across the room.

The confusion on Elizabeth's face slipped away, hardening into the assassin she'd been trained as. For someone who'd been dead for 200 years, her training had not lost its brutal edge as she shouted something in French, (which sounded a lot like, "die you scum-sucking traitor") and flung one arm away from her body.

A streak of Light blasted from her hand just as Rillin shouted a warning to us. He rolled backwards with her on the floor, her blue gown tangling with Rillin's legs and the jackets in a jumble of body parts and clothing.

Kian and I hit the deck, unwilling to test whether we were still immune to Elizabeth's particular brand of lethal Light. The streak of lightning-like power barely missed us, crackling past our heads just before it shattered like glass against the far wall, but not causing any damage to the building.

Had it been Eila throwing, it was very possible she would've taken out the wall. But Soul Light in the hands of Elizabeth was designed for one thing and one thing only: killing the soulless.

I rolled hard to a stack of crates in the far corner, using the old boxes as cover as Kian launched to his feet and blitzed across the room. He snagged Ana by the waist, hauling her with him behind another pile of forgotten ice equipment as she let rip a string of angry curses aimed at Elizabeth, who was now struggling with Rillin. "They are friends! Allies! *Coeur de Feu! Arrêtez!*" demanded Rillin, trying to calm her.

Kian, pressed with Ana against the boxes near me, looked at me and said, "So, she seems . . . pissed."

"YA THINK?" I demanded. "She remembers us watching her die. That we did nothing. To her, we are still those two Rysse clansmen from the harbor. For God sake, this ice house looks as old as she is. She's got no clue how much time has passed. To her, it probably feels like she was just IN the harbor with Rysse. Hours ago."

Kian cursed, "Shit, I didn't think of that."

"I DID!" hissed Ana. "What are you two? Morons? If she sees a car, she'll probably think it's a dragon!"

Kian eyed his girl, "There are no such things as dragons, even back in the 1800s."

"I'm BEING SARCASTIC!" howled Ana.

Elizabeth was still struggling in Rillin's arms, but her strength was fading fast. She yelled at Rillin in French, "*They are with him! They fight for HIM! They knew I was going to . . .* "

Elizabeth's voice suddenly trailed off.

I suspected she was beginning to remember the full extent of the harbor events. I could hear her heartbeat begin to race and her breathing sharpen. Though Rillin kept softly assuring her she was safe and she was okay, Elizabeth began to scramble once again in Rillin's arms, but this time panic was clear in every inch of her body. As I watched her from my position behind the crates, Ana and Kian not far from me, I could tell that her memories were surfacing.

She remembered dying.

Rillin carefully let her go, and she scrambled onto her knees away from him, trying to stand, but her legs gave out and she dropped to the floor. Sobbing and gasping, she clawed at her chest, as if she remembered the sensation of the Core Collapse. Of how her breathing had halted and her heart had stumbled to a stop.

Ana, beside Kian, swallowed hard, and Kian wrapped one strong arm around her. While watching Elizabeth struggle to deal with her darkest memory was difficult, it seemed more intense with Kian and Ana – as if they too knew this level of agony. As if they too were on the floor alongside Elizabeth.

Rillin slowly approached Elizabeth, kneeling down next to her but careful not to touch her as he spoke to her in French, "*I know you are confused, but please trust me. You are safe,*" he whispered. "*You are not alone and I will never, ever leave your side."*

Elizabeth's sobbing began to soften, her voice so dry and ruined by time that it sounded like the broken plea of an animal. On her hands and knees, her hair had tumbled down alongside her neck, shielding her face from us as she cried, her shoulders shuddering with each breath. Slowly, Rillin eased closer to her and reached out, sweeping Elizabeth's long, wild hair back over her shoulder.

"I am so sorry I left you in the woods," he whispered. "I thought I was protecting you, but I've regretted it ever since. Please, please trust me. I swear to you, I am still the Trial you knew back in the palace. I am still your *Monstre*."

Rillin shifted and opened a pocket on his hip, pulling out the small wooden owl he'd kept for centuries. Elizabeth drew a deep breath, her tears easing as she watched him, her golden eyes all the more intense now that they were rimmed in pain. "Never again will I fail you," he whispered, holding the owl out to her.

Elizabeth slowly sat back onto her hip and Rillin placed the small bird in her hand. She studied the little creature, turning it carefully in her hand. Finally she looked back up at Rillin, "What happened to me?" She looked over to where Kian, Ana, and I were semi-hiding, "Is Rysse dead? Did it work?"

Rillin looked uneasy. "There is much to tell you."

She gripped the bird tightly and her lip trembled as she asked, "Christian? My son?"

Rillin took her hand in his. "I'm so sorry."

Elizabeth choked back a sob and Rillin pulled her slowly to him, sliding his wide arm around her. She had begun to shiver, and I, believing she was finally not going to try to kill me, eased from my hiding spot and retrieved Rillin's jacket from the floor. I walked over to Elizabeth and handed it to Rillin, who draped it over her shoulders. Elizabeth seemed too stunned to really acknowledge me, but Rillin eyed me, as if knowing exactly what I was about to say.

"I'm going to go look for Eila," I said, leaving no room for argument.

Rillin nodded. "We can't stay here long. The police will be crawling all over this area soon."

"I know. I'm sure she's close."

Just then, someone banged on the back door. I instantly had my gun drawn, Kian quickly at my side, his Sig also clutched in his hand. "Who is it?" I called.

"It's BANE! Open up!"

"Thank God," I muttered, grateful Eila and her escort had finally made it to the ice house. I hurried to the door and yanked it open, revealing Bane, finally back to his human form. Flung over his shoulder, however, was the body of another guy. He stepped out of the storm and into the cavernous area, but I was immediately aware that Eila was not with him.

"Where's EILA!" I demanded, just as Bane dumped the body of Marcus Howe onto the floor. The agent, who at this point HAD to have nine lives, moaned, obviously not dead.

Bane spun on me, looking shocked. "What do you mean, 'WHERE'S EILA?' She was headed HERE! I SAW HER head this way with Nikita and the shifter. She was ahead of me – she should've been here before me!"

"You LOST my best friends?" demanded Ana, stomping out from behind the box where Kian had left her. She stormed past Rillin and Elizabeth, both still seated on the floor and now watching us. Rillin's hands ran slow circles over Elizabeth's back as she trembled slightly - probably from the cold and adrenaline fading in her body.

Ana got right in Bane's face. "You are supposed to be some epic-shit LESSER and you LOST Eila? How the Frak do you LOSE a Lunaterra?" Ana winced, glancing at Rillin. "I mean, BESIDES Rillin, how do you lose a chick that can toast your butt with supernatural Soul Light?"

Rillin just shook his head.

"We were able to kill all of the Linked fighters, but the police were coming," snarled Bane, now getting into Ana's face. "I sent Eila to come HERE so I could help clean up all the evidence of the fight before the police arrived. And Eila was killing it out there. She and Nikita and MJ in that lion form were lethal. They were fighting, side by side, with our crew. They were solid. They should BE HERE. The fighting was over and the streets between here and Faust were totally deserted. She SHOULD BE HERE."

Ana's brow wrinkled, "Lion form? What lion form?"

I shoved past Bane, ignoring Ana's questions. I was furious he'd lost her.

I headed for the door, but Kian grabbed my arm. "I'm going with you."

"Me too!" demanded Ana. Kian began to argue, but she pointed sharply at him. "Don't even start! I'm going!"

He sighed, "Fine. Bane, you stay here with Howe. Keep an eye out while Rillin takes care of Elizabeth. We will need to split as soon as we get back." I eyed the black armored truck sitting silently not far from Rillin. "We'll have to use the truck until we can switch to something more subtle."

"We were able to toss in the Iron Scrolls, a few books, some of Eila's and Rillin's weapons, and a few papers, but that was it," offered

Kian. "I was worried we'd lose everything in the attack."

"Good thinking."

Bane glanced at Elizabeth, shifting a bit uneasily. If he was shocked to see the former dead girl alive and well, he hid his reaction well. "Chris – " he looked at Elizabeth, realizing she might not be aware of Christian's death yet. "Uh, Eila's *grandfather* kept a garage here in town. It's how we got the armored trucks – he gave them to us for Faust. Pulled them from his garage."

Ana looked intrigued, "He's got a garage? With cars and stuff?"

"Yeah. Big one."

Ana bounced on her feet for a moment, clearly excited about the vehicles. The girl had octane in her veins, no doubt. Kian, rolling his eyes, pulled his jacket from the floor and slipped it over Ana's shoulders, "We don't have time to go car shopping, darling."

"Buzz kill," muttered Ana.

Kian simply zipped up the jacket, ensuring his fiancée would be warm, "If I say to disappear, Pix, you wink out. Instantly. Got it?"

"Yeah, yeah, whatever. I'll do the whole *blinding* thing if need be, so chill. Ain't no one gonna see me if I don't want them to."

Somedays I wished Eila had the same ability as Ana - to literally make herself invisible in the minds of those who were looking right at her. I checked my gun and holstered it behind my back as I asked, "Is Howe gonna make it?"

Howe, as if in response, moaned once again. Bane glanced at the agent. "Yes. I found him in one of the alleyways a couple blocks from Faust. He must've been able to drag himself out of the armored truck that Therophel crushed, and out of the building before the collapse. He's banged up and got his bell rung, but he's gonna make it."

Kian looked at me, "Do we want him to?"

Ana poked her soul shark in the chest, "Leave Marcus alone! Jeezus, we need to find Eila and MJ! And, well, maybe Nik, if she isn't a total turd."

I yanked open the outer door and the wind and snow hit me like a hurricane. "We'll be back with the girls and MJ," I said to Rillin.

"Find her," growled the knight, his lost princess tucked in next to him. "Bring her back."

"I will," I replied, then turned my attention to Elizabeth. She watched me from her spot next to her Trial, and I added in the best French I could muster, "*Don't worry. You are among friends.*"

She didn't make a move to reply.

I turned, pushing my way out through the door and into the night, Kian and Ana by my side, determined to find my girlfriend and the rest of our crew.

CHAPTER 36
NEW BEDFORD, MA
MONDAY, 12:33AM

Two hours, eight minutes, and a handful of seconds.

That's how long it took to finally spot a few of MJ's massive paw-prints that hadn't been obliterated by the snow. It was also roughly two hours and three minutes longer than it took for my fear about Eila's safety to become a living, breathing entity that was following me everywhere in the darkened streets of New Bedford.

In the time it took to finally locate the alley, we'd dodged a dozen police cruisers, several fire trucks, and at least six emergency vehicles. Thankfully, Kian and I could fade into the shadows, but Ana simply used her blinding ability to disappear from all those who looked her way, including Kian and myself, which at some points got really strange.

"They were here," said Kian, walking carefully around the footprints, the blizzard finally having eased into icy wind and fast moving clouds. "They were all here."

I scanned the ground and noticed more footprints, but also what looked like larger indents in the snow - as if someone attempted a snow angel but failed badly. "What do you make of these?" I asked, pointing to the two areas that were compacted on the ground - one much larger than the other.

Kian came over and examined the area. "Not sure - could be where two bodies were lying, though one has to be huge. Possibly MJ."

I swore, searching the alleyway for any clues.

"Hey - there was a truck here," called Ana from the far end of the alley, where a brick wall turned the narrow way into a dead end. "Tire marks. In the snow. Not a big tread, so . . . maybe a moving truck? Or a van?" She sighed, leaning back against a huge dumpster tucked into the corner. "Oh my God, where ARE they?"

"EILA!" I called into the night, no longer giving a crap if anyone unsavory heard us. I needed to find her, safety be damned.

Kian, of the same mind, started yelling as well, calling out to E and MJ in the night.

"NIKKI!" screamed Ana, but then she swore sharply and jumped away from the dumpster, eyeing the beat up piece of steel warily. "Holy crap, something just moved in there!"

"What?" demanded Kian, and I ran for it, flinging open the top.

Staring back at me was a young, twenty-something dude dressed in a Hole Foods sweatshirt and pants, his matching logo baseball hat all askew on his head. A young hooker, dressed in an ultra short skirt and skimpy top complete with long fur-lined leather jacket, sat scrunched up next to him. Both were staring back at me, their eyes wide, their hands tied behind their backs and their mouths gagged with scarves. They both stunk to high heaven.

"What the . . .?" whispered Ana, stepping up next to me, Kian at her side.

"Oh great. As if this night couldn't suck any more . . ." muttered Kian. "Lemme guess - you two were making out in a dumpster for kinky kicks, yes?"

The guy and the girl exchanged a look before turning back to us and yelling through their gags. Unable to understand a damn thing they were trying to say, Kian and I reached in and hoisted them out of the dumpster, depositing them on their feet in the alley.

I yanked the gag off the boy. "Who are you?" I demanded.

"I'm, uh . . . I'm Tucker. I, uh, drive that Hole Foods truck over there," he turned flicking his head towards the empty corner. He froze, eyes wide. "OH MY GOD, WHERE THE FUCK IS MY TRUCK? Holy crap, my boss is gonna kill me!" He spun on the girl, "I KNEW this was a rotten idea, Kasie, but oh no. YOU said this alley was perfect! YOU said no one would bother us! You said it would be ROMANTIC!"

Kasie, incensed that her *Romeo* was somehow blaming her, starting snarling something through her gag, probably a few well-chosen threats aimed at certain areas of Tucker's manhood.

Kian rolled his eyes and spun the girl to him, causing her to startle. "Allow me," he muttered, untying her gag. She let out a quick *thank you*, then spun to the Hole Foods guy once again.

"Tucker, you are such an asshole!" she snarled. "Don't you dare blame me for this shit show! How was I supposed to know we were gonna get grabbed by that kid!"

"WHAT kid?" I demanded, yanking the girl by the arm to get her attention.

She let out a squeak, shocked. "I, uh - the kid. The one who jumped us when we were in the truck. He forced us out, said we looked *yummy*, whatever that means, but then knocked us out. Smacked us right in the head with something - maybe a gun? That's all I remember until I woke up in the dumpster and heard you guys screaming someone's name."

"Did you see anyone else?" I asked, hopeful. "A couple of girls and a lion?"

The dumpster duo looked at me as if I'd lost my mind. "Dude," asked Tucker, slowly. "What are you smoking? This ain't Ringling Brothers. I don't care if it sounded like the circus had come to town thanks to all the sirens a little bit ago. There ain't no lions in New Bedford."

"But the kid that jumped us did have a pet, I think," added Kasie. "Either that or it was a rat, cause I didn't see it in the darkness, but I heard it squeak and the kid said something to it." She glanced around the area, "Crap, I hope it wasn't a rat."

Kian and I exchanged a look. This line of questioning was getting us nowhere and the clock was ticking. I nudged Ana, "Can you read them?"

She rubbed her hands furiously, "Damn straight I can."

"Do it," I replied, and both Tucker and Kasie let out a shout as Kian pushed them both to their knees, replacing the gags in their mouths. The girl fought against Kian, which was pointless, but the guy looked like he was gonna piss himself any moment.

What a prize he was.

Ana knelt down in front of the guy and raised her hands to his face. "Just try to relax, Tucker. This won't hurt."

"Unless you try something stupid and my girl gets hurt. Then I snap your neck. Got it?" added Kian. The guy nodded rapidly.

Ana touched his temples, and the guy slowly relaxed as Ana closed her eyes and began to relay what she saw in Tucker's mind. "His attacker is, wow, maybe fifteen? Short-cut brown hair, nice smile, great skin, solid square jaw. He's wearing a blue jean jacket. And when he talks, it looks like he has . . . FANGS." Ana blinked, stunned. She glanced back at Kian.

"Keep going Pix," he replied, and when she shut her eyes again, Kian looked right at me as he and mouthed the word, "*Wrecker?*"

"*Maybe,*" I mouthed back.

Ana sighed, her eyes tightly shut and her hands still on Tucker's head. "I . . . I don't have a visual on what he saw after he was knocked out, obviously, but he could still hear, whether or not he was conscious," whispered Ana. "He does have an auditory memory of voices. Hang on . . . Yeah, I hear Eila and Nikki. Eila mentions MJ and the possibility of flying. That they are trapped, but I think they were hiding, or running, from the cops. But then Eila says . . . "

"Eila says WHAT?" I demand.

Ana opened her eyes and looked back at me as she released Tucker, who swayed on his knees. "Raef, I think Eila may've gotten hurt. I heard her say 'ouch.' And I heard Nikki . . . scream. After that, I heard what sounds like a struggle. Then I can hear the doors to a vehicle open and slam shut and then a truck engine drives away. That's all there is in Tucker's memory. Everything else was just police sirens in the distance." She glanced over at Kasie, "Oh, and I totally thought she was a hooker, but she's not. She's his girlfriend."

"YOU THOUGHT I WAS A HOOKER?" demanded the girl.

I flexed my hands, digging my fingernails into my palms as I tried to calm myself and think clearly. "If . . . IF this kid took the truck and kidnapped Eila, Nikki, and MJ, he could be anywhere, but the fangs . . ."

"He's gotta be a Wrecker, Raef. He has to be. He could've grabbed her for Waite's bounty."

"Wrecker?" asked Ana, "You mean that whoever took Eila was one of those people Maia was talking about? ARE YOU SERIOUS?"

"We'll discuss this later, Pix," Kian replied, nodding to Kasie and Tucker.

She glanced at them. "Ah. Right." Ana dusted her hands on her pants, "Well, if a *Wrecker* grabbed Eila for the bounty, why'd he grab Nik and MJ?"

"Opportunistic thief, that's why," Kian replied. He looked up at me, "He won't hurt her, Raef. She's only valuable alive."

"I know," I replied, fury and terror twisting inside me like a hurricane. "But it means he probably knows where Waite has been holed up. He'll take her right into the lion's den."

"What is it with you people and lions?" demanded Kasie.

Ana set her hands on her hips and glared at the anti-hooker. In response, Kasie pressed her lips together and scooted closer to Tucker, both of them now eyeing all of us quietly. Ana turned back to Kian and me. "But we have no idea where the Gate is. How the heck are we gonna find Eila?"

"Everyone knows where the Wreckers live," I replied. "New Orleans. Terrebonne. James said he was headed there as well when he first warned us about the bounty and the second Polaris attack."

"James could be in on it," Kian replied.

"Or he is innocent and totally unaware of what is going on," added Ana. This kid - this *Wrecker* - is in a truck, which goes maybe 60 miles per hour if we're lucky."

"Try more like 55," muttered Tucker.

"I am SO not a hooker," added Kasie under her breath, still miffed.

"You're thinking we can catch up to him," Kian replied, an eyebrow raised. "Raef, he could be going anywhere."

"Yeah, but he may also be heading home. He could be going down Route 1. I mean, shit - we may be able to spot him. It's a HOLE FOODS truck."

Tucker nodded. "This is true. It does have a big pink donut on the side. With sprinkles." Somehow the kid's brain was warped enough to make him believe he was actually part of our conversation. He shook his head, a huge smile on his face. "Wait until I tell my boss this story. A stolen truck, some kid who you guys think wrecks stuff, and a triple kidnapping. And her," he pointed at Ana. "What are you? A psychic or something? This shit will be the stuff of legend! My friends are gonna go nuts. Best night EVER!"

Kasie gave him a shove with her shoulder and Tucker nearly face planted in the snow. "Best night EVER? Oh my God, Tucker, you are such a freak! We were attacked and tossed in a dumpster. A DUMPSTER! What are you thinking?"

Kian, Ana and I exchanged a knowing look. No way we could let these two go with any memory of the night's events.

I turned slowly back to the two arguing lovebirds, interrupting their blame game. "You know, just so we have all the details straight, Ana here wants to read you again. Both of you. So when we file the police report, we are sure to have all the details right. Sound good?"

Kasie shrugged, "Whatever."

"Heck yeah!" announced her date.

Ana flexed her hands, kneeling down once again in front of

Tucker. "So, yeah . . . just relax and let your mind go *blank.*"

As Ana worked, Kian pulled me aside. "Any chance Sparky had her phone on her when she got grabbed?"

"You think we may be able to track her!" I yanked my phone from my pocket.

"It's a long shot, but yeah," Kian replied. "I mean, most kidnappers would immediately ditch the phones, so . . ."

"Connecticut," I breathed, looking at Eila's little phone symbol on the digital map in my hand. "They are almost to Danbury."

Kian smiled. "Hooray for dumb kidnappers."

CHAPTER 37

NASTY DONUT TRUCK, GOD-KNOWS-WHERE
MONDAY, 4AM. MAYBE.

This was what a hangover felt like. Either that, or someone affixed a marching band behind my eyeballs and the drum line was throwing down. I blinked, which was more like winking out of sync thanks to the pounding in my skull. Moaning, I tried to roll over, but quickly realized my wrists were locked together in front of me, though my hands and arms were well bandaged. Trying not to panic, I rocked sideways, but my body came up against something massive and hairy.

I forced my eyes to crack open, thankful for the darkness around me, and came face-to-fur-covered leg with MJ's massive form. "What the hell happened?" I muttered, trying to get my bearings and wiggle my wrists out of the bindings. Slowly, I realized that I was in some sort of van or truck, and MJ was still in his black lion form, wings and all. He was seated, but he'd placed his massive front legs on either side of me, as if caging me in – or watching over me. I turned slightly and rolled into Nikki, who was also wedged next to me.

She groaned, rubbing her face with her tied hands. I finally realized our wrists were bound by plastic zip-ties. Neon orange ones. How tasteful.

MJ's gaze dropped to the two of us briefly, then back to whatever it was that had his attention outside the truck. "I think I'm dead. Or, rather, I want to be," croaked Nikki, her voice dry. "Jeez, what happened?"

"Faust. We'd gotten out of Faust and were supposed to meet up with the guys but then . . . I got stung by something, I think, anyway," I slurred, my mouth not catching up with my brain. Dear God, my tongue felt as though I'd licked the underside of one of the cafeteria chairs at school. *Bleh.*

MJ snorted, and tossed his head away from us. Slowly, so as not to barf and ignite the trombone section in my head, I rolled to my stomach to see what had MJ flustered. That's when I was finally able to see out the open back doors of what was definitely a box truck housing the three of us. A boy with dark hair, younger than us by a couple years, was tossing a few pieces of wood into a campfire, not far from the truck.

Slowly my memories came back, piece by piece, all falling into place. We'd been drugged, kidnapped, and tossed into a . . . *wait a minute.*

I glanced at the boxes near my head, Hole Foods donut logo clearly visible on the cardboard sides even in the darkened interior. "Jeezus, we've been kidnapped by a kid who makes minimum wage," I moaned, quietly. "We'll never live this down."

The kid heard me and turned from his fire-making, his eyes meeting mine. He smiled broadly, revealing – *holy snizzle* – FANGS.

Even more alarming, they seemed to be engraved, like scrimshaw. I froze under MJ, trying to reel in my panic. If we'd been grabbed by Edward Cullen's younger, more dweeby, vampire cousin, I was gonna just tap-out altogether – scream "Uncle" and hand over Destiny to Fate's greedy, sadistic hands.

"You're awake," declared VampKid, dusting off his hands. "Thank God I didn't kill ya. I was a little iffy on the dose."

Next to me, Nikki rolled to her stomach and I noticed MJ shifted his paw closer to her side, as if to steady her. She *did* look a bit green. "What . . . what happened? Who the heck are you?"

"I knocked you out and kidnapped you," proclaimed the kid in a slight southern drawl, crazy proud. "My name's Jared. This here is Sprout," he nodded to an empty spot near the fire, confirming that he did, in fact, have a screw loose. "And don't worry," he continued, oblivious to the fact that we couldn't see his invisible pal, "the cobwebs in your head will fade. Soon. Maybe. Actually, I'm not too sure how long it will take you to get your sea legs back, exactly, since humans aren't really destined to wake up once I nab them. Your big shifter pal, here – he's been up for a couple hours now, watching over ya like a big ol' broody hen. He's been less than civil, if I may say so, growling like a rabid bear if I come too close to the truck. I was able to bandage up your hands, though, before he woke up and started acting like a jerk. "

How, HOW do I get myself into this shit?

Jared turned back to the fire, poking at the burning logs with a long stick. A piece of oak crashed to the side among the flames, sending a burst of sparks sailing into the night air as he rambled on, "Ya know, I had a mind to dart your creature in the ass again and knock him out, only he took up that damn position over you the instant he woke up. Been like a statue above the two of you ever since. I figured if I knocked him out, he'd fall down and crush the two of ya like roadkill, and then where would I be? Lord knows, I can't trade you to Waite if you're dead."

The world began to spin and I rested my head against the cold, puckered metal of the truck's floor. "Wait . . . what?" I breathed, the drugs he gave us still messing with my focus. "You want to trade me? In exchange for what exactly?"

"Money," snarled Nikki. "He's a bounty hunter, Eila."

Jared's laughed, "Bounty hunter? Heck no, though if this works out well, I may just take on the title. Let's just say I'm driven to succeed in the venture."

"So your pot o' gold at the end of the rainbow? Does it come with hot chicks?" Nik asked, slowly easing herself to sitting.

"Maybe," Jared replied with a huge grin.

"Pfft – they must be comatose," I muttered, and Nikki snorted a chuckle. "Ya know, the term 'driven to succeed' usually doesn't include kidnapping," I continued, rubbing my forehead. I was never, EVER going to drink. Like, ever.

He shrugged, "Potato, tomato – still's the same to me."

Nikki glared at him, snarling, "IT'S *potayto, potahto,* you dumbass! Now let us GO!"

I dragged my 400-pound head back up to look at the kid. I couldn't even think straight. I felt like I'd been hit with the flu AND partied too hard. "Seeing as I'm in no shape to kick your ass at the moment, you got any water?" I moaned.

He blinked. "Uh, yeah. I sure do. I went down to the stream just down the hillside and brought some back. You want some to drink?"

"No, I wanna wash my hair."

"Really?"

"NO. I'm thirsty!" *Ugh* – yelling was REALLY not a bright idea. I pressed my hand to my face, trying to ease the migraine. Nikki did the same, shushing me as well, clearly dealing with her own death metal band playing in her head.

I heard the sloshing of water, and MJ's low, answering growl nearly caused the truck to vibrate. While I always thought Marsh was big, MJ's new form made his old Shuk form look like a lapdog.

Jared's voice was low as he approached the truck, wary of MJ. "Now look here, you oversized feline – she asked for water, that's all I'm bringing her. I know damn well you heard her, so stop all that angry cat-critter nonsense." MJ watched him closely as the kid put the cup down on the truck's open back end, then backed away quickly to the fire. I reached out a shaky hand and managed to get a drink, spilling some across my face. I handed the remainder to Nikki, who sipped it slowly.

The kid watched the three of us, his head cocked to one side, as if fascinated by our motley gang. He suddenly straightened, snapping his fingers. "Oh, I've got some food too. It's fresh. Hunting around these parts is good." He shuffled over to a bag on the ground and pulled something out. It was maybe a foot long, and lean, with a little tail.

And furry.

He held it up. "Anyone like weasel?" he asked, the dead critter hanging from his hands and swaying slightly. "Tastes damn fine, even raw."

That's when I puked on MJ.

* * * *

An hour later, we'd exited the truck and I'd managed to wash off poor MJ's vomit-covered paw, apologizing repeatedly for barfing on him. He'd simply watched me with those huge, dark eyes, and rubbed his massive head against my arm – a signal that it was fine and I was forgiven. I suspected he was maintaining his shifted form for our protection, but somehow Jared was under the assumption that MJ was stuck as a lion. I wasn't about to correct him.

Seated around the fire our would-be kidnapper had built, I took in as much detail as I could about our surroundings. Tall oaks cut spindly profiles in the darkened woods, and through the occasional gap between moonlit trees, I could make out a hint of rolling hills surrounding us for miles and miles. The sound of rushing water echoed in the distance, but it wasn't like that of the ocean. It sounded more like a raging river, or waterfall.

This was nowhere near Cape Cod. Where were we?

All in all, we seemed to be in deep farm country – like, pitch black, can-ya-paint-my-tractor-for-my-wedding-so-I-can-marry-my-cousin, MIDDLE of freakin' nowhere. By the absolute stillness of the surrounding countryside (save for our young kidnapper, who wouldn't shut up), I guessed it to be late. Way past midnight. Which meant that somewhere between running from Therophel and waking up in a donut truck (which depressingly lacked donuts), I'd lost at least five or six hours.

How far could we travel in that time? Where the heck were we? Was this upstate New York? Pennsylvania? A nicer version of Hell perhaps, given the way my LUCK RAN?! More importantly, how could I run Jared over with the truck when he wasn't looking? Come to think of it, could a Hole Foods vehicle even kill a vampire?

Why had no one TOLD ME there were vampires??

We needed to get back to Raef, Kian, Ana, Rillin . . . and even Elizabeth. I prayed they were okay – prayed they'd gotten safely to the harbor. As I sat by the fire, I silently willed my soul into the night, hopeful that somehow Raef knew I was okay and that I was determined to get back to him. Oblivious to my thoughts and plotting, Jared rambled on about the information he'd learned in the past couple days, about me and those I kept company with, including Raef. Apparently I was a hot topic of conversation among the supernatural world, thanks to Waite's bounty and all the juicy details he'd dumped online about me and my crew.

The more time I spent with Jared, however, the less I was worried about being kidnapped because one thing had become abundantly clear: this kid was no master criminal. With my hangover fading, I set to doing what Rillin had trained me to do: take in all details, assess the enemy, find his weaknesses, and attack when opportunity is best. Be smart. Be fast. Be deadly. Although, given that Jared looked kinda young and a bit clueless, I wasn't sure I could bring myself to murder the moron.

"Word is, y'all been running with soul sharks. That true?" Jared asked, peeling another strip of cooked flesh off the weasel. He scarfed it in a couple bites, his engraved fangs flashing in the firelight. When I didn't answer him, he continued on, his eyes traveling over me, Nikki, and MJ as if debating whether or not to filet the flesh from our bones when Ralph the Rodent was nothing but cartilage. "I also heard through the wayside that you're actually cozy with one of them sharks you run with. Like, knocking boots and whatnot. They say that he and another one of your, uh, *friends*, are First Army. And another one – big dude, which I guess they had but he got away – they say he's a Trial."

"*Was* a Trial," I replied hotly. "And the boot knocking is none of your business."

"Whatever," he replied, cracking the tail off his meal and sucking on it like a candy cane. Behind me, I could hear MJ actually gag through his lion lips. "Point is, there ain't no bounty on the three sharks. Technically, the bounty is only on you," he pointed at me. "So, just to be clear, I didn't intend on kidnapping all of you when I started this road trip, but I had to improvise pretty damn fast once I saw the fighting going on in New Bessfort. So, I hope we can be friends."

"FRIENDS?" demanded Nikki, horrified. "You kidnapped us! You are trading us to Lawson Waite! You can take your friendship and shove it!"

I sighed. "New Bedford," I replied, correcting him and ignoring the "friends" request. I studied our strange kidnapper through the firelight. "What *was* your original plan, seeing as kidnapping us wasn't your criminal activity of choice?"

Jared's eyes trailed over to Nikki as he mercifully tossed the tail in the fire. "I came looking for Maia Moriarty."

I raised an eyebrow, "Maia? What the heck do you want with Maia?"

"She owns Faust, right? Or rather did - looked to me like the whole building went to Hell."

Beside me, Nikki shifted, leaning more towards MJ as she got more comfortable. Jared seemed in no rush to drag us kicking and screaming to Waite, and as he spoke, a sadness seemed to fall over him. "Yeah . . . she owns Faust. What's it to ya?" Nik replied.

"I came here to cut a deal with her. Her fighters, her crew, for, um . . ." Jared rubbed his face, frustration clear in his voice. "Well, I hadn't figured out what I could give her in trade yet, I'll be honest, but I just figured she could name a price and I'd figure out a way to get it for her. Even if I had to raid every ship from here to Africa, I'd find a way to pay her." He studied the fire as he shrugged, "Doesn't matter now though. Ain't no place safe, which is why I grabbed you instead." He pulled his eyes from the fire and looked right at me. I knew that look because I'd seen it in the mirror. Repeatedly.

Anger. Frustration. Pain. Vengeance.

All of it was in the eyes of the boy across from us.

"What do you mean, there's no safe place?" I asked quietly.

He leaned back against a tree trunk, the pupils of his eyes flexing from round to narrow slits every once in a while. "My home was raided four days ago. Many of my kind killed. The only ones me and the other 'cussers were able to save were the youngsters, but our elders, our parents . . . they were still inside the village." He shook his head, "I need leverage. I need a way to bargain back Mayhem. To get back my home. As I was traveling up here, I found out that he wants you. More than anything, he wants YOU. I don't know why and I don't really care, but if you are his finest treasure, then I'm gonna bring you to him."

Mayhem? Something stirred in the back of my mind, like an itch I couldn't quite reach. I felt like I knew that word . . .

"How did you know where Faust was located?" asked Nikki, oblivious to my thoughts.

"Girl, we all know where Faust is located," he replied. His face hardened into something more menacing, and despite his young appearance of maybe fifteen, he'd managed to kidnap the three of us.

Underestimating him would be unwise, despite him being, as Nikki put it, a *dumbass*. "Truth is, I don't want this to just end with a trade. I want him dead. Want his fighters dead too. They say Maia Moriarty is a bokor – a mistress of black voodoo who commands a crew of *Mortis*." He hissed the word, as if it burned his tongue to even speak it. "They say that no one crosses Faust. They say Moriarty is fearless. I needed her and now she's gone. Her crew is scattered to the wind." His eyes drifted to mine and a chill ran down my spine.

This boy had seen things that had damaged his soul. Things that changed who he was on the most basic level. I knew those type of things as well. I'd seen them in a way that could never be unseen, even if I lived a thousand years.

"Look, I got no beef with you," said the kid, standing up and dusting off his hands. "You're just collateral damage. All of you. So don't take this personally. War's war."

We all watched him from across the fire, silence settling in around us for a while before he glanced at my hands, "I should check your bandages."

I held out my hands, still zipped together, offering them up to our strange abductor. Beside me, MJ growled as the kid started to approach. "It's okay, MJ."

Jared warily watched MJ as he knelt before me, taking a strange, golden star from his back pocket. "Hold still," he instructed as he took the star, no bigger than a silver dollar, and used it to cut the zip-ties free of my wrists.

He noticed me studying the golden device, and paused. Holding it up in the firelight, it glowed warmly in his fingertips. Up close, I could see writing all over the eight-pointed star. It almost looked like an old coin.

"It's a doubloon," he explained. "Cut into a throwing star. Highly effective as a weapon, even at a distance." He tucked it back in his pocket, giving it a pat. Carefully, he took my hands and silently began unwrapping them. As I watched him, a million thoughts ran through my mind. Could this kid be of use to us? Did he know where Therophel was holed up?

His touch was careful as he unwrapped my hands. I asked, "You said I'm leverage. I'm assuming you mean leverage against Lawson Waite, correct?"

Jared nodded.

"But you don't want the bounty money?" I asked.

"No."

"Are you trying to get the Gate? For yourself?"

Jared paused, looking very confused. "What gate?"

I looked at Nikki and MJ. "If you're not after money or the Gate . . . Are you trading me to get back your parents? Your home? Is that who raided you? Lawson Waite?"

The kid nodded sadly as he pulled more gauze from his pockets, my hands finally unwrapped. "At one time we did do business with him. Midas used to get pure coca leaves from Lawson Waite - he was our supplier. Brought everything up from the Caribbean, but then he dumped us, suddenly, about two years ago. So we started buying cut cocaine from some idiot named Garnet or Gardett . . . I think he owned the Crusty Crab restaurant or something."

"Garrett? The dude who owned the Pink Crab?" I asked, floored. Garrett and his damn nephew had tried to hijack Cerberus when we visited their island in the Caribbean. Raef had killed him . . .

Jared nodded, "Yeah, that's him, though he seems to have ditched us as well. We haven't been able to make contact with him since mid December, so we had to start looking for another supplier again, which sucked. But then Waite contacted our elder, Midas, and was like, 'Hey, I can start running your coca leaves again, so let's make a deal.' He came to Mayhem with an entourage of Mortis, which was a little weird, but whatever. We had a big celebration planned, so all the adults and elders were inside Mayhem when Waite suddenly unleashed his Mortis on the place and . . . " Jared stopped talking, unable to say anything further, emotion choking him.

I knew the feeling well.

I flinched as he rinsed my hand with water from his Hole Food's cup. He glanced at me as I bit my lip, "Sorry. They look painful - what happened to them? Did you fall through a glass window or something?"

Though my arms and palms were healing, they were still terribly sore. Unwilling to divulge information about my Light casting ability, I simply replied, "No. I was injured during the raid on Faust. We were attacked as well - by the same *evil* which attacked your people."

Jared paused, stunned. "You mean Waite? Lawson Waite was inside Faust? Was he inside when it collapsed? Is he dead?" Jared looked hopeful, and I realized that he had no clue who Lawson Waite really was. I looked at Nikki and she knew exactly what was running through my head - this kid and I had a mutual enemy. This kid and I wanted the same thing.

"Lawson Waite, the man, is dead. The creature who had possessed his body, however, is very much alive."

Jared's face fell to confusion, his hand stilling over mine. "What are you talking about. I saw Lawson Waite attack Mayhem. I saw him command an army of Mortis as they shredded our homes. He IS Human. I KNOW who he is."

I shook my head, "You saw the illusion, Jared. Faust wasn't attacked by a human. We were attacked by Therophel, who'd been using the body of Lawson Waite for God knows how long. Actually, he may've possessed Waite when Waite dumped Mayhem a few years ago. Maybe that's WHY he dumped you guys - he was no longer a human, but an angel with an agenda. Why run drugs anymore?"

"Therophel," whispered Jared, understanding hitting the young kid. "You mean the Fallen Angel? The creator of the Mortis race? THAT Therophel?"

I nodded, but Jared let my hand go, the new gauze hanging off my hand, only partially applied to my wound. He staggered backward, shaking his head. "No. No, you are wrong. I know the history. I know the legend - Therophel was cast to Hell long ago. He was banished from heaven for creating the Mortis race, condemned as Fallen and stripped of his power. He does NOT exist! He cannot exist!"

"The history is wrong," I replied, quietly.

Jared shook his head fiercely. "NO!" he shouted at me. MJ slowly rose to his feet, wary of the kid's anger. "NO! You are WRONG! Aztael and Therophel are dead. Gone. My family has proof. My family has the Soul Gear - we have the bone of Aztael!"

"You still have the Soul Gear?" I breathed, watching Jared now pace back and forth, agitated. He didn't seem to hear me, so I got to my feet and grabbed the kid, my hands burning. "LISTEN TO ME! Do you have the SOUL GEAR?"

Jared yanked hard out of my grasp and snarled in my face, his fangs brilliant in the firelight. "YES!"

"You're . . . you're a Wrecker," I breathed.

"What the Hell is a Wrecker?" demanded Nikki. "I thought he was a vampire!"

Jared stopped pacing and glared at Nikki. "Vampire? I ain't no vampire!" he snapped, looking horrified, but then he paused, looking surprised. "Wait a second – you don't know what a Wrecker is?"

I said nothing, too stunned to reply. The kid in front of me had access to the Soul Gear. Mayhem . . . Mayhem was his *home.* Where Midas' vault was located. The place that Waite raided. I whispered to no one in particular, "He's after the Gear," but Nikki and Jared were still arguing with one another.

"No, I don't know what a Wrecker is, you dweeb," snapped Nikki.

Jared, floored, leaned a little forward, "I'm a Kappa."

Nikki shook her head.

"A river child?" Jared demanded, getting flustered.

"What the heck is a River Child?" growled Nikki. "Speak freakin' English!"

"A *mermaid*!?" snapped Jared. "I'm a mermaid, you idiot!"

Nikki froze, but then a devil-like grin lifted to her lips. MJ's mouth dropped open as Nikki choked out a laugh. "Oh. My. God. You're the Little Mermaid?"

"I'm not from The Little Mermaid, damn it!" he snapped, but then a slow smile crept onto his lips as he showed off his fangs, "Unless I can eat that useless, flute-playing prince-dude. Then we're talking."

As if on cue, I heard a soft, chirp-like chuckle, and we all stiffened. Jared smiled, showing off his fangs once again as he nodded in the direction of the odd laugh. "Like I said, this here is Sprout. My shadow tail."

With a happy chirp, Sprout hopped into the firelight looking NOTHING like a chubby fish-sidekick.

I was demanding a refund from the theater (if I ever made it out of this alive), 'cause this crap wasn't even close to the movie.

CHAPTER 38
NORTH PASTURE HILLS, PENNSYLVANIA
MONDAY, 5:30AM

I leaned against the side of the armored SUV, the stillness of the little roadside rest stop doing nothing to calm my mind. In the distance, nestled between rolling mountains, was a sprawling farm complete with huge red barn. Twirling into the still dark skies, a spindle-like windmill turned lazily, catching the early morning air. It seemed to mark the center of the farmlands, the heart of the people that lived there. A single porch light softly illuminated the chipped paint on the front porch that ran around all four sides of the farmhouse. Despite the pre-dawn shadows blanketing the the valley, the entire setting seemed well-loved and inviting.

I couldn't help but wonder what it was to build a life in such an unburdened hamlet.

Did the people below, sleeping soundly in their old house among the expansive fields, realize how blessed they were to be human? Did they understand that the simplicity of day to day life was not a gift automatically granted to all of us? Did they take the time to taste the tart-tinged sweetness of a perfectly ripe apple from the orchards, or remember their child's first steps with absolute clarity? Did they have any clue that their life, whether simple or taken for granted, was glorious?

Did they know that there were so many of my kind that lived in the shadows, envious of their humanity?

I watched over the farmlands. Someday such a peaceful life might await Eila and me. The beautiful farmhouse and the rolling hills represented all that I ever wanted for me and for my girl, should she desire it. Though darkness loomed on the horizon, there was also this beautiful future that I had started to believe was possible. That I had started to HOPE for.

Rillin once told me that hope was the most dangerous gift of all, but I also knew it to be the greatest ally when faced with the impossible. As I looked over the valley, I pledged that this war with Therophel would fall under the might of my rage and be cut down by my determination. Because hope, this time, was my weapon. I intended to never forget the little farm tucked in between the Pennsylvania mountains. A moment of peace and tranquility before a gathering storm.

I needed to get Eila back. I needed her by my side in this war. I needed her hope, especially if mine faltered.

Her phone had shut off hours ago, and despite our best efforts, we could not restart the tracking. All we knew was its last known location, roughly where we were now - a spot in Pennsylvania, almost two hours from the New York border. Though we'd started closing the gap between us and Eila's abductor during the night, the armored

SUV was not the fastest of vehicles. Constructed as a titan on wheels, heavily plated with an iron hide, it had aggressive torque and a dauntless engine, but it was not built for speed.

I'd thought of ditching it and trying to snag another vehicle from some unsuspecting owner, but Rillin pointed out that the armored vehicle would be a potent defense against enemies.

Like me, Rillin was worried about Eila, but he channeled the stress in a different manner. I watched him in the field not far from the small bathhouse that Kian and Ana had entered. His body, and Elizabeth's, were nothing more than paper cutouts under the park light as they parried with one another, going through some basic hand-to-hand combat moves. He stayed on task, his focus on the young woman in a pale blue dress and leather jacket, whom he kept close and whom he kept trained. Elizabeth moved like oil, smooth and endless, as if her body knew exactly what she would demand even before she consciously asked. He moved, she moved. She pushed, he pushed.

It didn't matter that Elizabeth and Rillin had been apart more than a century and half. It didn't matter that she'd been in a tomb since 1851. Elizabeth Lisle Walker was just as graceful and dangerous as she'd been when she faced Therophel so long ago, as if time dared not touch her. She didn't shy away from the strange changes in the world since her Core Collapse in the harbor, trusting Rillin to lead the way and introduce her to all that she had never seen before. Trust, need, pain, passion; all bounced and flowed between the knight and his young queen, as if they were meshed as one. As if decades had never stood between them.

Not far from them, Marcus sat on a worn picnic table, his phone in his hands as he tried to locate probable areas that Eila's abductor may've pulled off and hidden the truck . . . if he'd stopped at all. Marcus said that most kidnappers who took someone for a ransom would keep their prisoner in decent shape. He believed that this Wrecker kid was definitely not a career criminal, since he was dumb enough to take the main highway south thus far. Howe said that a true criminal would keep a stolen donut truck off the main roads, lest it be identified by the cops. The Wrecker's route south was a critical bit of information that Eila's phone had given us, right up until it died.

As I watched the former FBI agent work on his phone, I was grateful for his understanding of this type of thing. While I admit that I debated ditching him numerous times since leaving New Bedford, he was once again proving to be an asset.

Honestly, it was a miracle he was alive.

I stepped away from the truck, my eyes darting to the bathhouse for a moment, hoping Kian and Ana would be ready soon. I eased next to the picnic table, but Howe's eyes never left his phone, his fingers tracing over the map on the screen. They stopped on an area of the map that looked to be a few hours from us, due south. "If I was a betting man, I'd bet they stayed in this general area for a bit."

"East Yonder?" I asked, taking the phone. "I've never heard of it."

"That's not surprising - it's a dust fleck on a map," replied Howe. He finally looked up at me. "My best guess is that this kidnapper kid is following I-84. East Yonder is right along the route, and according to what I could find, it's super small. Very remote. If this kid stays stupid, he's gonna take I-84 all the way to Terrebonne parish, which means he's still got a twenty-hour haul ahead of him. He's gotta stop for food and gas in the most unnoticeable places possible. Especially with Nikki - her face has been on the news all over the country. Hence, my best guess is East Yonder."

"What if we beat him there? Lie in wait? In Terrebonne?"

Howe rubbed the thin five-o'clock shadow on his cheeks, sighing. "Normally, I'd alert the federal agencies all along the I-84 corridor, but given that you guys don't want to let the cat outta the bag about your supernatural side . . ."

"That's not an option. What if we flew? Grabbed plane tickets and went right for New Orleans?"

"You could, but what if he veers off somewhere else? What if we think he's headed to Terrebonne but he's actually going to Atlanta? Or Texas? No, our best bet is to keep moving, even when he's stopping. We'll eventually overtake him and, God-willing, he'll still have that damn Hole Foods truck."

"Or Eila will overtake him and contact us."

Howe nodded, "Your girl is one ballsy chick, I'll give you that."

"Runs in the family," I replied, watching the field as Elizabeth spun towards Rillin. He snagged her, wrapping one broad arm around her shoulder and pinning her back against him. She struggled, but he held her tightly, saying something into her ear, and she nodded, her arms changing their angle and she finally broke his hold. He gave a tight nod of approval, then signaled for her to do it again, and she did.

Elizabeth, though initially confused and still a bit weak, was a furious fighter. True royalty, unfettered by fear or compassion. She had only allowed Rillin to hover for the first hour after she'd awoken, after which she demanded to be given a weapon and all the details of what we were facing. She didn't flinch as we informed her that Therophel was once again on the warpath. Like a true, honed assassin, she'd turned a small dagger over and over in her hand as she rode in the back of the armored SUV with Rillin, the two of them going over the paperwork and Gate designs, their voices hushed.

She said she knew how to kill Therophel, because she knew the true history of how Aztael was murdered - a story told to generations upon generations of Lunaterra. She said that the Lunaterra wanted to use the Gabriel Gate, but they were wary of it. They had seen it shred Aztael, fusing his essence to the actual Gate itself, transforming the granite into shimmering white brimstone – the bone of Fallen Angels. She said that the Soul Gear was actually carved of the Gate, and without it, the Gate could not operate. It was a failsafe, created by the Lunaterra, to thwart enemies who might somehow get access to the Gate.

She said that she could replicate the process if she could access the Gate, the Soul Gear, and Therophel. She said she could kill him with Eila's help. When I pressed her for details, however, she skirted answers, which made me uneasy.

Behind me, the sound of footsteps on gravel had Howe and me looking over our shoulders to see Ana and Kian walking towards us. I stepped away from the picnic table, Howe going back to his phone as I walked up to the two of them.

"You ready to hit the road? Howe thinks the Wrecker kid may've pulled off in a small town called . . ." My voice trailed off as Ana just strolled right past me, heading to Rillin and Elizabeth in the field. "Or . . . not," I muttered, somewhat stunned that I had been so thoroughly ignored. I watched Ana walk through the field and stop in front of Elizabeth, talking to the Lunaterrian princess.

"What's going on, Kian?" I asked, not taking my eyes from Ana. Rillin was now listening alongside Elizabeth.

Kian folded his arms as he watched his girl ramble on, "Pix says she's got an idea of how to get in contact with Sparky. Basically, tell her where to meet us, if she can get away from her kidnapper."

I snapped my attention to the soul thief beside me, "Are you serious? What's her idea?"

"No clue, but she told me that if she's right, I owe her an 808 Demon engine for her Trans Am, whatever the hell that is."

"You BET on whether or not she can contact Eila? Are you kidding me?"

Kian glared at me, "First of all, I got duped into the bet because my sneaky fiancée was using her sass and lips to mess with my mind. Secondly, I want you to know that I really hope we find Eila, but at the same time I really want to win this bet."

I narrowed my eyes at Kian, "What were the terms, exactly?"

"If she can pull off this idea of hers, I have to install the Demon engine. Me, with her dictating what goes where, and I *hate* manual labor. Now, if I win and Ana's idea doesn't fly with Rillin and Princess Fireball, I'll get Ana the Demon Engine and she has to install it herself."

I was confused, my eyes going back to Ana, Elizabeth, and Rillin, who were now in deep conversation. "Kian, you are such a moron - she gets the engine either way. How is that wining in your mind?"

Kian smiled, "'Cause she'll have to install it . . . naked."

I rolled my eyes as Ana, rubbing her hands excitedly, wandered back over to us. She smiled wide, "So, Key - I hope you don't mind hard, dirty work, 'cause I am totally finding my bestie with Elizabeth's help!"

"Pfft - says you," Kian replied. "You sure you didn't take a hit of Baz's weed?"

I ignored Kian, asking Ana, "What's your grand plan?"

She smiled at Kian like a cat who ate the canary before turning to me. Behind her, Elizabeth and Rillin were still in the field talking to one another. "Remember how Christian said that the Lunaterra were connected, like, through their thoughts? That they operated as one - like a hive - and were controlled by the ruling family?"

I raised an eyebrow, glancing to Kian. He simply raised his hands, "Don't look at me, this is her half-baked theory."

I looked back at Ana, "Yes, I recall that conversation in the Breakers. I also recall Christian saying that Elizabeth wasn't connected to the mind of the others, which was why she wandered off into the woods when she was little and he first met her."

Ana nodded, "True, BUT I was thinking about it, and what if Elizabeth can connect with Eila? You know, because E is her descendant and whatnot. Plus, Eila and Elizabeth are really different from their ancestors. I figured maybe their weirdness and bloodline can link them . . . mentally."

Kian blinked, "You're thinking that Elizabeth may be able to contact Eila? Like, talk to her?"

"Well, not talk, but more like send her an idea. An image," Ana replied.

My heart hammered with hope as I asked, "What did Elizabeth say?"

Ana smiled, "Lizzie says it's worth a shot. Tell her what place you want her to try to communicate to Eila. She'll need a picture, though - something she can replicate in her mind."

I looked over to Howe. "East Yonder? That's the town you think they may be near, right?"

Howe nodded.

"Pull up photos of the town. Of any sign, too, that says East Yonder. They need to be memorable. Something vivid."

"You got it," Howe replied, getting to work on his phone and sliding off the picnic table to head to Elizabeth and Rillin.

Ana, quite happy with her brilliance, swiveled slowly to Kian. "So, just to recap, Key: I want a Demon 808 engine. And I'll expect the installation to be perfect."

"If this mind meld thing works, Pix," Kian replied, a wide smile on his face. "Otherwise you'll be working in your birthday suit."

CHAPTER 39

SAME DAMN TRUCK, SAME DAMN SPOT

MONDAY, 6:52AM

Despite the falling temperatures outside, I managed to keep Eila and Nikki warm through the night as we slept in the back of the donut truck. Between my thick black coat and heavy wings, I was able to cocoon both of them – Eila snuggled against my side with her black cloak, and Nikki cradled between my front paws. She had twisted her body towards my neck in the night, her chilled hands finding their way into my feathered mane, and her sleepy breath sliding along the side of my face.

It seemed to me that everyone thought I couldn't shift back into my human form. Truth was, I knew I could phase, but given that we'd been drugged and kidnapped by a bayou-born mermaid – sorry, *Wrecker* – I felt that I was a far better defense for the girls if I stayed in my lion*ish* form.

Of course, the fact that our resident Fish Boy was sleeping like the dead in the front seat of the van made me wonder how brilliant of a kidnapper he was in the first place. He had to be the only criminal on the planet that could steal a pastry truck that was totally devoid of any freakin' food. Despite Eila's best efforts last night at trying to convince Jared that we'd faced off with Therophel, the Wrecker wasn't buying it. He had a plan, and he was sticking to it - drag us back to some sorta mermaid empire in the bayous of Louisiana and trade us to Waite and his Mortis so they'd leave Mayhem.

It didn't matter how much Eila and Nikki tried to convince Jared that he was screwed and that Waite was gone and Therophel was alive and on the warpath. Jared didn't believe them because he was a stubborn moron. Sick of listening to the girls' lectures, he finally flung us all back in the Hole Food's truck, threatening to cut us with his dagger dollars if we didn't get in the truck willingly. He'd tied Eila's hands again, bound my wings, and jammed all three of us in the back of the truck. Nikki had managed to nearly knee him in the balls as he shoved her in the truck, but she'd missed, and she fumed about her bad aim for a long while afterward. Eventually the exhausted girls nodded off against me. But I refused to sleep or let my guard down, though now, as dawn slowly warmed the sky through the windshield, I knew I was running on fumes.

Sprout, the freaky Shadow Tail, was currently sleeping in a box of napkins not far from me, having burrowed his way down through the paper goods like a ferret when we retired for the night. According to Fish Boy, Sprout could basically take on any form, flattening to the ground like a true shadow, or coiling in on himself to form a three-dimensional shape. Apparently his preferred shape was that of a comical-looking two-foot slug, complete with toothless smile except for two stubby fangs.

I will admit, Sprout was pretty dang cool to watch, like smoke trapped in glass – one part ghost, one part weird pet. Every feature and chubby wrinkle was made of the same black shadow matter, making him look like a monotone sculpture, but flowing like ink dropped into a cup of water. Everything about him was tinted like the night sky – eyes, mouth, fangs – *everything*.

A traitorous part of my mind wondered if I, too, would someday find myself split from Marsh, or rather this lion form, leaving me with my own Sprout as a sidekick. The thought chilled me to the bone, especially since the only other pet I ever owned - a Betta fish I named Lassie - bit the dust not long after I bought him. Me and pets, shadow version or not, were not a good combo.

Weirdly, my mind spun to the realization that I was definitely going to miss school. I was a bit relieved, actually, given the fact that I had a math test with Mr. Rohrbach third period, which I totally didn't study for . . . mainly because I was ripping desks through windows, smoking questionable herbs with killers, and dodging pissed-off Fallen angels ALL WEEKEND LONG.

Shit, I was gonna miss the assembly tonight in the school cafeteria. They were handing out college scholarships and I'd applied to a few, some of which I thought I had a pretty decent chance of getting.

Typical.

This was totally typical for me.

Need to go to an awards ceremony? End up kidnapped by a mermaid.

Determined to focus on the situation at hand, I forced my attention to the truck's front windshield, figuring it to be around six or seven in the morning given the pale pink sky lazily tinting the trees. We'd been gone ten hours so far, if my math calculations were correct (and Mr. Rohrbach said I wasn't working to potential! HA!). Of that total, I was estimating we'd traveled at least five.

Last night I had a tough time scenting the air, thanks to Jared's smoke-ridden campfire. When I woke this morning however, the air was clear of ash, and I could instantly tell we were nowhere near home. The constant scent of the ocean was now long gone, replaced by the rich odor of turned soil, budding leaves, and chilled running water. We'd gone south, that much I knew. By the lack of hard ice on the windshield and the scent of early spring, I was guessing we were possibly in Maryland, but I needed to figure out exactly where we were if we had any chance of escaping.

I also kept my nose to the breeze on the off-chance that Jared wasn't the only one planning to cash in on Waite's bounty. All I smelled, however, was Eila, Nikki, and Jared, who really needed to brush his teeth. Sprout didn't smell at all, though he'd chirp at random in his sleep . . .

I glanced down at Nikki, studying her face as she slept, her auburn hair tangled in unruly waves around her throat, and her lips in a hard line. Eila, tucked under my wing, had a determined wrinkle to her brow, as if she was plotting her escape, even in her sleep. The girls smelled like spicy cinnamon and cool lavender to my lion nose – it was a beautiful mix of scents that I'd never detected in my human form, which was a bummer.

Jared, however – he smelled like most teen boys. Nasty.

All in all, this whole kidnapping thing could've been way worse. I could've been kidnapped with Talk-Is-Overrated-Rillin and Shoot-First-Ask-Questions-Later-Kian, which would probably result in us all being cooked over an open fire by Jared and Sprout. With Eila and Nikki however, I knew we had a shot at ditching Jared because the three of us had one thing in common: we were sneaky as shit.

I stole another peak at Eila.

Raef had to be losing his mind right about now . . .

If there was an upside to this ordeal, it was the fact that this whole "trade-Eila-to-Waite" plot didn't feel very well planned out. The only bit of brilliance I could grant to Jared was the fact that he was slick enough to bind one of my wings with strips of fabric (aprons, I think), making flying impossible. 'Course, I hadn't tried to fly *at all*, so that could be a crash course in what not to do anyway – pun totally intended.

I gotta admit, I was diggin' my new Alpha form.

I felt Nikki shift between my paws and I looked down to find her green eyes blinking up at me. She seemed disoriented for a moment, so I didn't move, terrified I'd cause her to panic if she didn't recall my new, massive shape. Her confusion soon fell away, however, and she silently reached her hand up to trace my wide muzzle, her fingers playing with my whiskers. Her touch felt like icicles prickling over my face and my muzzle twitched in response. She smiled, a bit gleeful she was tickling me, then rubbed both hands over the same area, soothing the sensation away.

"You look like a badass," she whispered. I did my best to smile, which probably looked more like a snarl. She glanced over her shoulder toward the front seat, where Jared had begun snoring, then mouthed the words, *"Where's Eila?"*

I carefully lifted my ebony wing to reveal Eila, who was still out like a light.

As I lowered my wing back down, Nikki reached out and

touched the feathers, causing an intense sensation to race over my body. I shivered.

Nikki's mouth spread into a wicked grin, and I narrowed my eyes at her, shaking my head ever so slightly. She reached for my wing again and I shifted it back, just out of her reach. "Big baby," she whispered, pouting, but then her lips twisted, as if she was thinking. "*Can you fly?*" she mouthed.

I glanced over my shoulder to my bandaged wing and she sat up, nearly squishing her dream-worthy chest into my face as she struggled to see what I was looking at. The girl was going to kill me one of these days. It didn't matter that I was a lion . . . I was a dude, through and through.

"Right. Forgot he did that," she whispered into my fuzz-covered ear. She looked back towards the front of the truck, one hand wrapped around my neck as she waited to see if her movement woke our young kidnapper.

Nothing but dead silence radiated from the front seats, the snoring having stopped. From our angle, we couldn't see Jared, but I knew he was still up there. His smell was unmissable. Pressed against me, I could feel Nikki's heart begin to race as she turned back to my wing and began quickly tugging at the fabric, a desperate attempt to free me.

A hand appeared over the top of the front seats, and I quickly pulled Nik back down between my front legs just as Jared's head appeared over the headrest. He glanced sleepily our way, Nikki now frozen like a statue on her back and under my head, one hand still wrapped up in my mane.

Jared yawned, displaying the wicked length of his engraved fangs. He scrubbed his hands through his dark hair, "Man, these front seats are like hay bales. I think I slept on a seatbelt buckle or somethin'." In response to his voice, a delighted squeak emanated from the napkin box as Sprout began shuffling around inside.

"Perhaps we can upgrade from sleeping in a fast food truck in the future, eh? Maybe a suite at the Ritz or a fancy RV?" asked Nikki, sarcasm dripping from her voice.

"I don't got money for such things, woman," replied Jared just as Sprout's snailish head popped up from the box. He shimmied his way out of the carton and across the textured floor of the truck, causing Nikki to suck in a curse. She quickly tucked in her feet as she watched him slide by, but then he stopped right in front of her. Staring at her for a second, he finally offered a crooked smile, then bobbed his head and chirped something which sounded like a freakin' question.

Nikki narrowed her eyes at the blubbery shadow. "Unless you are asking how I like my cappuccino, I ain't in the mood, Worm Tail, so move along."

Sprout's head sunk and he made a pitiful sound as he slowly slinked his way to Jared, his body bunching and elongating in a slow rhythm as he slid up the back of the front seats. He let out one long, mournful snail wail, then disappeared into the cab seats with a dramatic flop.

Good grief, what a total drama queen.

Jared watched his sulking tail as it whined miserably on the front seat, then turned to Nikki, his face hard. "Ya know, that was really rude. He simply said 'Good Morning!' And if you girls want a hotel room, I suggest you both hit a strip joint and spin the pole. I'm sure you could make some good money for our little road trip."

I gave a low growl as Nikki produced a specific finger. I was impressed her arm had healed so well and with such excellent dexterity.

Jared frowned, "Damn, girl – don't get so uptight. Was just suggesting, is all. A girl like you with all that," he gestured to Nikki's body in general. "Those curves and lips would make a killing. Especially with that mean-ass glare of yours."

I flexed my wide paws, producing black claws which scraped against the steel floor of the truck, a clear warning to stay away from us. Nikki, however, was rarely a damsel in distress, and offered a few choice words about the fact that Jared's tail was pretty short and stubby, causing our young Wrecker to scowl and Sprout's head to pop back up over the seat, his mouth gaping in horror.

I chuckled, which sounded more like choking on a hairball.

Sprout, now majorly indignant, snapped his mouth shut, muttering something in his squeaky language as he disappeared down into the seat. The driver's door clicked open, then slammed shut again. Jared sighed, looking out the side window. "Well, now you've gone and really pissed him off. He's gone off to sulk."

"Jeez, who's slamming doors?" mumbled Eila from her hidden spot next to me. She shifted and pushed up on my wing. I raised it slightly, so as not to let all the warmth out, but enough for her to see. She twisted against my side, so she could see Jared.

He smiled broadly back at the three of us, all tucked against one another, and offered me a thumbs-up. "Two ladies at once. Gotta give ya credit, my friend . . . 'specially 'cause you is technically the pussy in this particular situation."

I just shook my head. We'd been abducted by Middle School 101.

Eila rolled her eyes as Nikki crawled out from under me. "So, what is the plan, Weasel Breath?" Nik demanded. "Drive us all the way to Louisiana in this sugar shack on wheels, then what? Meet up with Waite . . . who doesn't EXIST anymore?"

"Weasel Breath doesn't really have a plan, Nikki," Eila responded, easing out from her warm spot. She wrapped her arms tightly around her as she climbed past me towards Jared, undaunted.

Shocked she was coming near him, Jared shifted back. "You stay right there, ya hear? I ain't above knocking you out again, so you best keep your distance and follow orders."

Eila continued to approach him and I got to my feet, causing the truck to rock back and forth. In the tight confines of Hole Food's premier shipping vehicle, I wasn't going to be the best help, but I could probably swat Jared's pea head from his neck if I got the chance.

Jared, his eyes now slits, bared his teeth. "Stop there."

Eila finally stopped moving, thank God, and leaned back against the truck's sidewall. "See, I don't get why you don't keep us drugged. To me, this makes for some seriously poor logic in allowing us to be awake, so there's gotta be a reason for it."

If she didn't shut up soon, I was going to sit on her.

Jared studied Eila for a moment before answering. "First off, I didn't drug ya. I knocked y'all on your butts with my venom. You and your shifter I tagged with some of my throwing stars dipped in my venom, but your Feon here," he glanced at Nikki. "Well, I bit her. Ran outta tipped doubloons and, quite frankly, she's one spicy tamale, ya feel me?"

Nikki looked horrified. "Oh, my GOD! I'm gonna have mermaid cooties! Where'd you bite me, you JERK?"

Jared smiled, flicking his finger towards the lower section of

Nikki. "In your hip. Truth be told, I was aiming for your neck, all cool and vampire-like, but you swung back and nearly clocked me in the eyeball, so I had to shift body parts, as it were."

Nikki's hand went to her hip and tugged her pant waist down, flashing me some purple lace as she searched for the bite mark. "Don't bother," said Jared. "My venom seals the wound almost instantly – cauterizes it, so no mark is left. Highly useful in knocking out a victim so you can eat them. Alive."

Eila swallowed, suddenly not so confident.

Jared leaned on the seat back, looking at all of us. "And so, yeah, I can drug you, but I don't because, quite frankly, I'm not the only one after your butts if the scuttlebutt I heard on my travels up here is to be believed. If we are put upon by unfriendly sorts who'd rather the bounty for themselves . . . well, quite honestly, I'm gonna need y'all to defend my position, as kidnapper and such. Fair is fair – I caught you first."

Wow. Just . . . wow. I thought Baz was a moron, but Jared had him beat ten-fold.

Eila laughed. "What makes you think we'd help you in such . . . instances?" she asked. "Why not ditch your sorry butt and make a run for it?"

"And go where?" asked Jared, suddenly seeming less like an idiot, and more like a truly calculating thief. "Y'all are far from your allies. You run from me, you got nowhere to hide. Stick with me, however, and I may be able to get us down south without running into too much trouble."

"At which point, you'll swap us for your beloved Mayhem?" demanded Nikki.

Jared hooked his elbows over the seat, his face darkening, "See,

I was thinking about this last night. Originally, I was intending to only trade Eila to Waite, but I'm hoping to sweeten the deal with your shifter. I know I sure as heck would want a flying cougar under my thumb and playing fetch on demand if I could."

"He's a LION," snapped Nikki, now on her feet in front of me.

Jared looked at her as if she had ten heads. "Woman, he's black as coal, got wings like a raven, and a mane of feathers. Let's face it – he ain't neither lion or cougar, but some messed up contraction of bird and big cat. Don't rightly care what ya call him, as long as he's worth something to Waite."

I growled low, the sound deep like distant thunder. Yeah, I liked this form and I couldn't wait to really see what I could do with it . . . including stomping the life out of Jared.

"And what about me?" she demanded.

"I intend to keep you. Hand you off to Midas to help fortify and repair Mayhem."

"So, this is all to get Mayhem back, correct? To rescue your people?" asked Eila. "Big bad Jared brings us to Waite in a donut box truck and thinks Waite is actually gonna trade back Mayhem. You are a bigger fool than I ever thought possible."

Nikki snorted, "I don't know, Eila. I thought he was a massive fool from the get-go."

Eila just shook her head, "Lawson Waite was a ruse - a body, simply used by Therophel. He's GONE. You are dealing with Therophel now and he's just gonna kill you and take the three of us. Your Mayhem is a lost cause. Your family, your parents, are dead. He takes everything. Trust me, I know."

Jared leaned forward, rage in his eyes. "You know nothing! So just . . . shut up! I'm getting my home back! I'm finding my mom and the elders! They're not dead. They can't all be dead! Waite is just a man. I'm not falling for your bullshit lies about Therophel."

"Damn it, LISTEN to me!" snapped Eila. "You and I are not enemies! We are after the same end game - we want Therophel DEAD. I know what he's after - I know the power he seeks. If he accomplishes his goal, all our worlds could be destroyed. He already has the Soul Gear - that's why he raided Mayhem, I guarantee it! If you hand me off to him, you hand him the key to our destruction. YOU will ensure your family, whatever is left of them, dies. YOU - it will be your fault!"

Jared snapped, all control gone as he vaulted over the front seats and slammed into Eila. I tried to move to stop him, but there was no way I could maneuver in the truck. "TAKE IT BACK!" he screamed. "TAKE BACK YOUR LIES!"

"I'm not lying," roared Eila, and she elbowed Jared hard in the chest. The Wrecker flinched, but then grabbed her by the neck, snarling wide as he displayed his fangs close to her face. "I'll rip your traitorous tongue from your mouth," he growled, but Eila didn't flinch.

"Maybe," she replied cooly, "but I doubt you can manage it before I split your chest in half with my Light." Jared glanced down between their bodies, the gauze around Eila's hands having been literally incinerated in less than a second. Aimed at his heart, her open palms were glowing brilliantly under the ashy remains of the bandages. "Test me," she whispered in a razor sharp tone, "and you will die."

Seething he stared her down for a moment before shoving away from her. He punched the steel wall of the truck over and over, howling in rage. Outside the truck, Sprout scrambled onto the windshield, clearly triggered by his master. He pressed his shadowy face against the glass, squeaking loudly as if yelling at us to all calm down.

"I cannot go back empty-handed," Jared breathed. "I cannot leave Mayhem to the hands of such a killer."

Eila let the Light fade from her palms as she lowered them. "You don't have to go back alone. We can help you, but not if you are using us as bait. Not if you don't trust us. Not if you don't believe us. Release us - let me contact my crew. You and I want the same thing, Jared, but we will never destroy Therophel if we are divided."

Jared rested his head against the wall of the truck. "I kidnapped you. Why would you help me? Why should I trust you?"

"Because I've lost people I love too, Jared. Because I know the rage that lives inside you,"

Jared looked over his shoulder at Eila, and she held out one ash-covered hand. "I can help you get Mayhem back, if you help me destroy the Gabriel Gate and kill Therophel. We want the same thing. This is me, Eila Walker, pledging to you that I will help you get your home back. That I will help you rescue your people."

He looked at her outstretched hand. "You wish to make a deal. A bargain?"

Eila nodded. "What say you, Jared . . . Uh, I don't know your last name."

"Marlowe," he replied, and Eila blinked, as if something about the name surprised her.

Jared, however, didn't seem to notice as he finally reached out and grasped her hand, giving it a firm shake. "My name's Jared Marlowe," he replied, "and you, Eila Walker, have a deal." He tugged E a little closer, "and you better know what the hell you're doing."

She yanked her hand free. "I need my phone. I had it on me when you took us, so fork it over."

Jared crossed his arms, "Yeah, well, I tossed that sucker hours ago. Got run over by one of those huge trucks."

Eila flexed her hands, no doubt controlling her urge to strangle the fifteen-year-old. "Fine," she whispered, trying to act calm. "I'll just need yours, then."

Jared leaned back against the sidewall of the truck. "I don't have a phone, but the kid I jacked for the truck might've. His backpack is on the floor in the front."

Eila tossed her hands, exasperated. "Fine. I'll get it. Let's get the heck out of here."

Jared rubbed the back of his head, his fingers catching in his brown hair as he suddenly looked less sure. "About that . . ."

"Oh, lord . . . what now . . ." muttered Nikki as E climbed ungracefully into the front seat, flashing me a peek of butt crack as she fell over the backrest into the front.

"I'm pretty sure we're outta gas," Jared replied, and Eila popped up in the front seat, setting a backpack in front of her and digging through the contents. She tossed a sweatshirt and track pants at me. The pants caught on my ear, nearly blinding me.

"You're gonna need to phase, MJ. I can't take a stroll with you looking like *that* beside us." She glanced at Jared, "And I don't care about the gas - we need to ditch this truck anyway. I'm sure it's been reported stolen." She went back to digging through the contents of the bag.

"So . . . where are we?" Nik asked.

Jared winced, "South . . . somewhere?" He looked through the windshield, as if studying the surrounding landscape.

I shook off the track pants from my furry head as Nik snapped, "SOUTH SOMEWHERE? Are you serious? We're LOST? How can you drive all night and not know where you're going?"

Sprout, still on the hood of the truck, had calmed down and was now thoroughly enjoying one of the windshield wipers as a back scratcher. His smokey shape shivered happily every time he slid along the wiper, and he let out a curious *purr* as he massaged himself.

Eila upended the backpack and dumped it on the seat. "Shit. No phone. How did that kid NOT have a freakin' cell phone?"

"EILA! Idiot doesn't know where the heck we are!" snapped Nikki, still glaring at Jared.

Eila finally gave up on the bag and tossed it back to the floor. She looked at Sprout, then back to Jared and Nikki. "We're near a town called East Yonder. I saw the welcome sign that looked like it was last painted in the '40s," she replied with a shrug. "It was right on the side of the road. We can't be far from the town. They've got to have a pay phone . . . or a cell phone we can steal."

"See?" demanded Nikki, "That's what you're supposed to do when you drive somewhere, Jared! Pay ATTENTION to road signs!"

Jared looked an Eila, his head cocked. "I didn't see a sign anywhere. When did you see it?"

"I saw it . . . when . . ." Eila blinked, as if confused. "Actually, I don't remember where I saw it exactly. I just remember seeing it. I have a clear picture of it in my head. Like, a perfect snapshot. I even know what the town looks like - small, pretty with a church in the middle. Big white church spire sticks up above the trees. Heck, it looked like a photograph it was all set so perfect."

The truck fell silent.

I'd been up longer than the girls and there was nothing I saw that remotely resembled a sign or a cutesy town.

Nikki looked a bit worried as she replied to Eila, “I didn’t see anything like that. In fact, now that I think about it, we were unconscious coming down here. And there is nothing but trees as far as the eye can see from our crappy parking spot. You couldn’t have seen any town or sign. Are you sure you’re not getting a dream confused with, you know, *reality*?”

Eila paused, looking down at her arms for a while, as if searching for something. But then she rubbed them quickly, shaking her head. “No. I wasn’t hallucinating. I swear I saw it. I remember it clearly.”

“And you said it’s called East Yonder? The town?”

Eila nodded. “I . . . I *know* I saw it. I know I did . . .”

Eila seemed lost in thought as Nikki turned to Jared, “We need to get up above the treeline to see what’s around us. Maybe Eila’s just confusing a dream with reality thanks to your STUPID VENOM giving us a world-class hangover, but if by some chance she did somehow see a sign, we need to know.” She glanced at Sprout, still happily enjoying the wipers. “Can your weirdo tail climb?”

Jared looked at Sprout through the glass. “Okay, first of all, my venom’s the shit, so don’t even go there. Secondly, yes - we both can climb, but Sprout can get way higher because he’s, ya know, vapor. He’s basically my instincts and desires when I’m on land.”

Nik held up a hand, “Wait, wait . . . you’re saying that Sprout is your id - like, literally a piece of your psyche?”

“I don’t know what an id is,” Jared replied.

“Like, when Freud said we are made up of three things - the id, ego, and superego. Id is, like, the devil in ya, while ego is your good side. Superego regulates both.”

Jared blinked, "Yeah, I don't think I have the ego part, so . . . whatever." He knocked on the windshield and Sprout squashed his face against the glass, chirping a question back at his owner. Jared yelled through the glass to his tail, "We need you to get up a tree. See if you see anything. Maybe a town."

"*Cheek nee tee tee?*" Sprout asked, trails of his foggy form rippling in the breeze that slid past the windshield.

"No. We're not going there to hunt. Eila Walker, here, thinks she saw a town and we're gonna see if she's right."

Sprout just shook his head, sliding off the van's hood. We watched him slink off towards a tall pine tree as Jared turned back to us. "Deal's a deal - I'm gonna let you out of the van, BUT Eila's right," Jared looked at me, "Lion boy needs to jam back into his human form."

I wrinkled my lips, showing off my teeth. In the front seat, Eila nodded. "MJ, you gotta be human. I can't explain a lion if someone sees us, let alone one with wings."

I groaned, pushing the clothes around with my paw.

"Hopefully those will fit," she added.

We looked back out the window and watched as Sprout began twirling up a tree like a zephyr. Jared pulled keys from his pocket, along with Eila's little silver light sword. I hadn't even realized he'd taken it from her. Jerk.

He tossed the weapon into Eila's hands. "I'm gonna assume that does something funky, 'cause it has the work of your Feon pal written all over it. Trust is trust and a bargain is a bargain. I'm letting you have that back as proof I'm willing to trust you."

"Thank you," she replied, tucking it in her back pocket as Nikki watched.

Jared moved past Nik and me to the back of the van and finally unlocked the doors from the inside, pushing them open into the early morning sun. He paused, surveying the surrounding forest. "We are a full day's drive from Terrebonne and the Barrie forts. Let's find out where we really are and then you can contact your crew and tell them where to meet us."

"Works for me," Eila replied, climbing back over the seat to where Nik and I were waiting.

"And Eila," Jared added, "We don't have a lot of time to waste. Daylight's burning and I don't know how much time our elders have left inside Mayhem. And Barrie, while warded, is basically unprotected save from the other 'cussers like me. As soon as we have your crew, we are hauling back there, got it?"

"Understood," she replied just as Sprout called loudly from his treetop perch.

"What's he saying?" Nik asked.

Jared smiled a bit, showing off the tip of one fang, "He says there's a town not far from here. And it's got a church, white one, right in the center."

TERREBONNE MOONCUSSER

LAST LIGHT

ARE YOU BRAVE, ONE LAST TIME?

K. R. CONWAY

DAYBREAKER

12/1/2017

LAST LIGHT

ACKNOWLEDGEMENTS

Truth: Writing the "thank you" portion of any book is not easy. Doing so is basically one part total panic (because you KNOW you're going to forget someone), and one part feeling entirely inadequate as to how to convey such MAD, MAD gratitude. I'm going to try to do my best:

For my mom, who has been my cheerleader from the day I was born even though I looked like a beat up soccer ball. She has ALWAYS been my champion. When I've (more recently) wallowed in writer self-loathing, she smacked me about and pushed me onward, loving my characters. I'm so very, very grateful for her existence in my world and the universe because she is one heck of an awesome woman. #GirlPower

For Sabine and Spider (aka Charlotte) who have the patience of saints, especially when they've spent hours (yes, HOURS) on the phone with me, helping with story edits and plot issues. They are my core Beta team and without them, this series would not exist. Oh, and they were the ones who said "Split the book!" when they found out how huge it was becoming, so . . . go blame them. #MountHolyokeForever

For Nancy, Nate, Kat, Kim, and Laura who also jumped in to help grab goofs and errors. Not only was I flinging them pages like a printer gone mad, but they'd foolishly ask, "When do you need these back?" to which I'd laugh, "YESTERDAY!" So yeah – they'd stay up late, trying to catch all the errors as well. I'll owe them new eyeballs someday at the rate they read stuff. #GodLoveThem

To my EPIC fans, especially Siobhan and Erica, who are my dynamic duo from across the pond! I can't express how much I write this series for you, all of you. At the end of the day, I write out of sheer passion for the characters and the demands of the fans. #ThankYouFans

To Selina, who went from a casual friend to a close partner in crime. She was my dose of humor and sanity when I felt entirely overwhelmed. I'm so happy we've become pals! Oh, and no pressure but WHERE'S THE BOOK? #SouthofMontgomery

To Laura (see previous editing slave) who would abduct my son on a regular basis so I could write. Woman, MASSIVE thanks! You've been my best bud forever and I'm so glad our kids have fun together! Someday I will write you into one of my books as a hooker-assassin-horse thief, as requested. #MyKidWantsChickens

To my realtor, Jaime (yes, REALTOR). I am forever grateful for all the work you did to get me and my family into our new home (and my new office)! I find the view from the windows a perfect muse to my madness. #ThatCrazyWriterIsNowMyNeighbor

To my doctor Francis Farraye, at Boston Medical Center. Thanks for keeping me alive and kicking so I can "burn the candle at both ends with a blow torch." As requested, I wrote you into this novel with your dual requirements of youth and hotness. I'm sure the fact that your character is a cannibalistic mermaid with a shadow tail named Edgar may be a bit of a shock, however. #YouMadeMeAWhat

To the wild assortment of weirdos I work with at the Bourne Bus Yard. You make driving the Loser Cruisers a fun (if not psychologically questionable) career. I'm super-duper grateful for your snarky observations and dry humor, which I pilfer daily to toss into books like this. And yes, the kid-eating, bus-zombie manuscript is in the works. Not. #TrafficHell

Lastly, to my family – my husband, kids, parents, grandmother, aunts, uncles, brother, and so many, MANY others. I'm grateful everyday to call you part of my heart and soul. LOVE YOU ALL! #GeneticWeirdos

ABOUT THE AUTHOR

K.R. Conway is the author of the acclaimed Undertow series, which includes Undertow, Stormfront, Cruel Summer, True North, Last Light, and Daybreaker (2017).

At twenty-two, she started writing professionally for multiple magazines and newspapers. Thirteen years later, she wrote her first novel on a whim, basing it on her favorite Cape Cod places and pastimes. She called it Undertow.

Conway has a passion for working with teenaged storytellers (often in school and library settings), and is well known for her crazy classes. She is the founder of the Cape Cod Teen Writers Conference and a member of SCBWI. She holds a degree in Forensic Psychology with dual honors from Mount Holyoke College.

A Cape Cod native, she lives in Sagamore Beach with her family. She can often be found combing the sand with her kids, hunting for sea glass and jumping from lifeguard stands. Audiobook versions of the novels are available on Audible, iTunes, and Amazon.

Website: www.CapeCodScribe.com
Twitter: @sharkprose
Instagram: k_r_conway
Facebook: KR-Conway

LAST LIGHT

26641152R00215

Made in the USA
Columbia, SC
18 September 2018